The Scottish Ploy

Quinn Fawcett

The Scottish Ploy

A MYCROFT HOLMES NOVEL

A TOM DOHERTY ASSOCIATES BOOK

NEW YORK

THE SCOTTISH PLOY

Copyright © 2000 by Quinn Fawcett

This book is printed on acid-free paper.

A Forge Book
Published by Tom Doherty Associates, LLC
175 Fifth Avenue
New York, NY 10010

www.tor.com

Forge® is a registered trademark of Tom Doherty Associates, LLC.

Library of Congress Cataloging-in-Publication Data

Fawcett, Quinn.
    The Scottish ploy : a Mycroft Holmes novel; authorized by Dame Jean
Conan Doyle / Quinn Fawcett.—1st ed.
        p.   cm.
    "A Tom Doherty Associates book."
    ISBN 0-312-87282-8 (acid-free paper)
    1. London (England)—Fiction. 2. Kidnapping—Fiction.   3. Actors—
Fiction.   I. Title.
PS3556.A992 S36 2000
813'.54—dc21   00–031711

First Edition: December 2000

Printed in the United States of America

0 9 8 7 6 5 4 3 2 1

Author's Note

The character of Mycroft Holmes is used with the kind permission of Dame Jean Doyle.

Although phrenology is no longer regarded as a legitimate study, in the latter part of the nineteenth century, it was considered serious science; many well-known medical and professorial experts of the day devoted much time to it. That Mycroft Holmes, an educated and logical man, should be interested in phrenology may not be easy to accept for modern readers, but it is consistent with the work of the best minds of the period.

This was also a time of attempting to develop new treatments for the mentally ill. In Vienna, Breuer and his young colleague Freud were treating such disorders with hypnosis, and in France many asylums were made less prisonlike than they had been before. In America, the mentally ill and defective were approached as medical cases, treated somewhat more humanely in terms of housing and daily care than many in Europe, but sterilized for genetic reasons.

In dealing with the political climate of European diplomacy of the last century, I have attempted to stay within the limits of national positions even when a few of the particulars of this tale were my own invention.

As regards the London theatres, most are still in the same location as they appear in these pages, but they are much changed from the 1890s. Many of the buildings suffered extensive damage during the Blitz of World War II, and most had been modernized to use electric instead of gaslight long before the war. I have referred to *The London Stage of the Roaring Nineties* (1963) and *London by Gaslight* (1977) as my primary sources for theatrical information.

For
CLARENCE and PATTI

The Scottish
Ploy

Prologue

"*TOMORROW AND TOMORROW and tomorrow,*" said Edmund Sutton in a tone of unendurable fatigue and despair; I sat transfixed, although I had heard him rehearse the role for three months and thought myself inured by repetition. Around me in the darkness the audience was hushed, caught up in the performance they were watching. "*. . . to the last syllable of recorded time . . .*"

Beside me, Mycroft Holmes shifted in his seat, his dark-grey eyes fixed on the actor who was his double when he was not essaying roles like MacBeth. "He has them," he muttered to me; he, too, was aware of the audience, all but mesmerized by Sutton's interpretation.

". . . *who struts and frets his hour upon the stage and then is heard no more . . .*" Suppressed emotion lent the words pathos that wrenched my heart. Sutton turned away from the audience, delivering his lines upstage. Every word was audible, although his voice seemed no louder than when he had begun the short, tragic speech. ". . . *and fury, signifying*"—a brief pause as he turned back, marked by a faint, despondent smile—"*nothing.*"

"Masterful" whispered Mycroft Holmes, his praise as genuine as anything I had ever heard him say. "Astonishing. A most propitious opening."

I nodded, not wanting to break the spell with words. I was as moved as Holmes was, and startled to be so. Who would have thought, I asked myself, that there could be such a tremendous change between learning lines and acting them? But I should have known: I had seen Sutton in many roles for our mutual employer, most convincingly as Mycroft Holmes himself. I kept my eyes on the stage, watching the fight begin, knowing the play was nearly over.

As the curtain came down and the applause began, the spell broke and I clapped along with the rest, waiting for the curtains to part again for the actors to take their bows.

"I think we may agree he acquitted himself very well," said Mycroft Holmes as the cast once again appeared, this time in a long line, to accept the enthusiastic response of the audience. "He looks tired," Holmes remarked as he studied Sutton's face. Underneath the makeup that added a decade of hard use to his face there was very real fatigue.

"Small wonder," I said. "I'm exhausted and all I've done is sit." I clapped more vigorously for Lady MacBeth, a woman of dainty proportions who possessed a voice that wrung the heart with every word: her madness had filled me with horror, and now, here she was, smiling and flirting with the audience. I recalled that Sutton had said she had a rare temper and an eye to older men with money; as she had performed I would never have believed it, but now, I could see what Sutton meant. There was something about her handsomeness that had an edge to it, and a quality to her manner that I did not find wholly pleasing.

"Beatrice Motherwell not to your liking?" Mycroft Holmes asked archly.

"She . . . is a bit . . . overdone," I allowed.

The curtain opened three times for the cast, and then the applause died and the audience began to depart. The lights, which had been bright, were dimmed as an obvious hint to the audience that the theatre was about to close. It was not so long ago that Henry Irving had ordered the house lights—as Sutton called them—dimmed during performances; I saw such a strategy had the double purpose of speeding the audience as one would hurry a lingering guest. As I rose I looked around the theatre, thinking again that I was sorry this excellent production was not scheduled for a longer run; the Duke of York's Theatre was an appropriate venue, but the short run lessened the advantage of the theatre's prestige. I reached for my cloak, which I had draped over the seat behind me, and swung it around my shoulders. "Where now, Mister Holmes?"

Mycroft Holmes smiled. "Why, we return to the flat. We still have work to do tonight." He must have seen disappointment in my eyes, for he said, "We will save our comments for later, when he arrives at my flat. It would not do to let it be known that Sutton and I have any association beyond that of player and . . . er . . . playee." He chuckled at his witticism. "But he will join us as soon as he may, and you will be able to heap upon him all the praise you wish."

"He deserves praise," I said, a bit stubbornly. "I should like to congratulate him now. But I do see the wisdom of your precaution."

"No doubt, my boy, no doubt." He had tugged on his cloak and was making his way to the aisle. No one impeded his progress; such a tall, portly, imposing figure could cut through crowds as easily as a steamship might pass through pleasure-boats. I followed along in his wake as we made for the door.

Sid Hastings was waiting a short distance down the block, away from the cabs and carriages that gathered at the front of the Duke of York's Theatre. He lowered the steps as he saw us approaching and touched the brim of his hat with his whip. "A good evening, sir," he said to our mutual employer as we climbed into the cab.

"That it is," said Mycroft Holmes with great satisfaction. "A fine evening indeed." The misty chill of the November night had no effect upon his expansive good humor. "Take us back to Pall Mall, if you would. And then return for Mister Sutton. He should be ready to leave in ninety minutes." He gestured to the horse between the shafts. "Working out, is he?"

"He's not Jenny, but he's learning," said Sid Hastings.

"You miss her," Holmes said, sympathy coloring his tone.

"Just so," said Sid Hastings as he signaled his horse to walk on.

We rode a short while in silence, and then Holmes sighed. "I sometimes wonder if it is not unfair of me, to keep Sutton as my double, for surely his labors on my behalf have stopped him from achieving the recognition he so richly deserves. I knew from the first that he was remarkably gifted, and tonight has only served to deepen my conviction in that regard. When I see so superior a performance as he has just given, I can find it in my heart to question my demands on him." He shook his head. "And yet, I cannot spare him, since he is willing to do the work I require. Where else would I find such an accomplished actor who is my height and of a similar build, whose talent is so great as Sutton's, and whose loyalty would be so dedicated as Sutton's has been?" He stared out into the night. "I know he is irreplaceable. Just as you are, dear boy." He pulled at his lower lip, a sure sign of consternation. "Yet I am aware of how much Sutton has given up for me. This performance has only served to remind me."

"It was an impressive performance," I said, wondering if he had noticed any trace of himself in Sutton's interpretation of Mac-Beth, for I thought I had seen something of Mycroft Holmes—distorted and corrupted by ambition—in the air of leadership and capability with which Sutton had invested the role at the beginning of the play; the bearing and the age he assumed might or might not draw from our mutual employer, but the authority he portrayed was familiar to me.

"Sutton has a great deal of talent." Holmes leaned back against the squabs and stared into the middle distance. "As well as I know the play, he showed me new facets of its brilliance tonight."

"He impressed me as well," I admitted. "He was remarkable in what he did."

Holmes nodded. "When he arrives, we will toast him with champagne." The decision pleased him. "It is the least we can do, given his performance."

"Very good, sir," I said, glad that there was no pressing business to demand our attentions at the crack of dawn, for we had recently brought to a successful conclusion some very tricky negotiations involving the Turks and the Russians regarding British access to the Black Sea. It also deserved a toast I thought, and was about to say so when Mycroft Holmes sat up.

"We will drink to the Russians and the Turks as well," he exclaimed, as if reading my thoughts. "You acquitted yourself very well, Guthrie, and deserve applause as much as Sutton does; you, also, delivered a most commendable performance."

"Hardly, sir," I said. "I merely carried the necessary messages and had a few documents signed. They were willing to do what we required so long as it was not made public, which was very much to my liking. Nothing like essaying one of Shakespeare's greatest roles, and in front of an audience. I think I would rather face half a dozen of the Brotherhood's men, fully armed, than a theatre full of people." I chuckled to show I was exaggerating for the purpose of humor, but not by much.

The mention of that nefarious organization brought another change to my employer's demeanor. "Do not say that, even in jest," Mycroft Holmes warned. "The Brotherhood has seemed to be inactive for the last four months, which worries me."

"Do you suppose they are up to something?" I asked, anticipating his answer.

"I must always keep in mind what an implacable enemy the Brotherhood can be. Nothing I do is safe from their schemes, nor can we relax our vigilance in regard to their activities. We have supposed they are inactive, but that may be wishful thinking. The Brotherhood are utterly ruthless and single-minded in their determination to bring down all the governments of Europe." He coughed as if to announce a change of subject. "We're nearly to Pall Mall," he observed. "Not before time."

"Very likely not," I said, aware that Holmes was restive, and wondering why he was. "Has anything happened this afternoon that I should know of?"

Mycroft Holmes frowned and shrugged. "Nothing I am aware of," he conceded. "But I cannot rid myself of the sense that—" he broke off, then quoted, "*By the pricking of my thumbs/Something wicked this way comes.*"

"Sutton would tell you it is bad luck to recite lines from MacBeth," I pointed out.

Pall Mall was light of traffic at this hour, with perhaps half a dozen cabs and a small berline coach making their way along the street. Few pedestrians were about, and the constable making his rounds ambled rather than strode. Out of habit I watched all the movement near the building where Mycroft Holmes had his flat, and around the front of the Diogenes Club, directly across the street from it.

"Actors' superstitions, as is calling it 'The Scottish Play' to avoid the curse of the name," Holmes said impatiently. "It is the one thing about Sutton that troubles me, but I cannot suppose any other actor would be more rational about such things. If it is the worst he does, he is a gem among men." As Sid Hastings drew his cab up to the kerb, Holmes added, "Good luck or bad, my thumbs are pricking, and that bothers me."

"Small wonder," I said as I got out of the cab after him.

Before mounting the stairs to his flat, Holmes turned around and looked at Hastings. "Once you bring Mister Sutton back here, you may go off duty. I will not need you until nine in the morning."

Sid Hastings nodded. "Very good, Mister Holmes." And with that, he turned his cab around, heading off into the night.

"Does he ever sleep?" I wondered aloud, for I had never known Sid Hastings not to answer Mycroft Holmes' summons at any hour.

"I suppose he must," said Mycroft Holmes. "He has not complained," he added pointedly.

I stared down the dark street, listening to the retreating sound of Lance's hooves. "Well, more power to him," I said.

"Come, Guthrie," Mycroft Holmes said. "Let us make the most of this rare opportunity and celebrate Sutton's achievement, and our own. Tyers will have a meal ready for us shortly, and there is champagne."

"An honor, sir," I said, and followed him up to the top floor, thinking as I went, that for a portly man of forty-nine years, Mycroft Holmes could set an energetic pace when he chose to.

Chapter One

"GUTHRIE! GUTHRIE MY boy! Come down at once! At once!" The sound of my employer's voice in the front hall of the Curzon Street house where I had rooms brought me bolt awake and running for my dressing gown and slippers for all that it was a few minutes past three in the morning. I strove to bring my thoughts into order as I presented myself at the top of the stairs. Below, Mycroft Holmes was waiting, dressed formally and wearing a dark cape with shoulders shining with rain; I surmised he had been to the theatre again earlier in the evening.

He held his silk hat in one hand and a pistol in the other. "Make haste, Guthrie. Make haste. I need you to dress and come with me immediately."

I asked for no explanation, nor did I expect one. "I'll dress as quickly as possible, sir," I assured him, and turned back to my room. It was two nights after our evening at the theatre; Holmes had ventured out to the play again. That alone would not account for his appearance here, at such a time of night. No caprice would bring Mycroft Holmes to summon me at this hour, I knew; I rarely saw him with a pistol, but on those occasions when I had, it had boded ill. My alarm increased as I flung my dressing gown aside, shivering a little in the sudden chill.

"Make haste," Holmes shouted up at me again.

This very order—uttered thrice—brought me fully awake, for it was rare that Mycroft Holmes issued such commands in so brusque a tone; when he did, it meant that the urgency was genuine and immediate. Spurred by this certainty, I rushed back to my room and grabbed for my clothes on the wooden valet even as I tugged off my night-shirt; I ignored the gooseflesh rising on my arms and shoulders as I sorted out my clothes, then pulled open my drawer for underwear. I tossed them atop the rest. For an instant I longed for a cup of strong tea and a bit of oatmeal to help wake me, but I abandoned that wish as I heard my employer climbing the stairs, a sound that goaded me to swifter action. "What is the matter?"

Holmes was standing in the door, a large figure of imposing presence that even after more than seven years' association still had the capacity to impress me. "I have not half an hour since received a message that alarms me. I fear that Vickers has come to light again."

"Vickers," I repeated, pausing in the act of pulling on my singlet. "I had hoped we had seen the last of him. The Brotherhood, too."

"And I, dear boy, and I," said Mycroft Holmes heavily.

I knew by the tone of his voice that this was not good news. "What has happened?" I tugged my shirt over my head as I listened.

"Earlier this evening, I was summoned from the theatre at the second interval to wait upon—well, shall we call him a man of the highest rank and leave it at that?—who solicited my help in evaluating the work of Sir Marmion Hazeltine, which I assured him I would do with as much dispatch as possible. The person making this appeal is hopeful that Sir Marmion may have found a way to deal with the mad in a more constructive and humane manner, and to diagnose their ills more scientifically. I will, of course, do as he asks."

"Of course," I said, thinking that alone would not bring him here at such an hour or in so urgent a state of mind.

"Shortly before I left the castle, an informant from the Admiralty sent me word that Vickers has been summoned here for a meeting with other members of the Brotherhood—German members." He sighed. "There is no legitimate reason to refuse them entry to the country."

"But why not?" I asked as I fumbled with my buttons.

"The men are not officially listed as *non grata*, for the Crown does not recognize the existence of the Brotherhood, at least not in any way that would extend to diplomatic dealings. It would be a dreadful mistake to accord them such legitimacy as declaring them *non grata* would do. It is bad enough that they exist; it would be worse if we should lend them even the suggestion of legitimacy by recognizing them in any official way, which such a declaration would do." He cleared his throat, a sure sign of distress. "The trouble is, they are being very clever, and this puts me in a doubly awkward position, which I must suppose is their intention." He stumped over to my single chair in the bow of the window and looked out on the street. "I have been cudgeling my brains for some acceptable excuse to keep them out of the country, but without success. To deal with Sir Marmion on the one hand, the Brotherhood and the Germans on the other is not an easy prospect."

"Can nothing be done? Is there not some way to delay the Germans until you have delivered the information on Sir Marmion for your . . . your inquirer?" I asked as I stepped into my under-drawers. It was cold enough that I could feel the goose-flesh on my back and arms; I noticed that the small cat my landlady had taken in had come into my room, and sat staring, in the way of cats. I had found that cat myself, in these very chambers, covered in red paint; for that service the cat, a handsome, brindled creature now called Rigby, occasionally displayed a contemptuous affection for me: this was one such moment.

"No, not without causing embarrassment to a German noblewoman, and possibly leading to difficulties with the Turks," Holmes said with a brief, cynical chuckle.

"Oh, yes, the Turks," I said, continuing to dress.

"They are a complication, making swift action now all the more necessary." He pulled at his lower lip. "The crux of the matter is that German noblewoman."

"Good God!" I expostulated as I put on my trousers, tucking in my shirt-tails and adjusting the braces before I reached for my waistcoat. "What a coil! How comes a German noblewoman to be caught up in this?"

"Well might you ask. We have had word from Scotland. Concerning Sir Cameron." He glanced back toward the stairs. "We won't be overheard, will we?"

More and more tangles! What had Sir Cameron to do with this? I wondered, not doubting for an instant that the sottish Scottish knight could be part of this imbroglio. "No; only by the cat," I said in answer to his question. My landlady was not only the soul of discretion, she was a woman who valued sleep; she would not deprive herself of rest in order to eavesdrop.

Holmes looked reassured. "Well, you do recall that Sir Cameron's second wife is German?"

"Yes; I thought they were estranged." I had assumed that since I had first encountered the bumptious Scot in Munich on my first mission for Mycroft Holmes. "She has almost never been seen in his company. Not that I blame her."

"Just so," said Mycroft Holmes drily.

"Have they reconciled?" I asked, thinking it unlikely.

"Not as yet. But it seems she has come into a tidy fortune from her uncle, and now Sir Cameron is all alacrity to reestablish—er—rapprochement with her. Apparently she is of a similar mind—although I cannot fathom why. She has made the first move for reasons I can only speculate upon. His acceptance, on the other hand, is easily guessed: it would suit him very well to have his hands on her money." His smile was without humor. "His advantages are readily apparent should they reconcile. Hers are less so, which makes her pursuit of him so puzzling, although that is precisely what it appears is happening. She, it would seem, is encouraging him, which has to be something new in their marriage. Until now she has been at pains to avoid him. Yet as of two weeks ago she has sent word that she intends to visit him. She has said she will come to England to see him, to determine if she wishes to renew their—um—intimacy."

"That is a bit embarrassing," I said as I knotted my tie, then opened my sock drawer and pulled out a rolled pair. "But I do not see what that has to do with this emergency."

"Her uncle, it turns out, had some close associates," said Mycroft Holmes grimly. "In the Brotherhood. They will be her traveling companions according to the telegram she has sent to him. I have only just learned of this, or I would have advised against permitting her to have them escort her. It would have been much better to have her accompanied by half a dozen officers of one of the better Scots regiments."

"Is it too late to make such an arrangement?" I was standing on one foot, my sock held at the ready; Rigby watched inscrutably.

"I fear it is. Should I make such recommendation at this point, it would lead, I fear, to precisely the suspicions I would like to avoid."

I faltered as I pulled on my socks and looked for my boots. "Are you certain? That they are part of the Brotherhood? Are your sources accurate? This is not the sort of accusation you would want to make without persuasive evidence." I retrieved them from under the bed, and shoved my feet into them. "Considering what has happened to Sir Cameron, I wouldn't think that—"

"As certain as I may be without seeing their blood signatures on their oath. Your caution is laudable, my boy, but in this instance it is also misplaced," he answered, a grim note coming into his voice as he got out of the chair. "And there is the report on Sir Marmion, which should not be delayed. Are you ready?"

This shocked me; I nodded, and rubbed my chin. "I haven't shaved, sir," I said as I realized it for myself.

"Tyers will lend you a razor when we reach Pall Mall. It is a good thing you keep a change of clothes at my flat; you may not return here for a day or two. We haven't time for shaving now. Sid Hastings is waiting for us and time is passing. Come along, Guthrie. And be careful." He was already at my door, holding it open for me; Rigby slipped out of the room ahead of us. What could I do but don my coat, take my cloak from its peg on the door, and follow Mycroft Holmes down the street?

Sid Hastings brought his cab up to the kerb and let down the steps. "Gentlemen, do come in," he said calmly, as if this were mid-afternoon and not the dregs of night; we climbed in and closed up the front of the cab. "Walk on, Lance." His new horse, a slapping bay with Cleveland blood in him, obeyed his signal properly, and soon we were moving along at a good trot to Pall Mall, the hollow clop of the horse's hooves echoing eerily in the empty streets.

The dark streets were wet from the mizzle that came in off the Thames. I took a deep breath of the night air, as much in the hope it would waken me as to avail myself of its benefits. After going several blocks in silence, Mycroft Holmes spoke. "It is the most damnable thing," he said with emotion as he swung around, holding his pistol at the ready.

"Damnable? The Brotherhood?" I had not been privy to the thoughts that led him to this expostulation, and heard him now with a sense of apprehension; I could not see whatever it was that had alarmed him.

"Damnable," reiterated Holmes, squinting into the foggy darkness. "We are being followed," he declared. "Two men on horseback."

Again I looked and saw nothing, although I did hear the sound of a pair of horses not far behind us. "Are you certain?"

"Guthrie, dear boy, I left the theatre early in part because I was given a warning that there might be an attempt on my life tonight; the summons from the castle was fortuitous in that regard. There was a pair of horses behind me then, there was a pair of horses behind me when I left the castle, and there is a pair behind us now. If you listen, you will hear one of the horses has a loose shoe. You will hear no wheels, so you must assume the horses are being ridden, not driven." He shook his head, still twisted about in the cab in order to keep a watch on what was behind us. "And there is other trouble to deal with tonight. It is a difficult situation."

"What trouble?" I asked.

Mycroft Holmes did not answer directly. "The Brotherhood are busy again, as I told you. Vickers has been out of the country for almost a year, and I had reason to hope he would remain abroad, fixed in Germany, where we had our last report of him; after all he suffered as the result of our pursuit of him, I would have supposed he would wash his hands of Britain. Any prudent man would. But prudence is not one of the Brotherhood's virtues, is it?" He did his best to chuckle at this observation, an effort that ended on a sigh. "I have it on good authority that he intends to meet with these German Brotherhood members while they are here, which indicates he will be back, and protected by their position and rank. His return can only mean that the Brotherhood are resuming their efforts to find like-minded friends in Britain. They have more than enough of those already. The timing of the visit is suspicious." He pulled at his lower lip, a sure sign of consternation. "If the Turkish delegation had not set Sunday week for the start of their visit, I could view the Brotherhood's activities with a less jaundiced eye. It is all too pat. I have wanted to believe that this is mere co-incidence. But as it is, I cannot allow myself the luxury of hoping for the possibility that these incidents are only happenstance."

"You aren't surprised at this, are you, sir?" I asked, recalling the many times he had given warning to his colleagues in the government regarding the activities in the Brotherhood. "That the Brotherhood are trying once again to reestablish themselves in England?"

"No, not surprised," said Mycroft Holmes heavily. "It was only a matter of time until Vickers found a way to work mischief again, and with the Turks coming, the opportunity must seem too promising to pass up. There is tension enough between Eastern Europe and the Turks to offer the Brotherhood the very opportunities they seek, and Vickers is not one to miss such a chance. In his position, I would probably have done the same thing. Still, I hoped we would have a little more time to prepare for their return." He slapped his thigh through his cloak, a dark frown on his broad brow. "Well, it is not to be."

"I suppose not," I said, coughing diplomatically. "The situation must be urgent, for you to fetch me at this hour."

"Unfortunately, it is." He lowered his voice. "I received word tonight—along with the warning of a possible attempt on my life—that Jacobbus Braaten is arriving in five days at Dover. He is the first of the Brotherhood to come; he is here supposedly to confer with a group of Oxford dons. I have no doubt he will do it, and try to sound

them out, to determine if he might have an ally or two among them."
He stared into the night as if he could see the pernicious Dutchman
approaching through the mists.

"Jacobbus Braaten!" I exclaimed. I had not heard him mentioned
for more than three months; of all the many villains in the Brotherhood, Jacobbus Braaten was without doubt the most baneful. When
his steam-launch blew up last year, I hoped we had seen the last of
him.

"You will have to be very careful around him, if you happen to
encounter him again. I have heard he holds you responsible for the
explosion and his limp." Holmes gave a quick smile. "That was excellent work, Guthrie my boy."

"It wasn't deliberate," I had to admit. "I had to escape from him
as best I could. Breaking his leg was a fortunate by-product of my
improvised bomb."

"And a wise decision it was, putting those explosive on the
boiler," Mycroft Holmes approved. "I wish he had not survived, but
so it is."

The pair of horses behind us dropped back a way, so that the
sound of the hoofbeats was only a distant counterpoint to our words.
Sid Hastings remained unperturbed.

"If Braaten is coming, we must suppose the Brotherhood is serious about regaining its standing among the radicals in England." I
could feel my apprehension increase in spite of my intention to remain
detached from the threat. "No wonder you are apprehensive about the
Turks being here at the same time. Braaten has sworn to exact vengeance for Constantinople."

"The Turks would say Istanbul," Mycroft Holmes reminded me.

"Constantinople," I insisted. "Though it does not matter what
the city is called: if Jacobbus Braaten is determined to exact a price
for his misadventures there, nothing we do can change it."

"The Brotherhood has never been anything less than serious
about its goals," said Mycroft Holmes in a voice made deep with the
burden it implied. "You have as much reason as I to know this. You
have seen them at work."

I nodded. "I have never had cause to believe they would not go
to any lengths to achieve their ends. Indeed, I have every reason to

know they are ruthless and relentless." I shoved some unpleasant memories out of my mind for the time being: it was not the Brotherhood's past villainy that demanded my attention, but the plans that might be underway for new acts of mayhem. "Particularly Jacobbus Braaten. He's worse than Vickers."

"I know Vickers has spent some time with Braaten; two of our agents have confirmed it, one at the cost of his life," Mycroft Holmes went on as if he were discussing a social event rather than the plotting of dire men.

"Was that the information you had from Amsterdam last month?" I ventured, recalling the very correct Dutch officer who had called at Holmes' flat unannounced.

"That was the beginning of it, yes," said Holmes, his attention fixed on the road ahead. "I very nearly dismissed the report as being groundless; thank goodness Sutton had the presence of mind to review the communications the Dutch officer brought with him, or I might well have overlooked one of the crucial notes amid all the rest. I had not been as acute as I should have been. There was very careful phrasing in the text, so constructed as to seem innocuous. It was so welldone that I fell into its trap." He began to twiddle his watch-fob. "I had read the missive one way; Sutton showed me it had an alternate meaning."

"Did he," I said, curious but not particularly surprised, for Sutton was very sensitive to nuances of language—the result of his occupation.

"I admit it." Mycroft Holmes cracked a chuckle. "I'm not often caught napping, but this time I very nearly was. I cannot express the scope of my gratitude to Sutton; there are not words of sufficient obligation." He glanced back, as if to ascertain we were not being followed, and then he looked directly at me. "You will have to tread carefully; we must not alert any of the Brotherhood to the fact that we have been apprised of their scheme."

"Of course, sir," I said, a bit perplexed that he believed that I should need such a warning. My past experience with the Brotherhood made me keenly aware of the danger they represented. "You need have no doubts of me."

"Certainly not, dear boy," said Mycroft Holmes as we reached the turning into Pall Mall. "You will see that the Brotherhood are—" He stopped as the cab pulled up at the front of his building in Pall Mall, across from his club. "Come up, come up." He opened the door and let down the steps, saying to Sid Hastings as he did, "If you will return at eight, I will have work for you."

Sid touched the brim of his hat in salute. "Eight it is," he said, and signaled Lance to walk on just as I got down and flipped up the steps.

"Tyers is waiting for us," said Holmes as he began to climb the stairs. "I have arranged to have an Admiralty courier to be at our disposal from now until midnight. He is expected directly, and will arrive at the rear of the flat to decrease the possibility of observation. We may well have need of him." He reached the first landing; I was close behind him. "Be alert, Guthrie. I am very much afraid that we are swimming in deep water this time."

"We have done so before, sir," I said, gamely keeping up with him.

"Ah, but this time we are at risk as we have not been before. To face Vickers and Braaten at the same time is to compound the danger. To fight them in England is a peril of its own." He was almost to the second landing when he stopped abruptly. "If you are willing to face the Devil, you will have my greatest thanks."

"Surely it is not so desperate as all that," I said as we headed upward to his door; I glanced back down the street, wondering if I should see the pair of horses that had been following us.

"I would like to believe it is not, although all my senses warn me that it is." He was about to knock when Tyers opened the door for him, as neat and self-possessed as if this were three-thirty in the afternoon instead of the darkest hour of the night. "Ah, Tyers. You see me returned in good time. What news?"

"The Turkish gentleman is waiting in your study, Mister Holmes," said Tyers as calmly as he might have told us that the post had been delivered on time.

Turkish gentleman? I thought. One coming in advance of the delegation perhaps?

"Yes. Thank you, Tyers. I trust he has been provided a better-fitting pair of boots?" Mycroft Holmes shrugged out of his cape and handed it, his hat, and silk muffler to Tyers. "And he has had something to warm him?"

"Yes, sir. You were quite right in saying he would need a sticking plaster; he has a blister the size of a nut on the base of his heel." He took my overcoat from me. "I have water on for tea. We'll have you warm soon enough, Mister Guthrie."

"Very good," I said, feeling awkward to be noticed. I stifled a yawn and made myself stand very straight. "I beg your pardon. I am not entirely awake yet."

"What time did you go to bed?" Mycroft Holmes asked me as he motioned me to come with him down the hall to his study.

"Just after one," I said. "I was busy with the translations you requested from the German newspapers. I must say, I did not find anything suspicious in the pages, other than that the price of pork seems to be rising more than usual for this time of year." I still had the uneasy feeling that there was something I had not seen, something so obvious that when Mister Holmes pointed it out to me—as I was certain he would do—I would be mortified for not perceiving it instantly.

"What do you think such a fluctuation could mean?" Holmes suggested as he tapped on the door of his study. "Mister Halil Kerem. Do you mind if we enter?"

A muffled answer came from beyond the door, and then Mister Kerem himself opened the door, dressed in good English clothes, with a silken tie that was a trifle over-bright and a bit too wide, but otherwise quite acceptable, although clearly he was not a diplomat. He was wearing one boot and holding the other in his hand. "Mister Holmes," he said in very good English. "I am eternally grateful to you for taking me in. May Allah give you many worthy sons for your kindness."

"It is I who am grateful, Mister Kerem. You have alerted me to a most urgent problem that needs prompt attention." He motioned his guest to return to the over-stuffed chair he had clearly just vacated—a sock was lying on the floor in front of it—and strode in to take his usual place on the old-fashioned settle in front of the hearth.

"Come, Guthrie, let me present you." He signaled to me. "This is my personal secretary and general assistant, Mister Paterson Guthrie: Mister Halil Kerem."

"It is an honor to meet one who has the privilege of serving Mister Mycroft Holmes," said Mister Kerem, in that effusive and flowery way they consider good manners among the Turks.

"The honor is mine, to meet one who has come so far to be of use to Mister Holmes," I said in what I hoped was enough expansiveness.

"Guthrie is going to make notes on our conversation so that I may be certain that I have your information down in all its particulars," said Mycroft Holmes, glancing up as Tyers appeared in the doorway. "Yes? What is it?"

"Tea is almost ready, Mister Holmes," said Tyers, unflappable as always. "Do you want anything more than toast and marmalade to accompany it?"

"That will suffice admirably, for the time being. We'll want breakfast directly, but tea first, if you would," said Mycroft Holmes, giving me a moment to retrieve my leather-bound portfolio in which I kept paper and writing implements. "You will join us, of course, Mister Kerem?" It was not actually a question, only courtesy due a guest, but the Turkish gentleman considered his answer.

"I am generally fond of tea," he said, "but not with milk. Sugar will suit me very well." He smiled as he disposed himself in the chair again. "You are kind to ask. So often you English put in milk without bothering to ask."

"Yes. Well." Mycroft Holmes laid his arm on the table as he took his seat. "Perhaps you will be kind enough to tell me of your misadventure this evening, so that I may offer you what assistance I am able to?"

Tyers stepped back and closed the door; I could hear his footsteps as he went toward the rear of the flat.

Mister Kerem did not like being prodded, but he took it well enough. "At such an hour, I can well comprehend your testiness. I will bring myself to the point at once." He paused. "It is slavery, Mister Holmes—slavery."

I had begun to write, but his mention of that most heinous institution caused me to stop my efforts and wait for further instructions: I glanced at Mycroft Holmes to see what his response might be.

"My dear Mister Kerem, much as I lament the enslavement of my fellow-humans, I am powerless to interfere with Turkish sovereignty. It is a deplorable state of affairs, I grant you, but it is also beyond my powers to correct. If you wish to stir up public sentiment, it is a journalist you want, not a minor official such as I am." He spoke smoothly enough, but I saw he had begun to twiddle his watch-fob, a sure sign of agitation on Holmes' part.

"Not in Turkey, Mister Holmes," said Mister Kerem as dramatically as an Italian. "No. Nothing of the sort. Slavery here in England." He waited a second or two, and added, "You must stop it."

"Slavery here in England?" Holmes said in a tone of utter revulsion. "Nothing of the sort, my good man. Nothing of the sort. There are laws . . ." His voice trailed off and an uncharacteristic expression of doubt settled on his features. "Why do you say this?"

"Because my own brother was taken from our family," said Mister Kerem. "A lad of sixteen. And he is not the only one."

FROM THE PERSONAL JOURNAL OF PHILIP TYERS

The arrival of the Turkish gentleman, Mister Kerem, has alarmed MH in a singular manner—so much so that he went himself to fetch G at this late hour for the purpose of having him record what is said; MH himself was returning from a most private interview with HRHE when my note reached him. It appears to me that MH is more troubled by Mister Kerem than circumstances would seem to justify, which gives me to wonder what more MH knows of the situation that he has kept to himself . . . I must believe that MH has some special understanding that has been alerted by recent events.

This evening I reported to MH that this flat was under observation from the rear. In a flat opposite this one from the service alley, there has been a man in what must be servant's clothing who has done nothing but watch the alley and the stairs leading to this flat. I thought at first I might be mistaken, but now I can have no doubt. I have informed MH of this and he has acknowledged this intelligence with a nod . . .

What has puzzled me is the generous welcome MH has ordered to offer Mister Kerem. It is not like him to be so unquestioning regarding those admitted to this flat. No doubt he will explain it in good time.

I will have to find a way to warn Sutton not to approach this flat from the front, or to come in disguise. I expect him within the hour, when we will have to improvise, for MH does not want Sutton seen at this flat, except in his disguise as MH himself.

Chapter Two

I SAW DOUBT war with apprehension in Mycroft Holmes' features, and I realized he must have heard something of this before now, or he would not have been so quickly ambivalent. I glanced toward our visitor, and addressed him myself. "Why do you say this, Mister Kerem? Have you proof? It is a most infamous accusation you are making."

"Alas, I have only tangential proof, not anything direct but what I have been told, and what I have surmised," said Mister Kerem. "It is not to my liking to have nothing more substantial to offer you, but—" He shrugged in a hopeless way. "You may find it incredible, yet what I know I will impart, and pray Allah will give you more wisdom than He gave me."

"That is very good of you," said Mycroft Holmes, recovering himself somewhat. "Do you say there are those in England who support this most nefarious of trades?"

"I fear it is so," said Mister Kerem. "My brother tried to warn me, I think, but I did not listen. I could not attribute such villainy to any European. It seemed so far-fetched: a European in the slave-trade to Europe, where, as you say, such business is illegal. But when he vanished, and then the policeman investigating his disappearance was found hacked to death near the harbor, I knew I had been a fool. I should have given my brother as much faith as I gave my various employers." He gazed into the middle distance. "He was a good boy, my brother. Yujel. Not a name that comes easily to English lips, but as good a name as any in Turkish." He attempted to smile and failed utterly.

"This Yujel was taken, you believe?" Mycroft Holmes asked with a crispness of tone that implied he was not eager to be detracted by memories.

"He was," said Mister Kerem. "There was a man in our town, a foreigner, a European, who said he was looking for places to plant orchards, but he spent most of his time watching the young men." He made a resigned gesture. "As what man does not?" Mister Kerem glanced at me and then at Mycroft Holmes, one eyebrow lifted knowingly.

I could think of nothing to say to this, but fortunately my employer was not as nonplused as I.

"Indeed," he said in a very urbane tone. "Tell me more of this foreigner who claimed to be planting orchards."

There was a burst of sound from the kitchen. Tyers must be busy, I thought, and continued to write.

"Well, he was much like many Englishmen. He might have been a Dutchman, or even a Swede. He was fair and his face was florid. He walked with a limp. He was of middle years, and he spoke with an accent that some said was French, but I did not think so. His words were harsher." Mister Kerem cleared his throat. "I did not speak to him more than once myself, and that briefly and in English, so I cannot tell you very much about that. I only saw him a few times."

I realized the man he was describing could be Jacobbus Braaten, a notion that chilled me.

"Did you have any reason to think he was planning an abduction? Was there anything obvious about him?" Mycroft Holmes asked; if he had noticed the man's resemblance to Braaten, he gave no indication of it.

"Not as such. Why should I suspect such an infamous thing?" Mister Kerem frowned. "This man was a stranger, and so we all watched him, but we also ignored him."

"How do you mean?" I asked, for although I had had a brief sojourn in Turkey, I could not claim that I understood the Turks.

"I mean that he was kept apart, not so obviously that he would be offended, but enough to indicate he was a stranger among us. He was aloof by nature, I supposed, as so many Europeans are. So no one extended themselves to befriend him, but also no one was wholly unaware of him." He paused. "I do not intend to confuse you."

"Of course not," said Mycroft Holmes smoothly. "I know the insularity of which you speak. Turks are not the only ones to practice it." He essayed a chuckle. "The English villager is much the same."

"It may be so," Mister Kerem conceded, returning to his topic with full deliberation. "I cannot think what I am to do. I have come this far and now my trail grows cold, and I fear this can only mean dire consequences for Yujel, though I try not to despair of finding him. I know my brother came here on the *Princess Fatima* and arrived five weeks ago. Other than that, I can find nothing to point to what has become of him."

"Did you go to the police?" Mycroft inquired, with a quick glance in my direction to make sure I put down the answer fully and accurately.

Mister Kerem scowled. "They did not listen to me. One of the senior officers told me I was mistaken. They would do nothing."

"And so you sought me out. Now why is that?" Mycroft Holmes asked in a voice so bland that I was instantly on the alert.

"I was told by an official at the Admiralty that you might be able to help me." He shrugged. "So I determined to find you." He looked down at his feet. "It was no simple thing, I can tell you. I must assume you have enemies, Mister Holmes?"

"What public servant does not?" Mycroft Holmes answered, dismissing the possibility with such sangfroid that I was more alarmed than before. "You learned my direction and came to me with some difficulty."

"Yes," said Mister Kerem. "I was chased by hooligans down an alley. They threatened to beat me and rob me—"

"That, lamentably, might have happened anywhere in London, and for no reason other than you are a stranger here," Holmes told him. "Why do you say that it was connected to me?"

"Because one of the men warned me to stay away from you." Mister Kerem looked a bit shamefaced admitting this. "I was very much shocked."

"So might you be," said Mycroft Holmes, and rose. "I am going to see what has become of Tyers and our tea. Do you Guthrie, look after our guest."

I mumbled some words that might be assent, and I made a bigger show of opening my portfolio to take more notes. "You were saying about this European man, whom you believe is responsible for the disappearance of your brother . . ." I left the end open, so that he would be inspired to expand on his suppositions.

"It was a most dreadful thing," said Mister Kerem. "I had paid no heed to anything my brother told me, yet he had expressed his apprehensions most clearly."

"How was that?" I asked, and paused at the sound of something breaking and a muffled oath from the back of the house. I recovered and went on. "Precisely what did he say?"

"He said that he had seen the man watching him," said Mister Kerem in the dramatic manner he had used before. "He knew that the man wanted more than kisses."

"But a look and his suspicions would not be enough for such conviction as you have now, surely," I said, hoping to draw him out.

"You do not understand how it is," said Mister Kerem in exasperation. "If you had seen this man, you would have known that he would attempt anything nefarious."

"You did not listen to your brother, but you had similar apprehensions?" I pursued.

"I did not comprehend the whole of the danger," said Mister Kerem.

I considered my next question. "You did not respond to this threat until your brother's misfortune—is it possible there might be another explanation?"

"It was the foreigner who took him," Mister Kerem insisted with some heat.

"You believe this because he was a foreigner?" I asked, and saw that I had offended the Turk.

"That would be inhospitable," Mister Kerem declared, sulking.

I wondered what I might do to recover the advantage I had had only moments ago. Fortunately, Mycroft Holmes chose that moment to return, carrying the tea-tray and smiling affably.

"I'm sorry to have taken so long," he said to the room at large. "There was a minor accident in the kitchen and Tyers is busy setting things to rights." He put the tray down. "I think you'll find you'll be more the thing, as my grandmother used to say, when you've had a cup of tea. There will be baked eggs in a short while."

Mister Kerem shook his head, somewhat mollified. "I am distraught about my brother."

"Small wonder," said Mycroft Holmes. "I am distraught about mine, when he goes missing." He glanced at me. "Would you be good enough to lend Tyers a hand for a moment, Guthrie? I fear he may need some assistance."

"Of course," I said, rising and preparing to leave the two of them alone. As I set my portfolio down, I saw Mycroft Holmes signal me to be gone for at least five minutes. I gave him a slight nod to show I understood and said, "Whatever Tyers needs, I am his to command." I hoped I had not overdone it.

"Excellent fellow," Holmes approved, and gave his full attention to Mister Kerem.

Walking down the corridor to the kitchen at the rear of the flat, I began to wonder what my employer thought my absence would accomplish.

Tyers was fitting a cut section of wood veneer over a broken window-pane; he glanced my way and favored me with a single nod. "The courier was shot as he came up the steps," he told me. "The first shot was wide of the mark." He indicated the shattered pane.

"Is the courier . . ." I did not want to ask if he had succumbed.

"In the rear. Behind the rack of disguises Mister Sutton has provided," said Tyers, as if this were an every-day occurrence, requiring nothing more than the most minimal attention.

"How seriously is he injured?" I asked, appalled.

"He's bled a great deal, but the wound is clean; if he escapes a bad fever, he should be right as rain in a month or so. He is wrapped in blankets and resting comfortably. I will shortly go to inform the Admiralty of this unfortunate event, and ask Doctor Watson to step 'round for a look at the lad." Tyers managed a slight, inscrutable smile. "We don't want this getting out, do we?"

"Good Lord," I exclaimed. "I should hope not!"

"Exactly," said Tyers, implying a wealth of misfortune in that single word. He picked up the dustpan which had been lying before the cooker. I had not noticed it until now, and I saw it was full of shards of broken glass. "I'll be back in half a tick," he said, and went to dispose of the dustpan's contents.

Left to my own devices, I paced around the kitchen; the familiar smells of bread and grilled meats awakening my hunger. I recalled that Mycroft Holmes had mentioned breakfast and my mouth watered. I could feel the heat coming from the cooker; I hoped this meant that breakfast would soon be forthcoming. Even as I realized this, I was shocked at my lack of feeling, for surely I must be callous beyond all reckoning to care more for my next meal than the Admiralty courier who lay in the next room. Had I become indifferent to human suffering as a result of my work for Mycroft Holmes? I did not want to think so.

Tyers returned, wiping his hands after he hung up the dustpan in its place. "Good to see you're keeping your head, if I may say so, Mister Guthrie," he told me as he cut half a dozen rashers of bacon and put them into a pan to cook.

I was astonished. "Why do you think so?"

"You haven't gone blubbery on me, thank God fasting." He turned the bacon as it began to spatter. "There's more to this Turkish cove than meets the eye. You mark my words." He opened the oven and peered in. "Almost done," he announced.

"And the courier? What do you make of his . . . misfortune?" I asked.

"He is lucky to be alive," said Tyers, busying himself with readying plates for breakfast. "I am sorry he was injured, of course. But he is in the service of his country, and men have paid a far higher price than he for such." He opened the drawer containing the eating utensils. "Get the serviettes for me, will you, Guthrie? They're in the second drawer on the left."

I retrieved the serviettes and offered them to Tyers, who indicated the tray he was preparing. "Just there, sir, if you would."

"Mister Sutton hasn't arrived yet?" I said, thinking of the courier.

"Not yet," said Tyers. "He's a knowing one. He'll take care to come disguised."

"Did a message reach him?" I was mildly surprised, wondering how word had been got to him.

"No, it didn't," said Tyers.

"So. You have set out the cock, have you?" It was a signal device that Mycroft Holmes sometimes used to warn Sutton to put on a disguise. The little red weather-cock had seen better days, but it was innocuous enough to make it possible for its use without attracting any attention. "Why could you not get a message to him?"

"He'd left the theatre," said Tyers. "This way, he'll take precautions." He took a plate of scones out of the warming oven, and then pulled the butter out of the ice-chest and set them on the breakfast tray. "Marmalade and butter. Should we include honey, do you think? The Turks like honey." He did not wait for an answer, but went to fetch a stoneware jar of it from the pantry. "Better put it out, just in case," he said.

I felt as if I had nothing to do. I stood beside the table where the tray waited. "Should I check on the courier?" I asked.

"If you would. Take him some of this." He handed me a mug filled with an aromatic toddy of brandy, honey, and a mixture of herbs. "Make sure he drinks it."

"That I will," I said, taking the mug in hand and going out the rear of the kitchen.

The rack of clothing from which Mycroft Holmes and Edmund Sutton assembled their disguises took up most of the side of the long, dark chamber. The windows that looked onto the rear steps and the service alley were kept dusty deliberately, so that no one could easily look in and see what was stored here. Not that it mattered at this hour. I saw the gaslight was shining softly, hardly more than a glow, giving just enough illumination to save one from tripping over the array of shoes accompanying the clothing. I parted the items on the rack, going between a dove-grey morning coat and a multi-caped coachman's cloak.

The courier was lying on a narrow cot, a candle standing in a dish on the table behind his head. His shoulder was thick with hastily wrapped bandages, but I could see that a red stain was seeping through. The man's face was pasty, with sweat on his upper lip and forehead. His eyes were half-closed and he was breathing with an effort. He was a trifle younger than I, with a shock of light-brown hair slicked close to his skull and the indentation of spectacles on the bridge of his nose.

I pulled the blankets up to his chin. "There you are, sir," I told him as I bent over him. "They'll warm you up."

The courier's eyes opened, but did not truly focus. "What?" he asked. "Who?"

"I am Paterson Guthrie, Mycroft Holmes' confidential secretary. He sent me to check on you." It was near enough the truth that my conscience did not twinge at this slight mendacity. "I have brought you something to drink. It will help you to feel better directly." I held up the mug so he could see it. "Tyers has just made this for you. I will help you drink it." I dropped down on one knee beside the cot, and reached out to raise his head so he could sip the strange-smelling brew Tyers had made. "Here. Try it, there's a good fellow."

The courier drank as I tried to hold the mug for him. Some of the liquid rolled down his chin, and I was annoyed with myself for failing to bring a serviette to wipe his mouth for him. He sighed, and more of the liquid sloshed out. Then he tried to swallow and ended up coughing.

"Take it easy," I recommended, moving the mug so that it would not spill any more while he recovered.

"Sorry," he muttered, and his head rolled to the side, off my supporting hand.

I feared the worst had happened, and I put my hand to his forehead only to hear him moan. "You lie still," I told him, and rose. "You're pretty badly hit."

"I am," he agreed vaguely. "Cold."

"No doubt," I said, remembering how I felt after I had suffered a flesh wound the first time. "The doctor will call soon. Be sure he'll fix you up all right and tight."

The courier sighed again. I could not think of anything else to say. In a moment I went back through the hanging garments and into the kitchen, setting down the mug near the sink.

Tyers glanced at the mug and shook his head. "Is he complaining of cold?"

"Yes," I said, knowing it boded ill.

"Then we must hope Watson will come quickly," he said. "I shall be off in a shake." He had the tray almost ready. "If you'll carry this for me, I will be most grateful, Mister Guthrie."

"If it will mean more speed to help that poor wretch," I said, and reached for the tray.

"Tell Mister Holmes that I have gone out on an errand. He will take my meaning." He removed his apron and reached for his frock-coat that hung on a peg on the back of the door. "I think I will go to Watson first. Then to the Admiralty. I fear the courier needs help more urgently than I supposed at first."

"He may do so," I said, not wanting to sound panicked. "Best hurry."

"I will be back before sun-up," said Tyers, and went out the rear door as I turned toward the front of the flat.

Mycroft Holmes was nodding sympathetically as I came into the room. "Mister Kerem, any reasonable man must feel for your predicament."

"Do you suppose Englishmen are troubled by Turkish youths being sold as slaves in their brothels?" Mister Kerem countered. "I think not. I think Englishmen who want boys to serve them do not care how the boys came to that state."

"No doubt you are right," said Holmes with a subservient manner that was so startling to me that I almost dropped my tray. "Ah, there you are, Guthrie," he said as if he had only just noticed me. "In good time."

I put the tray down beside the tea-tray on the table. "Tyers has gone out on an errand," I told him as I made sure the tray was fully supported. "Baked eggs, bacon, scones, marmalade, honey, butter, and a fruit comfit." I pointed these out as I drew up my chair and chose a cup-and-saucer for my tea. I was now quite hungry and awake enough to know I needed food.

"At home I would have figs and yogurt," said Mister Kerem. "And coffee. But this is quite handsome." He took a plate and filled it with helpings of all that was offered.

"Mister Kerem has been telling me about this curious reverse white slavery. I think he may have stumbled across something quite significant. I shall have to make a full report of it to the Prime Minister at our next briefing." He had assumed that deferential manner that I knew to be most uncharacteristic of him. "It may demand our attention."

Something in the tone of his voice warned me to pay attention. I poured my tea and said, "It is an embarrassment to the government if it is true."

"No doubt," said Holmes, watching Mister Kerem as he began to devour his food. "I am shocked that so great an outrage as this should have existed for as long as Mister Kerem informs me it has, and we know nothing about it."

"Criminals can be very subtle," I said, trying to suit my remarks to his purpose.

"That they can." He took two baked eggs and three rashers of bacon, and began to eat them, chewing thoughtfully.

"May I pour you some tea?" I asked, seeing that his cup was empty.

"Yes, thank you, Guthrie," Mycroft Holmes answered, his face turned away just long enough to whisper, "Return to the kitchen."

Baffled, I did as he ordered. "I believe I have left the kettle on the cooker," I told Mister Kerem as I made my way to the door. Once there, I helped myself to a bit of egg still in the pan before going to check on the courier once again.

He was not improving. His breath was shallow, and his pulse, when I tried it, was thready. He was only half-ware of me, and that, too, was distressing to me. I put a second blanket over him and wiped his brow. Watson had better arrive quickly, I thought, or he will have wasted his journey.

As I turned to go, the courier spoke. "I . . . was shot."

"Yes, old fellow, I know," I said in as calm a tone as I could.

"It was . . . ambush." He panted now to get enough breath to finish.

"Yes; on the rear stairs," I said, paying closer attention now that I realized he was not wandering in his thoughts as much as I feared.

"It was . . . intended for . . . for Mister Holmes," said the courier. There was a febrile shine in his eyes, and an urgency that compelled my interest.

"How can you be certain?" I asked, fearing this might be a delusion resulting from his wound, and, at the same time, fearing it might not.

The courier blinked and strove to organize his recollection. "I heard . . . someone say, *That's him. That's . . . the other Holmes.*"

"The other Holmes?" I repeated, disbelievingly. "Are you certain that is what you heard?"

"It struck . . . me . . . as odd," he said, almost apologizing. "I stopped on . . . the stairs . . . because it was . . . odd." He was weakening quickly.

I put my hand on his sound arm. "Good work, lad," I said, wondering as I did what it might mean. The courier was fairly tall—he took up the length of the cot—and a cloak might give him the appearance of a more portly body than the trim young man possessed. But why should any assassin expect Mycroft Holmes to come up the rear stairs? Unless, I thought suddenly, they were looking for his brother, who, though as tall, was slighter. He had often come to the flat up the rear stairs, and he had his share of enemies among London's criminal element.

Withdrawing from the protected area behind the costume rack,

I mulled over my reflections and decided that there had to be some merit in my conclusion. Now I was annoyed that Mister Kerem was with us, for I could not discuss this deduction with Mycroft Holmes while the Turk was here. No matter how pressing his problem, I could not help but believe this was rather more urgent. I returned to the front of the flat and tapped on the study door. "Sir?"

"Come in, Guthrie. Come in," Mycroft Holmes greeted me sincerely through the door.

I did as he asked, noticing that the study was now quite warm. I could see that Mister Kerem was more comfortable now than Mycroft Holmes; the Turk was sitting at his ease, putting honey into his tea. "Tyers is still out," I said.

"He may be some little time," said Holmes as if untroubled by such a prospect.

"I hope he may be swift enough," I remarked.

Mycroft Holmes lifted a heavy eyebrow at my observation, but said only, "You must help yourself before the eggs are entirely cold."

"That I will," I said, and took up a plate, discovering as I did that my appetite had deserted me. I knew I had to eat something, and so I contented myself with a single baked egg and a scone. As I poured out the strong, black tea into my cup, I tried to think of some way I might gain a few moments with my employer to tell him all I had learned.

"Mister Kerem has presented a most persuasive argument," said Mycroft Holmes, again in a self-effacing manner that was at once amusing and unnerving.

"He has?" I said, taking my seat and putting my cup-and-saucer on the small end-table next to my chair.

"It is something that we must investigate, or so I now believe," said Holmes, refilling his cup and adding milk and sugar. "There are so many unanswered questions." He nodded to Mister Kerem. "This man has suffered a great deal, and I must conclude his is not the only family to be so disrupted."

"No, indeed," said Mister Kerem, drinking his very sweet tea with gusto.

"And it troubles me that we in England should have any role in this unsavoury business." He shook his head. "It must be looked into, and in a timely manner."

I was somewhat startled by this announcement, for while I knew Mycroft Holmes to be opposed to slavery in general, I did not suppose he would submit it to the Admiralty for action. "When might that be, sir?" I asked, trying to negotiate the conversational maze he had laid in my absence.

"Why, at the weekly review I attend," he said, waving this away with a negligent gesture, which told me more than anything that he was misleading Mister Kerem for some purpose of his own: he had daily dispatches from the Admiralty, and there was no weekly review he attended.

"An excellent venue, sir," I said, guessing this was expected of me.

"I should hope so," Mycroft Holmes said unctuously.

Mister Kerem smiled and finished his tea.

FROM THE PERSONAL JOURNAL OF PHILIP TYERS

The Admiralty courier is badly hurt, I fear. Watson has said he cannot remove the bullet here; I do not know if he can be saved, without such surgery, for the man's condition is deteriorating; Watson agreed. In any case, I despair of moving him safely, and not simply because of the gunman who might still be waiting to finish his work; the courier is so weak. If there is any reason to hurry, the welfare of that young man provides it. I will try to arrange for his removal to hospital at once. I shall not linger over these pages any longer . . .

Chapter Three

"I DON'T COMPREHEND how slaves can be brought into England. There are rules. Customs officials take a most dim view of abusing the law." Mycroft Holmes had finished eating and was sitting, sprawled in a posture most unlike himself, on the small divan under the window.

"I have heard tales of bribery," said Mister Kerem cautiously.

"Bribery, poppycock!" Mycroft Holmes protested. "It's one thing to look the other way for a handful of gems or to plate gold in brass in order to pay a lower duty on it. But human beings are not such objects. They act. They speak. They must have food and shelter."

"All this can be managed with planning," said Mister Kerem, dismissing Holmes' protestation with a wave of his hand.

"But you cannot be accusing Customs officials of overlooking something so egregious as this," Mycroft Holmes exclaimed.

Listening to him, I began to wonder why my employer had roused me so early. Surely this discussion, as upsetting as it was, could have waited until morning. Then I thought of the courier in the back of the flat and I knew there was more at stake here than was readily apparent. I was puzzled by the two events, for they had no apparent connection, yet from my work with Mycroft Holmes I had learned to be suspicious of anything presented as a coincidence. And that unfortunate young officer was proof that whatever lay behind these events was extremely serious. So I made myself listen to Halil Kerem, paying close attention to all I heard, certain that he would reveal the nature of his connection to the courier, no matter how tenuous it might be.

"So I was determined to find my brother," Mister Kerem said as he neared the end of his account. "I booked passage to London and arrived to discover he had disappeared."

Mycroft Holmes frowned. "You must have been aware that something of the sort could happen," he said, leaning forward as if implying his sympathy was colored by his opinion of the Turks— which it was, but not in the way Holmes' behavior would give one to assume.

"When searching for my brother," said Mister Kerem with great feeling, "I cannot be turned back by complications or disappointments."

"No; no of course not," said Mycroft Holmes, and looked up at the sound of the bell. "Tyers is still out, I suppose?" He looked at me. "Guthrie, would you be good enough . . ."

I put the remains of my breakfast aside and rose, saying, "Of course."

"I apologize for this interruption, Mister Kerem. The Admiralty has some business that needs my prompt attention." He motioned me away as the doorbell summoned me again.

I left the study and went down the hallway, hoping as I went that this early caller would be Doctor Watson returning. But as I opened the door, I saw I had been mistaken. There, in full evening dress and with a shining German order blazing on a scarlet sash, stood Edmund Sutton. All I could do was open the door and say, "Good morning, sir."

He stepped inside and said to me in very good German, "Good morning to you, my good man. Is Mister Holmes available?"

I answered in the same language. "He is with someone just now. If you would like to wait in the sitting room?" I indicated the way as if Sutton did not know it. "Whom shall I say is calling?" I was curious to hear the answer; I nodded toward the settee near the fire where a few embers still burned, making little headway against the morning chill.

"Say that Graf von Mutigheit is here," he told me without so much as the hint of a smile. "I will have a brandy, if you will."

I had to bite back a retort. "Of course, sir," I said, pretending to be Tyers, and left him. Before I fetched the brandy, I stopped in the study. "Graf von Mutigheit is here, sir," I told Mycroft Holmes. "He asked for a brandy."

"Then by all means get him one," said Mycroft Holmes with a kind of fussiness I might expect of a minor official, not a man who was near the apex of power in Britain.

"At once," I said, and was about to withdraw when Holmes stopped me.

"Tell the Graf that I will be with him in twenty minutes," he said, and glanced at Mister Kerem. "That will be sufficient for now, will it not?"

"Most certainly," said Mister Kerem with an expression that conveyed the opposite. "I am grateful that you have heard me at all."

"Oh, no need for that," said Mycroft Holmes with every show of modesty. "I'm a public servant don't you know. It is my duty to listen to all complaints."

With this fulsome sentiment ringing in my ears, I went to get Sutton his brandy. I did not linger in the kitchen, but poured out some of the best into a snifter, put it on a tray, and took it to the sitting room at the front of the flat. "With Mister Holmes' compliments and his assurance he will be with you in twenty minutes," I said in English.

"Very good," Sutton said, using a heavy German accent as he took the snifter. I saw he had flung his cloak over the back of the high-backed arm-chair in the corner, and although he must have been cold, seemed to be very much at his ease. If anyone were watching, they would be wholly persuaded by his performance. "You may go."

I bowed slightly and withdrew, thinking as I did that as recently as a year ago, I would have found his manner offensive and would have asked for an apology. But now I appreciated the value of these personae he invented; I no longer bristled at Sutton, for it now was obvious to me that the roles he played were the same as those he played in the theatre, but without the benefit of direction or script.

Once again I entered the study and once again I saw Mycroft Holmes doing his utmost to seem self-effacing and perhaps a bit ineffectual. I went and took up my portfolio again, beginning to write on the foolscap pad I kept in it.

"I can't think of anything more I can do, Mister Kerem," Mycroft Holmes was saying. "I will, of course, request that a finding be sent to the Turkish government when we have completed our investigation, but until then, I fear I am not going to be much assistance to you." He opened his hands to show how helpless he was; I did my best to stifle a laugh. "Bless you, dear boy," Holmes said, as if I had sneezed.

"Thank you, sir," I mumbled. I should not have had such a lapse, I realized. Sutton would be very disappointed in me.

"I fear I must soon give the Graf his assigned hour," said Mycroft Holmes. "I apologize for any inconvenience this may give you, but you see, the Graft's appointment is of long-standing."

"No, no. You need make no excuses. I understand perfectly," said Mister Kerem. "I am grateful to have had so much of your time, and I thank you for it." He paused. "Do you think there is any chance my brother might be found?"

"Early days yet, Mister Kerem," said Holmes with a shake of his head. "Still, something must be done."

"Allah is great," said Mister Kerem.

"Make a memo, Guthrie, to the effect that Mister Kerem's claims must be investigated, and as quickly as may be. If he is right, and there are slaves coming into England, Her Majesty's government must not tolerate it." He sounded more bluster than intention, but I duly made the note and kept my eye on Halil Kerem.

"Well, it is the best I can hope for," Mister Kerem said heavily. "I suppose I must content myself with your assurances."

"I will do as much as any man in my position can," said Mycroft Holmes, in a voice I knew was genuine, no matter how overwhelmed his manner suggested he was.

"For that I thank you," said Mister Kerem, beginning to pull on his shoes. "And thank you for your kindness. I did not know how hard walking would be." His laughter was brittle. When he finished buttoning his shoes, he got to his feet. "And thank you for this early morning meal. I had not realized how hungry I had become."

"Feeding the hungry is a virtue," Mycroft Holmes said with a piety I knew he did not feel.

Mister Kerem did not notice, for he said in perfect seriousness, "In both our faiths."

Mycroft Holmes rose. "If you wish reports on the progress of the Admiralty's investigation, you will learn more from that office than in applying to me. I can but put the gears in motion," he said.

"Thank you. I will," said Mister Kerem. "Now I will leave you to your German visitor."

"You are very good," said Mycroft Holmes in a manner that was as enigmatic as it was correct. He signaled me with a quick, covert sign.

I rose to escort the Turk to the door. "You may find a cab at the corner," I told him as I opened the front door.

Mister Kerem craned his neck in an attempt to look into the sitting room, and in that instant I was aware of the wisdom of Edmund Sutton's maintaining his German character. Had he made himself as comfortable as he was wont to do, Mister Kerem might well question the story he had been told only a few minutes ago. Finally he gave up, having had little more than a glimpse of Sutton. "The corner, you say?"

"Yes. You can spare yourself more discomfort if you don't walk too far on that blister," I said, feeling nervous, remembering how the courier came to be shot on the rear steps.

"True enough," said Halil Kerem, and put on his hat. In the first morning light, he cast a very long shadow.

For some reason I could not define, I was relieved to close the door on him.

Mycroft Holmes emerged from the study with an expression of aggravation on his powerful visage. There was now no trace of the timorous functionary about him. He put his hand on the doorframe and leaned on it. "What do you suppose that was all about?" he asked me.

"A Turk wanting to bring something to the government's attention?" I said, knowing it was not the answer my employer had in mind.

"Don't be daft, my boy. This was far more subtle than it appeared. That man sought me out, not the government, not the Admiralty: me. He had a purpose of his own." He stared at the framed maps on the wall opposite the door. "Most perplexing."

"No matter what the truth may be," I agreed; I could not rid myself of the sinister impression I had of Mister Halil Kerem. "And your behavior was also a bit . . . misleading."

"Misleading in what sense?" asked Holmes with the innocence of a babe.

"One would have thought you could not free a cur from the dogcatcher, as the saying has it," I said, a bit curtly.

Holmes smiled. "Well, do you know, Guthrie, when someone tries as hard as Mister Kerem to manipulate me, I want to reduce his hopes of any success in such matters."

I nodded. "Yes. And yet, I cannot help but suppose that there is more to it than you have intimated; your suspicions are roused, and you are on guard."

"How perceptive you are," said Mycroft Holmes, then straightened up. "How is the courier?"

"I have not checked him in the last several minutes," I admitted. "I did not like the look of him when I went to see him." I sighed. "He said something very strange: *That's the other Holmes.* He claims he heard it just before he was shot." I stopped, then offered my theory.

"It strikes me the reference was to your brother. If he, indeed, heard anything."

"An odd phrase to imagine; still, it may or may not have any bearing on his misfortune," said Mycroft Holmes, coming into the hallway. "I assume Sutton has arrived?"

"Grand as a Hapsburg and as gaudy," I said, smiling my appreciation. "Mister Kerem had a brief look at him. I think he was impressed at such a splendid fellow."

"The Graf von Mutigheit?" Holmes surged past me, his hand out in welcome. "Good morning, Sutton. Or should I say Graf?" He gave the actor a quick perusal. "Very good."

"For an improvisation, superior," said Sutton in the manner of the Graf. "I was nonplused when I saw the cock, I can tell you," he added in his own forthcoming way. "There has been some trouble, has there?"

"An Admiralty courier was shot coming up the rear steps last night," said Mycroft Holmes, looking tired as he spoke.

"Gracious!" Sutton exclaimed, no trace of the Graf left in him. "Seriously?"

"I am afraid so. Tyers fetched Watson." Holmes went toward the window and looked down at the early morning activity in Pall Mall. "I am not at all sanguine about it," he said. "Not with the Brotherhood trying to establish itself in Britain again."

"You have proof?" Sutton was alarmed, but he also sounded intrigued.

"I believe so," he said, and looked around as he heard a door slam at the rear of the flat. "If you will excuse me—" He swung around and started for the kitchen.

Perforce, Sutton and I followed after him.

Tyers met us in the kitchen. "Doctor Watson returned," he said without preamble. "He is with the courier now."

"Very good," Mycroft Holmes approved. "Have you been to the Admiralty yet?"

"No. I want to give them a report on the courier." Tyers went to the sink and refilled the kettle with water. "I am in need of tea. May I make some for you gentlemen?"

Mycroft Holmes nodded, and I was relieved, for I could feel myself begin to slump. "What did Watson say?"

"Only that he should not be disturbed while he is working on the lad." Tyers poked up the firebox and added more fuel to it. "This should not be long."

Sutton occupied himself by unpinning the order and sash from his evening clothes. "I think I had best change into something less conspicuous." He glanced at Mycroft Holmes. "If you will not need me for twenty minutes?"

"Go ahead. And you, Guthrie. Take Tyers' razor and shave; you might consider purchasing a second kit and leaving it here, as you do your change of clothes. You are beginning to look quite disreputable." He smiled to show he was joking.

"An excellent notion," I said, rubbing my stubbled chin. "I had nearly forgot."

"You know where I keep my razors, sir," said Tyers, a bit pre-occupied; I realized that he wanted a word alone with Mycroft Holmes and did not want to say so directly. Had I been fully awake, I would have seen this at once.

"That I do, and thank you, Tyers." I swung around and started out of the kitchen, Sutton right behind me.

We were both bound for the dressing room that connected Mycroft Holmes' bedroom with the bathroom. Sutton shrugged out of his coat and began working the studs out of his shirt before we reached it; I had come to see this skill at rapid changing of clothes as one of the unusual benefits of his profession.

"He's worried," Sutton remarked as he entered the dressing room.

I opened the drawer that contained Tyers' grooming and toilet items. There were three razors and I chose the one with the horn handle. "Yes. He is."

"He doesn't want us to worry," Sutton went on, his voice muffled as he continued undressing.

I went back to the bathroom, leaving the adjoining door open so that Sutton and I could continue our conversation. "That's obvious," I said as I got the lather-mug and the brush and started to stir.

"Is it just the Brotherhood, or is there more to it?" Sutton asked.

"I don't know," I replied, annoyed at myself for not being more on the *qui vive*.

"Then there is," said Sutton. A shoe clumped to the floor; a moment later so did the second.

"I suppose you're right," I said as I began to lather my face while staring in the mirror. There were circles under my eyes, seeming to be different shades because my left eye is blue and my right eye is green. I was vaguely aware that there was a touch of grey at my temples, hardly more than a few strands, but still, I thought. I had turned thirty-four in May; my mother had been far greyer when she was my age. This notion did not console me, for I knew I still had much to do in my life, and wanted no reminders of my mortality: gunshots and assassins took care of that only too well. I put the mug down, opened the razor, and set to work.

"Who is the Turk?" Sutton asked a bit later.

I was doing the short strokes under my nose, and so did not answer at once. "He claims his brother was brought to England, the victim of reverse white slavery," I said as I rinsed the razor and went to work on the area at the corner of my mouth.

"That sounds a bit far-fetched," said Sutton.

"So it does," I agreed when I could speak safely.

"Do you believe him?" Sutton asked.

"I suppose so—to the extent that I believe his brother is missing and may have been taken for immoral purposes," I said, tipping my head back and scraping at my under-jaw and neck.

"What does Holmes think?" Sutton waited for my answer, which was just as well, as I had to consider it while I shaved.

"He hasn't confided in me," I said. "But he was playing a role for Mister Kerem—you would have been proud of him—and I am convinced he had an excellent reason for doing so; he explained his intention to me after Kerem departed."

"What kind of role?" Sutton asked, emerging from the dressing room in golfing breeches and a roll-top pull-over as if he had just come in from the country and would soon be going back.

I had become somewhat accustomed to his periodic transformations and so I only glanced at him briefly before finishing my shave.

"You would have thought he spent every day in an office, dealing with nothing but paperwork."

"Well," said Sutton with a hint of a smile. "That *is* what he intends people to think generally. That is why he hired me."

"Yes, and established the appearance of a monotonously regular life," I conceded. "This was more than his usual illusion. He seemed reckless, even timorous, incapable of any real action."

"And you think he did it deliberately?" Sutton handed a towel to me.

I used it on my face and neck. "Yes. I do. As you would have done had you seen him." I put the towel into the hamper and closed my collar-button once again, then went to work on my tie.

"I wonder why," Sutton mused aloud.

Anything I might have said was lost; Tyers rapped on the outer bathroom door. "If you please, gentlemen, Mister Holmes would like you to join him in the withdrawing room."

That very formal chamber at the front of the flat was rarely used for any discussion among us, so I supposed we were to expect a visitor. I reached for my suit-coat and pulled it on as I went out into the hall, Sutton close behind me.

"Whom do you think is coming?" Sutton pondered aloud. "I was told nothing about a visitor."

"Nor I," I said as we reached the withdrawing room.

Although I had half-suspected an August Personage, I saw that we had a fastidious man of late middle-age seated on the sopha. This was not Doctor John Watson, who was no stranger to any of us, but another man, who also had the look of the medical professional. He did not rise as we entered the room, but instead subjected us to a swift, intense scrutiny.

"Gentlemen," said Mycroft Holmes, as if he had only just become aware of our presence, "if you would be good enough: this is Sir Marmion Hazeltine, come to offer his researches to us."

Sir Marmion's name was not unknown to me, given all Mycroft Holmes had told me. I nodded my respects to him. "I have long admired your work, Sir Marmion," I said, hoping Holmes did not mind my speaking up in this way.

The answer accorded me by Sir Marmion was a terse, "Most

kind," before he turned to study Mycroft Holmes' face. "You have a most extraordinary skull, Mister Holmes, if you will permit me to say it." He did not smile, but there was a lessening of the severity of his features, which seemed to be the most he would permit himself to demonstrate.

"From an expert of your reputation, Sir Marmion, what can I be but flattered?" said Holmes as he sat back in his chair. He indicated that Sutton and I should both be seated. "As to the matter before us, I must hope your researches have produced results?"

"In time, Mister Holmes. In time. For the nonce, I am gathering data—and I thank you for your efforts in that regard—and hoping to have reached useful conclusions before the end of next year." He coughed delicately. "I have been trying some of the techniques of Doktor Breuer of Vienna on the more difficult of my patients, and I have reason to think they may prove most useful in the future in alleviating the compulsion to commit crimes."

"That is a goal worth achieving," said Mycroft Holmes with very real sincerity.

"I hope in time we may end all crime and insanity from the human race," said Sir Marmion.

"Hear, hear," said Mycroft Holmes. "No doubt such a laudable goal cannot be achieved overnight, but in generations to come, we might improve ourselves to the point where we will not have those unhappy beings in such number as we seem to have now." He folded his hands. "The new century is but eight years away. The twentieth century! The promise of it astounds me."

"And I," said Sir Marmion. "When we see what science has accomplished in the last fifty years, I wish I might be alive to see the next fifty." He coughed delicately to show he was moved. "Still, that is not to the point." He picked up a leather portfolio and opened it. "Here is the information I was asked to provide you, Mister Holmes, with citations for the material appended."

Mycroft Holmes took the expandable folder with marbled covers Sir Marmion held out to him. "There is a deal of work in here, Sir Marmion."

"Alas, not nearly enough. We have so little information on the nature of the human mind," he said. "Doktor Breuer's work leads me to believe that there is much more to be discovered in regard to how the mind shapes behavior. I think you will be especially interested in the third case described in those pages."

"Very good. I shall study it with interest," said Holmes.

"I know you will hold all that you read in strictest confidence," Sir Marmion said fussily.

"Naturally. If I must discuss any of this with my colleagues here, you may rely on their discretion as surely as you may rely on mine." He put the file down on the table behind him. "It shall not leave this flat. You have my word on that."

"Most appreciated," said Sir Marmion, rising abruptly. "I will not stay. You have work to do, as have I." He went toward the door, Mycroft Holmes behind him.

Sutton and I rose as he departed.

"Works with criminals, does he?" Sutton asked quietly.

"And the mad," I said.

Sutton cocked his head. "Um."

FROM THE PERSONAL JOURNAL OF PHILIP TYERS

The courier has just been removed from the flat, taken out by Admiralty men who arrived in a drayage wagon and brought the poor lad down in what looked like a steamer trunk, to confound any watchers that may be posted in the alley or the street. Watson is escorting him to hospital, and has agreed to monitor the young man's case. He has said it is not a sure thing that the courier will survive, but he will make it mandatory that all efforts are made to help him. The Admiralty will keep him under guard while he recovers.

MH is most pleased, but it is not untrammeled pleasure. After his meeting with HRHE last night, this visit from Sir Marmion Hazeltine has provided the very material he has sought. MH has decided to spend the day perusing the cases Sir Marmion has brought him, although it means a slight delay in commencing the investigation of the slaving the Turkish gentleman reported; HRHE would expect MH to address the material promptly. And Sir Cameron is due in London tomorrow at noon.

Chapter Four

"AN EMBARRASSMENT OF riches," said Mycroft Holmes as he studied the pages before him.

"Sir Marmion's case histories, sir?" I asked as I continued my usual duties of copying out his memoranda of yesterday. We were back in his study and he was at the main table and I at the drop-front antique secretary.

"The number of them." Holmes put his hand on the expanding file and shook his head. "I am most impressed by his thoroughness, particularly in regard to the mad. I confess I do not always follow his deductions in regard to these unfortunates, but I believe that there are answers to be found." He pushed back from the table and stretched his arms out. "Dear me. One in the afternoon. How quickly time goes by."

"Very true, sir," I agreed, feeling a bit stiff. "There is a meeting scheduled for half-three today, as you will recall."

"The Germans," said Mycroft Holmes, with a ducking of his head as if in capitulation to the inevitable. "It will be awkward. If only Her Majesty and the Kaiser were not such close relatives."

"That can't be changed," I said, a bit wryly, for if anyone could make such an alteration, it would be Mycroft Holmes.

"No, probably not," he conceded. "But it does make our posture more problematic." He got up and began to pace. "Sutton will have to walk across the street to the club for me, I fear. The Germans will not be finished with us in time." He lowered his head. "Six more performances," he said, meaning for Sutton as MacBeth.

"Tonight, two performances tomorrow, then dark three days, then the last three performances," I said, realizing I had picked up the theatrical jargon of calling non-performance nights *dark* from Sutton.

"A pity in its way, but probably necessary." Mycroft Holmes took a turn about the room, stopping before the fire to warm himself, for this November day had remained sere from dawn until now. "He has received excellent notices. I am once again troubled that he is being deprived of greater opportunities because of me."

"You and he have discussed this, have you not?" I said, wishing that Tyers would bring a fresh pot of tea; the one Mycroft Holmes and I had shared for morning was down to the coldest of dregs.

"Certainly," said Holmes. "And Edmund assures me he is gratified to be my double and my creator of disguises, but when I think of his abilities, I wonder if he realizes how great his gifts are."

"If he is content, how can you question his decision?" I, too, rose and shook the knots out of my muscles. "Your memoranda are almost complete."

"Very good." Mycroft Holmes came over to the secretary and looked down on the pages I had stacked. "Excellent work as usual, my dear Guthrie."

"I should have had it done three hours ago," I remarked.

"We had a somewhat disrupted morning," Mycroft Holmes pointed out. "I hope that young courier survives. He should not have to give his life in this."

"If the Brotherhood is behind it," I said, "lives are the coins they play for."

"You and I know that, Guthrie. That courier does not. He came into this without sufficient warning, and that may be my fault." He went to the door, about to call for Tyers.

"You'll wake Sutton," I cautioned Mycroft Holmes, for the actor was sleeping on the day-bed in the sitting room, the curtains closed not only to keep out the sun, but to provide protection for Sutton in case this flat was still under surveillance.

"I trust not." Mycroft Holmes closed the door. "The Germans. What have you prepared for our meeting?"

"I have copies of all recent treaties and agreements between our governments," I said, indicating the file case on the second shelf of the secretary. "I have all correspondence related to this visit, except, of course, private correspondence."

"Of course," said Holmes, his heavy brows drawing together. That was what troubled him the most—that the Kaiser and the Queen might have a private understanding on these matters about which we knew nothing. "Well, gather them up, Guthrie. And put on your swallow-tail coat. I believe it is hanging in the closet opposite the front door."

I had got used to leaving my swallow-tail coat here, to save myself the dash back to Curzon Street to get it. "Yes. And my cuffs and collar are just cleaned." I essayed a smile. "I shall be ready directly."

"Good. We'll have a bite to eat and then summon Hastings." He took Sir Marmion's papers and put them back in the expandable file, then handed them to me. "Make sure they are under lock and key before we depart."

"That I will," I said, putting the file on the shelf above the German papers. "There."

"Very good." He called to Tyers again, not quite as loudly this time. "We need tea and some cold beef and mustard sauce."

"Shortly, sir," Tyers called back.

"Oh, and Tyers, if you'll nip off to hospital and inquire after the courier?" Mycroft Holmes asked for this as readily as he asked for mustard sauce.

"That I will, sir," said Tyers.

"You'll want to wash up," said Mycroft Holmes to me. "Tend to it, there's a good lad. I shall change my clothes directly."

Since I knew the difference between a suggestion and an order, I did as I was told.

Upon my return to the study, much improved from my efforts, I saw that Tyers had put out a tray on the table and brought a fresh pot of tea. I sat down to pour a cup for myself when I heard a rap on the door, and in the next instant, Edmund Sutton came into the room, his fair hair as mussed as a boy's, his tall, lanky frame wrapped in a paisley dressing gown. "Good afternoon," he said in a dazed voice.

"And to you. Tea?" I did not wait for his answer but began to pour a cup for him. "It's fresh."

"Wonderful. Not that I'd notice," he added. "The courier?"

"Is off to hospital. That took place shortly after you retired." I handed a cup to him, and pointed to the creamer.

He added sugar and a dollop of milk, then sat down in the straight-backed chair in front of the secretary and stared at the wall in a superb blankness of expression. "Did he live?"

"He was alive when he left," I said. "Tyers has gone off to make inquiry." I took a sip, and although the liquid was almost scalding, it was warming and I was glad to have it. "We're off in a short while."

Sutton nodded. "I'll make the traditional cross to the club at the traditional hour and return promptly. I'll need Hastings to get me to the theatre when I'm through. I have no wish to be late for curtain."

"Of course. I can't imagine that Holmes would refuse such a reasonable request." I sighed as I took another sip. "It is going to be a long day."

"It's the Germans, isn't it?" Sutton was waking up more visibly now. His blue eyes were sharper and his voice more resonant. "I shall come back here after the performance, in case Mister Holmes has more work for me to do."

"Fine," I said, hoping I would be in my rooms in Curzon Street and fast asleep by then. I was about to throw caution and manners to the wind and help myself to the cold sliced beef when Mycroft Holmes surged into the room in full diplomatic rig. I stood up. "Good afternoon, sir."

"Oh, sit down, Guthrie, do," he said. "I will have enough ceremony to choke a horse before this day is ended."

"Just so, sir," I said, and sat down again.

"Good afternoon, Sutton," said Mycroft Holmes, going to clap his double on the shoulder. "You have a pressing agenda today, I fear." He came back to the table and poured himself some tea. "The Germans will serve schnapps, of course, and it will go to their heads. They are *welcome* to Sir Cameron in their cups. No doubt they deserve one another." He paused. "I am in a foul mood. I apologize to you both for this spasm of mine. I dislike being watched, more so when I cannot identify the watchers."

"Well, eventually they will slip up and then you will know." I had hoped this would mollify his state of mind somewhat, but it did not.

"It is how to identify them that troubles me," said Mycroft Holmes. "They may be Brotherhood, they may be Turks, they may be Germans, they may be some group of whom I have no knowledge. It is demeaning enough to have them shoot at me, but when they go so far as to wound a courier it is beyond all limits." He drank down most of his tea and poured more; I was glad that Tyers had used the largest pot. "Sutton, you must be very careful. Keep a weather eye out for anything unfamiliar, and take no chances."

Sutton managed an engaging smile. "I won't. I have to perform tonight." He came up to Mycroft Holmes, saying, "Don't fret about me. I will be careful as a nun."

"Don't tell me you'll wear that habit you have in the back?" Holmes finally relaxed.

"I may, leaving here for the theatre, if I have time." He poured himself more tea. "Think a moment. If you are the target, I would do well to resemble you as little as possible once I leave your club."

"You have the right of it," Mycroft Holmes conceded. "Well, I'm sorry I won't see you in . . . in Orders, but I must applaud your strategy."

"Better than an evening with the Germans," said Sutton.

"Truly," Holmes agreed, looking somber once again. He glanced at me. "How soon can you depart?"

"Ten minutes if I have a bite to eat. Two if I don't," I said, looking longingly at the sliced beef.

"Guthrie, dear boy, eat. Who knows when you will have such an opportunity again? For we will have to be careful with the Germans. There are too many members of the Brotherhood with them, and it would not be prudent to dine too freely with them." He reached out and rolled one of the slices, picked it up and bit into it. "There. Now have as much as you would like," he recommended as he chewed.

"That I will," I said, and reached for the mustard sauce to spread on the next slice of beef. Considering how little appetite I had had an hour before, I found that this one taste of food made me famished. I drank more tea and had four more slices rolled up with mustard sauce before I took my serviette and wiped my fingers. "I am at your service, sir."

"I shall want to leave in five minutes. Gather your things and get your overcoat. It is drizzling and no doubt we will have rain within the hour." He waved me from the room, then addressed Sutton. "When you cross the street, have a care. Do not linger on the steps. Report any irregularity to Tyers. And have another superb performance tonight."

I went down the hall to the sitting room where I gathered up my clothes and shoved them into a valise I kept at Holmes' flat for that purpose. I would leave the valise with Sid Hastings, but I would carry my overcoat and portfolio with me.

"With all we have dealt with today, I suppose I should be grateful that it is only Germans we must face—not Hottentots or Chinese or Red Indians." Holmes grumbled as we met in the corridor. He had his tiered cloak over his arm and was pulling on his gloves. "We're going out the rear door, and through the alley. Be prepared to run."

"Aren't we tempting fate—going out where the courier was shot?" I could not bring myself to be at ease about his decision.

"We may be," Mycroft Holmes replied, "but a shooting in Pall Mall would cause a panic that I cannot accept. We will take our chances in the alley."

"But surely we should be armed," I said.

"The Germans would be offended." Mycroft Holmes gave me an abrupt stare. "If there is going to be trouble, best to be near the cab for escape, and in a place where there will not be confusion."

This seemed unlike my employer, but he had been putting forth an impression of himself today that was peculiar as any I had seen. "Would the attackers be so foolish? To attack in a busy street?" I asked, unwilling to think it possible.

"Boldness and foolishness are often judged by their success or failure," said Mycroft Holmes. "Get ready." He started toward the kitchen with an energy I found hard to summon in myself. I hurried after him, wondering if I should have my pistol in my pocket as a precaution.

"Is Sutton staying in the flat?" I asked.

"Until he has to go to the club in my stead, yes." As he secured the door from the outside, Mycroft Holmes made a swift scrutiny of the alley. "I think we will do well enough if we hurry."

I felt a trifle silly as I began to rush down the stairs. I was on the second landing when I heard the crack of a rifle and saw the wood of the railing next to me splinter. I faltered for only a moment, then plunged ahead, holding my portfolio to guard my head. Behind me, Mycroft Holmes moved with an alacrity that would have astonished me during my first year in his employment, but which I now recognized as typical of the man. Portly he might be, but active he certainly was. I increased my speed until I was afraid I would plunge headlong to the paving stone. At this hectic pace I was almost to the alley when a second shot rang out and I heard Mycroft Holmes curse.

Reaching the cobbles of the alley, I paused long enough to try to see where the shot had come from. Then I turned back to see Holmes wiping blood from his forehead. "Sir!" I expostulated. "You're hurt."

"And I don't want to be shot again, thank you, Guthrie," he responded, his terseness filling me with relief. "Keep moving. Hastings will be waiting at the corner." He was running, keeping up with me and sounding only slightly breathless. "Hurry!"

I complied, racing as fast as I could on the slippery, uneven stones. I rounded the corner and saw the cab waiting. In a last rush, I made for the cab, Mycroft Holmes immediately behind me.

"Guthrie!" Holmes cried suddenly, halting two steps behind me. "Stop! That's not Hastings!"

I skidded to a stop on the cobbles and looked in dismay. "Not Hastings?" I called out.

"Look at the horse!" he shouted, and turned with remarkable agility to run the other way. "It's not Lance!"

To be sure, the horse between the shafts, now I came to look at it, was a mouse-colored gelding, not Sid Hastings's new bay. Even as I followed Mycroft Holmes in his dash, I feared we were being herded into a trap, for as I swung back toward the alley courtyard, I saw the cab begin to move after us; as I ran, I dropped my overcoat, and would have tried to pick it up but that I heard the cab approaching. This goaded me on; as I rounded the corner once again, I almost tripped over Mycroft Holmes' foot; he had taken shelter at the edge of the basement stairs of the building opposite the back of the one in which he lived.

"Behind the dustbins, Guthrie!" he ordered me.

I needed no more incentive than that. I slipped into the first open shed and leaned against the wall. The sound of the horse's hooves grew louder, and I was compelled to attempt to shrink myself into the smallest possible space in the hope of remaining unseen while I railed inwardly at myself for not bringing my pistol. I clung to my portfolio and valise as if they could save me while I strove to keep out of the line of fire.

There was an exchange of shots, one from across the alley where Mycroft Holmes was hidden, and two from a rooftop. I heard a window open somewhere above me, but could not see who had done it, or where. I hoped the opener would not regret that action. Then there was a fourth shot, very loud, and a fifth. The cab stopped, the driver swayed on the box, falling forward.

Holmes emerged from his hiding place to catch the frightened horse before it could bolt; the animal and the cab provided him some protection. "Guthrie! Get onto the box!"

I was aware this might be reckless, but I answered his summons at once, hurrying across the narrow space that separated me from the cab. I tossed my valise and portfolio into the box-well, sprang onto the rear of the cab and scrambled up to the box. The driver was slumped forward, a large patch of red spreading across his brown stuff jacket. I mastered my revulsion and moved the man away from the reins, taking them in hand and pulling the horse to order. "Done, sir!"

I felt Holmes get into the cab, and then heard his tap on the frame. "Back out of here. They won't shoot the horse. Too much attention."

Making the kissing-whistle I had heard jarvys use to back their horses, I began to coax the mouse-colored gelding back out of the alley. It was a tricksy business, for the horse was sweating, mincing, and flinging his head in distress. Finally we reached the road and I guided the cab into traffic, looking about for Sid Hastings as I went.

"Go 'round to the *Fatted Calf*," Mycroft Holmes told me, his voice calmer now.

"Sir, I have a dead man here in the box with me," I exclaimed, looking about to see if anyone had taken notice of this distressing fact.

"All the more reason to go to the *Fatted Calf*. It's where jarvys gather; if anyone should ask, say you are seeking help for him."

"Help?" I repeated incredulously. "He's dead, sir. There will be no help for him." I looked about in case I had been overheard, but it seemed I had not.

"Ah, but few will know that if you appear to be tending to a stricken man. You are in clothing that, however scuffed, indicates a station well above the jarvy's. So if you behave as if he has been taken suddenly ill, I doubt anyone will question you. Take the rug out of the well and put it over him, as if to keep him warm."

I did as he ordered, all the while repressing the scandalous urge to laugh. I noticed that one or two passers-by looked at us in curiosity, but no one attempted to detain us. I took this as a good sign for now, but wondered if the people in the street would be equally inattentive were I the one injured, or worse? And I began to wonder who had shot the driver of the cab.

The *Fatted Calf* was a pub off Tottenham Court Road, an old building with an almost black front, and a large yard behind where jarvys put their cabs while they had a meal and a pint. I found a slot where the cab could go, steered it there and halted the gelding.

Mycroft Holmes got out of the cab at once, shaking off his clothing as he stood beside the vehicle and I climbed down from the box, my valise and portfolio clutched in my hands. "Leave it as it is, my boy. He will be found soon enough, and I will wager you a month's wages that it will be discovered that the man was no jarvy. I would reckon he will be unknown to all the jarvys in London." He watched as I came down from the box, and as I stepped onto the flagstones, he began to swat at my coat. "Most untidy. We will have to give the Germans a plausible explanation for your unkempt appearance, and when we return this evening, do you give your coat to Tyers to repair."

I looked at my valise. "My suit-coat is in here, Mister Holmes," I reminded him. "It is not as correct attire as this coat would be, but it is neat enough, and might be better than this."

Mycroft Holmes considered this; I saw the bloody line on his face had dried, and felt intense relief that he had not been seriously injured. "It is the lesser of two evils," he conceded at last. "Very well. Change your coat. But be quick about it. We do not want to be discovered here." He bent down and opened my valise, pulling out the coat inside and reaching up for the one I was removing. This he thrust into the valise and then he closed it as I shrugged into the other coat. "Come. Walk quickly but not too much so."

I did as he said, missing my overcoat as the damp wind cut through me. "What about Sid Hastings?" I asked as we walked.

"I hope nothing has happened to him," said Mycroft Holmes as we came to the front of the pub and crossed the street away from it. The sidewalk was busy, but not so crowded that we could not keep up a good pace. "We will flag down a cab a bit later. We do not want to be remembered in context with that dead man."

My stomach did a lurch at my recollection of his demise. "What of him?" I asked, rather more pointedly than I had intended.

"What do you mean, Guthrie?" Mycroft Holmes inquired as he picked up the pace. "The Germans had better appreciate our efforts to meet with them." As a joke it fell sadly flat. "Not that you or I will tell them about it."

"I should hope not," I agreed, but I would not be put off the point. "Do you know who shot that man back in the cab?"

"Of course I do, dear boy," said Mycroft Holmes as if the whole of it were obvious. "And so should you."

I frowned. "Tyers was out," I said, thinking aloud. Then I stared at him. "Gracious! You cannot mean that Sutton shot him? Sutton?"

Mycroft Holmes nodded as he adroitly dodged a flock of mudlarks rushing along the street, their high, young voices rising above the general rumble of traffic. "Whoelse?" He chuckled at my expression of dismay. "He is not nearly as incapable as you think him."

"No," I said as I increased my stride to keep up with Mycroft Holmes. "Apparently not."

FROM THE PERSONAL JOURNAL OF PHILIP TYERS

The physicians on the courier's case tell me his condition is grave, and not from loss of blood alone, but in the distress to his system he has suffered. They are planning to clean his wound in the hope of preventing a major infection, and they tell me the next forty-eight hours will tell the tale. Watson has said he is not as confident as his colleagues. From his years in the army, he has come to know something of these injuries, and he is more concerned about the cold the courier claims to be suffering from than from the wound itself. I have paid close attention to all he has said, for I put great stock in the wisdom of military doctors.

I have also called upon Chief Inspector Alexander, who deals with Customs in regard to all manner of illegal activities and given him a report in regard to Mister Kerem's claims. CI Alexander has given me his word to look into the matter as discreetly as possible. He has some useful connections in the criminal classes who are willing to betray their comrades if it serves their advantages. He himself does not put much credence in this accusation, but he is willing to investigate it on the off-chance there are vestiges of truth in it. I have asked him to keep us apprised of any developments he may have in the case, including any indication that Mister Kerem's fears are baseless.

I am now going to prepare a soothing draught for Sutton, who is much distressed at having to shoot a man; he saved MH's life, which he is glad to have done, but it does not mitigate the realization that a man who was living is now dead at his hands, a realization that is increasingly afflictive to him. He has to go to MH's club shortly, and then to a performance of MacBeth, both of which require that he have his wits about him. I suppose I should not be surprised that he has experienced such upset at his act, for it is never easy to kill another man, and no time is more difficult than the first. As an actor, he has performed killing many times, and dying, too, for that matter, but it is not the same as doing it.

MH and G should be with the Germans just now. If the meeting goes well, I should see them before eight of the clock . . .

Chapter Five

"THIS IS A great honor," exclaimed the German gentleman wearing the Order of Saint Karolus on the deep-blue sash that angled across his chest. He was between fifty and sixty, hale but marked by age. His light-brown eyes were almost tan, and his hair had faded from ruddy-brown to a shade the Dutch call mauve. He struck me as a fine painting might that has faded over time. Even his manner, which was cordial, seemed but an echo of earlier heartiness. He was in the library of the luxurious house just off Berkeley Square, currently the residence of a German industrialist, who was acting as the Baron's host during his stay in London. The industrialist, Dietrich Amsel, was conveniently from home, attending a meeting in Antwerp.

We had been escorted to the library by the household butler, a man of such self-importance that he minced along holding his head as if trying to escape a bad odor. He had ordered the upper servants to line the hall and to curtsy or bow as we passed by. I could tell Mycroft Holmes was somewhat embarrassed by this; he walked as if he wanted to be invisible. By the time we reached our destination within the house, my employer was trying to contain his annoyance.

"Baron von Schattenberg," said Mycroft Holmes, executing a perfect Prussian bow to the man.

"Mister Holmes: delighted. My aides, Helmut Kriede, Paul Farbschlagen, and Egmont Eisenfeld." Each bowed as the Baron said his name: Kriede and Eisenfeld were fair, blue-eyed men, neither of them more than twenty-five; Farbschlagen was dark-haired and grey-eyed, and seemed to be a few years older than his fellows. Looking at them, I wondered which of them were part of the Brotherhood, if, indeed, any of them were.

"And my aide, Paterson Guthrie. You will discover he has some ability in your tongue." Mycroft Holmes bowed again, and I winced, recalling my instructions to speak German like a novice, although I was fluent in the language.

"Good fortune indeed," said the Baron, and pointed to a table in the corner of the library, the one place not given to floor-to-ceiling bookshelves. It was flanked by windows, just now with draperies drawn against the dreary afternoon. I imagined that in spring and summer they would provide a pleasant prospect of the small park that lay behind the house.

Mycroft Holmes took the seat proffered, and signaled to me to sit beside him. "We had a minor accident in our cab on the way here, so I trust you will excuse the somewhat disordered appearance my aide presents."

"An accident?" The Baron halted in the act of sitting.

"You know what it is to be on the streets these days," Mycroft Holmes said, almost apologetically. "It is dark and everything is wet— mishaps occur."

"So they do," said the Baron, sitting down and telling his aides in rapid German to sit at the adjoining table. As he settled into his place, folding his pale hands on the table and crossing his legs at an angle to the table, he went on, "I am grateful you would take the time to help us . . . smooth over any possible difficulties we may encounter."

"And I am pleased you would ask for my assistance," said Mycroft Holmes with equal smoothness.

"It is always awkward, is it not, when an estranged married pair seeks to be reunited?" The Baron offered his conciliative, plausible smile. "Particularly when their respective countries must—perforce—be part of their considerations."

"Truly," said Holmes in a manner to match the Baron's. "And yet, do you know, I think it must be said that this prospective re-unification would be more easily done if both parties were willing to effect their meeting in Scotland."

The Baron laughed richly. "Oh, no, no, no, my new friend. No, Sir Cameron must not have so great an advantage over his wife. They must meet here, in London, where they are both away from their own grounds." He favored Mycroft Holmes with a slight nod. "You can see why we must honor her request."

"I see why it is one means of accomplishing their ends," Mycroft Holmes countered. "But I believe it is her uncle's condition, not hers."

"She is a good woman, willing to be guided by the men who love her," said the Baron. "Would that more women followed her excellent example."

Mycroft Holmes shocked me when he replied, "Amen," for he was not a man given to religious exclamations. "Still," he went on at his most amiable, "I am surprised that she has stipulated that she must be accompanied by her uncle, two cousins, and another relative whose degree of blood I have not entirely grasped."

"She is a woman of high rank and dignity. She wishes not to be alone with her husband until she is certain they will be able to resume their marriage." The answer was so easily given, I knew it had been rehearsed; Baron von Schattenberg looked directly at Mycroft Holmes and gave him a pleasant nod. "You must know what it is to have a woman of position undertake travel to a foreign country."

"Indeed," said Mycroft Holmes, and made an attempt to bring

the conversation back to the topic he wished. "And yet, I cannot help but feel there may be a more appropriate escort for her than the one she has proposed. The Kaiser would be open to providing men and women to accompany her who would more easily be welcomed into the company of our Queen."

I had to mask a near-cough to cover my astonishment. That Mycroft Holmes should say so much, and with such apparent candor, shocked me to the core. He might as well have accused the Baron directly of acting contrary to the wishes of the Crown. Opening my portfolio, I removed my notebook and pencils, as if preparing to record the rest of the conversation.

"It would not please Sir Cameron's wife to be treated as a complete stranger, for although she has never visited these isles, she is married to a most distinguished Knight, an acknowledged hero and popular leader. To subject his wife to the kind of treatment reserved for foreigners will do nothing to hasten their reunion." The Baron still spoke easily, as if he had nothing against such a suggestion, and sought only to end a minor misconception. "You must know that the establishment of a more regular relationship between Sir Cameron and Lady MacMillian must be the goal of all we do."

"Just so," said Mycroft Holmes, matching the Baron suavity for suavity. "Still, I cannot help but think that that which pleases Her Majesty must please Sir Cameron as well."

"It is possible, of course. But it is Lady MacMillian who has instigated these efforts, not Sir Cameron, and for that, I would suppose she is within her rights to conduct herself as she believes she must." Baron von Schattenberg shrugged. "Perhaps we should address other aspects of this coming visit and return to this matter of escort when we have concluded our other discussions?" Although his English was excellent, I could hear the language roughen; to me this indicated some tension or anxiety, but nothing in his manner supported such a likelihood.

"No doubt she is doing as she had been advised by her family," said Mycroft Holmes, making this observation carefully, since he was keenly aware that he might easily give offence.

"It is the work of her uncles to guide her with her husband absent," said the Baron pointedly but maintaining his affable smile.

"As she must be aware," said Mycroft Holmes, "in coming to see Sir Cameron, she puts herself in her husband's hands."

"Not until she arrives. Should she decide to return to Germany, she will need to have companions. It would not do for her to travel in the company of strangers." The Baron paused to snap his fingers; Eisenfeld jumped to his feet and all but saluted. "We have need of some schnapps. If you will ask the servants to bring the tray?"

"At once, mein Baron," said Eisenfeld, and left the room with alacrity.

While Mycroft Holmes and Baron von Schattenberg continued their fencing, I took a little time to study the two remaining aides, to see if I could discern anything in their demeanor that might hint of a larger purpose: Paul Farbschlagen was edgy, but he had the look of a man who was always so, from the redness at his cuticles and ragged nails, to the intensity of his grey-eyed stare; Helmut Kriede seemed a typically German mix of steely discipline and sentimental cordiality. Both of them watched the Baron as if he were their master and they his hounds. I had an uneasy moment when I wondered if I appeared the same to them. Then I had a swift recollection of the Japanese aides—Messers Banadaichi and Minato—who had been involved with the death of Lord Blackenheath, and I squirmed inwardly at the memory of how that ended.

"Guthrie," said Mycroft Holmes to me, his voice sharp enough to break into my thoughts, "do you happen to have to hand the information on Sir Cameron's arrival?"

I flipped through the sheets in my portfolio. "It says here he is arriving tomorrow at noon, according to your records," I said, proffering the paper with the information on it.

"Ah, yes," said Holmes, as though it had slipped his mind, although I knew it had not. This tactic had some other purpose than informing Baron von Schattenberg of Sir Cameron's itinerary; I gave my full attention to their discussion again. "Since he will be here tomorrow, we might best postpone our conversation until he may be included in it."

"Are you certain that will serve your purpose? He may well agree with our position," said the Baron with a keen smile.

"So he might," said Mycroft Holmes, somewhat wearily. "But if it will resolve our problems to our mutual satisfaction, then I think it is a better use of our time and energy to include Sir Cameron in our deliberations." He looked around as Helmut Eisenfeld came back with a tray on which stood a bottle of schnapps and two chimney glasses.

"In time to drink to our success, Mister Holmes: to the fruits of our efforts," said the Baron, so warmly that I supposed he assumed he had won this round. "To the reunion of Sir Cameron and Lady MacMillian." At this signal, Eisenfeld poured out two glasses of the clear, potent liquid; the Baron handed one to Mycroft Holmes and kept the other for himself. "*Prost!*" he exclaimed, and downed the schnapps in one go.

"Hear, hear," said Mycroft Holmes, and tossed his off as well.

Baron von Schattenberg held out his hand to Holmes. "Tomorrow then, at—shall we say?—four o'clock?"

"That is suitable to me, providing Sir Cameron has no objections," Mycroft Holmes said as if that would be an unlikely event.

"He must see the advantages of settling this matter," said the Baron.

Little do you know, I thought. What was Mycroft Holmes up to this time? I pondered the various possibilities, but nothing suggested itself.

"I am sure he will give you his full attention," said Holmes, and I knew then that he had some mischief in mind. Turning, he addressed me. "Gather up your things, Guthrie: portfolio and valise. It is time we left our hosts to their evening." He inclined his head toward the Baron. "Thank you for your hospitality, Baron, and for your candor. I will have much to tell Sir Cameron when we meet him tomorrow."

"I thank you for coming." He bowed, clicking his heels as he did. "It has been most . . . instructive." He made a motion, and Paul Farbschlagen moved to accompany us to the door of Herr Amsel's house.

It was nearly dark out as we left the house behind us, and Mycroft Holmes sighed. "I wish I knew what happened to Hastings." He looked about the street for a cab to hail. "I do not like summoning a jarvy I do not know," he said under his breath. "This is a most damnable situation."

"Do you want me to find a cab for us, sir? I could go to the corner and choose one not on this street." This was not an idle suggestion, for it would tend to ensure a safer ride than selecting a cab from those on this street: there were always cabs to be had at Berkeley Square. I had a notion my valise and portfolio could become uncomfortably heavy if we walked any distance.

"No," he said. "No, I think we might as well walk a ways, until I can sort out my thoughts." He buttoned his cloak and went into the thickening mists.

I followed after him. "Why did you cut the discussion short?" I asked when we reached Berkeley Square. I was aware I was only a few blocks away from my rooms in Curzon Street, and yet I was about to turn my back on them once again; I would not see my door for many hours.

"That was no discussion, Guthrie, and well you know it," he said to me as we turned along the Square and made toward Conduit Street and Saville Row, with the intention of making his way down to Vigo Street, thence to Sackville Street, to Piccadilly, to Church Place, down to Jermyn Street to Duke of York Street, to Saint James Square, and then to arrive at Pall Mall. "This was maneuvering, pure and simple."

I lengthened my stride to keep up with him. "It did have that feeling about it," I said.

"As well it should. You have been with me six years now, and you must know what you saw in there." He was not quite disgusted, but he was far from pleased. "That Baron von Schattenberg is too plausible by half!"

"Do you think he is part of the Brotherhood?" I could not keep from asking.

"If he is, he is a fool, since the Brotherhood seeks the downfall of all European nations so that it may assume power. As a Baron, he would be among those slated to be removed." He slowed his pace enough to blend in with the others on the street. "But he may have been promised advantages if he helps them, or they may be blackmailing him. Whatever the case, he will not entertain any suggestion I may put forth."

"Then why propose adding Sir Cameron to the discussion?" I

asked. "Sir Cameron is stubborn as a Derby pig and self-centered as a Bishop's cat." I made no apology for my animadversions.

"And drunken to boot," said Mycroft Holmes. "And once he decides a position is to his advantage he will not budge, though the earth crumble before him." He nodded twice. "Exactly. All we must do is show him that what Baron von Schattenberg expects is to his disadvantage and he will oppose it until the Thames flows backward."

"That he will," I said, comprehending now what my employer planned. "If they give him any of the schnapps, he will very likely consume it in quantity, as well, and that will only serve to add to his implacability." I could not help but chuckle. "I hope the Baron isn't too distressed."

"I hope that he is, so he will give away something—anything— that will give us some means of assessing the danger of the Brother-hood's current activities. The way things stand, we are operating in the dark." He stopped abruptly and held up his hand for silence; the throngs around us parted and rejoined as if we were islands in a stream.

"What is it?" I asked, nervous in spite of myself.

Mycroft Holmes shook his head several times, and I held my tongue. Finally he lowered his hand. "I think I was in error. For a moment I thought I heard the two horses from last night. The loose shoe—I thought I heard it."

"I'm afraid I didn't notice . . ." I began, and let the words trail off.

"With all the noise, it is an easy thing to mis-hear a sound," said Mycroft Holmes as if trying to convince himself. At the corner, we turned toward Pall Mall, making our way at a steady pace as night settled in over London.

By the time we reached the steps to his flat, Mycroft Holmes had stopped twice more to listen for the sounds of pursuit, and twice more assured himself that he had erred; I was jumpy as a springtime cricket, for every carriage passing in the streets now seemed the haven of sinister Brotherhood assassins, as had been the case in Constanti-nople, not so many months ago. It was most unnerving to believe there was an unknown and unseen enemy pursuing us. At least I had sufficient presence of mind to keep from being overcome by my anx-ieties, but they were preying upon me.

"I want you to come up for tea and a brandy, Guthrie. We still have much to discuss." Mycroft Holmes did not wait for an answer, but hurried up the stairs, none the worse for his walk. I trudged after him, keeping my thoughts to myself.

Tyers met us at the door, as I expected he would. "There is water just coming on to boil, sir," he said. "And I have asked Sid Hastings to come up after he has delivered Sutton to the theatre."

"Very good," said Mycroft Holmes. "I trust the afternoon courier arrived without incident?" He handed his cloak to Tyers as he spoke.

"Yes, and the pouch he brought has a dispatch from Amsterdam that may be more urgent than the rest." He took my overcoat and valise, but allowed me to keep my portfolio.

"Amsterdam, is it?" Mycroft Holmes said in alarm. "Jacobbus Braaten?"

"I was not informed one way or the other, sir," said Tyers, opening the door to Mycroft Holmes' study. "The fire is new-laid and I will shortly have your tea."

"Very good," Mycroft Holmes approved.

"I have put the pouch on your main table, as you can see," he added before closing the door.

Mycroft Holmes approached the table as if he expected the pouch to perform some untoward act. "Dear me," he remarked as he pulled back the flap. "Something on Turkish affairs as well as news from Amsterdam. I don't like it, Guthrie," he said as he sat down and proceeded to open the pouch—which was, in reality, a large leather brief-case with a double-lock on it.

"I can understand why you might not, sir," I said, going to the chair I usually occupied. My portfolio felt as if it weighed ten stone. I was delighted to put it down.

Holmes had opened the dispatch and spread it out on the table, reading it quickly and with amazing comprehension. Finally he slapped the flat of his hand down on the table and burst out, "He shall not!"

I looked up, startled by his fervor. "The Brotherhood, sir?"

"More specifically, Jacobbus Braaten. He has eluded his watchers and they now believe he may be on a ship bound for Ireland. From there, he is expected to cross to Manchester. He may already have done so." He sighed explosively. "So much for all the precautions we have in place at Dover. He and Vickers will be on English soil before Lady MacMillian arrives, and that troubles me. It smacks of more intent than simply returning the Brotherhood to Britain—it suggests they may already have some nefarious purpose in mind. Why that possibility should surprise me," he added with ironic humor, "I cannot think."

"There is still time to alert Manchester, isn't there?" I suggested, feeling a degree of apprehension I had not experienced since my last encounter with the Brotherhood.

"Possibly," said Holmes darkly.

"Then I shall prepare an order, if you like," I told him.

"Yes. Do that. It is little enough, but it is better than nothing." He lowered his head, brooding. "I am troubled that the Brotherhood has been able to act so quickly, and deceptively."

I rose to collect the embossed paper on which such orders were issued, and while I was at the secretary, Tyers returned to the study with the tea tray that contained—beyond the teapot, the sugar-bowl, and creamer—a basket of fresh scones and a tub of fresh butter, as well as a jar of potted ham.

"Set that down if you would, Tyers," said Mycroft Holmes, not bothering to look up from the paper before him.

"That I will," said Tyers, then added, "Sid Hastings has just returned. Shall I ask him to come up now, or would you rather speak to him later?"

Holmes put the paper aside, turning it face-down in the process. "Tell him to come up now. My question is pressing."

"Very good, sir," said Tyers, and left us in the study together.

"Are you going to ask him about why he was not in his appointed place?" I inquired.

"Yes. It is so much unlike him." His frown was more eloquent than words would have been. "What troubles me most is that he can be threatened. After all, he is a man with a family and I cannot ask him to put my interests, or those of the government, above those of his wife and children." He smiled, a trace of sadness in his demeanor. "Men like Hastings cannot make such choices without being broken by them. I would offer him a poor reward for his long devotion if I required that choice of him." He paused. "It is to his credit that he is so devoted to his family."

"I should say so," I agreed; I went to pour a cup of tea for myself and for Mycroft Holmes.

"No, Guthrie," said my employer. "Many men of Hastings' station are incapable of doing more than bringing children into the world and leaving them to grow up as mudlarks, or worse; we see the results of their indifference every day."

"Some of the highest ranks treat their children from the wrong side of the blanket worse than they treat their hounds," I observed.

"Sadly it is true. But not all men—high or low—are thus. Sid Hastings has always put the interests of his wife and children ahead of his own, and for that, he is a laudable example of what even a poor man may do to benefit his family." He accepted the tea I held out to him. "That is why I would never want to impose upon him, for such a conflict of loyalties would be hard for him to bear."

"So might it for any man," I said.

Mycroft Holmes shook his head. "Guthrie, dear boy, I wish I could concur. But, alas, I cannot. And neither can you." He reached for a scone, broke it and buttered the smaller portion, then popped it into his mouth.

"Every man has some loyalty," I said. "It may not be to family, but there is something that commands his allegiance." I meant what I said, and apparently Holmes understood that.

"You are still an idealist, my lad," said Mycroft Holmes with a faint air of self-deprecation about him. "I am grateful for that."

I took a mouthful of tea and swallowed, finding the heat most welcome. "Why do you say that, sir?"

Whatever his answer, I was destined never to hear it, for Tyers knocked on the door just then, saying that Sid Hastings was with him.

"Come in, come in," sang out Mycroft Holmes. "Have a cup of tea—Tyers, bring a cup for Hastings, will you?"

"Of course," said Tyers, and withdrew.

Sid Hastings seemed dreadfully uncomfortable standing before us, his cap in hand, his muffler loose around his neck under his thick tweed jacket. "I left my oilskin in the kitchen," he explained, staring up at the ceiling.

"Come, Hastings, don't be ill-at-ease. Have a seat." When Mycroft Holmes chose to, he could exude such bonhomie that any man would be hard-put to resist it; Sid Hastings sat down in the one straight-backed chair available.

"I'm told you wanted me to stay on duty this morning," said Hastings, turning brick-red at his own boldness.

"I was rather surprised when I did not find you at the agreed-upon place," Holmes said mildly. "It struck me as most unlike you, not to be at our appointed place. I hope it does not mean any misfortune had befallen your family?"

"No, no, sir," said Hastings, all but pulling his forelock. "All's well with them, even my daughter, thanks to you. We have naught to complain of, especially since you took an interest in our Fanny, as she calls herself now." He spoke of his child whose mathematical skills had secured her a position in a casino on the Continent where she was flourishing.

"Good of you to say," said Mycroft Holmes. "Give her my regards when next you write to her."

"Don't do that often," said Hastings. "But the Missus'll be sending her a letter at Christmas, as she does. Good with her letters, my Missus is. Writes regular. You may be sure we'll include your kindness to her." He had begun to relax a little. "We had a letter from her not long ago: she's saved more than an hundred pounds since taking up her post; she says she wants to buy shares in a railroad. I near to fell over when I heard that. Shares in a railroad! Who'd've thought she'd—" He stopped. "Not to take up your time, sir."

"I, for one, would have thought she would find a way to make her earnings work for her," said Mycroft Holmes. "Still, you're right— oh, thank you, Tyers"—this was for the cup-and-saucer Tyers brought from the kitchen—"we should discuss how you came to leave your place this morning."

"Well, I did what the copper told me to, didn't I?" Hastings said, a little too loudly.

"Did you?" Mycroft Holmes asked with no trace of blame in his voice. "What copper was that?"

"The one you sent," said Hastings, not touching the cup-and-saucer.

"Tell me about him," said Mycroft Holmes; I listened intently as well.

"Well, he was . . . just a copper. A proper constable. I know a right copper when I see one, and he was right to his boots. He said I was to go on until the afternoon, when I would be wanted again. He pointed to your rear door and said you were occupied with a Turkish gentleman, or you would tell me the same yourself. Since he was a policeman in uniform, I decided it was all right to obey him." He paused. "I shouldn't have, should I?"

Mycroft Holmes stared down into his tea. "No, Hastings. You did as you ought." He raised his eyes. "But I find it most perturbing to realize that the man who shot the courier and attempted to kill me is a member of the police."

FROM THE PERSONAL JOURNAL OF PHILIP TYERS

It has been a difficult afternoon and the evening is no less so: I have just given Sid Hastings a sandwich and sent him on his way, and must shortly seek out former Police Inspector Durward Strange. MH tells me that this is one of the few men who can be trusted to be wholly candid about police matters. It seems that MH is reluctant to go directly to Scotland Yard with his newest revelation for fear that if what Hastings says is accurate, admission of the danger would serve only to escalate it. Therefore, it is MH's intention to speak with PI Strange for the purpose of gaining as objective an opinion as possible. I understand that PI Strange is considered bitter by many on the force, and for that reason alone is not much sought-out . . .

Sutton is off at the theatre and will not return until well into the night. He has said that these last few performances are important to him, as they are very likely the last time he will essay such a major role in so important a theatre in London. He says it is not wise for him to become too recognizable, as continuing major roles would cause him to be, so he intends to make the most of this opportunity. He looks upon this as a grand gesture, one that will bring him the satisfaction of having made his mark among the important MacBeths of this decade. He is resigned to playing in less prestigious theatres and in less well-known works, but he is not above being pleased that his work has been well-received, and in so demanding a role as MacBeth.

Another package has been sent by Sir Marmion with the admonition that he must have its contents returned by no later than day after tomorrow. I have conveyed this to MH, who has said it is most frustrating to have so monumental an opportunity and so little time in which to take advantage of it. He has sworn to read the material provided until Sutton returns.

G has returned to Curzon Street for the night and will likely not be back here until six-thirty tomorrow morning to resume his duties. I have told him he will not be disturbed except in an emergency, which is a prudent thing to do, as it is most important that G, who is MH's right hand and second pair of eyes, be fully alert in these next few days.

Chapter Six

I WOKE AT seven-thirty in the morning, and, having realized the hour, was filled with chagrin. I should have been at Mycroft Holmes' flat before now, ready to work. I dressed in haste, had nothing more than a muffin before I bolted out the door into a rainstorm that washed over the city with Biblical enthusiasm. Splashing through the street, I attempted to hail a cab, and finally succeeded. "Pall Mall," I told the jarvy. "And quickly. I'm late."

"Right you are," said the jarvy, and set his horse in motion through the downpour.

Arriving at Mycroft Holmes' flat some twenty minutes later—our progress having been slowed by an overturned drayage van—I rushed up the stairs, and presented myself with apologies.

"Do sit down and recover yourself, Guthrie, there's a good lad," said Mycroft Holmes, who wore a dressing gown of plush hunter-green velvet over his trousers and shirt as he sat finishing his breakfast. "I slept in a bit myself. I didn't rise until nearly seven. Just as well that you took a little time to get here."

I did my best to appear satisfied with his casual remark. "You're very kind, sir: I should have been here sooner."

"Not on my account. Besides, tonight will probably be a late evening, so it is all one to me. Not that there is nothing to occupy your morning." He pointed to his stack of notes. "Sort those out and copy them, if you will," he went on as he cut into the last part of a thick slice of ham slicked over with the soft yolks of three eggs; two slices of toast with butter and marmalade spread on them awaited his attention. "I must have these files back to Sir Marmion shortly; he required that as part of the loan of them. It was a busy night, reading through them all. I feel as if I have been inundated with paper."

"No doubt," I said, studying the file which must have contained more than a hundred closely written sheets. "Has this been worth your review?"

"In what sense do you ask?" Mycroft Holmes pushed back from his table and gave me a direct stare.

"In the sense that the science that Sir Marmion explores may be applicable to your own work, of course." I was somewhat surprised by the questions.

"All science is applicable to what I do, Guthrie. You would do well to remember that. In the case of Sir Marmion's studies, however, there is an immediate importance to his researches that touches all of us. I must tell you that it is my belief that we must improve our understanding of the human mind if we are ever to use it to its fullest potential, and use it we must, or we will be overwhelmed by those who do not hesitate to capitalize on the power of their minds." He folded his hands on his chest and favored me with a thoughtful look. "Imagine what we might do if we could but comprehend the workings of the human mind, its strengths, its weaknesses, its unexplored capabilities. Once we had such knowledge, there would be no more madness, no more criminality, no more senility or apoplexy, and, once the mechanism was comprehended, no more poverty, for each man should know how to employ the strength of his thoughts, not be subverted by their weaknesses."

"A laudable goal," I said, making no apology for my skepticism.

"You think it is not attainable." He waved his hand to stop my protestations before I could make any. "Well, for now you have the right of it. But for the future, I do not agree. A capable, disciplined mind: the mind is the secret, Guthrie. All our potential is locked within it; science shows us that if it shows nothing else. Sir Marmion seeks to give us some access to it, and I, for one, applaud his efforts, and the efforts of all who seek to comprehend the whole of it. We have discovered so much in the last decade, we must persevere to the limit. I will not be stopped by fashions in thinking, nor by public outcry, for there is too much at stake." He rose from his chair.

"And what if the highest potential of a mind is for greater criminality, or more fecklessness?" I asked. "There may be such predilections even as there is talent for music and science."

Mycroft Holmes nodded. "Indeed, there may be such, and if there are, the sooner we know them, the better. In those cases Sir Marmion may provide the key to identifying those inclinations early enough in life when they might be redirected into more useful applications." He came over to me. "For example, if Sir Cameron had received appropriate instruction early in life, he might not be the drunken, cocksure wastrel he is now."

"It is possible," I allowed in a tone that said I did not think it likely.

"You do not think it could be so; you are not persuaded by what you have heard in this regard," said Mycroft Holmes, wagging a finger at me as if he were a schoolmaster and I a wayward student. "Yet I tell you each man has it within him to be a tyrant or a saint, to be a beacon of achievement or a sink of depravity. It is all a matter of emphasis and application, and of education." He began to pace the room. "I repeat: the mind is the secret. Do not deny the truth of it. You, of all men, should appreciate the power of the mind."

"I do not question it," I said. "I do question its diligence, and the ends to which it is employed."

"That is precisely what Sir Marmion's studies seek to address," said Mycroft Holmes. "And speaking of Sir Cameron," he went on in another voice, "I fear we must prepare to meet him at his London club. He has telegraphed early this morning that he does not wish to be met at the train."

"That is not reassuring," I said as I went to gather up the notes Mycroft Holmes wished me to transcribe.

"No. It suggests he had been drinking or has a doxy with him he does not wish anyone to see. It will not do, to have him arrive in this havey-cavey manner. Not that we would seem to have any choice in the matter." Holmes pulled at his lower lip. "And there is the meeting with Baron von Schattenberg. It would not be to our advantage to have Sir Cameron attend our deliberations drunk."

"No, it would not," I said, thinking of all the times we had had to deal with just that eventuality.

"I think I am going to ask Sutton to put on one of his disguises and go watch Sir Cameron arrive. If he follows him to his club, there will be ample opportunity to discover what state he may be in." He pointed to the notes. "Well, first things first. You may have two hours for that task, and then Tyers will return the file, as Sir Marmion requested."

"That seems an excellent notion; I had best begin at once," I said, and pulled my chair to the table before going to get the inkwell, pens, and nibs for the work ahead of me. "The cream-laid?" I asked, wanting to know what grade of paper he wished me to use.

"That is quite satisfactory," said Mycroft Holmes as he picked up his plate and put his silverware on it. "I'll leave you to it. Tyers will bring you your tea directly."

"Thank you, sir," I said, preparing to set to work.

"Oh, and Guthrie," Holmes said from the door. "Did you happen to notice if you were followed here this morning?"

I shook my head. "It was pelting down rain so much that I thought only of trying to stay dry." This admission bothered me, as if it indicated a failure on my part.

"Well, no matter, I suppose," said Mycroft Holmes, and closed the door.

For the next hour I worked at as rapid a pace as I dared, copying the notes that my employer had made and doing my best to sort them into like groups, but that proved hard-going: the language of phrenology was not always easily grasped, and I did my utmost to make sure I misinterpreted nothing of Mycroft Holmes' observations; the quality of his handwriting—often somewhat erratic in his notes—was affected by the speed at which he had jotted down his responses to the material and gave me occasional starts as I attempted to decypher the hastily made reflections. In addition to the riddle of Mycroft Holmes' fist, I struggled with the notions put forth on the pages, and thought it would be easier if I had the benefit of one of the charts to which the notes so often referred.

When Tyers finally brought my tea, I had completed roughly half the work, and I could hear Holmes singing in the bath.

"What is this passion he has for Bellini?" I wondered aloud, for Holmes was giving his own rendition of *Druid's Chorus* from the first act of *Norma*, relishing the repeated vow that the city of the Caesars would fall.

"Better this than the German ones," said Tyers with a shrug. "Or what he does to Rossini."

I chuckled and nodded. "*La Calunia*," I said knowingly, mentioning the famous aria from *The Barber of Seville*. A year ago, Holmes had struggled with it for almost four months before returning to the strains of Bellini.

"Will you want anything more than tea and toast just now, Mister Guthrie, or will this do?" Tyers smiled at me, his face so benign that I could not but thank him for his concern. When I had done that, he remarked, "I don't know how it may seem to you, but I cannot help but think that Mister Holmes has too much on his plate. You might suppose it was a deliberate attempt at obfuscation."

I nodded. "Yes. It does seem a bit that way to me, as well. But obfuscation of what? By whom? To what end?"

"Ah, if we could discern that," said Tyers as he prepared to leave me alone, "then it would no longer be obfuscation, would it?"

"I suppose not," I said, and poured my tea.

I had just finished copying the notes for Mycroft Holmes when the door opened again and Edmund Sutton strolled into the room. He looked like some minor functionary from a government office, or perhaps a senior clerk at a large counting house; I would have guessed his age at a decade older than I knew him to be. The most persuasive part of his ensemble was a pair of rimless spectacles perched on his nose, making his eyes seem much closer together than they were. He had slicked his hair to his skull with macassar-oil and affixed a moustache like a caterpillar to his upper lip. He affected a slightly stooped posture as well. I could hardly see MacBeth in the man at all. "Good morning, Guthrie," he said, taking the chair nearest the hearth.

"Good morning, Sutton," I replied. "I understand you are off to keep an eye on Sir Cameron."

"So it would seem," he agreed. "I should be invisible enough in this get-up, wouldn't you say?"

"I should think so. I wouldn't look at you twice, and I know you," I said, making as neat a stack as I could of the pages.

"Is that the phrenology material?" he asked, as if the possibility had only just crossed his mind.

"Yes. The files must be returned shortly, and Holmes wanted his notes copied before then." I picked up the teapot and realized it was nearly empty. "Shall I ask Tyers for more?"

"Not on my account," said Sutton. "I have had three cups already this morning." He fell silent, then said, "What do you make of it?"

"Of what?" I asked as I readied the files for their journey.

"Of phrenology," said Sutton, touching the tips of his fingers together in an almost perfect mimic of Mycroft Holmes' gesture.

"I know very little about it," I said carefully.

"I may say the same," Sutton reminded me. "But I am not sure the human character is so easily revealed as phrenology suggests." Now that he had said it, he stared at me, his chin up, looking down his nose. "If all that was needed to grasp the whole of a man's nature was to study his head, would that not have been learned long ago?"

"Possibly," I said, wanting to draw him out. "But why should anyone have bothered?"

"Why bother now?" Sutton countered. "The trouble is, I'm an actor; science is not as engrossing to me as it is for many another. As an actor, I know that there is more to a character in a play than what is on the surface of him. In great drama, the most notable roles are so faceted that they can sustain many diverse interpretations without losing the coherence of the playwright's work. There is much concealed, shaped by memory and circumstances. How could it be less complex for living men? How can all that befalls a man be writ on his skull and capture more than a sketch of the man who abides in it? Yet phrenology would make it so." He stopped. "Or so it seems to me."

I had the feeling I was being pulled into the end of a debate, one that had gone on between Sutton and Mycroft Holmes. "I understand your concerns," I said. "If I had a better grasp of the science, I would have an answer for you."

Sutton smiled a bit. "You aren't wholly convinced, either, are you?"

"Not wholly, no. But there is no denying that Sir Marmion has done some excellent work with the mad. His success with those held in asylums is beyond cavil. That cannot be regarded as mere chance." I put my hand on the package I had just finished preparing. "It is impressive to see the progress he has made with those who were thought beyond all reach. He may not have the entire puzzle solved, but he has solved a few of the knottier problems."

"Um." Sutton rose. "Well, I must be off. Sir Cameron's train is due in shortly. I will return in time to deliver my report, and before you have to meet with Baron von Schattenberg." He went toward the door, his walk changed from an easy stride to a stork-like tread, his head carried forward on his neck. "Shall I need my bumbershoot?"

"You may. It was raining heavily when I arrived," I said, resisting the urge to applaud his departure.

Ten minutes later I handed the prepared package of files to Tyers and went back to the study where I found Mycroft Holmes, newly dressed, his hair still damp from the bath, standing in front of the hearth, hands spread to the heat. "You've done well, my dear boy," he announced, cocking his head in the direction of the stacked sheets.

"It's good of you to say so, sir," I replied, and sat down in the chair I had occupied for most of the morning.

"Sir Marmion will have his files back in good time and you and I will have an opportunity to plan for our next go-round with Baron von Schattenberg." He continued to look pleased, which suggested to me that he had arrived at a strategy to deal with the situation. "I am most grateful for all Inspector Strange told me—in strict confidence, of course."

I was not quite following his thoughts here, but I sat still, waiting to hear what more he would say. "There may well be a few policemen who have become enmeshed in certain organizations that purport to address political wrongs that are actually occupied in fomenting violence and civil unrest. I am told that even when the alliance is not divided that police sympathies tend toward those organizations because of their public positions of maintaining order at all cost." He came to his chair and sat down again, his face expressive of his ambivalent thoughts. "Although I cannot yet prove it, I am convinced some of those organizations have direct ties to the Brotherhood, which would explain how they have managed to work undetected for so long—few policemen are willing to act against their fellows, as such an investigation must inevitably require."

"What does Inspector Strange have to say about the extent of this riot?" I was dubious about this possibility, for it struck me that anything so wide-spread could remain secret for long.

"He has only guesses, and is reluctant to try to seek out anything more material, for he has discovered that any proof that might have existed has been mislaid or destroyed. Those who could give relevant testimony are missing. He says that there were even policemen who tried to investigate the groups in the past, and they all—with one exception—came to a sticky end." Mycroft Holmes studied his hands. "You may guess, if you like."

"Your source of information?" I suggested.

Holmes nodded. "The one exception is Inspector Strange himself. He is not anxious to become caught up in the very intrigue he left behind four years ago."

"But you believe him?" I could see there was apprehension in his somber grey eyes.

"I would rather I did not, but I do." He rocked back on his heels. "Policemen serving as paid assassins. In England!" The idea clearly distressed him. "You might expect such a thing in Turkey, or in Sicily, or perhaps in Russia, but not here."

"What do you plan to do?" I asked, wanting to know for my own benefit as well as his.

"I plan to watch my back, and so should you." He folded his arms. "If the men who have been following us are policemen, then dealing with them becomes much more problematic than it was."

"If we have, in fact, been followed." I was becoming uncomfortable with the many notions now crowding my head.

"We have, in fact, been shot at," Mycroft Holmes said firmly as he fingered the small scab on his face. "And it was a policeman who sent Sid Hastings away. He is not one to be fooled by an imposter; no jarvy is."

"But why should anyone be taking such action now? Do you think it is the Brotherhood?" I knew the answer before I heard it from him.

"My dear Guthrie," he said, all insouciance, "who else is likely to take so great a risk at this time?"

I could not help but agree, lowering my head as I did. "Where does that leave us?"

"In a bit of a pickle, I should think," said Mycroft Holmes. "I hope you have your pistol with you. I do not want you going out without it."

"If that is what you want, I shall do it," I told him, trying to convince myself my anxiety was the product of my imagination and not the information Mycroft Holmes had conveyed to me. "My pistol is in my valise."

"Good man," said Mycroft Holmes.

"I will load it, if you think it best," I went on.

"Of course I think it best. Why should I want you to carry an empty pistol?" He pinched the bridge of his nose between his thumb and forefinger. "Do not try my patience, if you please."

"I did not mean to try your patience, sir," I told him. "You do not generally want me to carry loaded weapons to diplomatic meetings, such as the one we have scheduled this afternoon?"

"Ah, yes," said Mycroft Holmes. "Forgive me. Ordinarily you would be right, but it would be best, I think, to make an exception today. In case the Brotherhood has plans for us."

"You do expect them to take action, don't you?" I said, shocked in spite of myself.

"Regrettably, I do," he said. "If Jacobbus Braaten is coming to England with Vickers, you may be sure they will want to remove any . . . obstacles from their path." He laid his hand on his chest. "I am accounted something of an obstacle by them. As are you," he added keenly.

"Perhaps," I said. "But why draw attention to their presence by so overt an act as killing us? Would not the police—" Before I could finish, Mycroft Holmes interrupted.

"If the police are truly being influenced as Inspector Strange indicated they are, we must not look to the police to aid us, or at least not in any way we would expect." He began to twiddle his watch-fob, a sure sign of agitation on his part. "If the Brotherhood wishes to return to England, they know they must stop me, or render me ineffective against them. Had I not learned of the role the police might play in this, I might well have relied upon them in a most improvident manner." His voice dropped. "You have fought the Brotherhood more than once, Guthrie. You know what they are capable of doing. Still you do not want to believe how ruthless they can be."

I considered my answer. "I would prefer not to think anyone so lost to human sensibilities as these men are," I told him at last.

"I cannot blame you for that," Mycroft Holmes said with sympathy. "But I must ask you to remember what they have done before, and to realize their goals have not changed."

"Yes," I said, then sighed. "It is all such a muddle. Sir Cameron and his wife. Baron von Schattenberg and his aides. And on top of it, Mister Kerem's tale, which is another matter altogether."

Mycroft Holmes raised one heavy eyebrow. "Is it? I wonder."

I recalled what Tyers had said about obfuscation, and was tempted to mention it to Holmes, but said instead, "How could they be connected?"

"I don't know. Yet." He dropped his watch-fob and began to walk about the room. "They may not be. But my thumbs are pricking again."

"Not very scientific," I quipped, trusting he would not be offended.

"Not that we have determined thus far," he agreed, becoming affable once more. "But damnably reliable, for all of that."

"Indeed, sir," I said, aware that Mycroft Holmes' general level of sensitivity in such matters had been honed by years of testing. I stopped myself asking him if there was a bump for such predispositions on the skull.

"Just at present, I am—" He broke off as the sound of a ringing bell and pounding fists came from the front door. "What on earth?" he asked of the air.

"Mister Holmes! *Mister Holmes!*" came the urgent cry from a man whose mother tongue was not English.

"Mister Kerem!" Holmes exclaimed, motioning to me to answer the urgent summons. "Take your pistol, Guthrie. This may not be what it seems." He held the study door for me as I went to retrieve my pistol—unloaded as it was—from my valise, and rushed to do his bidding.

Halil Kerem stood on the top step of the stairs, his overcoat open, his suit in disarray, his hair wet. He sagged as I stood aside to admit him. "It is too much," he said as he trudged into the flat, hardly moving as I put my pistol in my pocket and closed the door.

"What is too much, Mister Kerem?" Mycroft Holmes asked from the study door.

For an answer, the Turk began to weep in a ghastly, shuddering way no Englishman—or Scot—would ever do. Through his tears, he said, "The police. They have found my brother. Mister Holmes. He is dead. My brother is dead."

FROM THE PERSONAL JOURNAL OF PHILIP TYERS

Returned from the asylum betimes, having put Sir Marmion's file into his hands myself, to find MH closeted with the Turkish gentleman, Mister Kerem, who has learned but an hour since that the police found the body of his missing brother in an alley in Shoreditch. He was not identified, but it seems there is a tattoo on his shoulder, for the corpse was quite naked and showed evidence of much abuse. Mister Kerem wishes to discover if the tattoo the police said the body has is the same tattoo as his brother's, which will settle the matter beyond all question. I have brought tea and brandy—although Mister Kerem, being a follower of Islam, does not drink—for MH, G, and the Turk.

I have a note from Sir Marmion to MH which I will deliver when it is more convenient; just now the task of consoling Mister Kerem seems to occupy all MH's attention . . .

I must remember to tell MH that in my journey to and from the asylum I was followed . . .

Chapter Seven

THE THREE OF us had crowded into Sid Hasting's cab and were bound for the morgue at Saint Elizabeth's Hospital, where Mister Kerem believed his brother's body had been taken. The rain had not diminished, and low places in the road now contained standing water that rose in what seemed a bow wave as we passed through them.

Mister Kerem had regained a modicum of self-control, and although he shuddered from time to time, he had stopped crying, for which I was exceedingly grateful: I supposed Mycroft Holmes shared my sentiments.

"If you will be good enough to call back for us?" Mycroft Holmes said to Hastings as we drew up at the carriage-entrance to the building. "I do not know how long we shall be, but there should be time enough for you to find a pub and eat a pastie."

"Thank you, sir," said Sid Hastings. "I shall be here again in half an hour, if that is satisfactory."

"Quite," said Holmes as he alighted from the cab and held the door for Mister Kerem and me to step out into the relative shelter of the extended and pillared roof. "I feel so much out of my element," he confided to me in a rush. "This is so much more my brother's area of expertise."

I had to agree that his brother dealt more often with cases of this sort, but I said, "You have more than enough skill, sir."

"That is what I'm afraid of," said Holmes drily as led us forward.

An orderly standing in the doorway looked at us in mild curiosity, not knowing if any of us needed his assistance. He was smoking a pipe, and was preparing to set it down when Mycroft Holmes signaled him to remain where he was. "Need to find someone, do you?" he asked, doing his best to be helpful.

"We know what we seek, thank you," Mycroft Holmes told him as we went into the hospital.

The smell as we stepped through the door was of carbolic and that underlying sweetish odor of sickness that all hospitals possessed. Ahead was a counter behind which an uniformed attendant waited, his ledger open and ready.

"Good day," said Mycroft Holmes as he went up to the counter. "I have here with me Mister Halil Kerem who believes you may have his brother's body in your morgue. He has come to identify it."

The attendant behind the desk scowled at us. "I don't know about that," he said, giving what was obviously a routine response for him.

"It is of some urgency, as I understand it," said Mycroft Holmes.

The attendant made notations in the ledger. "The police will be here in an hour or so. You may sit on the benches until they come."

"Must the police be here for him to make an identification?" Holmes asked, knowing it was not required by law—only that there were two witnesses to the identification, which Mycroft Holmes and I would be.

"It's easier if they are." The attendant was prepared to ignore us entirely.

"Easier for whom?" Holmes was beginning to lose patience.

The attendant did not answer; he seemed wholly engrossed in his ledger.

Mycroft Holmes laid his forearm on the counter and leaned forward; although he lost none of the affability he had extended in his initial greeting, there was no denying the authority he projected as he said, "My good man, Mister Kerem is in great distress. He is a stranger in this country, come to find his brother. Now he has been led to understand his brother may be the victim of a crime. It is his most earnest hope that the police are in error and the man you have here is not his brother. But unless you admit him—and us—to see the body, he must continue in the agony of uncertainty. Surely you have had other men come here to identify bodies?"

The attendant had backed up and now stood pressed against a filing cabinet. "In the basement. The second hall on your right. Take those stairs," he said, pointing to our left. "There is an orderly. He'll show you the body."

"Excellent," said Mycroft Holmes. "Thank you for your help."

The attendant nodded once, and tried to restore his importance as we went to the stairs, descending into the basement down a broad flight of shallow stairs. It occurred to me that the reason the descent was made so easy was that stretchers had to be carried up and down them with some frequency, a recognition that seemed somewhat ghoulish. At the second hall on the right the air was distinctly colder than on the floor above, and there was a searching, persistent odor of death that shocked me, not because I did not expect it, but because I did.

"Those double doors," said Mycroft Holmes, and I remembered he had been here before. "The attendant will be at a small desk on the other side; he will show us the body in question. Let me deal with him, Mister Kerem."

"Of course, Mister Holmes," said Mister Kerem.

I glanced at the Turk and saw puzzlement in his face. I supposed he was trying to reconcile his first impression of Mycorft Holmes as a bureaucratic nonentity with the manner in which Holmes had secured our admission to this place. I made a mental note to myself to mention this to Holmes later, when we were private again. Now I gave my full attention to the attendant, who looked up in surprise as we came through the door.

Without any preamble, Mycroft Holmes addressed the middle-aged fellow who sat behind the desk, a racing-book in his hands. "You have an unidentified body here, that of a young man. He has a tattoo on his shoulder."

"What is that to you?" The attendant was less officious than his colleague above-stairs, but he was also less easily impressed.

"This man"—Mycroft Holmes indicated Mister Kerem—"has reason to believe the body may be that of his missing brother. We have come with him as witnesses, in case it is."

The attendant rose from behind his desk. "I'll show you. But I warn you, he isn't a pretty sight, not if it's the lad I'm thinking of."

"I am prepared," said Mister Kerem. "Allah is Merciful."

"That's as may be," said the attendant as he led the way along a row of draped tables. "The killers weren't, I can tell you that. Had to have been more than one of them, the way he's beat-up."

I almost winced at this unfeeling remark, but thought it just as well to let it pass, to save Mister Kerem any more unpleasantness than was necessary. Perhaps the attendant was trying to prepare us for the body. I supposed the attendant had to subdue any trace of sympathy or he would become incapable of working here. Perhaps, I thought, in a clumsy way, the attendant was attempting to prepare Mister Kerem for what he would see.

The attendant stopped at the eleventh table. "This is the lad, then," he said. "He went through a lot before he died, the poor sod. The face is pretty bad. I'll turn him over for you so you can see the tattoo." With that, he whipped back the drape, revealing the battered and mutilated body of a young man with dark, curly hair. His eyes were gone, and his nose and ears. Three of his fingers were missing, as were his testicles.

Mister Kerem said nothing; an instant later the attendant turned the body over.

I saw Mycroft Holmes start in alarm, then at once mask the consternation he felt. He leaned forward to study the tattoo, the line between his heavy brows deepening. Whatever it was he saw, he did not like it.

"Is it the tattoo, then?" The attendant looked from one of us to the other.

"It is," said Mister Kerem in a voice so neutral it was hard to distinguish his words. "This man is my brother," he said more firmly.

"You are certain?" the attendant said to make sure. "The tattoo is enough?"

"It is enough," said Mister Kerem.

"Very good," said the attendant, and motioned to us to turn away while he put the body on his back once again and concealed it under the drape. "If you're sure, we can fill out the forms now, and you may send for the undertaker as soon as the police will permit it."

Mister Kerem looked shocked. "Can I not remove him myself?"

The attendant shrugged. "Not until the police say you may." He stepped away from the table. "I'm sorry. But your brother was murdered, and the courts call a body part of the evidence. It's the law."

"How can they?" Mister Kerem looked very much distressed. "They cannot be so . . . so hardhearted as to keep me from doing my duty—"

The attendant did his best to calm Mister Kerem. "Let's get the paperwork taken care of first, shall we. Then we will see what the police demand. The sooner this is done, the sooner you may have him." This was true enough as far as it went, but was more of a polite gesture than an assurance of swifter action on the part of the police.

"If I must," said Mister Kerem, glancing at Mycroft Holmes. "You can help, can you not? You got us here."

"I'll see what I can do; first you must provide the information asked. Then we may have reason to encourage the police," said Holmes, and pulled me some small distance aside while the attendant extracted a form from his desk and cast about for his inkwell and pens. "Did you see that tattoo?" he asked me in a whisper, keeping a covert eye on Mister Kerem and the attendant, about fifteen feet away from us. His voice was not much more than a breath, but his intensity made it seem louder.

"Most unusual," I said. "A winged serpent in a kind of circle."

"The winged serpent had a man's face," Mycroft Holmes declared. "The colors are quite vivid."

"Did it have a face?" I took his word for that. "What is the significance?"

"It is the inner circle of the Brotherhood," said Mycroft Holmes. "Their elite."

It took a moment for me to encompass the implications. "Oh, no. You cannot think that that young man—" I began, horrified at the notion.

"No, I do not think he was one of their elite. But he certainly has had contact with one of them. And recently. That tattoo is quite new, to be so bright." Mycroft Holmes blinked his eyes as if to sort through a number of visions, each more unpleasant than the last. "I wonder how much Mister Kerem knows of this?"

"Surely he must know *some*thing," I said, giving voice to the fear that had touched me as soon as Mycroft Holmes identified the tattoo.

"If he does, his presence here is more distressing than anything he reported to us." Holmes made a swift, dismissing gesture. "Well, we must take a page from his book: we must not reveal anything to him."

"Is that why you have changed your manner?" I ventured.

"In part," he replied. "Kerem has singled me out for some reason. I hope I may cause him to do something to reveal what that reason is. If you will assist me in that effort, I will be most appreciative, dear boy."

"As you wish," I said. "Shall you feign ignorance about the tattoo?"

"Of course, about its age and its significance. I will do my best to learn all that I can from Mister Kerem. And so shall you," said Mycroft Holmes, his grey eyes like the North Sea in winter. "Follow my lead, Guthrie. And be alert."

"That I will, sir," I said, and moved with Holmes as he went back to stand by Mister Kerem.

"I have supplied as much information as I can," Halil Kerem

said. "I do not know how my brother came into England, nor in whose company. If I did, I should surely inform the police." He was talking as much to the attendant as to Mycroft Holmes. "I know only that Yujel is dead and now our family must mourn his loss."

With a discreet cough, Mycroft Holmes asked, "Do you happen to know how long he has had that tattoo? And how he came to have it?"

Mister Kerem rounded on him, his face working with emotion. "Tattoo! *Tattoo?* What does that matter now? It was useful only to identify his body." He added something in Turkish that did not sound complimentary.

"I understand your upset, Mister Kerem. I would be distraught at the loss of my brother, too. But we must start somewhere, and that tattoo is an obvious place. It is certainly one of the first questions the police will have." He had returned to his bureaucratic persona; he did not quite dither, but he came close to it. "While you have been providing answers for this man"—he inclined his head toward the morgue attendant—"I have been trying to anticipate the questions the police will ask, in order to hasten their release of the body to you. The tattoo is so unusual, I am convinced they will fix upon it as having bearing on this case." He managed a nervous little smile. "The sooner they are satisfied, the sooner you may arrange for . . . the funeral."

"Very well," said Mister Kerem, making himself speak calmly while he used an over-large handkerchief to wipe his eyes. "The tattoo was an old one. He received it when he was eleven, as I recall. It was administered by a man who has done tattoos all his life. It is supposed to protect the man who has it." He stopped, his voice becoming unsteady as he again fought back tears. "Yujel was proud of it. He showed it off whenever he could."

"Just so," said Mycroft Holmes. "So his having the tattoo was known to many?"

"I would suppose," said Mister Kerem, turning suddenly to the attendant. "Is there anything you can do to give my brother a bit more dignity?"

The attendant laughed. "Dignity? Why, he's *dead,* saving your feelings, sir. Dignity is nothing to the dead. They have no need of it, no, nor of anything else." He saw the outrage in Mister Kerem's eyes. "If it would make you happier, sir, I'll put his body near the back, away from the rest."

"Thank you," said Mister Kerem stiffly. "On behalf of my brother."

"I don't want to add to your grief," said the attendant apologetically.

"Of course not," said Mister Kerem. "You have been most helpful." He spoke mechanically now, as if he could not continue to speak if he admitted any emotion.

"Now, you two gentlemen," the attendant went on, "you will need to sign here as witnesses of this identification. The police might ask you about it, or they might not. Just your name and direction, if you would?" He held out the pen to Mycroft Holmes, who took it and scrawled his name on the line indicated, and added his direction as the Diogenes Club beneath. When he offered me the pen, I dipped the nib in the inkwell, wrote my name and Curzon Street. "Very good," said the attendant as he took out an old square of blotting paper. "Thank you."

"Are we finished here?" Mister Kerem asked.

"I should think so, Mister Kerem," said Mycroft Holmes in a self-effacing voice that seemed comical to me, "perhaps we should report to the police now. Let this fellow get on with his work."

"Yes," said Mister Kerem. "This is an oppressive place, and I do not want to remain here." He took a half-crown from his pocket and handed it to the attendant. "For seeing that my brother's body is shown more respect."

The attendant took the coin, paying no heed to the critical look Mycroft Holmes gave him. "Why, thank you, sir," he said, and pocketed the coin.

"For that, be certain Mister Kerem's wishes are honored," said Holmes in an emphatic way.

"That I will," said the attendant, and I, for one, believed him.

As we climbed the stairs to the ground floor, I studied my employer's demeanor, for it was apparent he was wrestling with various concerns. I was reluctant to intrude upon his thoughts, but I knew I should say something to him, if only to make it apparent to Mister Kerem that we had his interests at heart. "Do we go to Scotland Yard?" I asked as we emerged on the ground floor.

"I suppose that would be wisest," said Mycroft Holmes. "They must be the ones dealing with the case."

His tone told me that he was not eager to do this, and I wondered how much his apprehension about police corruption was coloring his response now. "To whom should we speak?"

"We must learn first to whom the case is assigned. Then we will know." He shook his head. "You do not think that this murder will command the attention that others might."

"Why not? A foreign national found horribly killed," I said. "The yellow press will take to it as happily as to a royal scandal."

Mycroft Holmes addressed Mister Kerem. "You must pardon my secretary. He has a biased view of the press."

"I do not," I protested.

"Mister Guthrie has the odd notion that the press is interested in truth," said Mycroft Holmes, lifting one eyebrow.

"That is what they claim," I reminded him. "I have come to doubt that."

Holmes went on ruthlessly. "He forgets that what is truth to the press is news. It is news that the press seeks, and it is news it trumpets. A case such as your brother's may strike the press as news, in which case it will be blazoned on every broadsheet from Fleet Street. If it is seen as just another unfortunate killing, they will ignore it." He paused in the doorway to the carriage. "I want you to prepare yourself for either eventuality. Do not be disappointed in anything you read, Mister Kerem. The press are a capricious lot."

"On that we agree," I said with feeling, and stepped through the door into the rainy bluster of the afternoon.

Sid Hastings appeared as if conjured from the steady downpour. "There's a hot brick for your feet, Mister Kerem," he said as he lowered the steps for us; I got in, followed by Mister Kerem.

"Thank you," said Mycroft Holmes as he climbed into the cab. "We'll go to Scotland Yard, I think. If you will leave us and call back in an hour, I would be most appreciative. I will need you to be prompt in fetching us. Our duties are not finished. We still have the meeting with Baron von Schattenberg to attend this afternoon."

"That I will; we'll get you where you're going, no fear," said Hastings as he set Lance in motion. "Oh, sir, I think I should tell you: we are being followed."

Mister Kerem looked alarmed, but Mycroft Holmes nodded his acceptance. "Tell me as much as you can."

"There are two of them. On horseback. They picked us up in Pall Mall and I saw them again as I drew up for you now." Hastings threaded his way into the traffic, glancing back once. "Yes. Still there."

"Two of them, you say?" Holmes asked.

"On horseback. I can't make out much more than that." Hastings sounded apologetic.

"One horse has a loose shoe?" Holmes waited for the answer.

"Sorry, sir. I can't tell. Too much noise," said Sid Hastings.

"Well, try to keep a watch on them, if you can do it without being obvious," said Mycroft Holmes, and sat back out of the rain.

We rode most of the way in silence, as if speaking might somehow put our followers on alert. The jumble of traffic kept Hastings busy, and when he finally let us down, he said to Holmes, "Still there."

Mycroft Holmes nodded. "We'll see you in an hour."

"Right you are," said Hastings as he went off.

Scotland Yard was a warren of activity through which Mycroft Holmes led us until he reached an enclosed desk and addressed the harried gentleman behind it. "Inspector Wallace," he said. "Perhaps you could help us?"

The Inspector winced at the sound of Holmes' voice, and scowled when he turned to see who was addressing him. "Oh, Good God," he expostulated. "You."

"I," Mycroft Holmes agreed.

"What do you want?" Inspector Wallace was suspicious and made no effort to conceal it.

Mycroft Holmes did not answer directly. "There was a murder, a young man, foreign, with . . . significant mutilations. This man's brother, in fact." He put his hand on Mister Kerem's shoulder. "We have only just come from the morgue, and now we would like to speak to the officer assigned to the inquiry."

Inspector Wallace had begun to thumb through papers on his desk. "That would be Inspector Lionel Featherstone. You can find him up on the first floor. Ask for directions at the top of the stair."

"There—you see how little you had to fear?" Mycroft Holmes said with an inclination of his head. "Thank you, Inspector Wallace. I'll remember your kindness."

"No need," said Wallace with unseemly haste as we went off toward the stairs to the first floor.

There was more confusion as we reached our goal, but finally we were pointed to an office off the central corridor where we found Inspector Lionel Featherstone deep in discussion with three uniformed constables. At the sight of us, they all fell silent, staring at us as one. Lionel Featherstone was of moderate height but built like a steam-engine and seemed to contain as much energy. He wore a non-descript suit of clothes in a color between dark-brown and navy-blue. His face was guarded, but his eyes were lively, brown-shot-with-green hazel.

"Inspector Featherstone? My name is Holmes. I do some work for the Admiralty." He managed to make this sound as if he were a minor aide or other supernumerary. "This is my assistant, Mister Guthrie."

"Oh, yes?" said Inspector Featherstone, clearly reserving his opinion.

"I have come here with Mister Kerem to discuss your progress in the investigation of his brother's murder." He waited a moment. "I am afraid my time is limited, so I will not be able to stay with you for much more than forty minutes." He pulled his watch from its pocket and read it. "If you will spare us the time?"

Inspector Featherstone waved the constables away. "Find out about any grudges that might have been held against the victim. We'll meet again in an hour." As his men filed out of the small office, he gave his attention to Mister Holmes. "All right: what can I do for you, Mister Holmes."

Mycroft Holmes regarded the Inspector for a long moment. "Mister Kerem has just come from the morgue at Saint Elizabeth's where he identified the body of his brother. My secretary and I served as witnesses."

Inspector Featherstone nodded twice. "I see. And how did you hear about this?"

"What do you mean?" Holmes asked, glancing at Mister Kerem.

"I mean, no one has made a report on that body beyond filing its admission to the morgue and the assumption of foul play in the death of the young man." He tapped one finger on the desktop. "I am curious as to how you learned of this?"

Mister Kerem coughed a bit, then said, "I had a note left for me at my hotel. It told me the police had found the body, and so I assumed the police had left the note." He looked about in confusion. "If you did not, then who might have—?"

"The murderer, for one," said Inspector Featherstone. "Who else would know about it?"

Mycroft Holmes cocked his head. "This is most troubling. For if the note was left by the murderer, it means that the murderer knew you had come to London to search for your brother. How might he have known that?" He looked deeply concerned.

"I have no idea," said Mister Kerem, adding, "I should not have thrown the note away, should I?"

"Probably not," said Inspector Featherstone. "It would have been useful to have it. Still, we must make do with what we have." He indicated one of the wooden chairs in his office. "Perhaps you had better sit down and tell me more about this, Mister Kerem. Incidentally, my condolences on the loss of your brother."

"Most kind," said Mister Kerem, choosing a chair. "It is a great loss to my family."

Inspector Featherstone was pulling a notebook from his desk as he said, "It's always hardest when they die young."

Mister Kerem bowed his head in acknowledgment. "I wish to assist in any way that will help capture the criminal who did this," he said in a muffled tone.

"Of course. You shall." The Inspector selected a pencil. "If you don't mind, tell me how and when your brother came to England."

As Mister Kerem began to speak, Mycroft Holmes pulled me aside and said, "We will wait until this inquiry is properly underway and then you and I must leave."

"Baron von Schattenberg," I said. "And Sir Cameron."

"Exactly." Mycroft Holmes frowned, directing his stare toward Mister Kerem. "I shall have to inform the Admiralty of this latest development."

"Will not the police do that?" I asked, puzzled that he should make such a remark.

"I hope so," was Holmes' equivocal answer.

FROM THE PERSONAL JOURNAL OF PHILIP TYERS

Sutton has returned from his surveillance of Sir Cameron's arrival and is off to the theatre. He has informed me that apparently the Scot has decided to remain sober for his meeting, although he was hectoring the porters and his valet. Sir Cameron was taken to his hotel and, after changing rooms twice, is now in a suite to his taste; when Sutton came away, Sir Cameron had just ordered a good-sized dinner. He mentioned that he thinks Sir Cameron was being followed by more persons than himself. Sutton has three performances tonight—one as MH, two as MacBeth.

It being Saturday, no courier brought Admiralty dispatches today, although a note was sent round regarding the Kerem investigation. It would appear that Mister Kerem has been busy approaching his government's representatives in the hope of spurring some action on the part of the police. This means that the Turks will be watching to determine if we are being forward-looking enough in regard to the young man's disappearance. The government is worried about the possibility of trade in prostitutes, male and female, not simply because of potential embarrassment, but because of the problems it would imply for customs and all manner of foreign trade. . . .

MH and G should return shortly. I have clothing set out for them both. Barring any more unpleasantness, such as was encountered yesterday, the meeting with the Germans should finally go well, if Sir Cameron remains sober and reasonable. . . .

Chapter Eight

I FINISHED CHANGING clothes in record time, and was combing my hair when Mycroft Holmes came into the sitting room, very grand in his formal kit.

"I do hate these occasions," he said. It was a familiar refrain, and one that I had come to look upon as a rite: any time Mycroft Holmes had to make himself seen beyond his supposed circumscribed routine, he disliked it.

"Think of what good it will do. You may be able to keep Lady

MacMillian from bringing her uncles with her. That would make the momentary discomfort worthwhile, wouldn't it?"

"Very likely," said Mycroft Holmes. "We should depart on the instant," he added, going to the entryway and taking down his opera-cloak. "Are you ready?"

"Half a tick," I said, and slipped my comb into its handle, then turned to face him. "I have my portfolio ready, of course."

"Excellent," Mycroft Holmes approved. "Then we must be off. I do not want to arrive late, and give Baron von Schattenberg an excuse to be uncooperative. Once we are delivered to Berkeley Mews, I will send Hastings round for Sutton, to get him to the theatre while we are with Baron von Schattenberg and Sir Cameron." He pursed his lips in disapproval. "I believe Sutton will have the more pleasant evening, enacting a tragedy." Pointing to the corridor, he added, "Tyers will have a late-night supper ready for us upon our return. I do not mean to starve you, dear boy."

"No fear of that," I assured him as I picked up my portfolio and went to take my evening coat off its hook. "At your service entirely."

"Come along, then," he said, and led the way down to the street and into the last weeping drop of the storm. We went along to the corner where Sid Hastings was waiting for us. "Any constables talk to you, Hastings?" Holmes asked; he climbed into the cab while Sid answered. I got in behind him and pulled the steps up.

"No constables, no," said Hastings. "But I think we may be observed," he added conscientiously.

"Oh? By whom?" Mycroft Holmes asked as he slewed about in the cab trying to look behind us as Hastings set off into the afternoon traffic.

"I think there may be someone on horseback." He guided Lance through the confusion, his attention on the road more than whatever might be behind us. "It's hard to tell."

"Just one person?" Mycroft Holmes asked. "There were two before."

"That's my point, sir," said Sid Hastings. "If this one rider is following—and mind you, I don't say as he is—it isn't like before." He turned right at the next corner. "No. He's not coming after us. Sorry, sir. My mistake."

"It's all right, Hastings. I would rather you err on the side of caution than ignore what could be real danger." Holmes settled back against the squabs and looked over at me. "Are you prepared to deal with Sir Cameron?"

"Prepared may not be the word; resigned is more like it." I did my best to smile to show my intention was humorous, but I found it difficult to coax my face into that expression. "I am wary of him, sir."

"The voice of experience. He is difficult; no argument there," said Mycroft Holmes. "I keep thinking there must be some way to show him how his conduct might be improved, but I have yet to hit upon it." He stared out into the street. "I should remember to inquire after the courier who was shot. It troubles me that I have not been able to devote more time to working out—" He stopped. "Well, I cannot pursue it now. I have Sir Cameron and the Brotherhood to deal with."

"Not an enviable position, if I may say so, sir," I told him.

"You may, Guthrie; you may," said Mycroft Holmes.

I chuckled in spite of myself, but said nothing more until we reached Berkeley Square and turned down Berkeley Mews to Dietrich Amsel's house. Sid Hastings drew in and let down the steps, and I got out first, standing aside for my employer.

"Fetch us after you have delivered Sutton back to the theatre," said Holmes. "If we are not waiting at the door, have the butler tell us that you are here."

Sid Hastings touched the brim of his cap and pulled Lance around in the narrow confines of the street. "Wouldn't like this place to be a foot narrower, and that's the truth," he said as he left.

Mycroft Holmes' knock on the door was answered promptly by the butler, who relieved us of our overwear and informed us that Baron von Schattenberg was waiting in the drawing room. "Thank you; is Sir Cameron arrived?"

"Not yet," said the butler. "He is expected directly."

"Very good," said Holmes as he made his way in the butler's wake to the drawing room. I kept two paces behind my employer, knowing this was what the Germans regarded as appropriate conduct for an employee.

Baron von Schattenberg was as grandly arrayed as he had been yesterday, as if he expected to receive a formal visit from the Prince of Wales instead of Sir Cameron. He rose from the sopha by the hearth, bowing and smiling. "So we meet again, Mister Holmes."

"As was our arrangement," said Mycroft Holmes, without the effusiveness of the Baron. He nodded to the three aides, who were on the far side of the chamber as if seeking to make themselves partially invisible. "Good afternoon, gentlemen. I trust I see all of you well?"

"Indeed," said Baron von Schattenberg. "You are most gracious to inquire. We are all well here. And we are prepared to receive Sir Cameron, so that we may resolve the questions that have arisen in regard to his wife's visit." He indicated the sopha opposite the one he occupied. "Be comfortable, Mister Holmes. We are ready here to arrange matters to our mutual satisfaction; we are only waiting on Sir Cameron."

"So I was informed. Given the hour, he should arrive shortly," said Mycroft Holmes, more in hope than in certainty. He sat on the sopha as if it were a stiff-backed chair. "In the meantime, perhaps you can tell me upon which points you are willing to negotiate and upon which you are not. That will save us unnecessary bickering, and hasten our resolution of this matter."

"No doubt, no doubt," said the Baron. "A pity this cannot be accepted in a form that would most please Lady MacMillian, but—" He opened his hands in a display of helplessness.

Mycroft Holmes gestured his agreement. "You are not willing to have her visit Sir Cameron at his estate in Scotland: do I understand that?"

"Yes," said Baron von Schattenberg. "It is too early in their efforts to permit such a concession. She would have to relinquish most if not all of her autonomy to him, as her husband. She will not stay at his London house, either, and for the same reason." With elaborate casualness he added, "I assume you are aware that he has engaged a house in Deanery Mews?"

"I had heard something of the sort, but did not know what stock to put in it, it being such a capricious thing to do," said Mycroft Holmes, who, until that moment, had known nothing about Sir Cameron leasing a house in London. Since my rooms in Curzon Street were a mere five blocks from our current location, and Deanery Mews another five blocks or so beyond that, I resolved to nip round to have a look at the place as soon as possible.

"Capricious or not, I have confirmation that he has done this. He will occupy the house on the first of December according to the estate agent who arranged the matter. I am told it is his intention to receive his wife there." The Baron coughed. "Which is not entirely what is wanted. I am afraid that Lady MacMillian has said she must stay with her uncles at an hotel while she is in London. I had assumed this was understood already, but it now appears not. Lady MacMillian will not be assumed by his gesture. You must understand she is not yet willing to reestablish a household with Sir Cameron." He did his best to smile. "I hope you will explain this to him when he arrives."

"I will endeavor to do as you ask," said Mycroft Holmes, his jaw tightening. "I am somewhat surprised that he should take such an action, knowing as he does that this meeting is only the beginning of their reconciliation, if, indeed, they decide to reconcile."

"I perceive you comprehend the problem. It would be unwise of Sir Cameron to press Lady MacMillian too urgently; she will take it amiss. Her escort might then have to take action to protect her from Sir Cameron's importunities." Baron von Schattenberg flung up his hands. "Sir Cameron is a great hero, but such men are often impulsive and demanding." He nodded to his aides. "You will make sure that Mister Holmes has all that he needs while our discussion continues."

"Most kind," murmured Mycroft Holmes. "But Guthrie manages such things for me."

"Oh, yes," said the Baron. "A reliable English servant."

"Scots, actually," said Mycroft Holmes as I did my best not to bristle at the appellation he had used for me: servant indeed! I told myself that his comprehension of the language was imperfect, but that did not truly satisfy me. I had to assume the insult was done to rattle me and Holmes as well.

"Scots," said Baron von Schattenberg. "As is Sir Cameron." His unctuous smile was worthy of a cat.

"Yes," said Holmes, and I knew from his tone of voice that he felt insulted.

"No doubt your man can help you to understand Sir Cameron," the Baron approved, then shot a hard look at his aides. "Well, your man may sit near you, so long as he does not interfere with you or me or Sir Cameron, when he arrives."

"Very well." Holmes noticed a group of velvet-upholstered chairs behind him. "Guthrie, if you would be willing to sit there?"

"Of course," I said, and went to take the nearest of the four chairs. From this vantage-point I could watch not only Mycroft Holmes and Baron von Schattenberg, but the three aides, as well: I noticed that Herr Kriede was nervous, while Farbschlagen and Eisenfeld were not. I wanted to discover the cause but could think of no reason to account for it.

Baron von Schattenberg rang for refreshments, saying, "It is getting on in the day, and it will soon be the hour when you English have tea. I will not demand that you miss it."

"How good of you," Mycroft Holmes said, and did his best to look happily anticipatory of this treat. "I am sure Sir Cameron will welcome his tea, also."

"It is possible," the Baron allowed, and sat back on the larger sopha. "A pity we have to wait for him."

"He *is* the reason for our meeting," Holmes reminded him diffidently. "Once he arrives, we shall get down to it, all right and tight."

"Yes," said the Baron, and fell silent.

The only noises in the room were the clatter of the fire and the subdued whispers of the three aides. Sounds from the street did not penetrate to this part of the house, and it seemed to me that the Baron had chosen this room over the library for just that reason. I busied myself with opening my portfolio and taking out my notebook and pencils in preparation for the discussion to come.

Baron von Schattenberg stood and went to face the fire, which action provided him an excellent excuse to slight the others in the room. He sighed in appreciation of the warmth, and at last turned around to address those before him. "We see that Sir Cameron is not prompt. A most unfortunate trait in a man of his position."

"We do not know what has kept him," Mycroft Holmes interjected. "There are any number of reasons he might be delayed." I could tell from the edge in his voice what he feared one of those reasons might be: Sir Cameron's love of brandy.

"He would do well to send a message to us explaining his change in plans," said Baron von Schattenberg. "I am not used to waiting."

"He is only ten minutes late," Holmes said in a conciliatory manner. "The weather may be sufficient cause to account for that."

"So it might," said the Baron grudgingly. "The weather has been filthy."

Mycroft Holmes was spared the necessity of reply by the arrival of the butler with the tea-tray, which he set down on the table between the sophas. "Your tea, sir," said the butler, and bowed.

"*Danke*," said the Baron and waved the butler away.

"Cream cakes," said Mycroft Holmes, surveying the bounty on the tray. "A rare treat. Sir Cameron will be pleased."

"And raspberry tarts, which I understand he fancies as well," said Baron von Schattenberg, as if it were unreasonable to like such food.

"What would you rather have?" Mycroft Holmes inquired. "Sausages and cheese, perhaps?"

"That would be more to my taste," the Baron admitted. "Still, it is pleasant enough, in its way." He came to the sopha. "Let us hope Sir Cameron arrives before all is cold."

"Truly," said Holmes with sincerity. "It would be a pity not to enjoy this at its best."

That eventuality would not arise: there was a bustle at the front of the house, and then Sir Cameron's bellow, "Holmes! *Holmes!* Get out here!"

My employer and I exchanged glances as he rose. "If you will permit me, Baron?"

"Of course," said Baron von Schattenberg, apparently unaffected by the uncouth display at the front door.

"Guthrie. Come with me, if you please," said Holmes, not waiting to see if I was behind him as he left the room.

"HOLMES!" Sir Cameron's voice was louder than ever. "I know you're here!"

Mycroft Holmes answered the summons quietly. "Sir Cameron. What do you require of me?"

I paused a step behind Holmes to scrutinize Sir Cameron: he was a bit heavier than he had been the last time I had seen him, and his ginger hair was thinning, but he still cut a fashionable appearance in his formal clothing. Just now his face was flushed and he was white around the mouth. It took me a moment to realize that he was not inebriated but in the grip of fear, and then I wondered what had so discomfited him.

"I want something *done*," said Sir Cameron bluntly. "I want the blighters arrested."

"What . . . blighters?" Mycroft Holmes asked in an eminently reasonable tone of voice. "What has happened, Sir Cameron?"

Indignation and fear swelled in Sir Cameron's bosom. "Well might you ask. Some blighter took a shot at me! At *me*!"

Holmes' manner went from indulgent to serious in an instant. "When?" he asked.

"Just now. We were turning off Mount Street when there were two shots fired at my town-coach. The door-frame on the right side was splintered and my coachman was wounded in the shoulder." There was a suggestion of a stammer in his words, and he paced in a small ellipse, his hands caught together to keep them from shaking. I noticed a whiff of brandy about his person, and I assumed he had fortified himself from his flask.

"Are you certain?" Mycroft Holmes was intent now, entirely focused on what Sir Cameron was saying.

"As certain as a man may be," said Sir Cameron. "I won't stand for it! Shootings in London. In Mayfair!" He slammed his fist into his palm. "It's not to be endured."

Mycroft Holmes set about the task of soothing the mercurial Scottish peer. "Sir Cameron, if you will tell me all you can about the incident, Guthrie here will see a full report is tendered to the police within the hour."

"The police," Sir Cameron scoffed. "Fat lot of good that will do." He glowered at the butler who was standing a few steps away listening avidly. "See you don't pass this on to any of your cronies. I don't want to read about it in the *Mirror* tomorrow."

"I do not gossip, sir," said the butler stiffly, and pointedly left the room.

"Good riddance," said Sir Cameron. "There was something odd

about the shot—it was more like a hunting pistol—you know, the long-barreled Hungarian sort they use on boar and bear for the coup de grâce."

"No doubt you're right; we'll make due note of it," Mycroft Holmes told Sir Cameron as if this were nothing of significance, though both Holmes and I knew that Vickers favored a long-barreled Hungarian hunting pistol. "Still, if you want to stem the tide of gossip, perhaps we should tend to the matter for which we are here?" He made the suggestion tentatively, not wanting to provide Sir Cameron with another excuse to rant.

For once, Sir Cameron allowed himself to be persuaded. "Right you are. These Germans can't be trusted to hold the line. Smarmy lot, they are." He smoothed the front of his coat. "I'll give Guthrie my report when we're done here. The police can wait until we're finished with this meeting; it's not as if they can catch the assassin. If I know anything, I know he's long gone. He'd be a fool to remain nearby."

"A fool or brilliant," said Holmes distantly. "What better place to hide than among those walking on the street in the rain?"

Sir Cameron paid no attention. "I sent my coachman off to find a constable and then to see a physician to have his shoulder stitched up. He will give a first report." He made it seem as if these very sensible acts were the height of magnanimity on his part.

"It is probably best, as you say," Mycroft Holmes declared, relieved that he had not had to dispute with Sir Cameron over such precautions.

"Where are the Germans?" Sir Cameron went on.

"In the drawing room. If you will permit me to announce you?" Holmes said as he ushered Sir Cameron down the corridor.

"If you want to do the butler's job, what is it to me?" Sir Cameron said as if he had no part in the butler having left them to their own devices. "Let's just get this over with as quickly as we can. I have an engagement tonight and I do not want to miss it."

Mycroft Holmes concealed a sigh. "I should hope we may settle all our questions promptly, but that will be up to you, in large part."

"Then it should be a simple task, for I am a reasonable man." Sir Cameron declared with a fine disregard for the truth.

We were almost to the drawing room; Holmes made a last attempt to prepare Sir Cameron for what lay ahead. "They know about the house you let."

Sir Cameron stopped abruptly. "What business is it of theirs?" he asked, choler returning to his eye.

"They do not want you to have your wife stay there," Holmes said.

"And why should she? She has a suite reserved at Brown's, or so I believe. Does she want to change her plans?" Sir Cameron inquired. "What is it to her if I let a house in London?"

Mycroft Holmes held back the outburst I knew was threatening to erupt. "If not for her, then why—?"

"I can't spend all my time at an hotel or my club," said Sir Cameron petulantly. "It's much too public a place. A man needs a place of his own, don't you know? A private one. A place where he can enjoy himself without prying eyes upon him."

With a gesture of exasperation, Holmes whispered, "Do you mean to say you are going to install a mistress there?"

"Well, and what if I am?" Sir Cameron answered sullenly. "You can't blame a man for—"

The door opened and Baron von Schattenberg exclaimed, "Are you not going to present Sir Cameron, Mister Holmes? now that he has finally come?"

Mycroft Holmes recovered his aplomb with astonishing speed. "Of course," he said to the Baron. "It is my honor to present to you Sir Cameron MacMillian. Sir Cameron, the Baron von Schattenberg." He gave me a quick glance as if to be certain I was in place to deal with any faux pas Sir Cameron might make.

The Baron bowed and clicked his heels. "A pleasure, Sir Cameron."

"And for me," said Sir Cameron automatically. "I am sorry I was late, but on my way here my coach was shot at." He said it calmly, with an air of heroic resignation. "I knew I had enemies, but I did not think they would be so bold as to strike in the heart of the metropolis."

"Shot at!" the Baron marveled. "Did you suffer any—?"

"I am unhurt," said Sir Cameron. "Which is more than I can

say for my unfortunate coachman, who was wounded in the shoulder." He was dangerously near smirking now. "It is an outrage, of course."

"Most certainly it is," agreed Baron von Schattenberg with an alacrity that I found suspicious. "Come in, come in. There is tea and I can send for schnapps or brandy, whichever you would prefer."

Sir Cameron smiled. "That would be very good of you."

I shuddered at the thought of what brandy would do to Sir Cameron in his present frame of mind, and so I struggled to try to think of something to say that might warn him of the risk he was running. The best I could come up with was, "With so much to accomplish, do you think you want to—"

He did not allow me to finish. "I would welcome a glass of brandy to steady my nerves," he announced. "After the misfortunes of this afternoon, I do not want to make a decision based on my unwitting belief that I am under attack from old enemies instead of assessing my position from a less apprehensive posture." His smile was smug enough to annoy me but insufficient to give me cause to call his request into question. I looked at Mycroft Holmes and shrugged; he nodded to me.

"Then let brandy be brought," said Baron von Schattenberg. "It is only fitting that we offer our guest libation to his liking." He gave a quick look at Holmes as if to make certain that it was recognized that he, not Holmes, had the command of our current situation.

"For which I thank you," said Sir Cameron. "You must excuse Holmes," he went on glibly. "He is a Puritan at heart, and thinks himself above all indulgences. More's the pity."

"As you say," the Baron conceded. "I will see that you have the hospitality you prefer." He looked at Mycroft Holmes as if to accuse him. "Bring brandy," he ordered the butler, who was standing a short distance away. "And a carafe of hot water as well." He folded his arms. "When Sir Cameron is quite comfortable we will resume our discussion."

I was tempted to dispute the remarks Sir Cameron had made as well, but I saw Mycroft Holmes signal me to silence, and so I kept my peace. I busied myself with making notes that meant very little while the tea cooled in anticipation of the arrival of brandy, which would be most welcome when it was finally produced. When the butler came in with a tray containing an old bottle of French origin, I saw the three aides nod to one another, and knew then that they had anticipated some disruption in our meeting. That distressed me, but I contained myself, hoping that there would be some means to reveal this device for what it was.

"May I have some tea?" Mycroft Holmes asked as the Baron poured out a measure of brandy into a snifter of cut Czech glass.

"Oh, I think that is possible," said Baron von Schattenberg. "Herr Kriede, if you will do the honors? Pour yourself a cup first, and drink it down before you offer any to our guests. He has had such an ordeal that he deserves this courtesy."

"At once, Herr Baron," said Helmut Kriede, rising and coming to perform the duty requested by the Baron. He filled his cup with a flourish, stirred it thoroughly, added milk and sugar, stirred again and drank the whole. "There. You see?"

"You did not need to make such a display for my benefit, or for Sir Cameron's; we do not think we are in the company of our foes," said Mycroft Holmes. "But I thank you for your willingness to demonstrate your good-will."

"Thank you, Mister Holmes," said the Baron. "I wish you to comprehend the extent of our inclination to accommodate your expectations so that you will not balk at our requests regarding Sir Cameron and Lady MacMillian." He began to pour a second cup, paying only slight attention to what he was doing. "It is most unseemly that Sir Cameron has suffered any mishap that is the least associated with us, for that would tend to cast doubts on all that we do."

"Not at all," muttered Sir Cameron, whose visage belied his words.

"You see?" the Baron exclaimed. "Sir Cameron understands me. I do not mean to distress you, but you must realize that I am obligated to stand by my countrywoman in matters that may not be all you wish for."

"I do grasp that," said Mycroft Holmes, and gave an uneasy look at Sir Cameron, who was swirling his brandy in his snifter. "I do not wish to make Lady MacMillian's stay here unpleasant in any way, but I am concerned about her escort. The men she proposes to accompany her are not those who have wholly unblemished pasts, and this is perturbing to the Admiralty, and to Her Majesty's government. This leaves me in a difficult position, for I wish to find a way to welcome Lady MacMillian to London without the reservations we must have in the current circumstances. You have said, Baron, that she will not reconsider. I hope that this is not true, for I need her to—" He stopped abruptly as Helmut Kriede made a small, gasping noise then fell to the floor, the teacup he had been holding breaking as it hit the edge of the table.

FROM THE PERSONAL JOURNAL OF PHILIP TYERS

Sutton is off to the Diogenes Club in his guise as Mycroft Holmes. He told me just before he left that he would remain in the Reading Room of the DC for the purpose of removing himself from observation, for he is very much of the opinion that he is still being followed. If this is true, it is most disturbing, and I am at a loss to say what is best to be done . . .

There is a note from Sir Marmion, who has indicated that he is going to review the wounded courier's case, to determine if he has been receiving the best of care. While I do not doubt that the Admiralty provides its people with the finest treatment, I am also certain that Sir Marmion may be able to suggest other means to improve the courier's lot, and hasten his recovery.

MH and G are still with the Germans, which is not unexpected. I will not look for them for at least an hour or so. In the meantime, I have in hand an autopsy report for Yujel Kerem, which I shall present to MH upon his return. It appears MH was right in two of his conclusions regarding the young man . . .

I must step out for an hour or so to visit the butcher and the baker, for, tomorrow being Sunday, such shops will be closed, and I will be unable to find any of the meats and breads I can obtain during the week. At least the butcher has said he has put aside a standing crown roast of pork that I may bring here for tomorrow's dinner. Come Monday there should be fresh veal chops, and halibut from the fishmonger . . .

Chapter Nine

THERE WAS SILENCE in the drawing room of Herr Amsel's house in Berkeley Mews. No one breathed for the greater part of a minute, and then Baron von Schattenberg called aloud for the butler as Sir Cameron downed the entire contents of his snifter; for once I could not blame him. Mycroft Holmes dropped to his knee and took the man's wrist, then leaned forward and put his ear to his chest; it was apparent to all that life had departed, for Helmut Kriede's face was set in a rictus that cannot be long supported in life. The body carried odors indicating death had struck.

The butler appeared in the door, his annoyance at the summons giving way at once to horror. "My God!" he ejaculated as he saw the corpse. He rushed forward only to be stopped by Mycroft Holmes.

"Send someone to the police. Say it is urgent: there has been a death by poison." Holmes got up. "Then seal this room. Let no one enter or leave it." He regarded Baron von Schattenberg. "I hope this will meet with your approval?"

"Oh, yes," said the Baron, much shaken, his face gone pasty. "I will defer to you in this. It is your country." He turned away from Kriede's body. "But I do not like having to remain here. Is it necessary that we stay here? Can we not adjourn to the library and close this room for the police?"

Mycroft Holmes shook his head. "That would not be wise," he said as soothingly as he could. "We must provide no opportunity for any mischief to be done to the body, or to the scene itself."

"Come now, Holmes," said Sir Cameron in his bluff, bullying way, "No one's going to touch it. I think it's a damned good notion, going to the library. Nothing to be gained staying here."

"I regret to contradict you, Sir Cameron," said Holmes with a polite nod. "But we must be able to report to the police that the body is precisely as it fell, that no one has touched the cup-and-saucer, that, in fact, all is as it was when the poor man died. If we leave a guard here, no matter who that guard may be, there must be some opportunity for alteration of the scene, and that would muddle the investigation from the start. No, do not even pick up his cup, Herr Eisenfeld. Everything must remain exactly as it is." He motioned to me. "Guthrie, do you hand out sheets of paper to everyone, and we shall occupy ourselves writing down everything we can remember in the minutes that led up to Herr Kriede's death."

Sir Cameron welcomed this opportunity for complaint. "I saw hardly anything. I had just arrived and was still somewhat overcome by my experience in Mount Street."

Mycroft Holmes dared to interject his instructions. "It would be better if we do not discuss what happened until we have each one written his own impression of events. That way we may discover a detail only one of us observed." He pointed at me. "Guthrie, if you would?"

I had taken some sheets from my portfolio; I rose and handed them out to the Germans, to Sir Cameron, and to Mycroft Holmes. "Do you want me to do the same, sir?"

"Of course I do, dear boy. It is most essential that we triangulate our impressions, which this exercise will allow us to do," said Mycroft Holmes as he pulled out his pencil and set to work, providing an example to the rest, for gradually they all began to write. I, too, returned to my seat and put my mind to recalling all I had noticed from Sir Cameron's arrival to the moment Helmut Kriede fell dead. I tried to remember everything I had seen, and all the remarks I had heard. It was more difficult than I had thought it would be, for the presence of the corpse loomed in my attention, and my recollection shifted and slid like reflections on running water.

"This is preposterous," said Sir Cameron a short while later. "I have little to report. I arrived, I was received by you and Baron von Schattenberg, there was tea, you sent for some brandy, Baron, and then insisted on some nonsense with the tea. I didn't think it was at all necessary, but you Germans insisted, so it was done. The next thing I knew, the fellow was . . . was on the floor." He put down his paper. "I can tell you no more."

Mycroft Holmes schooled his demeanor to one of sympathy. "It is like you, Sir Cameron, to minimize the danger here. But it is important that you put such considerations aside, much as they do you credit. For it may be that the poison was intended for you."

Sir Cameron went very still; I watched the color fade from his cheeks. "What are you saying, Holmes?"

"I should think it is the obvious conclusion," Holmes said gravely.

"That *I* was the one intended to die?" Sir Cameron demanded. "How could that be possible?"

"Well, you sustained a most fortunate escape less than twenty minutes ago. Now it appears that a second assassin was in position to strike in case the first should fail." He looked at the paper with the few scrawled lines on it. "How could the killers have known you would have brandy instead of tea?"

I bit back a remark that anyone who had ever met Sir Cameron might suppose such a preference, but I said nothing on that head while Mycroft Holmes continued to deal with the Scottish knight.

"There is something in what you say," Sir Cameron allowed. "I may have been too hasty." He picked up his paper again. "I may be able to recall something more."

"Your report will certainly be worthwhile for the police." Mycroft Holmes went back to writing his impressions, and a few minutes later set down his pencil. "A pity we cannot have any tea while we wait," he remarked.

The others in the room stared at him with faces showing a range of emotions from irony to disgust. Baron von Schattenberg cleared his throat. "The police will want all the tea things, I suppose. Everything on the tray?"

"They will," Mycroft Holmes confirmed. "We do not know where the poison was, or whatelse is poisoned." He pointed to the pastries. "For all we know, they, too, are deadly."

Egmont Eisenfeld held out his paper to Holmes. "Do you think his face might be covered? It is most . . ." He made a gesture of repugnance to finish his thought. "The smell is bad enough."

Holmes considered this request. "I don't think dropping a handkerchief over his face would ruin anything." He pulled his own from his pocket, spread it, and put it in place.

"Thank you," said Eisenfeld. "It is less terrible, and it preserves his dignity."

I recalled the morgue attendants' remarks earlier this afternoon on death and dignity, and I saw at once that it was really the living who benefitted from these concessions to the dead, not the dead themselves, who were beyond all caring. I was startled at these responses, but I did not deny them, either. It perplexed me that I had taken so long to realize these things, after all the escapades I had passed in Mycroft Holmes' service.

"Guthrie," said Holmes, cutting into my reverie.

"Sir?" I gave him my attention at once.

"If you will collect all the papers so we may have them ready for the police?" Mycroft Holmes looked at the others in the room. "It will not be long. The police will be here presently."

"I hope so," said Sir Cameron. "The fire is burning lower and there is no more fuel to put on it. Do you think we could summon the butler for that service, at least?" He was becoming truculent again, fretting at any check on him.

"I think it would be best if we waited until the police come," said Holmes.

Sir Cameron gave a sigh of ill-usage. He stared at the Baron. "Where is my wife, sir? We might as well settle things, so long as we are stuck here." I knew his tone of old: he was attempting to pick a fight.

"It is what we are met to do," said Mycroft Holmes, surprising me and spiking Sir Cameron's conversational guns. "Let us try to make the best of our predicament."

This was all Sir Cameron needed. "Well, sir? Where is she?"

"She is in Holland," said Baron von Schattenberg with a kind of gratitude that struck me as questionable. "Her uncles are with her. If you can convince the Admiralty to permit them into your country, she can arrived day after tomorrow."

"Holland," said Sir Cameron, musing. "How long has she been there?"

"She arrived at her current location yesterday. I received a wireless last night, informing me that she was at her hotel." The Baron cocked his head. "She is anxious to see you."

"And she wants her uncles to come with her." He considered this. "What is the trouble with that, Holmes? The Admiralty do not object to her traveling with her relatives, do they?"

"It is not that they are relatives, although there is some question as to the degree of relationship of one of them," said Mycroft Holmes awkwardly. "We have been given reliable information that the uncles in question have affiliations that the government—" He stopped. "These uncles may have more planned than simply delivering your wife to London."

Baron von Schattenberg shook his head. "That is a ludicrous

idea. There is nothing unacceptable about Lady MacMillian's uncles, even the man who has been awarded that name honorarily."

"You are sure of that, are you?" Holmes asked, his manner highly skeptical.

"As sure as I am that my aide is dead on the floor," said the Baron.

"What is the trouble, then, Holmes?" Sir Cameron demanded. "What can the uncles have done that you will not let them accompany their niece—my wife—to this country?" He put one hand on his hip in a belligerent manner, glad to be in a wrangle at last.

Mycroft Holmes hated to have his hand forced, and by someone of Sir Cameron's stamp made it more intolerable; still, he knew he had to answer. "It is not your wife that troubles the Admiralty, I repeat: it is her traveling companions, and those they intend to add to their party here in London. There is a report—a very, very reliable report—that indicates the uncles are members of the Brotherhood."

I was astonished to hear him speak so bluntly, and in our present company. I hoped it was a ploy and not some desperate attempt to flush the culprit by a surprise attack. I wondered if he would reveal anything of Vickers or Braaten, or if he would keep that information to himself; I could not help but think he might have said too much already.

Sir Cameron stared in complete disbelief. "The Brotherhood? Absurd! They are men of high rank and great wealth. There is no reason for them to associate with such iniquitous men. What can they seek from the Brotherhood that they do not already possess?" He looked to the Baron von Schattenberg for support.

"They may seek power," said Holmes quietly, and added, addressing the Baron, "Please forgive my abrupt disclosure. I did not intend to put this before you in such a manner."

"I am at a loss," said the Baron. "I cannot put credence in this. If you are referring to the subversive organization known as the *Bruderschaft*, then I must tell you that your information cannot be correct. The organization is dedicated to the overthrow of those legitimately in power, or so we have been told. The men of the Brotherhood are scoundrels, all of them, unprincipled and treacherous. How could Lady

MacMillian's uncles be party to such barbarity? It is the height of absurdity to think they might ally themselves with such an organization. Her uncles have done much for Germany, for all Germans, not just their own class. They, themselves, are well-born and wealthy; men of highest repute and in excellent standing in the world. They have no reason to join so infamous a group." He shook his head slowly. "What could anyone have told you to make you believe so pernicious a lie?"

"The man who revealed this vouched for the authenticity of his information with his life. His body was found shortly after he provided us with his report. He was grotesquely murdered." Mycroft Holmes took a deep breath. "You must forgive me if I set store by such a sacrifice as our agent made. He had pursued these men for more than a year before they found him out, and they made him suffer for what he had done. If you wish a copy of the report, I will see you are provided with one." This last offer was startling; I wondered what Holmes sought to accomplish by it.

"Yes," said Baron von Schattenberg. "I would like to see your report."

"I will have it sent round tomorrow. And I promise it will be tomorrow, though it will be Sunday. I know this material is genuine and I believe what we have discovered deserves your immediate and concerted attention. When you have had time to review it, you may comprehend my many reservations about the escort Lady MacMillian has provided herself. In fact, you may want to undertake measures of your own where these men are concerned." He looked toward the window—shuttered in anticipation of the coming night. "You may not share my worries in this regard, but I would like you to have an opportunity to see the reasons I have them."

"I know a thing or two about the Brotherhood," Sir Cameron remarked. "Nasty brutes, the lot of them. Won't do to have them hanging about. I don't think my wife would permit such—"

The butler knocked on the door. "Chief Inspector Pryce has arrived," he announced.

"Let him come in," said Mycroft Holmes before Baron von Schattenberg could speak. He signaled me to come to his side, which I promptly did. I was still perplexed by all the revelations Mycroft

Holmes had provided the Baron; such a forthcoming warning was not in his usual style; it struck me that perhaps this murder might lend weight to the things he had learned about Lady MacMillian's proposed companions. At least he had not said anything about Braaten and Vickers sailing for Ireland: that was best kept as reserved information.

The door opened and Chief Inspector Vaughn Pryce came into the drawing room. Of average height, lean, about thirty-five or so, with a strong face, he was altogether a smoother customer than Inspector Lionel Featherstone; he looked about and said, "Good evening, gentlemen. I see there has been a development here. How did it come about?" He had a better accent and tailor than most policemen could boast: I remembered hearing that his mother, whose name he used, had been an entertainer before she married a very minor Earl from the north and earned the odium of all her husband's family. Did that account for the saturnine cast of his countenance, or had his police work made him cynical, as it had done for so many others?

"So you are Chief Inspector Pryce," said Mycroft Holmes. "My brother has spoken of you often. I am Mycroft Holmes. I am associated with the Admiralty."

"Holmes, Holmes," said the Chief Inspector. "Yes, I think I know your brother: tall, clever chap with a knack for turning up culprits."

Ordinarily Mycroft Holmes would protest such a demeaning description of his younger brother, but now he only said, "Sounds very like him."

"Does he have anything to do with this?" asked Chief Inspector Pryce. "No one said so."

"Alas no. This is a suspicious death that may have diplomatic implications, which must be the reason you have been sent to investigate," said Mycroft Holmes pointedly; he, too, knew that Chief Inspector Pryce had in the last year been assigned to crimes among the upper classes.

"Diplomatic implications?" Chief Inspector Pryce echoed. "How is that?"

Mycroft Holmes spoke before anyone else could. "Well, this house is owned by Dietrich Amsel, a German national, and the dead man is also German. The man who employed him is a Baron. We were gathered here this afternoon to arrange a visit for Lady Mac-Millian—you know Sir Cameron, of course?"

"By reputation," said Chief Inspector Pryce. "A privilege, Sir Cameron."

"You're most kind," said Sir Cameron in a voice that suggested that such homage was his due.

There was a long, uncomfortable pause, at the end of which Chief Inspector Pryce was moved to speak. "So you were here to make arrangements for Lady MacMillian. And this man just keeled over?"

"It seemed almost that way," said the Baron, as if the death of his aide was only now becoming real to him. "He drank some tea and collapsed."

"Um-hum," said Chief Inspector Pryce. "Why?"

"Did he collapse? It would appear to be from poison," said Mycroft Holmes. "Swift and paralytic, by the look of it. Monkshood, perhaps." He coughed. "Nothing has been moved aside from a small amount of action each of us has taken."

"I see," said Chief Inspector Pryce. "Did any of you notice anything beyond the ordinary? Before the man . . . collapsed?"

Mycroft Holmes answered again. "While we were waiting for you to arrive, I asked that we each put down our recollection of the moments leading up to Herr Kriede's death. My secretary Guthrie has the pages for you."

I opened my portfolio and retrieved the pages I had just put there. "I think you will find them useful, Chief Inspector," I said as I handed them to him.

He took them, a bemused light in his eyes. "How very . . . beforehand of you, Mister Holmes," he said, and I reckoned he was not best pleased by this.

"My brother has imparted to me the importance of preserving first impressions of crimes, as well as keeping the actual scene as undisturbed as possible. I have seen the wisdom of his admonition, and heeded it here. That was why I ordered the room closed and put us all to the task of recording our impressions of Herr Kriede's demise. I trust I have not over-stepped myself?" He caught his lower lip in his teeth, but this was his only outward indication of apprehension. "If it would suit you, we will now withdraw to the library, leaving this room to your attention."

Chief Inspector Pryce contained his growing annoyance and said, "That would be more convenient, yes, sir."

"Then come along, good Herren, Baron von Schattenberg, Sir Cameron," Mycroft Holmes declared. "The Chief Inspector has much to do."

The Baron was reluctant to leave. "Helmut Kriede was my aide, and he is dead in my service. I think I should remain here to see that he is not mishandled, or made ridiculous by your police."

"I wouldn't do anything of the sort," said Chief Inspector Pryce with an oily kind of sympathy. "But we must make certain tests in order to determine how he died, and from what cause. We need such information in order to mount a prosecution of the guilty party when he is brought to answer to the law. Poison can be difficult to identify. This man is the victim of a crime, and it behooves us to do all that we can to apprehend his killer, wouldn't you agree? If I tell you that nothing disgraceful will be done, that he will be treated with respect, will you leave the room while we do what we must?"

Baron von Schattenberg considered his answer. "Will he have to go to your morgue? Can we not send him directly to the undertaker, for embalming, before his body is shipped back to Germany?"

Mycroft Holmes turned to the Baron. "Do you think that is wise? Herr Kriede was murdered, and his body may tell us much."

"He was here as a diplomat," said Baron von Schattenberg sharply. "For that reason alone, we should be allowed to return the body to his family as quickly as possible. Or must I inform the Kaiser that Her Majesty's government will not adhere to diplomatic custom?"

"If you want him shipped," said Chief Inspector Pryce in a tone of some surprise, and with an uneasy glance at Mycroft Holmes. "I'll try to hurry the release of the body from the morgue. You'll want to make arrangements now to have the body picked up. It will probably have to be Monday: tomorrow few of our men work unless they must. I'm sorry, but I doubt I can speed the examination of the body more than that, not where poison's involved. He'll have to be vetted by our doctors, and I'll try to get one of them to tend to it tomorrow, so you may have him first thing on Monday."

"Thank you," said Baron von Schattenberg, much subdued. "His family will be distraught."

"More's the pity," said Chief Inspector Pryce. He was growing anxious to have us leave the room. "If you please, gentlemen?"

"One thing," said Mycroft Holmes as he went toward the door. "We do not know if anything was done to the food and the tea. Have your men check the food, the plates, the tea, and everything else on the tray for poison."

Chief Inspector Pryce sighed. "All right. Since the man died of poison, we'll endeavor to find out how it got into him." He bowed slightly to Sir Cameron. "Sorry to have to exclude you, Sir Cameron. A man of your . . . experience might be most helpful, but under the circumstances—"

Sir Cameron shook his head. "No, no. Best to leave things of this nature in you johnnies' hands. No fear. I know when it is best to lie doggo."

"I'm sure you do," said Inspector Pryce, his admiration making him smile, no matter how somber this occasion had become. "We'll need an hour or so to inventory the pertinent items for our investigation, and then, of course, the body will have to be removed." He looked away, shaking his head. "The young man is German, I suppose? Did you say he was German?"

"Helmut Kriede, yes, was German," said Mycroft Holmes from the door. He gestured to Sir Cameron to follow him, and then stepped into the corridor with the Baron and his two aides. I kept near at hand, wondering what might be best to do.

"The library, I think," said Baron von Schattenberg. "May we have some schnapps brought there?" This last was to the butler, who hovered nearby.

"If you wish. Do you want anything more?"

"I don't think so," said the Baron.

"I could use a strong cup of coffee, if you have it, with sugar," said Sir Cameron. "And something to tide me over until supper." He saw the distress in his host's eyes and added, "I know it may not seem suitable to be hungry at such a time, but I've learned through my various adventures to make the most of these moments. You worry about how it looks, you eating at such a time. Well, I'll tell you it looks a damned sight less peculiar than you going off in a faint because you're famished. Who knows how long the police will keep us here? It is a cold night, coming on to frost, I should expect, and we will have to be out in it. So it is only sensible to have a bit to eat now, in case we must be here for hours."

"You may be right," said Baron von Schattenberg, and nodded to the butler. "If there are any sandwiches you could send up, that should be enough." He started toward the library, his men following after him. "Is the fire built up?"

"I'll attend to that," said Paul Farbschlagen, going ahead of us to see if the chamber was warm enough, glad, I assumed, to have something to do.

Mycroft Holmes fell in beside the Baron, saying, "A most unfortunate loss, Baron. My most sincere sympathies to you." He sounded genuine enough, and I supposed he meant what he said. "If you need my help in anything relating to his death, you have only to ask."

"The body must be readied to be shipped home at the first opportunity," said the Baron as we entered the library, Sir Cameron lagging behind.

"I will do what I can. I will ask that the Admiralty prevail upon the police to hasten their investigation of the body—which I feel you would want them to do as thoroughly as possible—so that you may handle all the other arrangements. I am reasonably certain the body can be made ready to release to you on Monday morning, just as the Inspector said. I will inform you if there are to be any delays, and the reasons for them." He looked about him, taking stock of the library. "I think it would be wise to turn up the lamps. It is quite dark in here."

Baron von Schattenberg was walking as if his ankles could not bend, and I began to feel for him. He was upset, beyond all question, and his two aides were doing their best to conceal their distress, as well. Eisenfeld sat down at the side-table and occupied himself setting up the chessboard. Farbschlagen had gone to the hearth and was choosing more wood to burn; he moved automatically, as if by rote, and his hands shook as he stoked the fire. Sir Cameron made for the sideboard where a decanter of sherry stood, while the Baron drew an over-stuffed wing-back chair up to the fire and sat down, staring into the flames as if they were far, far away.

"Baron von Schattenberg," said Eisenfeld when the Baron had remained silent for the greater part of two minutes, "what shall we do?" He spoke in German.

I answered awkwardly, as I had been instructed to do, "We had best obey the police."

"*Ja,*" said the Baron distantly. "Until they leave this house, we obey the police." He said this last in English, as if to be certain everyone understood.

Farbschlagen moved away from the hearth where he had just laid two new logs. "We will be warmer in a moment."

I doubted that, although I understood Paul Farbschlagen's intent. "It is not easy to warm up after such an event," I said. "It is not only the flesh that is chilled." I noticed Mycroft Holmes was watching Sir Cameron, and I guessed he was not sanguine about how the Scot was behaving; being a Scot myself, neither was I.

"I must inform his family," said the Baron. "I must write a letter at once." He started to get up, but Mycroft Holmes stopped him. "Please. It is my duty."

"Then do it properly," said Holmes. "Collect your wits and bring your thoughts into order. Do not write so important a letter without calming yourself. Have a drink, and then get pen and paper."

"I must write to the German Ambassador here in London as well. I will need his help in the arrangements," said the Baron a bit distractedly. "This must be done properly from start to finish."

"Yes, yes. You shall do all these things. But first you must restore your self-possession. It will not do to let the police see you thus dismayed. They would likely draw conclusions you would not like. You are rattled, sir, as who would not be?" Holmes signaled to Paul Farbschlagen. "If you would, fetch a glass of sherry for the Baron. If we wait for the schnapps, it may be an hour before he is steadied."

"Is the sherry . . . safe?" asked Farbschlagen.

"I should think so," Mycroft Holmes said after considering it for a moment. "Poisoning the sherry is too random. Who knows who might drink from it? Whereas the tea-tray was bound for the drawing room and our consumption." He waited a moment. "Sir Cameron has suffered no ill-effects," he added. "Given the speed with which Herr Kriede collapsed, Sir Cameron should be dead by now if there is poison in the sherry."

"Thanks very much," said Sir Cameron, much affronted.

"You reputation for bravery is well-deserved," said Baron von Schattenberg as Farbschlagen went to pour a large tot for him.

Somewhat placated by this observation, Sir Cameron helped himself to another glassful.

FROM THE PERSONAL JOURNAL OF PHILIP TYERS

An Inspector Featherstone has just called to see MH, and I had to tell him that he is from home and will not return until later this evening. A solid sort of policeman, Featherstone, not too imaginative but not a lump, either. He is looking into the death of Yujel Kerem, and has some questions he would like answered as soon as is convenient. I have told him MH will be available to him tomorrow at noon, if he is not opposed to working on Sunday.

Nothing more from Halil Kerem. I have prepared an inquiry regarding him, and will present the results of the inquiry to MH by tomorrow evening. First: must be discovered on which vessel he arrived in England, and from what port. Then: to discover his place of residence and his activities since his arrival . . .

A note was delivered from HRHE, asking for MH's report on Sir Marmion's work. I must assume that whatever his reason, HRHE is in some haste to have the evaluation he seeks . . .

Sutton is off to the club, and then to the theatre. If Saint Martin's Lane were a bit nearer he would be tempted to walk the distance, but that might also cause someone to recognize him and make an association that would be to no one's benefit, so it is just as well that he rides in Sid Hastings' cab. These have been a demanding few days for him and will not cease to be so until the run of the play is over next week. In anticipation of that event, he has been reading plays this afternoon, trying to determine which of them he should do next, as the run of MacBeth is coming to an end. He says he would like to try something less traditional for his next work, something that will call upon him to expand his range. After tonight, he has three performances to go until closing, and he wishes to have some new project for the future. None of the plays he is considering is as famous as MacBeth, *but each has something to recommend it. I foresee another spate of learning lines and prancing movements.*

Chapter Ten

OF THE SIX men in the library, four were reading books. I was reviewing my notes, and Mycroft Holmes was playing chess against himself. It was growing chilly again, the fire having burned down, and if it were to be built up again, the butler would have to supply more logs. The hall clock had chimed eight a short while ago, and the sustenance of the sandwiches had worn off some time earlier. From behind the tome Sir Cameron had propped in front of his high-backed chair, there came an occasional hint of snoring that the rest of us strove to ignore.

Then the door opened and Chief Inspector Pryce came into the library. "I am sorry it has taken so long, but sometimes it is difficult to arrange matters on Saturday evening. There are other demands on the police on Saturday after dark." He regarded Baron von Schattenberg. "The morgue van departed about twenty minutes ago, with my recommendation that the examination be done tonight. I can't do much more than that."

"I am grateful that you have done so much," said the Baron, his voice dull. "This has been a very great shock to us all, and you have made our shock less dreadful."

"You may not feel that way when I come tomorrow to speak with you. I'll make it in the afternoon so you can go to church. Sorry to have to bother you on the Sabbath, but if you will let me have my interview then, I shan't have to ask you to come down to Scotland Yard to file your account and sign your statement in regard to this murder. Oh, yes, I have the records Mister Holmes advised you to make, but overnight something more may occur to you, and it will be of assistance to my inquiries if you will—"

"Tomorrow afternoon will be fine, Chief Inspector," Baron von Schattenberg informed him. "I will make myself and my aides available to you."

"That's very good of you," said Chief Inspector Pryce, startled at this easy cooperation.

"No, it is only expedient," said the Baron as if he carried the weight of the world upon his shoulders.

"Well, whatever it is, I thank you for accommodating this investigation. In return for your efforts I will do all I can to keep your privacy intact. More than that I cannot promise." He looked at the Baron with a steady kind of reassurance. "I am sorry your man was killed."

"As am I," said Baron von Schattenberg. "As soon as you have apprehended the criminal responsible for this, send me the information so that I may inform his family that justice will be done." He looked across the room to Mycroft Holmes. "I am told we may repose confidence in the English police."

"Yes, indeed you may," said Chief Inspector Pryce.

There was an awkward silence in the room, as if everyone was stifled by the audacious crime that had blighted the afternoon. Finally Mycroft Holmes spoke up. "I will take it as a personal favor if you, Chief Inspector, will keep me abreast of your investigation. I may have no official role to play in this, but I am involved."

Chief Inspector Pryce almost sighed. "Yes. Very well. For the sake of the Admiralty I will see you remain informed."

"You are very good, Chief Inspector." Holmes rose from his chair. "I trust you have no more need of us tonight. I will put myself at your disposal tomorrow; you may choose the hour. Guthrie and I will be glad to review our accounts with you." He bowed Prussian style to Baron von Schattenberg. "If I may assist you in any way, my dear Baron, you have only to send me word of it."

Baron von Schattenberg nodded. "And Lady MacMillian? We have resolved nothing concerning her visit."

"I will supply you the information we discussed and, if you still have questions, we will meet again. Otherwise, I am certain your good judgment will guide you in this matter." Mycroft Holmes looked in my direction. "Come, Guthrie. Tyers will be wondering what has become of us."

"No doubt of that," I said, preparing to leave. I had just picked up my portfolio when Sir Cameron roused from his stupor.

"And what of me?" he demanded. "I do not want to make myself a target for all the criminal scaff-and-raff of London." He rubbed his face as if pressing wakefulness upon it. "I must go to my hotel, but I require an escort."

"Guthrie and I are hardly suitable to your purposes," Mycroft Holmes pointed out. He looked to Chief Inspector Pryce. "Sir Cameron was shot at on his way here. It might be a sensible precaution to see him back to his hotel."

His brow flicked in a quick indication of annoyance; then his demeanor was once again that of polite inquiry. "This is news. Who shot at you?" Chief Inspector Pryce asked, sounding more puzzled than worried.

"How should I know?" Sir Cameron demanded, putting his large volume aside and getting to his feet. "I had nothing to do with it. I did not order it, nor did I bother to stop and ask questions. My coachman, who was somewhat injured in the attack, was ordered to report the incident as soon as he had received treatment for his wound."

"Your coachman was shot," said Chief Inspector Pryce, doing his best to glean the salient facts from Sir Cameron's remarks. "By an unknown gunman."

"Yes. In Mount Street. Just before we turned into Berkeley Square." Sir Cameron stared hard at Chief Inspector Pryce. "You can review his—my coachman's—description of the attack if you call at Scotland Yard, or whatever police station he went to in order to give his information."

"I'm sorry, Sir Cameron. I knew nothing of this," said Chief Inspector Pryce; he had an edge to his voice, as if he was not best pleased to learn of this now.

Sir Cameron bristled. "Well, whether you know about this or not, you must realize that I cannot safely set foot on the street without an escort."

"I can certainly see why you feel so," said Chief Inspector Pryce, and went on more briskly, "I will arrange for uniformed constables to escort you to your hotel. Once there, if you would be good enough to give them your version of what happened in Mount Street, I would appreciate it."

"Then you think there may be a connection?" Sir Cameron asked.

"I think it is possible there may be," answered Chief Inspector Pryce cautiously.

But Sir Cameron seized upon it. "There, you see, Holmes?" he demanded as he swung round to face my employer. "You were one to make light of it, but you were in error."

"For which I am most heartily sorry," said Mycroft Holmes, wanting to leave without having to endure more unpleasantness. "Guthrie, if you are ready?"

"At your service, sir." I stepped up briskly.

"Excellent," Holmes approved. He paused to regard Sir Cameron. "You have the police to protect and advise you. I know you are in good hands."

"No thanks to you," Sir Cameron reminded him. "I have been set upon by assassins twice today and little good you have done me."

"I apologize for any trouble I may have caused you," Mycroft Holmes said smoothly. "I regret I could not anticipate everything."

"I won't be fobbed off in this way," Sir Cameron said, warming up for a bear-jaw.

"Gentlemen, gentlemen," Chief Inspector Pryce intervened. "Everyone is upset, I know, and inclined to speak out of turn. By tomorrow you will be in better charity with one another. Until then, do you each give the other some leeway for a trying evening. Few of us show to advantage in such circumstances as these."

"Well-said," I told him. "We will endeavor to remember your admonition." I had to fight the urge to look to see if Sir Cameron were listening. "Well, then. Mister Holmes and I will expect to see you tomorrow after services."

Mycroft Holmes recovered himself. "Yes." He handed his card to the Chief Inspector. "My man Tyers will admit you whenever you call."

"Thank you, Mister Holmes," said the Chief Inspector, and looked to Sir Cameron. "If you will place yourself in our hands, I think we may keep you safe."

Mycroft Holmes did not bother to listen to Sir Cameron's response; he went to Baron von Schattenberg and said, "Please extend my condolences to Herr Kriede's family when you write to them, if you would. I shall count that as a kindness."

"Most certainly I will do so," said Baron von Schattenberg. "And I look forward to the material you shall provide me tomorrow."

The two men shook hands, and I managed to mutter an appropriate departing phrase, and then we made for the front door. I was mildly surprised to find Sid Hastings drawn up at the kerb, waiting for us, although Mycroft Holmes evinced no astonishment at all.

"Good evening, Hastings," said Holmes as he climbed into the cab. "I trust I see you well this evening."

"That you do, Mister Holmes; the better for your company, if I may say. The wait quite unnerved me, with the constables making us move and the people asking questions no one could answer. They said they removed a dead body a while ago." He pulled up the steps as I got aboard and started Lance on his way. "From what I saw, there was a rare dust-up in that house."

"Worse than that, I'm afraid," said Mycroft Holmes. "Yes, you are right: the police have taken away the body of one of the German aides."

"Blimey," said Hastings. "No wonder the constables were that set on having us all move along. I must have gone round Berkeley Square half a dozen times to keep them happy."

"They were being sensible," said Mycroft Holmes in a tone of approval. "Wouldn't you say so, Guthrie?"

"Yes. Quite pragmatic." I held my portfolio tightly against my chest, aware now that I had been edgy all evening.

"Shall I take Mister Guthrie to Curzon Street?" Sid Hastings asked as we entered Berkeley Square from Berkeley Mews.

"Do you want to go directly to bed, Guthrie, or would you rather have supper with me in order to discuss what transpired this evening? Which course would you prefer?" Mycroft Holmes inquired. He was rarely so accommodating and I was instantly suspicious.

"Is there some reason I should not dine with you?" I asked, eager to sort out his purpose for asking.

"None in the world, dear boy, unless you are too worn out to enjoy yourself." He was guileless as an infant.

"Then perhaps I should come with you. If we are to meet with Chief Inspector Pryce tomorrow, it would be best, I think, if we are willing to deal with him in a—" I said, trying to forestall any new ventures Holmes might propose.

"In a manner calculated to help him in regard to the murder that, at the same time, will not complicate his inquiries with considerations beyond his immediate concern," said Holmes in what I had come to think of as his diplomatic voice. "We would not want him to be led into areas of inquiry that would only make our work more difficult and would avail him nothing."

"No doubt you're right," I said, comprehending his intentions at last. "It would serve no useful purpose to have him caught up in the various problems you and Baron von Schattenberg are negotiating." I snapped my fingers. "That is why you are willing to give him what information you have on Lady MacMillian's uncles—you do not want these very delicate issues dragged through the tangle of a murder inquiry."

"Bravo, Guthrie," said Mycroft Holmes. "It will be difficult enough with Sir Cameron in the mix, but it is possible that with a little care we may keep our diplomatic considerations out of the police investigation." He paused, looked back, then said, "Two horsemen."

"Not again," moaned Sid Hastings in exasperation. "I thought I had lost them when I took Mister Sutton to the theatre."

"It would seem not," said Holmes. "Take a circuitous route back to Pall Mall, say, by way of Piccadilly, Coventry, and Haymarket. If they are truly following us, we will have some opportunity to verify it, and to observe them."

"If that is what you want, Mister Holmes, it is what I shall do," said Sid Hastings, going straight down Berkeley Street toward Piccadilly.

I wanted to swing around in my seat and stare out behind us, to see these two horsemen. I did not think I could recognize them—not if Mycroft Holmes had failed to do so—but I hoped I could discern something of their demeanor, and through it, their purpose in watching us.

"They are not fools, Guthrie," said Holmes with a philosophical shrug. "They are careful to fall back once they have been spotted."

In another, less acute man, I would have supposed that he had allowed his apprehension to take visual form, and that the two horsemen were nothing more than the product of a lively imagination. But my years with Mycroft Holmes—now numbering six—had taught me the greatest respect for his cognizance, and this was no exception. If he said the horsemen were there, then I could be certain they were, whether I saw them or not.

Piccadilly was crowded, a kind of melee going on among the carriages, cabs, coaches, vans, and all manner of other vehicles, with horsemen and crossing-sweepers added to the general confusion. I thought that any number of desperate persons might be in this mass and would go totally unnoticed. I was about to remark upon this to Mycroft Holmes when he ducked down in his seat and tugged on my arm so that I should do the same.

"What on earth?" I exclaimed as I did my utmost to comply with his urging.

"Look." He pointed to a new groove in the wood by the door.

"Whoever shot was standing on the sidewalk or in the street itself. You may see the bullet traveled up from below, so it came from the street. But where? And who?" He glared as another shot popped; had I not been alerted to it, I should have never have recognized the sound for what it was. "Small caliber pistol, I should think, and coming from the left." He raised his voice slightly. "Hastings. Are you all right?"

"There's a hole in my sleeve that wasn't there before, but it didn't touch the flesh, nor the bone." He seemed remarkably calm for a man in such an exposed position. "We're almost to the Circus," he went on. "There's too many people there for the shooter to risk it. Too many coppers, too," he added, chuckling. "He'd be a right fool to try anything there."

We went a little farther on without incident, and finally Mycroft Holmes sat upright once more; he released my arm. "There you go, my boy."

I straightened up and smoothed the front of my coat. "That was most unnerving," I said, trying to sound as jaunty as a man may under such circumstances.

"Wasn't it just?" Holmes agreed with a kind of sudden playfulness I found puzzling. "One would almost think that we are not intended to be hurt, only frightened."

"Why do you say that?" I asked, and added, "If it will please the shooter to be satisfied with fright, I will gladly tell him I am petrified."

"I say that the intention is to frighten because the shooter has been at pains not to hit the horse." Mycroft Holmes waited a moment, allowing me to take in what he had said. "If killing us was his intention, he could shoot the horse, or at least wound him enough to stop us, and then pick us off at his leisure." He shook his head. "But he chooses busy streets and he aims for the cab, not for us. We are being warned, Guthrie."

"I can see why you might think so," I admitted. "But what about the courier? What about the graze on your face."

"Ah, that was a different shooter altogether. That one used a rifle and was shooting to kill. Not the shooter now. And possibly not before in the cab." He settled back as we entered the traffic of Piccadilly Circus, then entered Coventry Street. "We have been shot at by someone on foot, not on horseback, or in a window. That in itself is most peculiar. But that there has been no attempt to interrupt our progress, I must look beyond my first assumptions for an explanation."

"Have you any idea as to what may be at work in this?" I was baffled by what Mycroft Holmes said, although I realized it made a kind of sense. "Who would do this?"

"That is more difficult to discern," Mycroft Holmes said. "I have been mulling the whole, and have not progressed much further than to realize there are two groups, not one, with whom we are dealing."

"Three, counting the Turks," I said somewhat lightly.

"Oh, the Turks are part of it—at least Halil Kerem is. I thought you realized that," said Holmes as we turned down Haymarket toward Pall Mall.

"How do you mean?" I asked, then answered for myself. "The tattoo."

"Yes. The tattoo. It was not old, as Mister Kerem said; it was quite new. The colors were still vivid and there was a slight swelling under the thing itself. It could not have been more than a month since the young man was given it." He gave me a quizzical look.

"But why would Mister Kerem lie?" I asked, watching the activity in the street with close attention.

"Exactly. He said the lad had a tattoo, and he gave a description of it to the police, although he could not possibly have seen it, not if his brother was kidnapped when Mister Kerem says he was, and Mister Kerem has been searching for him unsuccessfully as he claims." He pulled at his lower lip. "So I must ask myself: when did he see his brother—if the dead youth *is* his brother—for the last time, and why did he lie about it?"

"And what answers do you give yourself?" I asked, eager to be out of the cab and up the stairs into Holmes' flat.

"I have three explanations that suit the circumstances as I know them. I must suppose one of them is right, unless I have incorrect information to go on. I make allowances for the fact that I most certainly have insufficient evidence to suit my purposes. Therefore, little as I may like it, we must improvise." He did his best to look out the back in as unobvious a way as possible. "I can't tell if they are still behind us. The street is too busy; if it were daylight, I might manage rather better, but—" He settled into his seat again. "I think it would be wise for Sutton to provide Hastings with a number of hats and caps, so that as he travels, he may change his appearance."

I could not help but smile. "How would you disguise the cab?"

"Fortunately all cabs look very much alike, and their anonymity is a disguise in itself. If I can provide Hastings with a dark coachman's coat, a change of cap should be as useful a device as more elaborate measures." He regarded me seriously. "How often do you look at the face of a jarvy?"

"Perhaps half the time," I confessed.

"And that is considerably more than most," said Mycroft Holmes. "You understand that for most Londoners one jarvy is the same as another." He shook his head in ironic amusement. "Most passengers of cabs are more likely to remember the horse than the jarvy."

I had to admit this was true. "Yes," I said. "I think I should know Lance anywhere."

"Very likely," said Holmes. "So a cap or a hat will serve our purposes very well, I think. What do you say, Hastings? Are you willing to change your headgear from time to time?"

"If it's what you want, Mister Holmes, I shall do it." He sounded wholly unperturbed by this request, and he added a little later, "Nothing outlandish-like, though."

"Certainly not," said Mycroft Holmes. "That would defeat our whole purpose."

"Then tell me what you want me to wear and I will." He drew in as a house-removal van lumbered by, two Suffolk Punches leaning into their collars. "Come to think of it, I don't pay much attention to drivers myself, not unless I know them, like One-Eyed Taffy Snow."

"My very point, thank you, Hastings." Holmes leaned back a little, securing the lap-rug with the weight of his hands. "This has been a most fatiguing day, Guthrie. I am heartily glad it is almost over."

"Very good, sir," I said, holding on to my portfolio. "Do you expect me to come round tomorrow?"

"If you would, Guthrie. It's a frightful bore, but we owe Chief Inspector Pryce that much." He noticed a constable walking along the street. "There's another invisible sort, as Hastings has already demonstrated."

"When would you like me to arrive?" I asked, thinking I would take the time to have a look at Sir Cameron's house before wending my way to Pall Mall.

"Oh, ten o'clock would be about right, I should think. If you plan to attend services, there should be early ones that will answer your needs." Holmes looked up at the overcast sky. "There will be rain before midnight."

"You do not often attend holy services, do you, sir," I observed, knowing the answer already.

"When it is necessary I do. Otherwise, I prefer to keep my dealings with the Almighty on the clandestine side." He sat forward as we approached Pall Mall. "Traffic is still fairly thick," he remarked.

"It's Saturday night, isn't it?" said Sid Hastings. "Lots going on in London on a Saturday night."

"No doubt," said Mycroft Holmes as we neared his building. "Thank you, Hastings. I will have hats for you come Monday. Give my regards to your family, if you would be so kind."

"Right you are, sir," said Hastings, drawing Lance to a halt. "If you have need of me tomorrow, send me word. Otherwise I shall plan to be at your door first thing Monday morning."

"I appreciate your dedication," said Mycroft Holmes. "And I shall bear it in mind."

We climbed out of the cab; I resisted the urge to bolt for the stairs while Mycroft Holmes made his way toward them, his walk unhurried, his demeanor calm and at ease. To see him no one would suppose he had so much besetting him as he had now. I went up behind him, reminding myself that next year he would be fifty, and marveling at the activity he was able to sustain at such an age. A great many men of his age were used up, exhausted, whereas Mycroft Holmes seemed to have gained a second wind and was showing more endurance and stamina than men half his age.

"Good evening, sir," said Tyers as he opened the door. "I hope I see you well?"

"You do, Tyers. In spite of the unsettling events at Herr Amsel's house—I assume someone informed you of it?" Holmes shed his cloak and handed it to Tyers. "I am longing for a brandy and a proper meal. Those German sausage-and-cheese sandwiches aren't fit for sick cats."

"Just so," Tyers agreed. "I have a pork loin with baked apples, green beans, and potatoes *au gratin*. That should revive you."

"And a bottle of claret, I should hope," said Mycroft Holmes. "I knew I could rely on you, Tyers."

"For pudding, I have a meringue with fruit compote. For now, there is brandy in the study." Tyers paused. "Will you and Guthrie be working late?"

"I hardly know yet," said Holmes, with an apologetic sigh. "I hope it won't come to that."

"And I," I said, feeling somewhat guilty for saying it.

"Yes. I want you alert and clear-headed for tomorrow," said Holmes as he opened the door to the study in which was laid out a setting for our supper. "Have a seat Guthrie, while I pour the brandy."

"Thank you, sir," I said, taking my accustomed place and putting down my portfolio. "It *has* been unusually active, hasn't it?"

"Yes, indeed. I think our adventures today almost rival those that Sutton essays in *MacBeth.* There are bodies in plenty, men vying for power, and one ambitious woman in the middle." He brought two snifters back to the table, offered me one and sat down in his accustomed chair. "Now, about Mister Kerem. I believe I mentioned various ways to account for the inconsistencies in his story."

"That you did," I said, prepared to listen to the whole of it.

"Well then; if the tattoo is as new as it appears—and the examination will help in determining that—we must assume either that Mister Kerem was told about the tattoo in his search for the lad, and said he had seen it to lend veracity to his description. If that is the case, those who provided the description intended to use Mister Kerem to draw English officials into the search, and to that end gave Kerem enough to spur him on, but not so much that he could unravel the clues himself. That is one possibility. The second possibility is that information was provided to Mister Kerem after his arrival here, as a lure and a goad to his search. He may have been given a sketch or even a photograph of the tattoo. Again, it would make it far more likely that Mister Kerem would take whatever measures he could to bring the police and others into his search." He drank a sip of the brandy. "That is the second possibility."

"And the third?" I asked when Mycroft Holmes continued to stare into his snifter.

When he answered, his voice was remote. "The third possibility is that Mister Kerem arranged for the tattoo to be put on, which also means he arranged for the lad to die."

FROM THE PERSONAL JOURNAL OF PHILIP TYERS

MH and G are back from Berkeley Mews, both of them looking worn to the bone. I will presently give them the supper I have cooking for them, and will reserve a portion of the meal for Sutton, who will arrive here some time after midnight . . .

Inspector Featherstone sent his card around, saying he would like to call on MH tomorrow in the afternoon. I have sent him word that I will confirm or recommend another time for the appointment before noon. I trust Inspector Featherstone will be willing to visit at this flat rather than require MH to come to Scotland Yard. It is not wise for MH to spend too much time in such places, for who knows what criminals may see him, or policemen who are not as upright as they are sworn to be.

It appears that Lady MacMillian is preparing to leave Holland on the Monday crossing. Unless we can secure the assistance of Baron von Schattenberg, it will not be possible to turn back her uncles when she is admitted to the country. There is as yet no real proof of their mission here, but perhaps there will be enough doubt to make it possible to refuse them entry to England without causing the Germans too much official distress. With the tragedy earlier this evening, such support may prove difficult to secure . . .

MH has requested that tomorrow I send an inquiry to the Admiralty in regard to the courier who was shot in his attempt to deliver his dispatch. I will prepare the note before retiring tonight, and see that it is given to a Navy messenger at noon . . .

Chapter Eleven

CHURCH BELLS AWAKENED me. I lay in the state half-way between sleep and rising, aware of my sheets and blankets but still haunted by the last vestige of my dream. The steady whisper of rain augmented the call of the bells and gave me a sense of being suspended in space, which I relished for as long as I could persuade myself to indulge my torpor. Finally I rid myself of the last of my woolgathering and sat up in bed. It was not quite seven in the morning and the sky was just beginning to lighten, lending the clouds a cast of tarnished silver. As

I got out of bed, I sighed at the luxury of six hours' actual slumber—a rare event for anyone in the employ of Mycroft Holmes.

I washed and dressed, making as little noise as possible, for I was aware that Missus Coopersmith had not yet wakened; she would be up soon enough, readying herself for her weekly spiritual exercises. I held off donning my boots until I was almost ready to depart. Then I gathered up my over-coat, my portfolio, and my umbrella and went down the stairs as quietly as I was able. Once on the street, I opened my umbrella and set out at a steady clip for Pall Mall.

Turning from Half Moon Street into Piccadilly, I became aware of someone behind me in the rain, someone on a dark horse that kept a steady pace with me. I told myself my rush of fear was nonsense, that I had no reason to assume I was being followed. But I fought the urge to run. I could rush across the street to the Green Park and force the rider to come after me. I could confront him there, challenge him, demand to know why I was being followed. No sooner had this notion formed in my mind but I put it into action, racing across the thoroughfare, and wishing, for once, that there was much more traffic than was on the street this rainy Sunday morning.

The horse and rider came after me, and I began to wonder if the rider carried a weapon, in which case my impulse was far from useful as anything I might do. I dashed along the neat path toward a clump of bushes, with a vague notion of slipping into the protection of its many branches, when the horse broke into a canter and in a matter of seconds cut me off and brought me to a halt. I wished now that I had brought my pistol, or had a knife ready to hand. I crouched, prepared to do battle.

"Oh, Guthrie, don't be a goose," said a familiar voice, and a moment later, Miss Penelope Gatspy dropped out of the saddle, one hand on the rein, the other holding the brim of her elegant little hat; I am afraid I must have goggled at her, for she went off in a peal of delicious laughter. "I can't be so much a disappointment as that," she said.

"No. Not a disappointment. Not at all. Nothing of the sort." I made myself stop. "I thought you might be . . . someone else?"

"Jacobbus Braaten, for instance?" she suggested. "No, don't waste your breath protesting. My allies in the Golden Lodge have been following you and Mister Holmes as soon as we learned that Braaten and Vickers had sailed for Ireland. They will undoubtedly make for London as quickly as possible, and they will seek you out." Her cerulean eyes narrowed as she contemplated the possibilities. "You must be very careful. We can't guard you all the time."

I did my best to smile. "You have been following us?"

"Some of the time. There are six of us assigned to you, and two are on duty at all times. My comrade is in Pall Mall just now, waiting for you—and me." She began to walk along the path, leading her horse; I kept to her other side. "We began night before last. I began my watch yesterday morning. And I must say, you have been very busy."

I heard the note of exasperation in her voice and I could not help but bristle. "There has been much to do," I said, attempting to hold my umbrella in such a way that it shielded us both.

"Poor Sutton. He has been scampering from role to role," she added.

"That he has," I said. "It is his work."

"Petulance does not become you, Guthrie," she said, and wagged a finger at me just as a shot cracked.

Her horse screamed—it was such a sound as I hope never to hear again—and half-reared, then tottered and fell, blood pumping from a wound high in his neck. He kicked spasmodically, and struggled to right himself, only to fall back, his breath going out of him for the last time.

Miss Gatspy stood as if transfixed for perhaps two seconds, then came to her senses. "Come," she said, taking my arm and pulling me toward the bushes I had been running for. "Hurry!"

I felt rather than heard the bullet that slapped through my umbrella to whisk past my ear. This leant new impetus to my run. We tumbled into the half-barren branches of the bushes, paying no heed to the pokes and scratches the limbs and twigs bestowed on us. "Can you see?"

"Not in this downpour," said Miss Gatspy, her voice tight.

"Do you have any idea who is shooting?" I knew it wasn't prudent to trust her, but I could think of no reason to disbelieve her information.

"Agents of the Brotherhood, I would suppose. Jacobbus Braaten has said he wants you dead. You, Guthrie, not just Mycroft Holmes. He had put a price on your head among his men. He holds you responsible for his limp, and he wants vengeance." She pulled him deeper into the thicket. "If I were the killer, I would try to trap us in here. I don't propose to let that happen."

"I will follow your lead, Miss Gatspy," I said, and closed my ruined umbrella as tightly as the torn fabric would allow. "This is useless."

She took it from me. "Perhaps not," she said. "It may be put to some use."

"If you can find a means to turn it to our advantage, please go ahead. It is my honor to present it to you." I was appalled at how stuffy I sounded as I spoke to her. What had come over me? Was it the shock of seeing her horse die?

"Thank you, Guthrie," she said with a quick, tantalizing smile. "If we can reach those trees, I think we can—" She stopped as another bullet plowed through the thicket at about three feet above the ground. "That isn't sporting," she complained.

"You don't think this is a *game*, do you?" I demanded, very much troubled by her remark.

"No. And I think men who aim for their opponents' vitals want to inflict suffering as much as they want to kill them." She crouched down. "Come. That last shot wasn't aimed, it was intended to make us give away our position. We should be somewhere else."

"Won't that be doing just as they want?" I asked, doing my best to follow her through the brush, feeling the twigs gouge and snap at me as we went. If I was so assaulted, what must be happening to Miss Gatspy? Surely her porcelain skin would be scratched and bruised by the rough treatment our escape was providing? I tried to think of some way to express my concerns without making it seem I thought her incompetent.

"Hold still, Guthrie," she said suddenly, halting in the middle of the bushes. "I think he's worked around to our left flank. If we don't move, perhaps I can hear him. He will certainly not be able to hear us." She stayed in a crouched posture as she leaned toward the screen of branches and leaves of bright red and yellow. "Yes. There is someone out on the pathway. If he continues along, perhaps we can double back," she whispered.

"Won't he be expecting that?" I could not hide my apprehension. "You must be aware—"

"Quiet!" she ordered, barely audible.

I did as she commanded, remaining still and silent as a thin finger of water began to make its way down from the back center of my collar to my back, and then to slide down beside my spine; a second trace of cold wetness was forming under my ear and spreading along my shoulder. It was all I could do not to sneeze. I swallowed hard twice, but this did not diminish my impulse, which I feared must express itself in dramatic ways, exposing us to the deadly purpose of our hunter.

"You will have to make a break for it, Guthrie. Go down the south-east path. Do not get some foolish notion to come back to rescue me or you will ruin all. I will come to Pall Mall directly I have dealt with this brute." She had put her lips near to my cheek to tell me this, and I could smell the violet perfume she sometimes wore. "If you're ready, nod."

I nodded, as she told me, and then, as she struck me on the arm, I broke out of our hiding place and made for the path she had mentioned; I still held my portfolio, which I now raised over my head to afford myself a modicum of protection from the rain as I ran. I thought I heard a shot fired, but I could not be sure of it, for I suffered no injury, nor did I notice any sign of a bullet. At the end of the path, I entered a wider walkway that led out of the park to the path leading around to Saint James Park and then up The Mall. I was cold and wet, my over-coat was sodden, and my shoes were soaked through. Still, I had a strange elation that I decided must come from my fortunate deliverance. That thought had no sooner entered my mind than I was struck with the risk Miss Gatspy must be taking, and I hesitated, wanting to return to lend her whatever assistance I could. But she had insisted I go, and, more to the point, that I not return; I knew her abilities well enough to realize that if I did not follow her instructions, I might end in causing her more hazard than she had worked out for herself; that alone kept me walking toward Waterloo Place, though every step was painful to me.

"You look like a drowned rat, Guthrie. What happened?" Mycroft Holmes said as he opened the door to my knock.

"I feel like a drowned rat," I told him as I came into the flat. "And if it is all the same to you, I would like to request a bath and a change of clothing before we set about our preparations for today."

"All right," said Holmes, his mein quizzical as he closed the door. "Tyers," he called out. "Will you be good enough to ready a bath for Guthrie? And take out his traveling suit, if you would. What he is wearing will have to be dried." He motioned me in the direction of his dressing room where his bathtub stood. "Half an hour in hot water and a suit of dry clothes and you'll do."

I thanked him and added, "We will have another visitor this morning."

"Your Miss Gatspy?" Mycroft Holmes ventured.

I stared at him in open astonishment. "How did you know?"

"My dear Guthrie, only she causes you to behave in a manner compounded of hang-doggedness and smug self-satisfaction. How did you happen to encounter her?" He opened the door that led to the door into the kitchen. "Let us know when the water is ready, if you will, Tyers."

"That I will," said Tyers and worked to fill the fourth eight-gallon stockpot that was also used to heat bath-water.

"She was . . . was following me," I said, thinking as I did how absurd it sounded. "She was."

"If you say so, I believe you, Guthrie," Holmes said, amusement lending a glint to his deep-set dark-grey eyes.

Thus encouraged—however sardonically—I plunged ahead. "According to Miss Gatspy, the horsemen who have been behind us are from the Golden Lodge. They have been sent to guard us and have done so ever since they learned of Jacobbus Braaten's and Justin Oliver Beauchamp Vickers' plans to sail to Ireland in order to reach England." I folded my arms, disliking the tightness this caused in my wet garments; I gave him a quick summary of the results of our morning meeting, and all that had transpired in the Green Park. "She said Braaten has put a price on my head for laming him."

"That was a worthy act, Guthrie. In his way, Braaten is acknowledging it. So is Miss Gatspy, for that matter." He stepped back and reached into the long wardrobe that stood behind him. "Let me loan you a dressing gown," he offered. "You can get out of those damp clothes while Tyers fills the tub. I don't want you catching a cold in the middle of this tangle."

"Nor do I," I said with feeling.

"Well and good, then," said Holmes, and handed me the green velvet dressing gown he often wore. "It will match one of your eyes, at least." With that sly reference to the disparity in my eye color, he went out of the dressing room and along the corridor to the front of the flat; I heard him humming an air from *Le Nozze di Figaro*—the one that begins, *La vendetta, oh, la vendetta.*

It did not take me long to get undressed, and although I felt a trifle disconcerted in such a garment, I tried to take its generous proportions in good part; I resembled a half-raised plush tent, I decided as I wandered out into the hall and down again to the study.

"You know, Guthrie, there is something you ought to consider," Mycroft Holmes said, suppressing a smirk at the sight of me. "You *do* look as if you had borrowed your big brother's clothing."

I smiled, a bit stiffly; I am a good eight inches shorter than the very tall Mister Holmes, and slighter as well. "I suppose it's to be expected, sir," I said, and before he could comment further, I added, "What is it I ought to consider?"

"That your encounter with Miss Gatspy was a careful demonstration of theatrics, intended to make you inclined to trust her once again." He said it blandly enough, but he was watching me to see my smallest response.

"Yes," I said. "I thought about that, but I decided it wasn't likely."

"Ah, Guthrie," Mycroft Holmes sighed, half-seriously, "you must not let your infatuation with that woman cloud your—"

"You will have your jest, sir," I said, surprised at my own audacity. "I came to that conclusion because the shooter killed her horse. As a valuable animal alone, it was hardly the act of someone attempting to show a false heroism."

Mycroft Holmes considered what I said. "There is merit in your argument."

"I should hope so," I said, pleased to have gained that praise.

"The Golden Lodge might ask its members to be willing to sacrifice their lives, but destroying a fine Thoroughbred, that is another thing altogether."

"You are persuasive," said Holmes. "It does sound unlike them."

"I cannot think Miss Gatspy would be party to such under-handed dealings," I said. "She tried to protect me from danger."

"Now *that* is more persuasive still," said Mycroft Holmes merrily. "Why waste a horse when all she need do is smile and you will—?"

I stood very straight, the deep folds of the velvet dressing gown hanging around me. "I trust I am not so callow as to be undone by a pair of fine blue eyes," I said.

"I trust so, too, Guthrie," said Holmes. Then he deliberately changed the subject. "I anticipate another visit from Mister Kerem before nightfall."

"Why should he come here?" I wondered. "He now may go to Inspector Featherstone. Why should he pull you into his coils?"

"Why indeed?" Mycroft Holmes said. "That is what I am at-tempting to puzzle out. Why should he come to me now that he has the attention of the police? Yet I have a note delivered shortly after seven announcing his intention to call around at three. I cannot dis-cern his reason from what he has written, so—" He shook his head, and then, with a change in his stance, indicated a stack of notes. "When you are bathed and dressed, I have a few items for you to copy. I realize it is not customary for you to perform such a task on Sunday, but—"

"I will have to do them tomorrow morning if not today," I said, shrugging. "I am at your service today, in any capacity you should want."

"Excellent. And when Chief Inspector Pryce arrives, I intend to learn at least as much from him as he is determined to learn from me. I rely upon you to listen closely to all he says. Take no notes, for that will put him on his guard. I wish to discover what his assumptions may be, and how he is inclined to interpret the death of Herr Kriede." He was all business now—no more tweaking or risibility. I heard him out with due attention, knowing how much reflection must have gone into his memoranda and his plans for today.

"Your own thoughts: have they changed?" I thought back to the previous evening with a mixture of dismay and agitation of spirit that reminded me that I had not achieved any sense of resolution in regard to the poisoning.

"Yes and no. Go bathe and we will discuss it when you return," said Holmes with a wave of his long-fingered hand. "I can hear Tyers pouring in the first pot of water."

Now that I listened, I could hear it, too. "I'll be back in twenty minutes," I said, with every intention of taking no longer than that. But it was almost thirty-five minutes later that I returned to the study, in dry, warm clothing, and the ache in my scrapes and bruises beginning to fade. As I entered the room, I halted as I caught sight of Miss Gatspy seated in the Turkish chair that Mycroft Holmes had pulled out from its corner for her use. I did my best to speak calmly. "Good morning again, Miss Gatspy. I want to thank you for your timely intervention this morning."

"You're welcome, Guthrie," she said, extending her hand to me.

I took it, and barely touched it with my lips. "I hope you did not encounter any more difficulties in extricating yourself from the—"

"Oh, cut line, Guthrie, cut line," said Mycroft Holmes in mock exasperation. "You frame your periods as if you were in one of those dreadful plays of Sardou."

"I do not mean to offend," I said, feeling a bit slighted myself.

"You do not. Only tell her you are grateful and leave it at that," said Mycroft Holmes, to be seconded by a nod from Miss Gatspy herself.

"I am grateful, Miss Gatspy," I said, attempting to bring this whole exchange to a conclusion.

"My pleasure, Guthrie," she told me, then looked back at Holmes. "So, as I told you, I am going against the leaders of the Golden Lodge in revealing our presence to you, but I think it is to our mutual interests to work together until this latest ploy of the Brotherhood is stopped."

"Will that create any problems for you? Going against them?" Holmes was concerned.

"It may, but nothing to compare with the problems we would all have if Braaten and Vickers succeed in reaching London," she responded. "You, of all men, should see that."

"Of course. I concur." He indicated my usual chair. "Sit down, Guthrie, and get your portfolio and pencil." He smiled in that ghastly way he had when he was contemplating evil.

I hastened to do as he ordered, and did my best not to be distracted by Miss Gatspy's nearness. Mycroft Holmes did not often receive females, and so it was a disconcerting event when we were graced with a woman's presence. That this particular woman was an accomplished assassin only added to the air of uneasiness we experienced. As I opened my notebook, I tested my pencil on my thumb and very nearly broke off the lead. "Sorry," I muttered as I prepared to take notes.

Mycroft Holmes studied the far wall in an abstracted manner. "What do you think the chances are that they will reach London? Realistically?"

"Realistically? I would think they are excellent," said Miss Gatspy energetically. "You must know that these men have been at least a jump ahead of your intelligence since the first move was made by Lady MacMillian." She folded her hands demurely. "The Golden Lodge has watchers in Liverpool, in Port Talbot, and has a ship patrolling along the Cornish coast. There are any number of places they might come ashore with no more halt than a sailor would have at the local pub. We must suppose that is what they are doing, for they must assume that you have become aware of their intentions." She paused and looked over her shoulder at me. "Should I repeat, Guthrie?"

I felt color mount in my face. That she should imagine I could not keep pace with her! "I will let you know if I fall behind."

"Yes, it would be wise to guard the small harbors, but I will order the Customs officers to be alert as well. Braaten and Vickers may assume we will be kept busy by watching the shore and will therefore come to land at a major city." Mycroft Holmes began to twiddle his watch-fob. "You cannot be too careful with villains like these."

"No," she agreed. "It would not be prudent to hope that they will do what we wish them to do."

"And what is that?" I asked, goaded into speaking. "What does the Golden Lodge have to gain from thwarting the Brotherhood?"

"You mean beyond keeping Britain and the Continent from

rushing into war? I cannot think what other goals we share." Her large blue eyes shone with mischief and she gave a lingering sigh. "You have an obligation to protect British interests over all others, as I have an obligation to serve the Golden Lodge in any and all circumstances. Just now, our purposes march together, and it is to our mutual advantage to work together. One day it may not be so, but at present, we are allies by contexts; let us make the most of the opportunity we have been presented."

Steady applause came from the door. "Brava, Miss Gatspy," said Edmund Sutton as he strolled into the study, dressed simply but elegantly in dark wool trousers and a tweed hacking jacket over a roll-neck pull-over. "Quite a stirring delivery. I wish Beatrice Motherwell would do half as much with Lady MacBeth. It would be the crowning achievement of our production." He sighed. "Tyers said to tell you he will have tea ready shortly, and a light nuncheon-cum-breakfast."

"Good," said Mycroft Holmes. "I am getting hungry." He signaled to me. "Guthrie, as soon as we have eaten, if you will tend to the memoranda, I would very much appreciate it."

I felt as if I were a child being banished from adult conversation, and I knew that was an unworthy sentiment. "Of course, sir," I said.

"Until Chief Inspector Pryce arrives," added Holmes, and I had the oddest sensation that he had been aware of my thoughts.

"Yes. Until then," I said, and did my best not to look at Miss Gatspy.

FROM THE PERSONAL JOURNAL OF PHILIP TYERS

It is as Miss Gatspy said: there are two men on horseback watching this flat. They circle the block, always opposite one another so that they are not completely obvious. They do not keep a regular schedule of circuits, for that might alert those they seek to stop. It is reassuring that the Golden Lodge is willing to aid in stopping Vickers and Braaten from arriving in London. I concur with MH, G, Miss Gatspy, and the Golden Lodge that no good may be had from allowing those fell men into the country. They must be stopped now, before they can make a foothold for their despicable cohorts. It is a most clever device, trying to bring a few of their most successful agents to this country as escorts for Lady MacMillian. Who would want to offend Sir Cameron by refusing his Lady the right to company of her choice. Is she just a pawn, I wonder, or is she part of the plot they have concocted?

The nuncheon I have put together is not as substantial as a proper luncheon would be, but it is a bit too early for such fare. I will set out a dish of hard-boiled eggs for those who want them, but I will serve more toast, scones, and hot-cross buns for usual fare. That and tea should do them until one in the afternoon, when I will be sure there is a proper Sunday dinner laid out for them, with a standing rack of lamb in the Greek style with fruit jelly and a mustard sauce for a garnish. Then potatoes and onions roasted, and a ginger-cream sauce for the kale. That, with new bread and a ripe Stilton and port should satisfy them. And if all goes well, they will be able to dine without the interruption of a crisis. Or so I hope.

However, I may have to shuffle my plans a bit. It may become a busy afternoon, in spite of MH's assurances to the contrary. For a Sunday, the world is most restless. If Sir Cameron insists that he be given the opportunity to join in our discussion with CI Pryce, which a note from his hotel suggests is the case, then it becomes a more confusing day than what we have anticipated. Sutton will have to be absent during Sir Cameron's visit, of course. MH already expects Mister Kerem to arrive with his latest complaint; he has informed MH of his intention to do so.

There is also an invitation from Sir Marmion delivered not twenty minutes ago that I must present to MH when I take in tea and nuncheon. Barring any sudden decisions MH might make in that regard, I have no reason to assume that this summons will tend to interfere with what we have already set up for the afternoon. I shall hope that Miss Gatspy's colleagues will provide all necessary protection so that we need not expect our day to be enlivened by more shots fired. To that end, I will remember this in my prayers at Saint James' Church in Jermyn Street. I shall have time to attend services myself once I am done with those duties.

Chapter Twelve

ALL BUT ONE scone was gone from the tray, and two pieces of toast stood untouched; other than that, breakfast had disappeared in an enthusiastic frenzy of a meal. Miss Gatspy had refilled her teacup three times, and so had I; Sutton and Mycroft Holmes had done so twice, and were having the lasts of the meal, taking their time about it in order to encourage Miss Gatspy to talk as much as she wished to do about the intelligence that had fallen into the hands of the Golden Lodge.

"They are most dangerous men, those who are part of the Brotherhood. I thought I understood the extent of their intended destruction, but I did not. I could not credit their malice, not really." She smiled, her limpid eyes now filled with the burning blue fury at the heart of a flame.

"You have found something out?" Mycroft Holmes inquired as he helped himself to a half a bun.

"Indeed I have, and it is most troublesome," she replied promptly.

"My dear Miss Gatspy, when you say troublesome you strike terror into my heart," said Mycroft Holmes lightly enough but with genuine purpose in his voice. "Are we speaking of deadly?"

"We are," she said; I could not help but regard her with concern, for it would be like her to put herself at risk in such a situation.

Holmes studied her for a moment, then spoke. "Perhaps you would elaborate."

She nodded. "Certainly. You are aware of the precarious state of Turkey, I must assume? A man in your position must be informed of developments there."

"The remnants of the Ottoman Empire are rotten to the core. Nothing can be done to change that. Corruption is a way of life there. The steady decline in their fortunes has provided opportunities for every minor despot and each ambitious Prince to exploit the regions in which they are situated, all without any fear of repercussions from their various heads of state. The problems confronting the governments in that part of the world are many and significant and are not, generally, being addressed, for those with power are more inclined to want to use it to enhance themselves and their families; they neglect the very people they claim to guard."

"That is part of it," said Miss Gatspy, and paid no heed to the shocked expressions that greeted her remark. "The worst of it is subtle, not easily recognized by anyone, even those who might have cause to know a great deal about it, as you do. We of the Golden Lodge made a long study of the situation, and lost seven of our men before we happened upon the heart of the problem, if heart is a word that can be used for anything so atrocious as the activities of the Brotherhood in regions formerly controlled by the Turks."

"That sounds as if you are entirely satisfied with what you have discovered. You are certain you have hit upon the truth." Holmes scrutinized her face as she answered.

"I am. And you will be when I bring you a copy of the file we have prepared." She smirked at his shock. "Oh, yes. I am willing to show you the extent of our information, and to discuss it with you, if you should want elaboration on any point."

"But, naturally, you want something in exchange," said Mycroft Holmes when she fell silent.

"Yes. It seems only fair, does it not?" She drank down her tea. "You may not share our interpretations of the facts, but you will surely recognize the information we have to offer as being most valuable. And I know that you have access to intelligence reports that could serve the Golden Lodge well, if you would accept a trade." She put the cup-and-saucer back on the tray. "I must know if you are willing to respect what I impart to you."

"Of course, Miss Gatspy," said Mycroft Holmes at his most civil. "Or you would not still be here, no matter what good you have done Guthrie."

I had to resist the impulse to protest such uncharitable observations; undoubtedly Mycroft Holmes would respond with an inappropriate comment on his assumption that I had an attachment to Miss Gatspy—and while I was fully conscious of the debt I owed her, I did not consider this as being indicative of an attachment. Fine sort of man I should be, I thought, to have so little mastery of my emotions.

"Thank you for your candor. I hope you will understand why I have considered it necessary to exceed the mandate of the leaders of the Golden Lodge in these events." She smiled slightly. "I would not be a truly dedicated agent if I did not, from time to time, question the decisions of those who, unlike yourself, confine their activities to research and analysis of gathered information."

"Miss Gatspy, you will destroy my carefully cultivated reputation if you should say such things outside of this room." Holmes' voice was still unfailingly polite, but his intent was steely.

"Which I have no wish to do, as your capacity to spring into action without being seen to do so is one of the things I most admire in you." Her smile this time made it perfectly clear that she was almost flirting with him.

"Miss Gatspy, you quite unman me with such praise," said Mycroft Holmes as Sutton silently rolled his eyes.

"Mister Holmes, I am delighted to hear it." She settled back in her chair. "I cannot remain much longer, but I would like to establish a time tomorrow when I might find you in. I do want to place this information in your hands as soon as possible."

"Would ten in the morning be a suitable hour?" Mycroft Holmes asked. "If you are willing to leave the file with me, I need not detain you any longer than it takes you to drink a cup or two of tea."

"That will be satisfactory. I will send word to you by nine if I must change the time of our meeting," she told him. "With Vickers and Braatan coming, you cannot let them become part of Lady MacMillian's suite, for then any attempts to dislodge them could cause just the sort of incident we wish most to avoid. I say we because I think you want to keep this from public attention as much as we of the Golden Lodge do. For once, we are in accord with the Brotherhood."

"On that point, at least," said Mycroft Holmes as Miss Gatspy rose. "I do appreciate the care you have taken of Guthrie. I trust he will not need such . . . intervention in future."

"Don't blame him, Mister Holmes. He did nothing foolish. In fact, he was most resourceful, and kept his head commendably. If I were you, I should be proud of him." She turned to give me a look of encouragement.

I did not know what to say. "Most kind," I stammered out, and tried to think of a more cogent remark. Nothing came to mind as I watched Miss Gatspy take her leave, saying she would see us tomorrow before Tyers came to escort her to the door.

"A most perplexing addition to our case," said Mycroft Holmes when the door was closed. "I wish I could persuade myself that your Miss Gatspy is as altruistic as she claims to be."

"Do you doubt her motives?" I asked, a bit hotly, for I could not think ill of someone who had preserved me from danger.

"Perhaps not hers as much as the Golden Lodge's." He looked down into his empty teacup as if to divine the information he sought there. "I wish I could credit that shadowy organization with sterling intentions, but I would be a fool if I did."

Sutton spoke up. "Do you think this is another attempt to throw you off the scent?"

Holmes considered his answer carefully. "Not as such, no. I think it may be another layer to the puzzle." He scowled. "If only Lady MacMillian had not chosen this time to reconcile with Sir Cameron."

"But that is the crux of the matter, isn't it?" I said. "She is making it possible for the Brotherhood to reestablish itself in Britain, and unless we wish to offend both the Germans and the Scots, we cannot do anything without presenting convincing evidence." I shook my head, thinking of how much we would have to have in the way of proof before an official action could be taken.

"Yes. That is what is so disheartening." He rose and began to pace, a sure sign of dismay. "I have sufficient authority to order that Lady MacMillian's escort be refused entry to England. But if I do that, I embarrass the government and the Admiralty if I cannot also demonstrate why I have done so."

Sutton, who had been watching Holmes with some apprehension, said, "Do you suppose that is part of the ploy—to make you over-play your hand and discredit yourself so that the Brotherhood can resume operations here without hindrance?"

Holmes stopped where he stood and swung around to look at Sutton. "Of *course!* Of *course!*" he cried. "You have hit it. Why did I not see it?"

"You have been trying to deal with three confusing and diplomatically delicate crises," said Sutton. "I have been watching the drama, and it has made it easier for me to assess the . . . structure, you might say."

"However you designate it, I must tell you, you put me to shame," said Holmes, his countenance lightening for the first time in two days. "I had a sense that there was some underlying common purpose to all that has been happening since the question of Lady MacMillian's visit began; I was searching for a common thread in the nature of the events. Now I see that it was aimed at compromising me. Sutton, you are a prince among men."

Sutton blushed, and smiled at this praise. "This is the sort of thing actors look for," he said diffidently.

"And good thing that you did." Mycroft Holmes now rounded on me. "Guthrie. I need all my notes of the last three days. I want to review them from this perspective. If Sutton's thesis holds up, you and I must work quickly to keep the Brotherhood from having its way." He was filled with renewed energy, making his way about the room with vigor.

"I will do it," I said, and prepared to review the files in his antique French secretary. "What about Chief Inspector Pryce? He should be calling soon."

Holmes stopped still. "Ah, yes. Chief Inspector Pryce. I should have sent a note round to Strange, to get an assessment of him. With his history, he might be—shall we say maleable—in terms of loyalty."

"Because his father's family opposed his mother?" I asked, recalling the great uproar in the press at the time of Pryce's father's death, when his sisters had attempted to deny Pryce's mother any portion of her inheritance. I had been in school then; I and my schoolmates had followed the battle in the papers. How we had battened on any bit of scandal and relished the acrimony. The memory was now tainted by chagrin. "Would that be enough to make him support such villains as the Brotherhood?"

"Men have done so for less," said Mycroft Holmes.

I could not deny that. "Shall I prepare a message to be sent round now?" I asked.

"Wait until after our interview. Then I may have a better sense of the man." He glanced at Sutton. "Are you planning to go out this afternoon?"

Sutton nodded. "I have an appointment with a theatre manager at two. I should meet with him. I want to begin a new role as soon as possible."

"I'd recommend leaving out the back, and in disguise," said Holmes. "With half the world watching this flat, we want to minimize any attention you may be given."

"Don't fash yourself," Sutton said. "I will leave as inconspicuously as a spider."

"An interesting prospect," said Mycroft Holmes with a flicker of amusement in his eyes. "I will not see you until tomorrow, I suppose."

"Correct," Sutton told him, and went to the door. "You are going to go to the club tomorrow?"

"I will try. Unless something arises, I will make the crossing myself. Why?" He was mildly curious, and listened as much from courtesy than from need for information.

"I may have an audition tomorrow, if things go well today." He set down his teacup and made a sweeping gesture. "It is a small company, and they are planning a revival of *Volpone*. If the manager is satisfied with our meeting today, I will read Mosca for him tomorrow." His blue eyes brightened at the prospect. "It is a wicked part, not at all like MacBeth."

"MacBeth isn't wicked?" I asked. "What else would you call him?"

"Tragic," said Sutton as if this were obvious. "Mosca is wily, sly, and mischievous. Altogether a different sort of fellow."

"If it is to your liking, I will hope you get the part," said Mycroft Holmes. "You say it is a smaller company?"

"Yes, and not as well-housed. That does not bother me," Sutton said quickly. "I know it is wiser to be less visible than I am in *MacBeth*. The Bridge Street theatre is small—it seats only four hundred—and it is not as well-known as Drury Lane or Duke of York's, but it has a good reputation in theatrical circles."

"How large is the company?" I asked, recalling some of Sutton's earlier observations on the advantage of larger troupes of players.

"Just at present there are seven regular members," he said. "They plan to expand to ten."

"Good enough for many plays," said Holmes, and added, "I do appreciate what you have done, Sutton, and I want you to know how much I value your devotion."

"Well, you'd do as much for me, if our situations were reversed," Sutton responded.

I was not entirely sure this was so, but I held my tongue; Sutton would not like my observation and Mycroft Holmes would be insulted by it. "I'll wish you good luck," I said at last.

"Thank you, Guthrie," said Sutton, and turned away. "I will

change now. If you have any need of me between now and tomorrow afternoon, send word to my rooms and I will come as quickly as I am able."

"Thank you, Sutton. You are very good." Holmes cleared his throat. "If talent and skills are of any value, the part is yours already."

Sutton bowed as if taking a curtain-call, and then went out of the study, whistling as he hastened down the hall to the rear of the flat.

Mycroft Holmes said nothing for the better part of a minute and then said, "As soon as Chief Inspector Pryce arrives, we should go into the sitting room. I would rather he not see some of the material we have in here."

"Why not remove there now?" I suggested, reaching for my portfolio. "I can as easily review your notes in the sitting room as I can here." I prepared to gather up the papers. "You can keep this room closed during his visit."

"A most useful notion, Guthrie. Most clever of you." Holmes signaled his approval by taking half the stack of papers in his hands and going to the door. "Well, come along. There is work to do."

I did as he told me, taking the copies of the memoranda and slipping them into my portfolio as I followed him out of the study. In the sitting room, Mycroft Holmes drew up one of the chairs toward the hearth, calling out to Tyers for more wood.

"Shortly, sir," Tyers replied. "I have one thing to do for Sutton before he departs."

"Fine," said Holmes, putting down the sheets of paper and clapping his hands for warmth. "The cold gets into everything," he complained. "We should make the room a bit more inviting before the Chief Inspector arrives."

"No doubt," I agreed, opening my portfolio and pulling out the sheets I had put there.

"A bit of a puzzle, isn't he?" said Mycroft Holmes.

"Who? Sutton?" I asked, being mildly distracted by my preparations.

"No. Chief Inspector Pryce. For a man who endured so much notoriety a decade ago, he has weathered the storm remarkably well, don't you think?" His tone of mild interest persuaded me that my answer was of importance to him.

"It certainly appears so," I answered.

"Exactly, Guthrie. It does appear so." He sat down and took his notes in hand. "We might as well use our waiting time to advantage." With that, he put his full attention to the information contained in his notes; nothing short of an explosion would have pierced his concentration. Taking this for an example, I began my review of the notes, hunching my shoulders in an effort to stay warm.

FROM THE PERSONAL JOURNAL OF PHILIP TYERS

Sutton has just left, looking like a chimney-weep. I reminded him to be on guard, not only for the Golden Lodge guards, but any other person who seems unduly interested in this flat or in him. I have still to take wood into the sitting room so that it may be warm by the time Chief Inspector Pryce arrives. No doubt there will be a message for me to take to Inspector Strange when this meeting is done.

This morning's sermon was taken from the Book of Job, *where God speaks to Job out of the whirlwind, which cautions us not to speak without knowledge, or to question God's creation. I admit I have always found* Job *problematical, for if scripture is accurate, God had not yet created Adam when He laid the foundations of the earth. Indeed, if Mister Darwin is correct, the foundations of the earth were laid long before Man stepped onto it. How are we to encompass the whole of it? And should we repent if we cannot comprehend the whole?*

I expect the afternoon to be uneventful, but this may prove to be famous last words . . .

Chapter Thirteen

IT WAS TWENTY minutes past twelve when Chief Inspector Pryce knocked on the door; Tyers admitted him at once and showed him into the sitting room, offering to bring tea or brandy.

"Tea, if you would. I am technically on duty, and should not drink, though many of my colleagues would accept such an offer." Chief Inspector Pryce said nothing more until Tyers had left for the kitchen. "I spent last night reviewing the reports you had the presence of mind to get yesterday. They make most interesting reading."

"Do they?" Mycroft Holmes asked politely; he had risen to greet the Chief Inspector and now sketched a bow in the direction of the chair nearest the window. "In what way?"

"Most significantly, I noticed that only you and your secretary mention that the victim was nervous at the onset of the meeting. None of the Germans remarked upon that." He looked directly at Holmes. "I find that curious."

"Why?" countered Mycroft Holmes. "Why should this strike you as strange?"

"The Germans said nothing of it," Chief Inspector Pryce restated.

"Perhaps they knew the reason for his apprehension, and did not think it was solely connected to the events of the afternoon," Holmes suggested smoothly. "Or perhaps they knew his character to be of a nervous disposition, and so put no stock in his behavior. Guthrie and I, not familiar with the man, paid attention to what his associates did not."

"Very credible notions," said Chief Inspector Pryce, going toward the proffered chair at last, and sitting down. "And yet it does not wholly satisfy me. Why should the Baron choose this man to taste the tea, and why have it tasted at all? It strikes me as odd." He let the implicit challenge hang between them.

" 'Riddle me this'?" Mycroft Holmes responded. "I am afraid I cannot tell you anything much, my dear Chief Inspector."

"Your report says that Sir Cameron was of an unquiet state of mind," Pryce went on.

"He had been shot at not ten minutes since," Holmes reminded him. "He was somewhat testy because of it."

"As you would be; as we all would," said Chief Inspector Pryce.

"My point precisely," Holmes agreed. "And because of the delicacy of our discussion, the Baron undertook to reassure Sir Cameron that he was in no danger in Herr Amsel's house."

"Still, it is an odd sort of courtesy, and what a result to have," said the Chief Inspector; I saw that he was trying to lead the conversation toward a specific goal, but I did not know what that goal might be. I listened more closely to the interchange between the Chief Inspector and my employer, paying close attention to the nuances of their discussion.

"Yes; I would think that it is most unlikely that the Baron planned anything so disruptive to our occasion. He lost one of his men and all but guaranteed that Sir Cameron would reject any solution he might offer to their current impasse. With the efforts that were being put forth, one might almost suppose that there was a deliberate effort being made to sabotage our discussions." Holmes returned to his preferred chair and sank into it; the warmth of the built-up fire made the room quite cozy, although rain rattled on the windows and wind moaned along the river, heralds of another full-blown storm preparing to descend upon London.

"Which, I gather, has something to do with the coming visit of Lady MacMillian," said Pryce in a methodical manner. "I did not realize Sir Cameron was estranged from his wife." He let his remark dangle, tantalizing bait.

"For several years, yes. It was thought for some time that any rapprochement was unlikely. Lady Cameron is German, as you must surmise. She has recently expressed a desire for a reconciliation, and her visit is intended to be the first step in that process," Holmes said.

"Why so much negotiation? Why does not Lady MacMillian simply arrange to visit Sir Cameron at his home in Scotland and discover for herself if she wishes to renew her association with her husband?" It was a reasonable question, but Mycroft Holmes became wary at once.

"If only it could be so uncomplicated," he said, and I was aware by his manner that he had planned for this question. "But Lady MacMillian is a noblewoman in her own right and has recently inherited considerable wealth and estates in Germany. This makes her married state more than a matter of inclination and the heart: property and money are involved. Her family fear that if she should visit Scotland, Sir Cameron might—as German law provides—lay claim to all her fortune and her lands by right as her husband. In that event, there would be no legal recourse to deny him what he claimed so long as he did not formally separate from his wife. The family don't want this, nor do the Kaiser's government. So if there is to be any reconciliation, it cannot happen in Scotland, where Sir Cameron's authority over his Lady would be unalloyed. Here, in London, there is room for negotiation." He shrugged. "You, Chief Inspector, of all men, should be aware of how zealous families can be in regard to property and riches."

Chief Inspector Pryce pursed his lips. "I have had some experience of it," he said drily.

"Lady Cameron wishes to be accompanied by her uncles, an arrangement that is not satisfactory to Sir Cameron," Holmes went on, leaving out his own objections to the proposed arrangement. "So it has fallen to Baron von Schattenberg and me to work out a solution to the problem that is acceptable to all parties, in order to have the reunion a success."

"Sounds like a thankless task to me," said Chief Inspector Pryce in a tone of voice that suggested he was keenly aware of the difficulties this could bring.

"It has not improved with Herr Kriede's death." Holmes glanced up as Tyers brought the tea-tray into the sitting room. "Thank you, Tyers. Did the sweep get off betimes?"

"That he did. He will return tomorrow or Tuesday," said Tyers as he departed.

"Very good," Holmes said without any show of interest; I knew he had asked the question to account for Sutton's departure should Chief Inspector Pryce make inquiries regarding this flat during his investigation of Herr Kriede's death. "Assam, Chief Inspector, or Lapsang?" He indicated the two pots of tea on the tray.

"Lapsang, I think," said Pryce, pleased at the choice. "Sugar, no milk." He paused and added, "You are most fortunate to have a sweep work on Sunday."

"That I am. I did him a service once, and he is willing to extend himself on my behalf because of it," said Holmes smoothly.

"It must have been a most worthy service," said Pryce, encouraging Holmes to enlarge upon it.

"That it was." Mycroft Holmes leaned forward and poured a cup for the Chief Inspector, then rose. "I must excuse myself a moment. Guthrie, do you take over the work as host and answer what questions you can while I am out of the room."

"Of course," I said, wondering why Holmes was departing so rapidly. I went to pour a cup of the Assam for myself, with sugar and milk. I realized that I, too, would have to excuse myself in a short while. The amount of tea we had consumed this morning was prodigious. "What may I do to help you, Chief Inspector?" I asked, giving him my full attention.

"I would like to know what your first impressions of the death were. I have read your account, of course, but if anything now stands out in your memory, I should like to hear it." He tasted his tea and waited for me to answer.

"Well," I said, thinking over the events of the previous evening, "I was aware that as courteous as the Germans were being, they were under some pressure to resolve our shared problem with dispatch. Lady MacMillian has already left Germany and is probably in Holland, or so the Baron said. That alone added to the urgency of our negotiations."

"You do not want the woman to show up in London before the terms of her visit are approved," said the Chief Inspector.

"It is not so much the woman as her uncles who accompany her. They have certain connections that the Admiralty do not want to have turned loose in the city. It is lamentable that this is the case, but I cannot ignore the danger these men might represent." I assumed it was all right to say so much, for this had been mentioned in three of the reports Mycroft Holmes had provided yesterday.

"It is certain, is it, that these associations pose a real danger to Britain?" Pryce regarded me with polite curiosity.

"Yes, it is certain," I said. "We would not undertake this business if it were not." I put down my cup and leaned forward, elbows on my knees. "It may be that the shot fired at Sir Cameron before he arrived in Berkeley Mews is part of the puzzle. It served to put in motion the events that led to Herr Kriede's death."

"So I am informed," said Chief Inspector Pryce. "Which is what I find puzzling, for if the Baron did not know such an attempt would be made on Sir Cameron, how could he have anticipated that Herr Kriede would drink poison from the cup?"

"Exactly," said Mycroft Holmes from the doorway. "That cup

could have been given to anyone. I assume the poison was in the cup and not the tea?"

"It was, though why you should think so escapes me," said the Chief Inspector. He swung around to look at Mycroft Holmes as he went back to his chair and sat down.

"Merely the observation of the event. My notes on the death make mention of this: the tea had no detectable odor, and the spout was not discolored by anything more than tea. The cup, however, had a distinctly bluish cast to its interior after it fell onto the carpet. That was why I was most particular in making sure no one changed the scene of the crime. I made mention of that as well in my account, for it suggested to me that the cup had been the instrument of conveying the poison, and if the room were not guarded, another cup might be substituted for the fatal one." He paused. "I understand that the Baron would probably pour out the tea and have his assistants hand it round. In which case, it is likely that Sir Cameron or I would have been given the deadly cup."

Chief Inspector Pryce nodded. "Indeed. It seems very much that way to me. I am astonished that you should be willing to consider such a possibility with such sangfroid." He scrutinized Mycroft Holmes from beneath puckered brows. "Most men, contemplating their murder by poison would be in something of a dither."

"But I was not the victim, nor was Sir Cameron, as it turned out," said Mycroft Holmes. "The unfortunate Herr Kriede had the sad problem of drinking from the cup. I doubt he was aware of its contents."

"In spite of his nervousness?" Pryce inquired. "Any man facing such a possibility might well betray himself with a fit of nerves."

"But that was not the case with Herr Kriede, as I have said already. Whatever made him uneasy, it was not the prospect of dying by poison. I do not think anyone would take so great a chance as the Baron did to deliver a deadly draught to his aide in that haphazard fashion. Who is to say whether or not it would succeed? If it failed, then accounting for the death would be more trouble than the elimination of the man would be. As a German citizen, Herr Kriede would not have to be killed in London, but might have been sent home for more discreet disposal. So I do not consider Herr Kriede to be the intended victim." Mycroft Holmes folded his arms. "No, as regards Herr Kriede, I rather thought that he suspected something was amiss but did not dare to reveal it to anyone. I am in no position to surmise the cause of his response, or what triggered it: what that might be, I must point out that any guess I venture would be purely conjecture on my part."

"All right. I will not assume you to have discovered the truth. Have you any notion of what that disturbing information might be?" Chief Inspector Pryce asked.

"I am sorry to disappoint you, Chief Inspector, but prescience is not among my accomplishments," said Mycroft Holmes. "I have any number of guesses, but that is all they are, and as such they can do nothing to aid your investigation. In fact, they might cloud the very issues you seek to clarify." He poured Assam for himself. "If you are to find your way through this very confusing case, you will not want to load yourself with speculation on all fronts."

"Perhaps not," the Chief Inspector agreed. "Although I would reckon your suppositions would be nearer the mark than many another's would be." He finished his Lapsang. "Still, your point is well-taken. I will not ask you to venture your opinion yet. I may return to ask you more at a later time, if I may."

"I am always delighted to help the police in their inquiries," said Mycroft Holmes with the utmost cordiality. "I do think I should point out that neither I, nor Guthrie, had any opportunity to touch the tray or any of the objects on it."

Chief Inspector Pryce laughed. "You will have your joke, Mister Holmes. I would never consider you a suspect in such a case."

"Then you would not be doing your work well," said Mycroft Holmes sharply. "Everyone in that room, and the butler as well, should be considered possible killers until you prove they could not have done it. That must include Guthrie and me. And Sir Cameron, for all he arrived late and was still feeling the effects of having been shot at."

"If you insist," Chief Inspector Pryce said, his manner suddenly much more formal. "I will, of course, seek for confirmation of your statement."

"Very good," Mycroft Holmes approved. "If it should appear to anyone—the press, the Germans, or Sir Cameron—that you do not view all of us equally suspect, then there will be cries of bias and favoritism. This is not an accusation the police want to bring upon themselves."

"I suppose you're right," said Pryce, glowering down at his cup.

Mycroft Holmes made a gesture of encouragement. "There is trouble enough already in regard to Lady MacMillian. Her visit is most inopportune for reasons that are too complex to go into just now. I would advise you to keep in mind that the police will be closely watched during this inquiry, and that Sir Cameron is something of a darling to the press."

"That has not escaped me," said Chief Inspector Pryce with a wry smile. "When I called at his hotel this morning, there were half-a-dozen journalists waiting just outside the door."

"Not entirely surprising. Sir Cameron is a prime favorite of theirs," said Holmes with the patience of a much-tried parent.

Chief Inspector Pryce made a gesture of resignation. "I would prefer it if he did not feel compelled to tell them the whole of the story. But short of putting a guard on him in a sequestered place, there is not much I can do to stop him."

Holmes held up his hand, considering his next remark. "To that end, Chief Inspector, I may have a recommendation to make: I understand that Sir Cameron has taken a lease on a house in Deanery Mews," he said at last. "He himself confirmed that he had. You might want to suggest to him that he would be safer in that establishment than in an hotel, for the public may come and go in the hotel, but his leased house would be his castle. Lady MacMillian might not like it, but it would simplify the problem of guarding Sir Cameron. If someone wishes to try to shoot him again, it would be more easily accomplished at an hotel than in a private house. It would also be less expensive to stay at the house than to pay for both house and hotel." Again he waited to let the Chief Inspector deliberate on what he had just heard. "You might also remind him that it is safer to have his own servants about him than men he does not know who might be more venal than he would like."

Pryce managed not to chuckle. "You are a clever man, Mister Holmes, one the criminal classes might call a peevy cove. I am much relieved that you are on my side."

"So long as you are on the side of Her Majesty's government, I am," said Mycroft Holmes in genial warning.

"Whom else would I serve?" Chief Inspector Pryce asked as he got to his feet. "Well, I will not keep you any longer. I have still to talk to the Baron, and then I must be about making arrangements for the body. Is there anything you can do that might smooth the way for that?"

"I have prepared a memorandum for you to present to the coroner and to the Customs officer. It may prove useful." He went to the small half-desk in the corner and pulled out a sheet of paper with a few lines scrawled on it. "If there are any difficulties, have a message sent round and I'll try to sort it out for you." Handing over the paper, he added, "I don't suppose I have to admonish you to tread carefully."

"No, you do not," said Chief Inspector Pryce. "I have been given enough of these cases in the last year to know a proper mess when I see one."

"You will want to be alert in your dealings on this case. There is more at stake here than you know." He shook hands with Chief Inspector Pryce.

"Mister Holmes, I am not naive, nor am I in awe of the aristocracy. In this case, everyone is holding something back. Including you." This last was direct but not intended to offend.

Mycroft Holmes shrugged. "I regret that I cannot be more forthcoming."

"Oh, I don't want to compromise your work, and so long as it does not run at cross-purposes to my investigation, I will not do or say anything that might lead to trouble for you. But if the case should require that I delve into areas that it could be diplomatically awkward to explore, I will do as my conscience and my duty require me to do." He went to the door, Holmes following behind him. "Within limits you have been most helpful, and I shall keep that in mind."

"What can I be but grateful?" said Mycroft Holmes as he opened the door and let the Chief Inspector depart into the growing storm.

I rose from my place and went into the small entry-hall. "What do you think, sir?"

"I think that Chief Inspector Pryce is a very canny man. And I think that I must soon call on Inspector Strange, to get his assessment of the man, for I cannot make him out on such brief and official acquaintance. I will say he is a notch above most of the officers I have met, and that is not simply because he has better manners. You and I have encountered many rogues with public school accents and arms over the door who were hooligans or worse beneath their polish. No, this man perplexes me." He stood by the door for a short while, lost in thought, then turned and went down the hallway toward his study. "Come, Guthrie. We have notes to search. We may not be dawdling."

"As you wish, sir," I said, and went to fetch my portfolio and my sheets of paper I had taken from the file in the study. "I have the material here to hand."

"Very good. Come along and let us set to work again." He seemed full of industry, but there was a preoccupation in his eyes that was also in his voice, and that caused me to wonder what was on his mind beyond the task he had set for us. Had Chief Inspector Pryce caused him such perplexity that he was unable to concentrate on something as important as the possibility of his being the object of schemes set in motion by the Brotherhood? I could not believe it, but I did not want to challenge him on that account. Taking up the papers and my portfolio, I returned to the study and sat down at the table to continue my work. One thought occurred to me. "If Sir Cameron intends to keep his mistress at the house in Deanery Mews, won't this new arrangement force him to find other lodgings for her?"

"To tell you the truth, Guthrie," said Mycroft Holmes in a voice of exasperation, "I do not care if it inconveniences Sir Cameron's amorous escapades. I do not want another such incident as yesterday's on our plate, and I fear we will have just such a misfortune if he remains in public."

"Do you think the Brotherhood is behind it?" I asked carefully.

"I think it is likely, but that is not the same thing as proving it." Mycroft Holmes paced the room for a bit, then went off to his library, returning with four books in his arms, two of considerable age. These he set down on the table and began to read through them in a hurried way that indicated to me he was looking for something specific among the texts. I did not interrupt him, but did my best to continue my work, saying nothing to disturb him as I searched for the links he wanted established. Finally he rose, taking one of the older books, and began to read from it.

"*One of the services demanded of loyal Turks was the presentation to the Ruler of a youth of great beauty for the purpose of ensuring the good-will of the Ruler as well as securing an ear at the Court. This practice has been undertaken for generations and will undoubtedly continue for generations more.*" He snapped the book closed. "That was written in 1749, and it is as true today as it was when Sir Charles Greeleigh wrote it. I *knew* something of Mister Kerem's story struck a chord. If I had not had so much on my mind, I would have recalled this before now. The young man was a pledge to the Brotherhood. That was why he had the new tattoo on his shoulder." He sat down and opened another of the books.

"Does that mean the Brotherhood brought him here?" I asked, trying to follow his assumptions. "It would appear to be involved because of the tattoo. But you are suggesting this is more than a crime turned to their advantage."

"Oh, most certainly it is. They brought him here as a bribe. If only I had some inkling as to whom they intended to influence, I might then be able to discern more of their plan." Holmes bent over the pages of the second book, his brow beetled in concentration. "I know I have an account of a similar incident in France some years ago. If I can find it . . ." His voice trailed off.

"How will you go about gathering proof?" I could not keep from asking. "You say yourself that you lack crucial evidence."

"I am hoping that Mister Kerem will make an error, and that will lead me to the information I need." He rubbed his hands together. "I must prepare myself."

"In what way?" I perceived that his thoughts had raced ahead of what he had revealed to me.

"Once I find the account of that French case, I will know," said Holmes, and delved into his books again, keen as a hound on the scent of a fox.

FROM THE PERSONAL JOURNAL OF PHILIP TYERS

Word has come from hospital that the courier is improving at last. He has regained consciousness and although he is very weak, he is aware of his situation and his narrow escape. This is good news for the Admiralty as well as MH. I will plan to call round to visit the young man tomorrow morning, when I may obtain a full report from his physician. MH will want to review it . . .

The storm is growing worse, a proper gale. There will be trees down on many streets, I shouldn't wonder, and water standing in cellars all over London. I shall need to have the roof here inspected as soon as the weather improves, for I have detected a wet patch on the kitchen ceiling. No doubt there will be slates in need of replacement.

If there is any benefit in this storm, it is that Lady MacMillian cannot leave Holland while it continues, which means she will be kept, perforce, from arriving at least for another day or two, a most welcome respite . . .

A note has been delivered from Sir Marmion, giving MH access to his asylum tomorrow from three until five in the afternoon. This is a slight adjustment in plans, but not enough to cause any real inconvenience. The Germans have not yet asked for a new meeting to complete the arrangements for Lady MacMillian's visit, and I begin to think that such preparations are increasing the problems dealt with rather than lessening them . . .

Chapter Fourteen

FOR MOST OF the afternoon the French case continued to elude My-croft Holmes; I was aware of his increasing frustration, and I supposed that there was nothing I could do to assure him he would prevail, so I kept to my searching, and gradually, a notion began to take shape in my mind, a notion that continued to define itself as I read on. Finally I put the pages aside, and said, "The boy who cried wolf."

Mycroft Holmes looked up from the sixth book he had dragged in from the library. "What did you say, Guthrie?"

"I said 'The boy who cried wolf,'" I answered. I was suddenly aware of the ferocity of the storm, and it shocked me to realize I had not heard it plainly until now.

"A cautionary tale for children," Holmes agreed, nodding. "But what has it to do with your current task?"

"It is what I have seen in your notes. You have consistently remarked on the importance of warning others of impending danger, or the potential for danger. The circumstances you have discerned all deserved warnings, and all of those warnings are based on conjecture rather than on specific facts." I laid my hand on the stack of transcribed notes. "Take a look, sir. It is most interesting to see that in each situation you have been put in the position of issuing admonitions and recommendations for protection that could, in fact, come to nothing."

"Yes, I understand that," said Holmes impatiently. "What does that have to do with—" He broke off as he picked up the two sheets on which I had written my observations. "Oh. I *see*," he went on. "Yes, of course. If I issue too many warnings that come to naught, then no one will believe those that indicate a very real threat. Very clever, in many ways. It turns my own strengths against me. No wonder I could not discern it for myself: we are never so blind as when we must discount our own virtues." He rose and went to lay more wood on the fire. "When Sutton suggested that these seemingly unassociated incidents were intended to confuse me, I agreed with his decision, for I could see how it was so." He looked into the flames, musing. "I did not think they were set in motion to discredit me as well, and, of course, my enemies were counting on that. I thought physical danger was the aim, but this—I confess that had not crossed my mind. And it should have. I have allowed myself to regard myself with the high opinion I enjoy from others, and that is a mistake, although a flattering one."

"You have had a great deal thrown at you, sir, and from many directions." I knew this would not satisfy him, but I said it in the hope he would not be too self-critical.

"Which was part of the ploy, of course." He brushed his hands together. "I must give them high marks for deviousness," he said. "It is simple, elegant, and effective. I am ashamed to admit I had not seen it. I must confess that I was too willing to regard my handling of so many cases at once as enough of an accomplishment to provide me with the protection of my abilities, which has suited the Brotherhood very well." He frowned, his eyes distant. "I am relieved that you have discerned my folly." He looked over at me. "This is twice you have shown me the brink, Guthrie. I am most grateful, dear boy."

I contained my satisfaction. "It is hardly worth remarking upon, sir. It is what you employ me to do. At another time I should have hit upon this much sooner than I did, but I, too, have found the piling up of events confusing."

"Do not be too self-effacing, Guthrie. I doesn't become you. Accept my gratitude." He clapped me on the shoulder, his large hand gripping with surprising strength. "You and Sutton have been awake on all fronts, while I have allowed myself to be perturbed in a hundred ways."

"There have been many distractions," I agreed, repeating myself.

"As, of course, was the intention of those behind them." He sat down again. "I am unsure what I might do best just now." Taking a long breath, he went on, "I should review all my most recent actions, to try to winnow out the counterfeit threats."

"I think most of them are genuine," I said, feeling it incumbent upon me to be sure we did not underestimate our risks.

"Genuine perhaps, but more like traps set by a clever hunter: each capable of being sprung, but only if the prey is unwary enough to tread on one." He nodded to himself. "Now that you point it out, I see it plainly. How very clever of them."

I was not entirely listening. "Something just occurred to me, sir," I said, not wanting to interrupt him, but not wishing to lose my thought.

"Yes?" he said. "What is it?"

"We have been provided intelligence that suggests that Vickers and Braaten are coming to England by way of Ireland, and we think that they have already reached the Hibernian shores, isn't that correct?" I saw him gesture confirmation and hurried on. "What if they have already landed? What if all the bits of intelligence have been planted to throw you off, so that valuable time is wasted on searches that might prove fruitless because the prey is already gone? All the efforts made will lead to nothing, and the search might easily be—"

"Abandoned. Yes. And in the meantime, Braaten and Vickers will be at liberty to work their malign schemes without detection or hindrance until their damage is so great that they expose themselves. Very good, Guthrie. I can see you have learned to deal with these fell gentlemen on their own terms." He sat back. "They killed two of our men to mislead us." His face was stony; I knew he was much shocked. "None of this can be proven, and it cannot be bruited about, for fear of . . . er, crying wolf. You have put your finger upon the pulse of it."

I tried to smile; my hands were stiff from work and my head ached, but I still felt pleased with myself. "Thank you, sir."

"No, Guthrie; thank *you*. I should have found myself playing into this very clever trap had you—and Sutton—not had the presence of mind to see these patterns. Dear me," he went on, chagrined, "I was very nearly caught napping, and by the Brotherhood, at that."

"Not without cause," I said. "You have pointed the way; Sutton and I have only read the signs."

"But they needed reading," said Holmes. "All this is supposition, of course, but I am beginning to think that it is the most accurate assessment of the situation in which we find ourselves." He laid his big hands flat on the table. "So we begin again."

I sighed, knowing the task to be a daunting one. "With your transcribed memoranda?"

"Actually," said Holmes with renewed industry, "we should begin with the dispatches from the Continent, and the reports from our men there. I need to refresh my memory on what precisely was said, and what sources our men relied upon for their intelligence."

"That will take some time, sir," I pointed out. "Would you mind if I sent a note round to Missus Coopersmith, telling her I shall not dine with her tonight?" My landlady made it a point to have Sunday dinner with her lodgers at tea-time, and would not be pleased by my absence.

"I'll ask Tyers to attend to that now." Holmes was already on his feet. "And I shall instruct him that you will take your mutton with me. If you would prefer, I will send the note, saying I require your services, so it will not fall to you to explain to her."

"I will still have to explain how it happens that I am working on Sunday," I said. "She is a stickler for keeping the Sabbath."

"Well, in palmier times, I would endorse her habit. I think it is well for men to rest one day in seven. Unfortunately, our enemies are not so obliging as to permit us this luxury." He pulled a sheet of paper from the box set out on the table, reached for his pen, and began to write; when he was done, he handed it to me. "I have left you space where you may append a note of your own."

"I shall try to remain in her good graces." I dipped my pen in the inkwell and set down a few words, saying how sorry I was to miss an excellent meal, but I knew she would want me to do my duty; I asked her to give a morsel of meat to Rigby on my behalf, and promised I would try not to waken her when I finally came in. It was clumsily done, but it would suffice. I gave it back to Mycroft Holmes. "There you are."

"Wretched weather to go out in," Holmes observed. "Still, it can't be helped." He rang for Tyers, and when that worthy arrived, he said, "Have this carried round Curzon Street, will you, Tyers? Guthrie will be dining with me tonight and needs to inform his landlady of that fact."

"Very good, sir," said Tyers, and took the note.

"By the way, is it capon tonight?" Holmes asked.

"It is, sir, with crab-apples and ginger preserves for a relish." He gave a satisfied glance at the papers laid out. "You're making headway."

"At last, yes, I think we may say we are," Mycroft Holmes declared with an emotion that was perilously near satisfaction. "We are no longer on a tangent, which is all to the good."

"Truly," said Tyers. "Given the weather, should I summon Hastings to carry this?"

Holmes considered his answer. "No. No, I think not. Ask one of those Golden Lodge guards to make himself useful. They are already out in the storm, and they are mounted. One of them can manage the job while the other is gone for a short while. Even if the Brotherhood is also watching us, they should not pay too much attention to one man being gone, and on Sunday. The Golden Lodge's agents are better equipped than anyone to deal with the Brotherhood, in any case. And Tyers, see they both have hot rum for their trouble."

"Of course, sir," said Tyers, and withdrew.

I watched this exchange with half an eye; my thoughts were still dwelling on the stratagem the Brotherhood had developed to mislead Mycroft Holmes, and the more I considered it, the more apprehensive I became. The Brotherhood knew my employer's prodigious intellect and acute sense of detail, and had used these very qualities against him, inundating him with myriad bits of information with the intention that so much specificity would engross him so that he would not be able to discern the underlying purpose of their ploy.

"A penny for your thoughts, Guthrie," said Mycroft Holmes as he roamed around the room.

I shook my head. "It is just that I am troubled by the way in which the Brotherhood appear to have used your strengths against you, as you remarked earlier. I am also curious why they should chose to focus their attention on you: why not the Prime Minister, or some other, more visible, member of the government? I mean you no disrespect, sir," I added hastily. "But if their intention is to render Britain impotent in European affairs, there must be more obvious ways to do it, one that would cause wide-spread embarrassment and bring about more upheaval than your compromise would. This whole venture is aimed at you, to lessen your authority and to cause the Admiralty to doubt you."

"That was obvious once their ruse was recognized," said Holmes with a nod. "Revenge is a factor, of course. I have been a thorn in their sides for many years now. It is also possible that they do not want their activities to be obvious enough to throw the government into chaos, at least not right now. They may prefer to drain away British influence and then pull down the country when it has lost the confidence of Europe. In which case, they would have to fix their efforts on me, or someone like me. I suspect that Vickers played no small part in developing this device."

"It does not trouble you that they set out to destroy your credibility?" I was appalled at his self-possession. "Do you not feel smirched?"

"On the contrary, Guthrie. For the first time since this began, I feel my strength returning. I think that the Brotherhood may have overstepped themselves. They have undertaken to work against me so particularly that they have given themselves away." He clapped his hands together. "The dispatches are in the cases under the window, are they not?"

"I believe so," I said. "It is where I put them."

"Excellent," he said, going to lift the lid of the long case. He rummaged about in the long stacks of folders—for all the world like a hog after truffles—and pulled out two of the folders. "Here they are," he exclaimed, and pulled them out in triumph. "Guthrie, you take the Constantinople dispatches and I will take the European ones."

"What precisely am I looking for?" I asked, thinking my headache would not soon be gone.

"I am not certain. But you will know it when you see it. Your recent ten days in Asia Minor should serve you well." His enthusiasm was increasing. "You and I will find the key. I am convinced of it. Persevere, my boy, persevere."

I opened the folder and looked at the collection of reports, telegrams, bulletins, and other such material that made up the contents. Just looking at the names brought back the whole of the experience to me, and I had to swallow hard against the many impressions that welled up in me. This was no time for maundering, I told myself, and I set myself to the methodical perusal of all the various collection of facts, rumors, and conjectures that had come to the Admiralty from Turkish territory in the last two months.

An hour later, when I had sorted nine of the dispatches into three stacks, Mycroft Holmes interrupted my concentration. "Your note has been delivered."

"Oh. Thank you." I looked about me, noticing how dark the day had become, with the storm continuing and the muted shadows of afternoon closing in. As I pinched the bridge of my nose, a snout of flame winked a few feet away: Mycroft Holmes had lit the nearest gaslight. A moment later, a second lamp flared, and soon the study was bright and cheery.

"Have you discovered anything thus far, Guthrie?" Holmes inquired as he came back to the table to sit down.

"Not a great deal," I had to say. "This stack contains information that would appear to have nothing to do with our current situation. This stack might have some bearing on current developments. And this stack has information dealing directly or indirectly with the Brotherhood. The second dispatch is the most telling of the four in the pile."

"Good work, Guthrie," said Mycroft Holmes. "This is what I have come to expect of you."

I saw that he had reviewed nearly twice as much as I had, and I took the praise as being as much for my efforts as my results. "You have not been behind the times in your work."

"Ah, but European dispatches are much more readily evaluated regarding the Brotherhood than are those from the East," said Holmes. "I rely upon you, because of your recent activities, to comprehend the contexts of the dispatches better than I would be able to do without extensive cross-referencing." He regarded his own work. "On the other hand, I see European dispatches almost daily."

"But you are persuaded the two are connected?" I knew it was tempting to see activities of the Brotherhood everywhere, and to attribute all our difficulties to their nefarious intervention, but it was also oversimplifying a very complex world.

"Beyond doubt," said Mycroft Holmes. "And I should think you would agree, seeing that you and Sutton discerned it." He stretched and yawned. "And speaking of Sutton, as he is not here, I must soon ready myself to cross the street to the club."

"In this storm?" I asked.

"In any weather," said Holmes. "Besides, we English must honor our storms: as winter is the guardian of Russia, so storms are the guardians of England." He cocked a brow at me. "I should think a Scot could agree on that point."

"I'll concede you have a point, sir," I said with a hesitant smile.

"I'll accept that," said Holmes. "When I come back from the club, you and I will dine, and then we'll see how much more there is to do."

"How late do you think we will have to work?" I could imagine the work going on long into the night, but I didn't want to say as much.

"It will depend on how quickly we find what we are looking for," said Mycroft Holmes merrily. "If we do not come upon the information we seek, we'll put a stop to this at ten, if that will suit you?"

"That is a good hour," I said, not looking forward to the task of getting home. I realized some of my reluctance was linked to my mishap in the Green Park; I solaced myself with the realization that no assassin would want to be out on such as night as this one, and that the very tempest that distressed me also protected me.

"My dear Guthrie, I know I demand a great deal of you. You have dedication and loyalty that cannot be found everywhere; you have a first-rate mind and you can think for yourself, which is a rarer combination than you might suppose. If we were not in such a muddle, I would gladly send you home as soon as we have eaten, but we cannot do that, not with Braaten and Vickers prowling like wolves at our door." Mycroft Holmes began to pace again, this time twiddling his watch-fob, a sign of his dismay. "We were very nearly trapped this time, and that concerns me. It also alerts me, for which I am grateful, for it means that we have a narrow opportunity in which to prepare to deal with whatever it is that the Brotherhood is planning: we may be certain that their return to England is but the first step in a much larger plan, and one which will be increasingly difficult to stop, like an avalanche in the Alps, that can bring down tons of snow once it begins to move. This is just another such avalanche, and we have a small snippet of time in which to halt its progress, or lessen its severity. It behooves us to do all in our power to end their intrigue before it is fully in motion. We must not flag now that we have the chance to stop the damage." He picked up a few of the dispatches, frowning down at them. "I cannot help but wonder why they should link the crumbling Ottoman Empire with Britain, and how they seek to manipulate the two to their advantage. When I have found the answer to that, we will be on the way to ending this gambit."

"Could that link be another attempt to mislead us?" I suggested.

"It is possible, but it seems unlikely, at least at this stage of our discoveries. I am concerned about Eastern Europe in all this. There are ancient animosities in that part of the world that might be used to topple governments or bring about endless, small wars that would leach the countries of resources as well as disrupt the commerce and industry of the entire region; any country so vitiated would be a prize for the Brotherhood to pluck." He took a deep breath. "Remember that Lady MacMillian's estates are in the eastern part of Germany, in the Czech region."

"Yes, so they are. And they have had difficulties in that region, if my memory serves," I said; I had not thought of that until Holmes mentioned it. Now it seemed as obvious as a guinea in a coal scuttle. "The Czechs have not had an easy time of it of late."

"No, they have not," said Holmes. "Nor have the Slovaks, or the Poles, or Austro-Hungarians, particularly on their eastern and southern borders." He came up to me. "It would take so little to ignite that region, from Greece to Latvia."

"But the danger would not—" I stopped. "Oh," I said. "The *treaties.*"

"Exactly: the treaties," said Mycroft Holmes grimly. "The Brotherhood could embroil all Europe in war if they could drag the larger powers into the regional fighting because of the treaties. So far the major powers have struggled to maintain the stability of all Europe. Even Nicholas wants stability for Russia—you will recall he sponsored those talks on arms limitation?—so that there may be real reforms in his vast country. But if Eastern Europe erupts, who shall be safe? Britain has been able to use her influence to keep the Continent fairly peaceful."

"And should continue to be able to do so for a good many more years," I said, knowing this was among Mycroft Holmes' highest goals.

"Yes. So long as England is stable. But if the Brotherhood gets into the government, then who is to say how long that stability can survive? We might be pulled into any number of conflicts from which we would be unable to extricate ourselves, no matter how urgently we might wish to. This gambit with Lady MacMillian is just a rehearsal, and in miniature, at that, for how it might play out." He came to a halt near the fireplace. "We must make them see that England will not be party to any such petty disputes as they may try to create."

"A pity that Sir Cameron is being played for a fool," I said, not without irony.

"That it is, Guthrie," said Mycroft Holmes with a sigh. "But what are we to do? I do not think he would heed any warning we offered him."

"Is there someone he might listen to?" I asked, unable to think of anyone myself.

"I doubt it," said Holmes. "He is not inclined to listen to any counsel but his own."

I took this in, and then said, "Do you think Lady MacMillian is part of this? Is she acting for the Brotherhood knowingly?"

"I have no notion," said Holmes. "And that worries me, I must tell you." He stared down into the fire. "If she is only a tool, then we need not worry about what she says to Sir Cameron. But if she is part of their association, then she becomes much more dangerous and problematic."

"Do you plan to speak with her yourself?" I did not think he would wish to make such a direct approach, but he had used such disarming methods in the past.

"Not unless all else fails," said Mycroft Holmes.

"Why would it? We have discovered their ruse and they do not know it," I said, with more confidence than I felt. "Does not that give us the advantage?"

"Briefly, perhaps," Holmes allowed. "But they will have more than one means of achieving their goals, or I am mistaken in my understanding of the Brotherhood." He touched the place on his wrist where there was a darkened scar—the same place Brotherhood initiates had their tattoos. I wondered again how he came to have it.

"If the answers lie in the pages, we shall find them. And if we should be fined for working on the Sabbath, I'll pay my portion gladly." I meant every syllable, though I knew my good, religious mother would be shocked to hear me utter such sentiments.

"I don't imagine we will have reason to worry," said Mycroft Holmes. "Who is to report us: Tyers?"

I dutifully laughed at his remark, but I thought again of the men who opposed us, and what they would do if ever they managed to remove Mycroft Holmes from his post. They were not inclined to honor the Sabbath and keep it holy; in fact, they held all such exercises in contempt. They would be stopped by nothing short of arrest or death, and death was surer than imprisoning such dire men. I realized

I was more than prepared to kill them in cold blood, and that caused me a pang of anguish. What was I becoming? Standing against them was shaping me to their demands as surely as if I had joined their numbers. Flustered, I picked up the dispatches before me and forced myself to read.

"Guthrie," said Holmes, his voice a quiet rumble, "I do realize how much you do for me. I have complete confidence in you."

"You are good to say so, sir," I managed to reply.

"Actually, I am not," he countered drily. "It causes me to impose upon you most shamefully. I do want you to know that I am aware of what I do."

"You needn't apologize," I said, feeling color mounting in my face.

"I am not apologizing," said Holmes, a bit more briskly. "I am preparing you for yet more work."

Relieved, I chuckled, and put the dispatches aside to listen.

FROM THE PERSONAL JOURNAL OF PHILIP TYERS

The storm continues unabated. I am sorry for anyone abroad on such an afternoon as this, for it is nearly dark, although it is only four-ten, and the wind is furious. There will be damage from it throughout the City; I would not be shocked to learn that trees are down and windows broken. In half an hour it will be full dark, and the streets will be treacherous for anyone seeking to travel. I hope, for G's sake, that the worst will have passed by the time he leaves for Curzon Street.

I have provided the Golden Lodge guards with mugs of tea laced with rum, but it is hardly enough to keep out the cold and wet. This is most troubling to me, that they should keep at their posts in such vicious weather. If they are taken ill, I will be inclined to feel partially responsible, although they are acting at the behest of their masters in this duty. I may suggest that they keep watch in carriages rather than on horseback, if for no other reason than that a lone rider in such weather is conspicuous where a closed carriage—a Clarence or a milord—is hardly noticed by anyone . . .

Little as I want to admit it, I am bound to say that the flat seems emptier without Sutton here, rehearsing his parts and working on the clothes he provides for disguises. Even four years ago he seemed an intruder, and now he is all but part of the household. If he is cast as Mosca, he will have the advantage of knowing most of the play already. Still, it will be pleasant to have the entertainment of his rehearsing again. I am heartily tired of MacBeth *and would enjoy a comedy . . .*

I have a joint of beef to dress for this evening's supper, and some turnips to butter. That, pea soup, and a wedge of Stilton will be the fare. Tomorrow the butcher will bring the pork and veal for our dinners that I have already ordered. That, and a trip to the baker and the greengrocer should put all to rights until Wednesday. I suppose I must soon put in my order for a Christmas goose . . .

Chapter Fifteen

IT WAS AFTER ten when I finally took my leave of Mycroft Holmes and braced myself to go out into the storm. My hope of hailing a cab was not great, and as I looked at the empty, blowing length of Pall Mall, I supposed I had to resign myself to walking, and arriving at Missus Coopersmith's house soaked to the skin; my shoes were past praying for. I began to trudge toward Saint James Street, feeling my legs grow wet and my trousers sodden as I went. I had almost reached the corner when a very stylish covered sylphide came round the corner from King Street; the horse between the shafts was buckled into one of those patented Albermarle coats, which gave him some protection from the rain. I watched the dashing equipage with more than a trace of envy until it came along beside me, and Miss Gatspy called out, "Guthrie. Get in."

I stopped still in surprise, and then I hesitated. "What do you want of me?"

"To take you home." She gestured impatiently. "Come on. I'm getting wet holding the screen open." When I did not hasten to join her, she added, "I would have to follow you in any case, so why should you have to suffer unnecessarily."

I had no ready answer for this, and the prospect of a dry journey was too much to resist. I set my foot on the step and swung up into the carriage, pulling the screen closed behind me. "Thank you," I said, aware of the closeness of the interior. "I'm afraid I'll dampen your clothes."

"No doubt of it," she rejoined almost merrily. "But you would not be any drier in a block or two." She gave her horse the office and we went off at a jog-trot through the blustery night.

"I'm sorry to be of trouble," I said as we moved along.

"No trouble that I had not planned for," said Miss Gatspy, taking the turn onto Piccadilly with the ease of long practice.

"You're a first rate sawyer," I remarked, knowing that such a turn in a wind was not easily executed.

"I'm a crack shot, too," she said, letting her horse set the pace toward our next turn. "Are you and Mister Holmes making progress?"

"I should think so," I said, not wanting to give too much away.

"If there is anything I, or the Golden Lodge, may contribute to your efforts, you have only to ask." She was all but invisible in the dark interior of the sylphide, but I was keenly aware of her in spite of that. "I have offered before, I know, but I want you to know that it was not an idle gesture. The Golden Lodge is most concerned about the most recent activities of the Brotherhood."

I knew she was attempting to draw me out, and at another time I might have resented it, but after such a long, demanding day of research and speculation, I could not help but ask, "Does the Golden Lodge think it possible that Vickers and Braaten may already be in England?"

She turned to me, and although I could not see her features, I knew she was startled. "Vicker and Braaten in England?" she repeated, as if trying to learn a phrase in a foreign language. "Why would you think that?"

"There are some indications that suggest that—" I began.

"In other words, you aren't going to tell me why Mister Holmes has such suspicious, only that he does have them." She sighed in exasperation. "All right. I'll make inquiries, but I don't know if I can promise any results before Tuesday."

"That you are willing to help is most . . . most generous of you," I said, trying to find words to express my gratitude without saying anything my employer would not approve. "We have been unable to evaluate the conflicting reports we have, and—"

"You needn't bother, Guthrie," she said, not unkindly. "You have an obligation to Mister Holmes to keep his confidences. I understand that, for I find myself in the same quandary." She peered out at the street. "The turn for Clarges and Half Moon Streets should be along here."

"Take either one," I said, feeling I should contribute something to her efforts.

"I rather like Half Moon Street," she said, and held the reins more tightly. "Sit back, Guthrie. You will be home in a few minutes."

"Much sooner than if I had walked," I told her. "And much drier."

She shook her head. "You have a very odd idea of gallantry," she remarked, and turned the horse into Half Moon Street.

"I had not intended to be gallant," I protested.

"Yes," she replied, "I know."

We went the rest of the way in uneasy silence. As we reached Missus Coopersmith's house in Curzon Street and Miss Gatspy drew the sylphide up to the kerb, I tried to think of an appropriate way to thank her for providing me with his safe journey. "It was most accommodating of you to provide me this ride tonight, Miss Gatspy."

"It was, wasn't it?" she agreed archly as she lifted the screen so I could step down. "Guthrie," she said when I was out of her vehicle, "be careful. You may have had a lucky escape, but you cannot continue to do so."

"I will endeavor to keep that in mind, Miss Gatspy," I said; she pulled away from me before I was half-done, and swung her carriage about, then set off back toward Half Moon Street. I watched her go until I could not see the sylphide any more, then I slowly trod up the steps to Missus Coopersmith's front door.

"Mister Guthrie," said my landlady as I let myself in; she was seated in the withdrawing room just off the entrance hall. "It was good of you to send that note that you would not be dining with the house."

"I am sorry I could not join you," I said, shaking the rain from my shoulders and hanging my coat on the peg near the door.

"One would think you were a military man, the hours and duties that are set for you," she said, not quite complaining. She was a comfortable woman of middle years who was regarded as a widow although her husband was still very much alive and living up-country in India with a native wife and any number of half-caste children of his own; he had provided handsomely for my landlady, deeding this house to her before abandoning her, and his country, for his life on a tea plantation. "The government ask a great deal of their staff." She smiled as Rigby jumped into her lap and began industriously to knead her thigh through the folds of her skirt.

"So they do, Missus Coopersmith," I said in agreement; I wondered what her purpose was in this impromptu inquisition.

"I would not have stayed up, but there was a letter brought here by a man in uniform, to be given to you as soon as you returned." She lifted her brows in an expression of critical curiosity. "I pledged to put it into your hands myself." Saying that, she set Rigby aside, rose and came toward me, an envelope in her hand. "Now I have discharged my promise, I will seek my bed. I suppose you will break your fast with your employer in the morning?"

"Yes, Ma'am, I will," I said, taking the envelope and looking at it, noticing that it was entirely plain but for my name on the front. The flap had been double-sealed with a device I did not recognize.

"Well, thank you for your care, Missus Coopersmith," I said, as I noticed her tendency to linger. "I apologize for any inconvenience this may have caused you."

Reluctantly she went past me toward the corridor that led to her portion of the house; I was reasonably sure she would try to discover in future days what the enveloped contained. I resolved to think of an answer that would satisfy her without necessarily giving away any secret that could put me at a disadvantage. With this thought to accompany me, I climbed the stairs and went to my rooms; she had two other lodgers, all of us occupying the first floor: I supposed I was the last one in on this night.

My rooms were much as I had left them, which I found reassuring after such a day as I had had; after conducting a cursory search of the two rooms I occupied, I returned to my sitting room and turned up the gaslight in order to read the letter in the envelope. Using my pen-knife, I cut the end of the envelope so that the seals would remain intact, in case I should want to know more about them. A single sheet of cream-laid paper slid out into my hand, properly folded. I put the envelope down and opened the letter.

To Mister Paterson Erskine Guthrie, the letter began in a sloping, Continental hand.

This is to warn you that you are in grave danger. You have been duped and that may lead to your disgrace and ruin. Your close association with Mycroft Holmes cannot be to your advantage, for Mister Holmes is shortly to be revealed as an enemy of the state. There can be no question but that this will happen, and sooner rather than later. You, and those who work with him, will be indicted with him if you do not immediately sever all connections with this most dangerous man.

You may not wish to believe this, for you have been misled by his protestations of love of country, but it is all part of a subtle deception that has for years been the source of dissension and strife throughout the Empire. It is his purpose to destroy the very institutions he purports to defend. So successful has he been that only in the last few days has the full sum of the damage he has done been known, and it will not redound to your credit if you continue to support him in his fell purpose. You have already had some indication of his true allegiance. You have seen the mark on his wrist that is in the same place as Brotherhood initiates have theirs. You cannot think this is an accident, no matter how adroitly he may have accounted for its existence. Surely you must have wondered before now what the meaning of it may be, and surely you know the answer.

His mask of patriotism hides secrets of such perfidy that they cannot be mentioned here. Suffice it to tell you that this treason is beyond question, which you may discover for yourself if you will but search out the Admiralty intelligence officer Angus McDonald and see what his efforts have uncovered. You will be given irrefutable proof that your self-proclaimed devoted civil servant is more dangerous than any number of spies. The activities of Mycroft Holmes are beyond question the result of deliberate treachery, and you will know this for the truth when you evaluate the material McDonald had gathered in this regard.

The loyalty you have reposed in this man has been misplaced. You have been the tool of a cynical, ruthless enemy, and because of him, you will be forced to share his ignominy unless you turn against him at once and demonstrate your character as a true subject of Her Majesty by revealing all you know of this man's activities to the officer who shall call upon you Monday evening at eight in the evening.

If you confide any of this to Mycroft Holmes, you will be known as his accomplice and nothing you do or say will spare you from sharing his fate, if he does not decide to be rid of you himself.

> *Believe me*
> *One who is your friend*

I must have read the letter three or four times, and yet it still made no sense to me. I thought of all Mycroft Holmes and I had discussed earlier that evening, and suddenly our recognitions became more sinister. Not that I doubted him—far from it—I was struck by the desperation of this attempt to subvert my dedication to my employer and all his work. "What a farrago of lies," I expostulated at last. Even as I spoke, I began to ask myself if the writer intended I should believe, or if it was supposed to be an obvious trap, for the accusations were so overstated, surely it could not be expected by anyone that I would be convinced of their veracity? I began to mull the possibilities: the culprit actually planned that I would accept this passel of prevarications—that did not seem likely. Then was it assumed

I would tell Holmes about this denunciation? That might be part of the plan, a way to draw him into a tangle of deception and peril that would surely hamper his ability to deal with the current list of obstacles in his path. If I decided not to tell him, to act on my own, what then? Might I not become mired in the same bog as it was hoped Mycroft Holmes would fall into? If I met with this Angus McDonald, what would I learn? Or was there an Angus McDonald at all? Might he not be a fiction created to lure an unsuspecting Scot into a trap that would end in ruining his employer's career? The more I wrestled with the possibilities, the more confused I became. This I attributed to fatigue, and ordered myself to wash and go to bed, in the hope that a night's sleep would restore the tone of my mind and sharpen my wits, so with these many unappealing hypotheses for company, I bathed, drew on my nightshirt, and got into bed, where I lay, fretting, for three hours and more, until exhaustion finally bludgeoned me into restless slumber.

I wakened no wiser than when I had closed my eyes. The one encouraging note of the morning was that the wind had abated, although it was still raining. I rose and shaved, doing my best not to think of the letter that had so disrupted my sleep. While I dressed, I finally resolved to show the letter to Mycroft Holmes first thing this morning, and to follow his advice regarding it. My decision did not do much to shore up my state of mind, but it did ease my apprehension to have come to a decision—any decision. I left the house promptly when it was lacking fifteen minutes of seven, my umbrella and portfolio in hand, and I was relieved to find Sid Hastings pulled up to the kerb to take me to Pall Mall. It was still raining, but in a steady, misty way; the wind had died down, and most of the street-lamps were still alight, and would be for another half hour.

"Morning, Mister Guthrie," Hastings said as he let down the steps for me.

"Morning to you, Hastings," I replied as I settled back.

"Better day than yesterday," he remarked as he signaled Lance to walk on.

"The storm has passed," I agreed, for to me it was not much of an improvement on the previous day, not with that pernicious letter in my portfolio, seeming to me to be afire.

We drew up at the rear of Mycroft Holmes' building, Hastings telling me that Holmes preferred I entered that way today; this was not so remarkable that it troubled me, for I had often arrived at Holmes' flat by many and varied routes. I got out of the cab and nodded to Hastings, then climbed up the three double-flights to the second floor, where I knocked, then waited for Tyers to come to the door.

"Mister Holmes is in his library, Guthrie," Tyers informed me, giving me a glance that seemed dubious to me. I told myself I was being suspicious for no reason, and I did my best to smile at him.

"Thank you." I closed my umbrella and took off my over-coat, handing them to Tyers, and this time I had no doubt that he was troubled about my presence. "Is anything the matter?" I asked, confused by his manner.

"That is for Mister Holmes to say," responded Tyers in a kind of stiff courtesy that alerted me more cogently than ever that something was indeed very much amiss.

"I shall go to him directly," I said, and made my way through the rear of the flat to the kitchen and thence to the hall and the library. I knocked, wanting to be punctilious in my actions, and said, "It's Guthrie, sir."

"Come in, my boy. Come in," he invited, his voice heavy.

I did as he told me, and saw as I entered that he was standing in front of the small fireplace that gave heat to the room, his attention apparently wholly on the flames. "What has happened?" I asked, aware that something must be very much amiss for him to behave in this way.

Mycroft Holmes turned to face me. "I have had a most disturbing communication, one that I do not believe, but which others may do." He held out a sheet of paper to me. I took it, and saw the same, slanting Continental hand as marked the letter I carried.

Mister Holmes,
Too long have you bestowed misplaced trust in Paterson Erskine

Guthrie. The dedication he has shown you is sham, a deliberate deception to permit him to be privy to state secrets that are to be used by his true comrades against the interests of Britain. If you do not now act immediately to reveal his dissimulation, you may well be tainted by his downfall.

It would be folly to hesitate in taking action, thinking that you must give him a chance to show his loyalty and prove that this letter is nothing more than a misinterpretation of certain crucial facts that will be made available to you by noon. When you have seen for yourself what we have uncovered, you will share our appal. It is impossible for these incriminating disclosures to be kept from the public for long; unless you are swift in your denunciation of this man, you will not be able to preserve your reputation. You will bring embarrassment to the government and you will compromise the position of Britain in the world.

Do not reveal what you know to Guthrie, for he is a most dangerous man. You will be subject to every danger that a man of his ruthlessness can display. For your own sake, say nothing to him, and do not allow him access to you, or the consequences may be dire for you and your manservant. The police will know what is best to do, and the Admiralty, if given an opportunity to act quickly, will remove Guthrie from any position where he might be able to do you and your reputation any lasting harm. Let me assure you that this accusation is not made without foundation, as you will see when the corroborating materials are given to you.

You are known for your intellect. Do not fail to employ it now.

One who is your friend

My hand was shaking as I finished reading. Without a word, I opened my portfolio and brought out the letter I had received and handed it to Mycroft Holmes.

"Well," he said when he had finished. "Hardly inventive, is he?" He chuckled. "What utter poppycock."

"Just so, sir," I said, a bit stiffly.

Oh, don't look so glum, Guthrie. I would never be convinced by such a denouncement as this, nor would you. But we should be grateful that our enemies seem to think we could be. It would appear they have overplayed their hand at last." He gave a sigh of satisfaction that confused me.

"With such pernicious—" I stopped. "What do you mean, over-played their hand?"

Mycroft Holmes took the two letters and laid them on the end-table beside his chair. "They have made two mistakes in sending these. First, they have admitted they are in London. Second, they have used the same hand for both."

"Why is that significant?" I asked; I was still in turmoil and could not readily follow his thinking.

"Because it means that these so-called denouncements originate at the same source, and that, in turn, points the finger in one direction and one direction only." He picked up the letters again. "I know Vickers' hand, and this is not it. But as it is Continental, I would suppose that our odious Jacobbus Braaten wrote the letter, possibly to Vickers' dictation; the use of English suggests a native-speaker. But you can see that the style of the fist is European, can you not?"

I was astonished at his composure, and said so. "I hardly slept last night, for apprehension. You see this . . . this ominous letter, and receive one of your own, and you are very nearly satisfied with them. Have you no concern for what the Admiralty will say when they read these implications and charges?"

Mycroft Holmes actually chuckled. "My dear Guthrie, you can-not imagine the number of anonymous denunciations the Admirably receive every month, claiming to prove that various government min-isters, military commanders, and men such as myself, are involved in scandalous activities. Once in a very rare while, there is a reasonable cause to investigate, but for the most part, such ravings are put into files and kept for the purpose of comparing them to other such in-flammatory effusions." He sat down. "I will, naturally, send these along, with a note about Angus McDonald, for it may be that he has truly been dragged into this, or he may have taken part willingly."

"And what of the papers?" I asked. "The *Times* would not stoop so low . . . but there are less reputable journals that might—"

"There are laws that even the yellowest of sheets dare not trans-gress," said Holmes, a steely shine in his grey eyes. "Do not think they are unaware of the consequences of printing any accusation that might be detrimental to the Admiralty. They also know that if their credibility is destroyed in the courts, they will be unable to continue in business, for those publications survive on innuendo and veiled reports: 'Lord M has been seen abroad with a young dancer from the ballet; is he doing more than patronizing her art?,' 'What has the Member from H been doing in the gambling hells of Paris?,' 'Atrocious murder in Drury Lane—actor in custody,' 'What did Sir R's butler witness that earned him a dismissal?' That sort of thing. They would be mad to try to expose someone less in the public eye than most of those about whom they print titillating tidbits, for the public would not care and the courts would." He rubbed his big, long-fingered hands together. "No, I think this time the Brotherhood's arrogance will serve to bring them down at last. In England, at least," he added, frowning.

"Because of those letters?" I did not quite see how this was to be accomplished.

"In large part, yes. We are now on the alert for these men; we are not in disarray, as it is obvious they supposed we would be, and that gives us an advantage." He reached out to the bell-pull to summon Tyers. "I doubt they believed we would both be persuaded by these vicious ramblings, but I think they anticipated that they would create enough doubt in one or the other of us, that there would be a diminution of trust, and that could be used to keep you and me from participating fully in our various ventures."

"That did occur to me," I said, not mentioning that it had been after two in the morning.

Mycroft Holmes sighed. "And so, I think I had best account for the mark on my wrist, so that anything hinted at in that letter may be answered fully, at least in that regard."

I looked away in confusion; I had to admit that the mark in question had roused my curiosity from the time I entered Mycroft Holmes' employ and learned about the Brotherhood. Until now he had not done so much as mention it. I coughed. "It isn't necessary, sir."

"But it is, Guthrie, it is," said Holmes, and glanced up as Tyers came into the library. "We could use tea now and breakfast in half an hour. Sirloin and eggs, I think, and a baked apple in cream."

"Very good, sir," said Tyers. "I shall get to work at once."

"And Tyers, who is watching us this morning?" Holmes added as if unconcerned.

Tyers answered at once and without sign of being alarmed. "There is a man from the Golden Lodge in a buggy at the end of the service alley, and one in Pall Mall as well. I have not noticed anyone else, although there was an ironmonger's cart pulled up at the end of the alley a while ago. I did not recognize the name and I have not seen the cart before."

"To which house did this ironmonger go?" Mycroft Holmes inquired.

"To the home of Missus Helmstone, the old woman on the first floor, opposite, at the end, who is bed-ridden," said Tyers.

"Oh, yes," said Holmes, smiling slightly; it was not a pleasant smile.

"She is in the care of a nurse and her nephew," said Tyers as if reporting on the weather.

"I think," said Holmes, "it is time we inquired after Missus Helmstone. A pity Sutton isn't here this morning, but perhaps we can call upon Miss Gatspy when she arrives."

At the mention of her name, I looked around at Holmes, much astonished. "Did you invite her to join us?" I asked, rather more bluntly than I had intended.

"No; but I suppose she will make an appearance sometime this morning," said Holmes at his most bland.

"Oh." I was somewhat nonplused. I thought I should offer some remark, but none came to mind.

"It is consistent with her previous actions," Mycroft Holmes added, wicked amusement in his eyes.

"If you are joking me, sir, I will do my utmost to be amused," I told him; he continued to assume some attachment existed between Miss Gatspy and me—for such a perspicacious man, I was hard-put to understand how he could reach so ludicrous a conclusion.

"Oh, don't cut up rough, Guthrie. I mean you—or Miss Gastpy—no disrespect." He waved Tyers away. "Now, about this mark on my wrist. Draw your chair a bit closer, Guthrie, so you can see more clearly. You will observe," he said, rolling back his sleeve, "that it is a discolored scar about the size of a farthing."

I leaned forward to examine the area in question. "Yes. There is a bluish cast to the skin, almost like a perpetual bruise, and the scar would seem to be from a burn."

"Very good," Mycroft Holmes exclaimed. "It is a burn-scar. I received it when I was cast out of the Brotherhood."

FROM THE PERSONAL JOURNAL OF PHILIP TYERS

This morning continues raining, and there is no sign of it abating. Sid Hastings has gone along to the Thistle *to avoid being out in the rain. He will call back here in an hour to find out when MH needs him, and will keep himself in readiness for that time . . .*

The ironmonger's cart has returned, and is once again in the same position it occupied earlier. I have taken the opportunity of observing Missus Helmstone's rear windows twice in the last hour, but I have discerned nothing to indicate what may or may not be happening in that place. Perhaps the Golden Lodge observers have had more success in monitoring what is taking place there.

I must get to work on breakfast for MH and G. Then I must bring up another load of wood for the fires and my cooker . . .

Chapter Sixteen

I SAT DUMBFOUNDED, certain I had not heard Mycroft Holmes correctly. "I beg your pardon?"

"I was expelled from the Brotherhood, many years ago," said Holmes calmly, rolling down his sleeve and putting his cuff in place once more. "They found out I was spying on them. I was lucky to escape with only the burn and the gouge on my neck—I know you have seen that scar, too. By all rights I should have died on that foolhardy venture." He looked at me in mild surprise. "Guthrie: surely you have guessed that I once was more active in the field than I am today?"

I brought my astonishment under control. "Well, yes," I allowed. I had not thought he had done anything as hazardous as penetrate the Brotherhood. The enormity of his revelation all but took my breath away.

"I was very like all those fine young men we have sent out on missions the world over—you being one of them upon occasion—when I was in my twenties. And in that capacity I was expected to infiltrate many organizations whose purposes were to harm Britain." He put his elbows on his knees. "I was twenty-four—hard to believe now that I was ever so young, or so reckless—and I had been assigned to the Continent, to search for European organizations that might prove dangerous to British security. The Brotherhood had not been identified, specifically, but we had discovered that there was an underground establishment that was revolutionary in purpose and I discerned that its activities could become a threat to this country. I was authorized to pursue the matter, and so, unaware of the cutthroat nature of the Brotherhood, I posed as an idealistic young scholar in search of social reform." His laugh was rueful. "That wasn't so far off the mark back then. Most of my ideals had not yet been tested. That changed." As Tyers brought in the tea, Mycroft Holmes rose and went to the fire to lay another log on it. "Days like this, the damp gets into the bones."

"And the chill cuts deep as a knife," I said, following his conversational lead. "With winter coming, it will be worse."

Tyers shook his head. "Telling him about the old days, are you? About bloody time, if you ask me. He's been loyal for six years." With that he turned on his heel and left the room.

Holmes lifted his big shoulders. "Tyers is awake to everything," he told me as he came back to pour the tea. "Ah. Gunpowder. He will have his jest, I suppose."

I managed to smile. "If it was deliberate."

"You may rest assured that it was," said Holmes. "Here." He handed a cup of gunpowder tea to me then poured his own. "Yes. I stumbled upon the Brotherhood in Belgium, and over several months I attended various meetings they sponsored and listened with rapt

attention to all they said. They were impressed by my apparent enthusiasm; as time passed I fell in with them. I never imagined how
vast an organization they were, or how old. I thought at first that they
were radical sorts of Freemasons, and I almost turned away from them,
under the impression that they were an off-shoot of the more traditional semi-mystical lodges with political aspirations; I thought that
they were theorists, and that could not be dangerous to England. I
had all but removed myself from the case and gone on to other seemingly more pressing assignments when I met Vickers. He had just come
down from Cambridge, and was full of zeal; at the time I did not
comprehend the extent of it, or appreciate what it meant. He convinced me to stay, for he announced his intention to bring the Brotherhood to England. He said he would need a lieutenant and decided I
would suit his purposes to admiration; I thought this was an excellent
opportunity to obtain crucial information, so I notified the Admiralty—secretly, I thought—of these developments, and I promised
Vickers to do all in my power to aid him." His brow darkened. "I was
in too deeply, but I didn't know it."

"So all that you have told me about the Brotherhood is not the
result of reports and research," I said, and took a sip of my tea.

"Of course not. I would never have known where to begin had
I not experienced directly the full malice of the Brotherhood first-
hand. Having been privy to their *inner sanctum*, I know their intentions and what they are capable of doing." He passed a hand over his
eyes as if to wipe away an unbearable memory. "When I was initiated,
as part of the rite they killed a man they called a traitor. You have
seen for yourself, in Bavaria, what they do. I was aghast at what I
witnessed, but had to conceal my feelings, for I finally comprehended
the nature of the organization into which I had insinuated myself."
He looked away from me, his face now in profile to me, and hard to
read. "On the instruction of my superiors, I remained in the organization for almost a year, passing on everything I learned about the
Brotherhood. I was convinced I was undetectable. Then someone at
the Admiralty said something to someone else and somehow it got
back to Vickers. To this day, I do not know who the person was who
compromised me, or why he did it, but Vickers used the information
to the fullest; he denounced me and I was brought before their

council—I believe you have met a few of them—and they proposed to make an example of me."

I felt myself breathing hard, for although I knew he must have escaped, my knowledge of the Brotherhood was enough to make my pulse race. "But you escaped. Of course."

"In a manner of speaking," Holmes said obliquely. His next words were interrupted by a ring from the bell in the front. "Ah. I conjecture your Miss Gatspy has arrived." He looked somewhat relieved as he rose to open the library door, to find, not Penelope Gatspy, but Mister Kerem standing expectantly before him; he had pushed past Tyers, and come directly to the library.

"Mister Kerem," said Mycroft Holmes, recovering from his surprise.

"Mister Holmes, I come to ask your assistance yet again," he said without any of the conversational arabesques that are often a mark of Turkish good manners. "I trust I do not intrude." He stepped into the library, his raincoat over his arm, dripping on the carpet. "I am loathe to disturb you, but I can think of no one else to whom I might apply for help."

In the hallway, Tyers shrugged to show he had been unable to stop Mister Kerem even long enough to take his coat.

"Dear me," said Holmes, admitting Mister Kerem and closing the door. "What is the matter?"

"I have just come from the police and they have told me that I cannot take my brother's body home just yet." His distress was so obvious that I wondered how it could possibly be wholly genuine.

"I am sorry to hear it," said Holmes sympathetically. "I must suppose the police have reason to keep the body."

"They claim they need to examine it again. They told me that there are a few problems they have encountered in dealing with it. I have appealed to them, but they are adamant." He shook his head and stared down at his galoshes. "What am I to do, Mister Holmes? I must have his body aboard the ship by this afternoon or I must make arrangements yet again to carry the body to Turkey; the next ship does not depart until Thursday, and that is a long time to store a body."

"Indeed it is," said Mycroft Holmes. "But if the police require it to complete their inquiries, I should think you would want them to carry on. How else are they to find his killer?"

Mister Kerem sighed heavily. "It is a difficult matter, and one that it may be hard for an Englishman to understand. It dishonors my brother not to bury him quickly. The longer I must delay taking him home, the more the family will be shamed by it."

"The voyage will cause a delay in itself," said Holmes as delicately as he could. "Surely your family want your brother's killer discovered and his death avenged?"

There was a longish pause while Mister Kerem wrestled with these possibilities. "It is going to be most difficult to explain all this," he said slowly. "It is not how these things are handled in my country when such a crime has been committed." I was observing Mister Kerem closely, and I thought I saw an expression of cunning cross his features then, a kind of slyness that was gone so quickly I hardly knew if I had properly seen it, or if it had been nothing more than a trick of the light.

"Yes; that is the problem with dying on foreign soil," said Mycroft Holmes. "If it would make your situation easier, I could see if we can arrange to embalm him. That would lessen the . . . difficulty of transportation." He held up his hand. "I realize this may be at odds with your religion, but under the circumstances, it is the wiser course."

"Of course. I do understand that." He looked up at the ceiling. "I cannot think what to do. I must appeal to you."

"I will do what I can, Mister Kerem, but I fear it may not be much. If the police have issued the order, it is they you must address for action." He bowed slightly. "You should ask the police to advance their investigation."

"I have done so. I have told them about the ship. They do not listen to me. I am only a foreigner," he said bitterly. "They do not want to waste time on me. They would listen to you." He put such pathetic hope into his voice that I was sincerely embarrassed for him.

"I will do what I can, Mister Kerem," Holmes assured him. "But I am afraid it may not be enough to let you depart today."

"I must!" he declared. "If I remain much longer, I will disgrace my family and the memory of . . . of my murdered relative."

I wondered if Mister Kerem had forgotten what he had claimed was the lad's name and their degree of relationship, or if there was a Turkish tradition that forbade speaking of the dead by name. It struck me that given what Mycroft Holmes suspected, in the case of Mister Kerem, the former was more likely than the latter.

"You will have whatever poor aid I am able to give you, Mister Kerem. I regret to say it may not be much." He had achieved that ineffective manner again, one that hinted at a love of magnifying trivia as a means of lending power to his own position.

"I would appreciate anything, Mister Holmes." His shoulders sagged. "I must take him home."

"And so you shall," said Holmes. "I will do what I can to make that possible for today. So much must be the decision of the police. You must see my hands are tied if the police are not willing to release the body."

"I see that you are not eager to help me," said Mister Kerem bitterly.

"Who would be, on such a very awkward errand?" Mycroft Holmes countered. "I assumed all was in readiness before. I had not anticipated this change. What man wants to plow the same field twice?"

"Truly I do not," said Mister Kerem.

"No more do I, Mister Kerem. But I will do as much as I am able, and quickly." He nodded in a way that indicated their discussion was at an end. "I will send you word when I have something to report. Tell my man Tyers where you may be found this morning."

Mister Kerem drew himself up, insulted to be given such short shrift. "I am sorry to have bothered you. I am a desperate man."

"Your apology is accepted," said Holmes. "But if I am going to be useful to you, I must set to work at once. Forgive my hastiness, but I must immediately contact the police."

At once Mister Kerem was all approval. "Yes. Of course. You will notify the police of my wishes. I will not linger." He pulled on his coat for himself. "I will return to my hotel and await word from you. I thank you, Mister Holmes."

"I have not deserved your thanks yet," Mycroft Holmes answered, a grim note in his self-effacing manner.

"I am sure you will; until I hear from you, a very good morning," said Mister Kerem as he turned and went out of the library and down the hall to the front door, not waiting for Tyers to let him out.

"What other diversions shall we encounter today?" Holmes mused as he stared out the door into the hallway.

"Well, you did say you would try to help him," I pointed out.

"It is called setting a trap, dear boy," Holmes corrected me quietly. "I hope this may mean the police have begun to do their work as they ought. If Mister Kerem persists, they will not be able to detain the poor lad's body much longer, more's the pity."

I was puzzled by his remark. "You mean the tattoo?"

"Among other things, yes," said Holmes, and took his chair. "It's bad enough having to let the Germans send Kriede home: that we cannot delay. But this is another matter, and we must make the most of the opportunity we have."

I remained silent a short while, then asked, "Are you going to send word to Scotland Yard?"

"I am going to prepare a note to be carried round to Inspector Strange. I want his opinion on the whole situation before I go one step on Mister Kerem's behalf." He pulled open a drawer in the end-table and took out a sheet of paper and an envelope. He then retrieved pen and ink, trimmed the pen, and wrote a few quick lines before putting Inspector Strange's direction on the envelope. "I will have Hastings take this round at once. I will tell him to wait for the answer."

"And what will you do about the body?" I knew my employer to be a very capable man, but I doubted even he could order a corpse away from the police while they were still busy with investigating it.

"I will try to arrange for the release, as I said I would; I will also try to discover what it is that they are searching for, that they must keep the body here," Holmes told me. "I will also send a note to the morgue asking what the condition of the body is, and tell them that the family are waiting to bury their dead."

"I should think they would be glad to be rid of him by now," I said, knowing how putrefaction sets into a body.

"Very likely," said Mycroft Holmes. "I have to admit I am worried that they may have taken the corpse for burial in Potter's Field. That would be embarrassing at the least." He saw my dismay. "But consider, Guthrie. The boy is foreign, the victim of a murder found disposed of. The identification of the young man may not have reached the proper hands before an interment order was given. I would prefer to think that this is the case than that there is an on-going effort to be rid of the evidence." He put the envelope aside. "Remind me to give this to Tyers when he brings breakfast."

"If you forget, I will," I said, thinking it highly unlikely that such a possibility would occur. I wanted him to tell me how he escaped from the Brotherhood, but before I could bring it up again, there was a ring from the front as someone twisted the bell.

"Ah," said Holmes getting to his feet. "This will be your Miss Gatspy." He went to open the front door himself while I stood in anticipation of greeting the new arrival—no matter whom that might be.

I rose in anticipation of greeting the caller, wondering why it was that Mycroft Holmes expected her this morning. If I asked, he would subject me to more jocularity in her regard, so I thought it best not to inquire too deeply into the matter. I had bent to retrieve my teacup when I heard a voice that was no more Miss Gatspy's than mine is.

Mycroft Holmes came to the door with the new arrival in tow. "Sir Marmion Hazeltine has come to call, Guthrie." He raised his voice. "Tyers, there will be a third for breakfast."

"Oh, no, Mister Holmes," said Sir Marmion. "I must not stay so long. As I told you, we are soon to receive at the asylum a most dangerous madman. He is a criminal of the deepest stain, and, much as I am reluctant to do it, he will have to be confined in a small, dark chamber. It is for his protection and the protection of others. I wanted you to know this because I am going to be unable to receive you later today. I hoped we might reschedule for later in the week, say Thursday or Friday? The worst should have passed by then, and I will be able to explain my methods to you without fear of ruction."

"Do come into my library, Sir Marmion," said Holmes as he escorted him through the door. "As you see, Guthrie and I are hard at our chores. Tyers is preparing sirloin and eggs. Do join us. If we cannot meet this afternoon, surely you can spare half an hour for discussion."

"Well," said Sir Marmion, his resistance fading, "it is not my habit to take meat in the morning, but I should not refuse an omelette, if one can be made." He ducked his head in appreciation, gave a glance in my direction, then looked back again. "Egad, sir," he said, coming up to me in surprise. "Your eyes are different colors. Most unusual."

"Yes. Left blue, right green," I said, recalling how much my mother feared they would prove unlucky for being mismatched.

Mycroft Holmes went to the door. "Tyers, Sir Marmion will have an omelette."

"I shall attend to it, sir," came the answer from the kitchen.

"*Most* unusual," Sir Marmion said again.

"Does such divergence play any part in your theories?" Mycroft Holmes asked as he pulled a reading-chair from its place against the wall. "Tyers will use the butler's table to serve," he added as he left an open place among our chairs. He resumed his seat. "How does it happen that you are taking such a dangerous fellow as the one you described under your wing?"

"It was the request of the judge who sentenced him. Apparently the prison inmates are afraid of him, and for very good reason. Since I am fascinated by the working of criminal and degenerate minds, I offered my services to accommodate this one. My assistants are preparing a cell for him even as we speak." He looked at me again. "Did you know that Napoleon Bonaparte had eyes of differing colors?"

"I believe I read that somewhere," I answered, remembering how my schoolmaster would compare any minor infraction on my part to the calamities of that Corsican upstart: *beware of Guthrie. Next he'll be sacking Moscow.*

"It may be that such eyes contribute to independence of thought," said Sir Marmion. "As grey eyes, such as Mister Holmes has, are said to indicate profundity of soul." He turned his attention to Holmes once again. "I am certain that your skull could tell us much about the intellect."

"You flatter me," said Mycroft Holmes, whose tone indicated he did not want to discuss this any longer.

"Hardly that. But let it go for now." He sat back comfortably. "You will be interested to know that my studies have determined that hysteria in women can be diagnosed through phrenology, and much unhappiness prevented by timely massage and electrical applications."

Mycroft Holmes nodded. "It would please many married men to have such techniques at their disposal, I should think."

"Yes. In time we should be able to address any number of chronic complaints through proper diagnosis and anticipatory treatment, such as electrical stimulation of the affected area of the skull." He paused, as if awaiting questions; when none came he went on, "I hope to learn much from this criminal, so that no one with dangerous tendencies indicated by the skull may be free to go about the world creating havoc everywhere."

"How complete are your studies?" Holmes asked. "Have you sufficient data to support your theories?"

"What I have encourages me," said Sir Marmion. "But I will need a great deal more than I have now before I can present wholly persuasive evidence to the scientific and medical community." He coughed delicately. "Understanding the human character is certainly a worthy goal to which to aspire, don't you think?"

"I think it is," said Holmes, a great deal more carefully than Sir Marmion perceived.

"Then you should be willing to let me do a reading of your skull, to add to my collection of data. Skulls such as yours are hard to come by. I should be grateful of an opportunity to take such a reading. You must not blame me for reiterating my request: I can study ordinary skulls, and those of the man, in plenty. But men of such high calibre as yourself are rare in my studies, and therefore all the more worthwhile."

"You continue to flatter me," said Mycroft Holmes, not best-pleased.

"Hardly. I am eager, I admit, to increase the information I have to hand, and to widen the samples from which I draw my conclusions. Scientists are like this, wouldn't you agree?" His eyes were bright as jewels and his enthusiasms was all but contagious.

"Many are, some are not," Mycroft Holmes responded.

"Oh, come, Mister Holmes. You cannot tell me that you lack curiosity. I will not credit it." He peered at the side of Mycroft

Holmes' head, just above the ear. "I should think you are most in-quisitive."

"A requirement of my work, I'm afraid," said Holmes, pouring more tea for himself. "Tyers will bring a new pot and a cup for you, Sir Marmion. If you will excuse me?"

"Of course, of course. I am the intruder." He beamed on the two of us, beneficent as Father Christmas. "You have been more than kind in receiving me on such short notice."

"I am interested in what you are doing, Sir Marmion. It is you who is being kind." He did not smile, but his demeanor was cordial. "So you would rather postpone our visit because you are going to be taking in a dangerous criminal. It seems a prudent measure to me."

"It is, it is," said Sir Marmion. "The other inmates we have are easily overset and many of them become agitated when any disruption occurs. You may well imagine how some of them may respond to the presence of so dangerous a man as this murderer we are going to keep in close confinement."

"I should think one need not be mad to have such a presence be upsetting to one's peace of mind," said Mycroft Holmes just as Tyers came in with breakfast on his butler's table. He set this down in the center of our chairs, saying, "I have made another pot of tea. And the clotted cream was delivered not half an hour ago." He stepped back and left.

"Sirloin, eggs, muffins, preserves, clotted cream," said Mycroft Holmes, enumerating the food set out. "And an omelette under the cover, Sir Marmion," he added as he lifted the lid.

"A fine collation," approved Sir Marmion. "You are most for-tunate in your staff, Mister Holmes."

"So I think," said Holmes tranquilly as he leaned forward to take his silverware in hand and set to eating.

I followed his example, feeling wolfish myself. The eggs were perfectly prepared, poached until the whites were firm but the yolks were runny. I consumed them gleefully, and had more tea when My-croft Holmes offered to pour another cup for me.

"Mister Holmes," said Sir Marmion as he cut off the end of his omelette—a ribbon of yellow cheese oozed out onto the plate where his knife had freed it—"do you think you might be able to come to my asylum at two on Friday afternoon?"

Holmes considered this. "I should think it could be arranged," he said, "if no emergency commands my presence at the Admiralty."

"That is understood, of course," said Sir Marmion, and had more omelette.

I recalled that would be the evening of the closing performance of *MacBeth*; I had supposed that it was my employer's intention to attend: he had already purchased tickets for Wednesday night's performance.

"With that caveat, I should think we can plan to come to . . . is it called Hawthorne End?"

"The town is," said Sir Marmion. "The asylum is an old estate from the time of the Stewarts: Hawtrees, between East Acton and Park Royal. You will find it readily enough. Give your name at the gate and you will be admitted."

"And how many inmates do you house there at present?" Mycroft Holmes asked.

"There are ninety-three currently in residence," said Sir Marmion. "About half of them are seen as untreatable. They are the ones for whom I hold the greatest hope, for with phrenology to guide us, and galvanic shock to treat the afflicted areas, I believe in time we will achieve significant improvement."

"Very commendable," said Holmes a bit remotely; he seemed far more interested in his sirloin and eggs than in what Sir Marmion was saying.

"Someone must do something to stop the degeneracy that is dragging down our lower classes—most of the incorrigible cases come from the lower and immigrant classes—and this may be the most promising avenue of treatment yet." He paused. "I have even got hope for the man we are taking into our care today."

"The criminal you mentioned? I believe you said he is a murderer?" Holmes prompted.

"The very same," said Sir Marmion. "I should hope that we will be able to do him some good." He paused again, this time to wipe his mouth with his serviette, and then went on with growing enthusiasm. "Imagine how much better the world will be when we eliminate the criminal element entirely! when we have put an end to feeble-mindedness, and to all forms of mental aberration that have plagued mankind down the ages!"

"A most laudable goal," said Mycroft Holmes with a hint of irony in his voice.

"I shall show you how it is to be done. You will endorse my work when you understand it better." He took another bite, then put down his fork. "I must thank you for your hospitality, Mister Holmes, but I fear I must leave you now. I look forward to our next meeting." With that he rose, put down his serviette, and made for the door. "I think I will stop on the way back to Hawtrees and find out how that young courier is doing. I trust he continues his recovery. Your man will show me out; do not disturb yourself." And with that, he was gone.

"Well," said Mycroft Holmes after a thoughtful moment of silence. "He certainly has given us a lot to think about. We will discuss it when your Miss Gatspy arrives."

"Do you still expect her?" I asked, surprised at how wistful I sounded.

"Of course, dear boy," he said serenely. "Don't you?"

FROM THE PERSONAL JOURNAL OF PHILIP TYRES
Sir Marmion has left and MH is still closeted with G. It is half-ten now, and the rain is getting heavier.

I have tended to my errands; I carried a quick note brought by Hastings from Inspector Strange to MH. I will shortly make a strong pot of tea for the Golden Lodge fellows, and one for Sid Hastings as well, to help them ward off the damp . . .

Chapter Seventeen

WHEN THE DOORBELL rang shortly before eleven, Mycroft Holmes allowed Tyers to answer it. "I am not leaping to my feet again without purpose," he announced, and an instant later, rose as Miss Gatspy's familiar voice said, "Tell me where they are, Tyers, and I will find them for myself."

"The library, ma'am," said Tyers.

Mycroft Holmes had just turned to the door when Miss Gatspy came into the room. Her fair hair was drawn back into a sensible bun, as if she were about to ride to hounds; wisps of curls escaped around her face fetchingly. Her ensemble was more than appropriate for London's streets: a suit of mulberry wool with modified leg-o'-mutton sleeves and a neat shirtwaist blouse beneath ornamented with a bit of lace at collar and cuffs.

"Good morning, Miss Gatspy," said Holmes, bowing her to the chair Sir Marmion had vacated; the butler's table—and the aftermath of breakfast—had been removed a short time before. "I had almost given you up."

"So you *were* expecting me," she said. "I thought you might be."

"Actually," he said, almost drawling, "I supposed you would come somewhat earlier in the morning. But here you are at last."

"You have had a busy morning thus far, Mister Holmes," she pointed out. "You could hardly want me to appear while you were speaking with the Turkish fellow, or Sir Marmion."

"You've either been watching or your Golden Lodge associates have kept you informed," said Mycroft Holmes at his driest.

"It has been some of both, I'd say," Miss Gatspy remarked breezily. She turned toward me. "There you are, Guthrie. Are you well?"

"Well enough, Miss Gatspy. And you? Do I see you well?" How pompous I sounded, and how little I had intended to.

"I have the constitution of an elephant," she said. "Surely you must be aware of it?"

"I know you have much stamina," I said. "If you will sit down?"

"With gratitude," she said, and sank into the reading-chair Sir Marmion had occupied so short a while ago. "You must be very busy, trying to find the common thread in all your disparate activities of the last few days. May I ask what progress you have made this morning?"

"You may ask," said Mycroft Holmes, sitting down as well; I hurriedly resumed my place. "It has been a most interesting day," he told her.

"In what sense?" she asked. "A weed in a cabbage patch is interesting, if it is the right weed. I would guess your current problems are more complex than that."

I shook my head. "You know very well they are more complex."

"Guthrie," Mycroft Holmes admonished me, then said to Miss Gatspy, "It began with poison-pen letters. Perhaps you would care to venture an opinion on them?" He reached out for the folder in which he had placed the scurrilous letters. "The same hand wrote them, you will notice."

"Yes, indeed," she said as she read quickly and attentively. "A bit overdone, I should say," she remarked. "They smack of a trap."

"They do, don't they?" Holmes agreed affably. "I thought so, too."

"What do you plan to do about them?" she asked. "Is there anything the writer might reveal to the press that would cause the kind of embarrassment claimed here?"

"Who knows?" Mycroft Holmes asked with a shrug as he took the letters back from Miss Gatspy. "Anyone might read perfidy into anything, recounting it with such a bias."

"Now you are not being entirely honest with me," she said. "But no matter. A man in your position must have any number of secrets he would not like to see exposed. I will not press you for details, but I warn you that you should be prepared for a difficult period in the next several months."

"I think so as well." Holmes leaned forward. "I may need some assistance from the Golden Lodge—assuming this originates with the Brotherhood."

"Which I suspect it does," said Penelope Gatspy. "And so do you, or you would not bother to mention it to me."

"You are most astute, Miss Gatspy," said Mycroft Holmes with false contrition.

"Yes. I am."

For several seconds, no one spoke, and then I remarked, "Mister Holmes said he wished to discuss Sir Marmion's visit after you arrived, Miss Gatspy. You know already that he visited here earlier."

"Good for you, Guthrie," Mycroft Holmes approved. "Keeping us to the straight and narrow." He leaned forward, looking directly into Miss Gatspy's face. "I need to know: what does your organization have by way of information on Sir Marmion?"

She thought about her answer. "He was knighted in 1887, six years ago, for his success in dealing with the mentally impaired. He has spent more than twenty years studying the mind and the skull. His papers have been published in all the best theoretical journals and he has addressed the Royal College of Surgeons on the subject of phrenology as a diagnostic tool. He has an excellent reputation in the scientific community. Everyone has acclaimed the results he has had with his electrical treatment of hysteria. His studies in phrenology are at the forefront of the subject. He keeps an asylum to the west of London; there have been favorable reports on his work there. His techniques are studied by many others in the medical community. There is talk of providing permanent funding for his asylum. It is said that he has had better results with the treatment of melancholia and hysteria than almost anyone else in England."

"Yes. Your records agree with mine." He began to twiddle his watch-fob. "And yet, he told me he is taking a dangerous murderer into his care. He implied the man's a maniac."

"And so he might," said Miss Gatspy. "He has done so in the past. Why should this be of interest to you?"

"True enough; he has treated other criminals. And yet, you know, I am perplexed. You see, whenever a perpetrator of a capital crime is moved in this country, for any reason, I am informed of it, and I have received no report in regard to this criminal. I have gone over my records, and I can find no mention of such a man, nor of any decision to put him into Sir Marmion's care. Very few people know I receive this report; it is the sort of information one does not want bruited about, so it is not astonishing Sir Marmion was unaware of it. That, Miss Gatspy, gives me to wonder."

She was engrossed in what he said. "Can there have been a delay in providing you the information?"

"It is possible, but highly unlikely. And I have never seen any mention of any such a proposed transfer to Hawtrees, this year, of a murderer or any other criminal. I find this most baffling. So I ask myself, what is the purpose of telling me about this fictitious criminal?" He cocked his head as he glanced from Miss Gatspy to me and back again. "What is he seeking to hide? For he has no reason to boast of this to me."

"I should think not," I said to Mycroft Holmes.

"You must have some preliminary theses on the question," said Miss Gatspy, ready to listen.

"That I do," he admitted, and went on slowly, thinking aloud.

"I think there is some reason Sir Marmion does not want me to visit Hawtrees before Friday. He cannot or will not tell me the real reason. This suggests to me that something is happening there he is not eager to have discovered, or he has someone on the premises he must conceal for the next few days. That would make my arrival inopportune, and so Sir Marmion wishes to discourage me."

"But he does not want you to know that your visit would be awkward," said Miss Gatspy.

"That seems to be a part of it. Why is that? Does he have an inmate who does not want his presence known? But who could be there?" Mycroft Holmes raised his hand. "Someone I would recognize, perhaps? Someone who is not supposed to be there."

"You mean Brotherhood men," I said before Miss Gatspy could speak.

"I may be jumping at shadows, but it seems to me that if I wished to hide with impunity, a madhouse might be an excellent place to do it. Odd behavior would not be commented upon, and most persons are inclined to ignore the mentally afflicted." Mycroft Holmes rubbed his chin, his eyes fixed on the middle distance. "I had hoped that the Golden Lodge could shed more light on this."

"You suspect a possible connection between Sir Marmion and the Brotherhood?" said Miss Gatspy.

"Yes. Or any similar affiliation." Holmes dropped his watch-fob and shook his head. "I would like to make some headway somewhere in this mare's nest." He sighed. "It is like one of those infernal Russian dolls, each containing another until the very heart of the matter is revealed."

I ventured to say, "A mixed metaphor, sir," in the hope of amusing him.

"My dear Guthrie, I do not aspire to persiflage, only to the apprehension of criminals, and enemies of Britain," he said with awful hauteur.

Miss Gatspy seconded him. "I cannot blame you for your misgiving. You may have discerned something we"—by which she meant the Golden Lodge—"have not. I will ask our members to turn their attention to that possibility, if you like."

"It may be helpful, but only if it can be accomplished in a day, two days at most. By then I fear the damage—whatever it may be—will be done. I have the . . . the pricking thumbs of *MacBeth* warning me that whatever is planned, it must happen soon. Do not tell me that I am succumbing to superstition, for that is not the case; I hope I have more intellectual rigor than that." Holmes got out of his chair and began to pace. "If Lady MacMillian reaches London, again to mix the metaphor, the genie will be out of the bottle."

"How is that metaphor mixed?" Miss Gatspy inquired, dimples appearing in her cheeks.

"Pricking thumbs have no commonality with genies," said Mycroft Holmes, dismissing the question with a wave of his hand. "Do not bother me with these trivial considerations. I have too much on my mind." He stared at her, his expression polite but unrevealing. "You need not remind me that I brought it up. I am aware of it. When I am much pressed, my thoughts spring every which way, like hares in March. And pray do not bring up Professor Dodgeson's cunning little satire."

"Then I shall remain mum on the subject," said Miss Gatspy at her most obliging. She got up from the chair; I rose with her. "If there is nothing more, I must go and send my superiors word of your need for information in regard to Sir Marmion's background. Is there anything other than his possible ties to the Brotherhood that you would like us to examine?"

Mycroft Holmes stood still for nearly five seconds. "Yes," he said. "If you would, review the titles of his published papers. There may be something there that we have overlooked."

"All right," she assured him. "I will. For whatever your reason may be, I will do this. And I will bid you good-day until tomorrow, gentlemen," she said as she went to the door. "Don't fear. Tyers will see me out."

I watched the door close behind her, and listened while her footsteps faded down the corridor to the entry-hall. Only when she had left the flat did I sit down again.

"A most illuminating twenty minutes," Mycroft Holmes approved. "If only all my colleagues would be so succinct. I am glad to have all the help I can on this, providing it is genuine and not deliberately misleading."

"Why would she provide you with inaccurate information?" I asked, unable to think that Miss Gatspy would do anything so reprehensible in this precarious situation.

"I have no idea. That doesn't mean she would not do it, particularly if her superiors instructed her to do so. She is their lieutenant, Guthrie, not ours, and she must answer to them, not to us." Holmes went to the shuttered window and peered out through the narrow gap between them. "The courier. The Turk. The police. Sir Cameron. Baron von Schattenberg. Herr Kriede. Lady MacMillian's uncles. Sir Marmion. It is all a muddle, and deliberately made so."

"Small wonder it rankles," I said. "Put like that, and no one could make sense of it."

"But there must be sense in it, somewhere," Mycroft Holmes said emphatically. "As deceptive as the Brotherhood can be, I must believe that there is a uniting purpose in all this. I know their ways and I recognize their methods here. What eludes me—infuriating as it is—is what they seek to accomplish in all this confusion. I am certain that we will shortly have to take the brunt of their machinations."

"More pricking thumbs?" I suggested.

"No. Or at least not entirely. I have had over twenty years of opposing them," he said bluntly. "The Brotherhood knows if ever they are to gain a foothold in England again, they must confuse and mislead me so that I cannot recognize their presence. All this confounding of incidents and information is clearly their work, and to the end of allowing Braaten and Vickers to enter the country undetected. Once they have the support of Lady MacMillian's uncles, removing them becomes a most ticklish operation." He slapped his hands together. "It is not easy to know where to begin, but I do not wish to wait for them to act again. Next time they may try something more deadly than attempting to ambush you in Green Park." He sighed. "If a Hungarian hunting pistol were the weapon used, then I would know where we stand."

"No doubt; but that might have had a more fatal conclusion if Miss Gatspy had not—" I said, only to be interrupted.

"I will vouch for her pluck and her self-possession, Guthrie. You need not fly to her defense." He pointed to the file that contained the two letters. "In your reading, keep a watch for phrases like the ones used in the letters. They may point the way to our opponents."

"You did suggest that Vickers might have dictated them to Braaten," I reminded him.

"And I still think it is not unlikely. But until I have more proof than intuition, I want to use deduction and logic wherever possible." He took another sheet of paper and cleaned the nib of his pen. "I must send a note round to Inspector Featherstone, one to Chief Inspector Pryce, one to Inspector Strange—a second imposition for him. There are far too many police in these matters, and they are caught up in the deception, beyond doubt. But who among them is doing the damage? To what purpose is he doing it? And how?"

"Have you any theories on that head?" I asked him, aware that he was troubled by the layers of questions he had to consider in his work.

"I have one or two, but they are not fully supported yet, and I will no longer allow them to force my hand." He dipped his pen in the inkwell and wrote quickly. "I'll have Tyers carry these. Hastings can drive him."

I was already concentrating on the material I was to review, but I said, "Do you think Mister Kerem will be able to have his brother's body released?"

"I hope not," said Mycroft Holmes. "Once it is gone, we will have no chance of finding out who butchered that unfortunate boy. Whom I suspect is *not* his brother."

"So you have said," I muttered.

"Yes, and I am persuaded it is the truth," he declared, continuing to write. "There is too much that makes no sense on the face of it if he is supposed to be a relative. If he is not who he claims to be, then some of his actions make more sense. They are also more sinister. Go back to your review, Guthrie. The sooner it is completed, the sooner we may begin to stop the miscreants at their own game."

I gave myself to my task, reading with attention and occasionally setting a page aside for closer scrutiny. Mycroft Holmes completed his letters and summoned Tyers.

"The direction for each is on the envelope. Have Hastings run you round to these places. Wait for a reply." He gave the envelopes to Tyers. "I am sorry to send you out in this weather, but this must be attended to."

"I will leave in ten minutes," said Tyers, taking the envelopes handed to him. "I must be sure the fire in the cooker is properly banked before I leave."

"Yes, indeed," Holmes approved. "It would not do to start a fire."

"My very thoughts," said Tyers, and left us alone again.

"I trust you are not finding the day too dull, Guthrie," Mycroft Holmes said as he went to take two volumes from the shelves. "I fear we will need hours and hours of meticulous review before we accomplish our task."

"I prefer it to being shot at," I said, hoping again to amuse him.

"No doubt," he said, pursing his lips with distaste.

I put my attention to the pages, and hardly moved but to turn them for the next few hours. I was dimly aware when Tyers returned and handed Mycroft Holmes two notes, and I accepted the cup of hot tea that was brought in at about half-two. By the time Holmes dressed for his walk across Pall Mall to his club, I had completed all but the last half-dozen pages, and was ready to take a turn about the room to clear my head. I had just risen to my feet when I heard Sutton arrive at the rear door. Little as I wanted to admit it, I was glad the actor had returned to bear me company.

"Hello, Guthrie," he said as he came into the library, casually but elegantly attired in a cut-away coat and silk gloves. "I thought you and Holmes were to have gone to the asylum today, and I was to visit the club."

"Sir Marmion has asked that we reschedule the meeting," I told him, and proceeded to sum up the purpose of his visit.

"So Holmes is going to the club; just as well," said Sutton. "I hope I may get my tea out of this." It was a gentle jibe, not intended to wound; Mycroft Holmes heard it from the door and answered him.

"You may get your supper as well, if you are minded to wait for it." He was almost ready to leave. "How did the audition go, dear boy?"

"It went well, I thought. I have been asked to come round next week to read with the cast, and then we shall see. I am encouraged." He smiled broadly. "My recent favorable notices have stood me in good stead."

"Excellent," Holmes approved. "I know you are capable of delivering a fine performance. I wish I could provide you with a letter of reference, but . . ." He shrugged.

"No doubt the director would not know what to make of such work," Sutton said lightly. "I am grateful to you for your offer."

Mycroft Holmes laid his hand on Sutton's shoulder. "There are few actors who can claim that their performances have saved lives, even helped to preserve Britain from her enemies."

"You praise me too much," said Sutton, a little color mounting in his cheeks. "I have done the work for which you hired me."

"And modest, to boot," Holmes said as he started toward the front of the flat. "How is it out there? Any slacking in the rain?"

"Not yet," said Sutton. "They say it will be another day or two before we see the sun again." He came over to the reading-chair and dropped into it.

"We shall all be growing fungus by then," Holmes complained. "Still, I should think it would be prudent to keep my rain-gear to hand." He went back to his dressing-room and emerged a short while later ready to depart. "I shall be back at the usual time; you might show Sutton the work we are doing. I would like his opinion when I return," he said, and went out the front.

"I take it matters have worsened since I last saw you," Sutton said in his best languorous air.

"Yes, they have," I said, and did my best to explain recent events to him in as clear a fashion as I could. When I had finished, I said, "So you see why Mister Holmes is perturbed."

"Perturbed? I would understand if he were raving; I would be," Sutton responded. He had listened with abstracted attention, staring up at the ceiling and hardly moving; now he sat forward and clasped his hands together. "I should think dealing with Sir Cameron may be one way to address the problem now."

"Why should we do that?" I asked, wanting to have as little as possible to do with Sir Cameron.

"Because he is a pig-headed, self-centered lout who is accustomed to using bullying and sullens to get his own way," said Sutton. "If you want to buy a little time, persuade him he is being taken advantage of, and let him take on the uncles and Baron von Schattenberg. He doesn't care a fig for diplomacy, and he has a reputation for making his own way. If you cannot turn that to advantage, you are not the man I know you to be."

I stared at him, the sense of his recommendation so over-whelmingly obvious that I chided myself for not seeing it before now. "I think it could work," I said at last.

Sutton grinned. "Of course it could work. And it would give you not one but two fewer problems to deal with: Sir Cameron would be aiding rather than thwarting you, and the Germans would have to make their arrangements with him instead of using Holmes as the negotiator."

"I doubt Holmes would accept that," I said, a bit regretfully.

"Then you must point out the benefits of such a ploy—at least for the next few days. From what you say, that is the crucial period, isn't it?" Sutton exuded confidence and optimism.

"It seems so," I said carefully.

"And since that is all you have to go on," Sutton said, "it may be as well to plan around what you actually know than around con-jecture." He got up abruptly. "I am famished. Do you suppose that Tyers could make me a sandwich to tide me over until supper?"

"I don't see why not. Ask him," I recommended as I began to put my mind to the best way to convince Mycroft Holmes to take Sutton's advice in regard to Sir Cameron.

Sutton was almost out the door when Tyers came in, pale as new cheese, a note in his hand. "What the devil—?" Sutton exclaimed.

I got to my feet and went to Tyers. "What has happened? You look dreadful." I had a momentary impression of Miss Gatspy lying in a pool of her own blood, and a chill went through me. Then I made myself listen to Tyers.

"This was sent from hospital," said Tyers, holding out the note. "The courier died."

I stood very still, my mind struggling to grasp what I had just heard. "What did you say?" I asked as I seized the note and read it.

Dear Mister Holmes,

As per your instructions, I am regretfully informing you that the Admiralty courier brought to us for treatment of a gunshot wound took a turn for the worse at about one in the afternoon. It was not the expected outcome, for he had been improving steadily until this. His fever, which had been diminishing, suddenly shot up, his lungs became congested, and in spite of our best efforts he died at eleven minutes past four. A notice has been sent by messenger to the Admiralty.

Most sincerely,

Yr svt,

Humphrey Johnathon Albert Rawlins, physician, FRCS

"He was recovering," said Tyers. "Our report yesterday was so encouraging." His shock was lessening, which relieved me.

"Bullet wounds are unpredictable," I reminded him. "If there was a sudden increase in infection, no one could have saved him."

"Yes," said Tyers, shaking his head. "I do not know how I shall tell Mister Holmes."

Sutton took over. "Leave that to us. You go put a spot of brandy in your tea and do what you can to steady yourself." He all but guided Tyers from the room, then came back to me. "He's knocked all to pieces. Do you know why?"

"No," I admitted. "I am baffled."

"Then perhaps Holmes will be able to enlighten us when he returns," Sutton said, sitting down once again. "Well, come on, Guthrie. We have work to do."

FROM THE PERSONAL JOURNAL OF PHILIP TYERS

I don't know how I managed to get supper on the table tonight, but it is done, and MH is still conferring with G and Sutton. I am still struggling with the courier's death, which has affected me deeply. He reminded me so much of my nephew, who is in the Navy, that I have allowed myself to become attached to his case, and this is the result. Young Clive is a good lad, and eager to advance himself on behalf of his country, as this courier was. That so much promise would come to such an abrupt end. I have seen it many times before without undue distress, but now I am as distraught as I would have been, had that lad been my nephew.

The Admiralty courier came and went at the usual hour, and for once I was able to offer the young officer a cup of tea for his trouble. I know I am trying to make amends to the lad who was killed, but I can think of nothing else to do.

No word yet from the police regarding the various inquiries in progress, which may mean there has been no progress, or it may indicate that there have been obstacles in their investigations, or deliberate avoidance of responding. We have received a preliminary report from Scotland Yard on the shot fired at Sir Cameron; there is nothing of use in it . . .

MH is sending G home shortly, for he intends to get an early start in the morning, by calling upon Sir Cameron at his leased house, where Sir Cameron has taken up residence today. I can see how a man would have to recruit his strength for such an encounter . . .

Sutton will stay over in case Holmes has need of him tomorrow. He says he would rather be useful here than fretting in his rooms, waiting to hear if he has got the part for which he auditioned . . .

I do wish it would stop raining.

Chapter Eighteen

THE HOUSE IN Deanery Mews was a grand establishment three stories high, built roughly a century ago, and maintained in good order ever since. As we trod up the steps to the front door shortly before eight in the morning, I could see that Mycroft Holmes was not looking forward to our visit.

A harried butler answered our knock, doing his best to mask his confusion with excessive dignity. "I am afraid Sir Cameron is not at home to visitors, gentlemen. I will see he is given your cards."

"Oh, we are not making a social call," said Mycroft Holmes cordially. "We are here regarding the attempt that was made on his life. We need more information if we are to pursue the case vigorously. Ask him to come down for Mister Holmes of the Admiralty and Mister Guthrie. We do not mind him meeting us en dishabille, and you may tell him so."

Short of throwing us out the door there was nothing the butler could do but take our over-coats and gloves and reluctantly admit us to Sir Cameron's hired house. "I will inform Sir Cameron you are here," he said stiffly.

"Much appreciated," Holmes told him. He nodded toward three crates standing near the drawing room door. "I see Sir Cameron is providing some of his own furnishings."

"Yes. They arrived from Scotland last night," said the butler, more forthcoming than I would have expected him to be.

"I am sure Sir Cameron is pleased," said Mycroft Holmes. "If you will tell us which room has a fire lit, Mister Guthrie and I will repair there to wait for Sir Cameron. Tell him we are entirely at his service."

Nonplused, the butler left us at the door of a small sitting room just off the main corridor. It was a charming room on the east side of the house, and, were it not raining from low-scudding clouds, the room would be filled with light. As it was, there was a small fire on the hearth to take off the worst of the chill, and one of the gas-lamps was lit for our convenience.

"At least Sir Cameron should be sober at this hour," I said, trying to find an amusing side to this most annoying chore.

"Hung-over, most likely," Mycroft Holmes said, taking his place on a Queen Anne settee. "He is apt to be in a devilish temper."

"And when is he not?" I asked. "Drunk or sober, the man is—"

"—a boor. Yes, I know," said Holmes. "As we both have good reason to know. Still, I do think for once that may work to our advantage." He smiled in mild amusement. "I believe that there is much to be gained if only Sir Cameron can be nudged into digging his heels in on our account."

"I wish you had allowed me to bring my portfolio. I feel quite naked without it." I chose a seat at a small writing desk next to the window. "More dreary weather," I said, staring out at the rain.

"At least it is likely to slow the efforts of those seeking to shoot Sir Cameron or any of us. With such pluvial excesses, taking aim at any distance is hardly possible." He had surrendered his over-coat and gloves at the door, as had I, and now he rubbed his hands together to keep them from getting cold. "I hope Sir Cameron will order more wood for the fire. These old houses—like my flat in Pall Mall—have not converted to burning coal. I would prefer a wood-fire in any case. It is nicer to smell."

"I cannot argue," I said. "But heating a house with wood is costly."

"Guthrie, you remind me you are a Scot." He did his best to chuckle at his remark, but the sound was hollow and quickly died.

For ten minutes or so we remained in silence, waiting for Sir Cameron to make his appearance. When he finally came into the sitting room, it was clear he had just risen and probably had not slept alone, for there was a red mark in the shape of lips at the top of his chest where his nightshirt was open and his dressing gown of heavy hunter-green velvet did not cover.

"What in the name of the pox are you doing here at this ungodly hour, Holmes?" he demanded as he banged the door closed behind him.

"I am doing my best to protect you, Sir Cameron," Mycroft Holmes answered with the demeanor of conviction.

"So you say!" He tramped across the flowered carpet as if to deprive the loomed buds of life. "I am not accustomed to being dragged from my bed at dawn by a civil servant who has failed to do any of the things he is supposed to do on my behalf." He folded his arms and glared at Holmes; as usual, he paid no attention to me, and I was at liberty to scrutinize him: I noticed the puffiness around his eyes and the slightly sallow color of his skin, the sag beginning beneath his jaw, and the first touch of grey in his ginger hair.

"I apologize for inconveniencing you, Sir Cameron," Holmes soothed. "But we must ask you to consider again the matter of Lady MacMillian's escort."

"Her uncles? You're not here about that, are you?" He shook his head. "You have a bee in your bonnet about those uncles of hers."

"As you should," Mycroft Holmes said. "You have forgot the Married Women's Property Act, haven't you? You know that Lady MacMillian is entitled to claim all your marriage settlements so long as she is in the British Isles. With her uncles to assist her, she may be able to demand the income of her spousal grants, and no court in the land would refuse her. If she is not accompanied by her uncles, any suit she would bring would have a significantly smaller chance for success." He stood still, letting Sir Cameron think through the potential monetary loss any such claim would mean to him.

"She wouldn't," Sir Cameron blustered.

"Perhaps not," Mycroft Holmes allowed. "But you may be sure her uncles would."

Sir Cameron's scowl deepened. "You are telling me that my own wife wants to claim her marriage grants?" He took a turn about the room. "She has come into property of her own. What can she want with anything of mine?"

"Exactly," Holmes said. "You must see it is her uncles who are behind this scheme." He paused as if trying to soften a blow. "You have put yourself in a difficult position, coming to meet her here in London where you have your title but not your position to bolster you."

"What are you saying?" Sir Cameron's face was taking on a purple tinge as his temper mounted.

"I am saying only that were you in Scotland, you would retain more of your authority than you do here in England. I think it was a clever move, coming to London. It makes her uncles more able to pursue you on her behalf."

I watched Sir Cameron weigh the matters in his mind, and I saw that his venality was uppermost in his considerations. "Why should it be any different here than in Scotland? I am a knight and a gentleman in either place."

"Of course," said Mycroft Holmes with mendacious sympathy. "You are also an acknowledged hero; the public admire you. This admirable reputation makes you noticed in the world, and there are those who seek nothing more than to discredit those who have risen the highest in the esteem of the British people. It would be a most distressing development to see you made into the butt of vulgar jokes all because your wife's uncles attempt to claim what is rightfully hers, here, in the full glare of the press and the music-hall jesters." He paused. "I do not want to deprive you of anything to which you are entitled, but I fear that once Fleet Street gets wind of this, they will trumpet it about in a manner that will be more scandalous than accurate, and any efforts on your part to diminish the furor would probably lead to more uproar."

Sir Cameron cleared his throat. "What about that shot fired at me? Could that have anything to do with—?"

"With your wife's uncles? I cannot say for sure that they did or they did not, but it might be most prudent to return to Scotland, at least until we can determine what role, if any, those gentlemen had in your recent fortunate escape. It should not take too long. That way, you will have the authority in the meeting, not the uncles. You will not be at the beck and call of Baron von Schattenberg, either." Mycroft Holmes made his face into a mask of commiseration. "I know that retreat is repugnant to you, but if you are willing to leave London for a fortnight, then the Admiralty could determine what part, if any, Lady MacMillian's uncles played in that unhappy event."

This was more than Sir Cameron was willing to accept. "I am not going to be driven out of this house when my goods have only just arrived."

"No, certainly not," said Holmes hastily. "But if you go for a fortnight, your staff can have all in readiness for when your wife finally arrives, without her uncles to bedevil you."

Sir Cameron prowled the room like a caged animal. "I don't like it," he said at last. "I am not a fool to be hounded by ambitious men. No, I don't like it."

"What don't you like, Sir Cameron?" Holmes inquired, the very model of solicitude.

"I don't like having my hand forced by a pack of greedy Germans who ought to know better than to trespass on my good nature," he said roundly. "But I do see the wisdom of what you say, Holmes. I am not one to take risks foolishly."

I recalled the petulance and cowardice I had seen Sir Cameron display, and I agreed heartily and ironically with him.

"You have a keen grasp of these matters," Holmes agreed. "No doubt you will want to think over what we have discussed, so I will not keep you much longer." He went up to Sir Cameron, the very image of concern. "It is imperative that you wire your orders to Holland, and inform your wife, who is there with her uncles, that you will be unable to meet with her for two weeks. You may claim press of business, if you like, or any other reason that will not put her uncles on the alert. If you offer to pay for her accommodations in Amsterdam, I am certain she will consent to remaining there until you are ready to receive her."

"Sans uncles," said Sir Cameron.

"Naturally," said Mycroft Holmes. "You will have to make arrangements in that regard, but I doubt those men want to cool their heels for two weeks. If you are in London, they may come, regardless. But if you are in Scotland, they will not."

"They have no stomach for the lion's den," said Sir Cameron smugly. "Who could blame them?"

"Precisely," said Mycroft Holmes, turning the word to outrageous flattery.

"I could mention the weather, and advise them not to attempt the crossing while the storm is raging. In this weather, no one is going to cross the Channel unless it is absolutely necessary, in any event," said Sir Cameron, as if the weather was his personal ally.

"Very likely, Sir Cameron," said Mycroft Holmes, admirably concealing his growing exasperation. "But it would be wisest to inform Lady MacMillian that you will be away in Scotland for—"

"A fortnight. Indeed. I shall use the time to consult my solicitor. If Lady MacMillian has come into her inheritance—and she has—it is most unseemly of her to want to claim her marriage portion from me. This is what comes of giving women property rights. Their natural greed is allowed free reign and all of us who are married men suffer because of it." He tugged at the sash of his dressing gown. "It may be as you say, and her uncles are promoting her desire for possessions, but I know her, and she is a worldly German woman, and I would not put it past her to want to gain control of as much of my fortune and lands as she can."

This display of pettiness astonished me, even in one such as Sir Cameron. I had not thought he could cherish such small-minded resentments as he currently displayed. I was tempted to ask him if he were sure of himself, but I supposed he must be, and would be offended by any doubts I expressed; I exchanged a knowing glance with my employer and continued to watch their exchange.

"That may be the case; if it is, it would be wise to prepare yourself for that eventuality." Holmes hesitated, as if uncertain whether to continue or let well enough alone.

"Yes." He laid his thick hand on Mycroft Holmes' shoulder. "You have been a good friend to me this day, Holmes. You need not fear that I will forget your timely warning, or your efforts on my behalf."

"Thank you, Sir Cameron," said Holmes with a humility I knew to be foreign to him.

"You are a good man," Sir Cameron added, and turned away. "I will wait until this afternoon, and then I will inform my staff that I have had word from the north and must return at once to Scotland. I will leave my staff here to ready the place for my return, and I will take the train north tomorrow. That should be soon enough for our purposes, don't you think?"

"If you make sure to send word to Lady MacMillian, yes, I should think so," said Holmes. "If you like, I shall call on Baron von Schattenberg and inform him of these developments, so you will be spared one more chore."

"A fine notion, Holmes," said Sir Cameron. "You have a fairly sharp mind when you decide to use it."

I could see that Mycroft Holmes was both amused and aggravated by this supercilious praise. "I am pleased you notice."

Sir Cameron swung around. "I am not one of those dolts who thinks of nothing but himself, and cannot appreciate virtue in anyone but himself."

"You are good to say so," Mycroft Holmes responded, his grey eyes snapping; I thought he was about to laugh aloud.

"Yes," said Sir Cameron in fine self-approval. With bluff courtesy he cocked his head toward the door. "Well, I will not keep you. No doubt you have other duties than looking after me. You have been diligent on my behalf, and I will not forget it."

"You are good to say so, Sir Cameron," Holmes repeated.

"Credit where credit is due," said the man whose knighthood came as a result of Mycroft Holmes' determination and bravery, which Sir Cameron had managed to represent as his own.

"A fine policy," said Holmes, motioning to me to come with him to the door. "Guthrie and I have other errands yet this morning. We will leave you to your plans." He halted at the door. "If I were you, I should not venture out today. That assassin may still be searching for you, for the police have not yet made an arrest in that matter."

"What else do you expect of the police? Laggards, all of them, even that popinjay Pryce." He stifled a yawn. "Beech will show you out."

"Thank you for your time, Sir Cameron," said Mycroft Holmes as he opened the door and all but shoved me through it ahead of him.

"Think nothing of it," was Sir Cameron's magnanimous reply just before the door closed.

"Not one word, Guthrie, until we're outside," Holmes whispered ferociously, then nodded to the approaching butler. "We're leaving now."

"I will show you out, sir, if you don't mind," the butler said as if he suspected Mycroft Holmes might try to purloin the silver.

"Of course," said Holmes, meekly following the butler—Beech, as Sir Cameron called him—to the door. "I am sorry to have disturbed your morning," he said as we went out of the house.

Sid Hastings was waiting at the end of Deanery Mews; he gave Lance the office and came to pick us up, cheerful in spite of the rain. "Hardly anyone came into the Mews while you were inside. There was a tradesman, but he went around back."

There was nothing remarkable in this, and I wondered aloud why Hastings had seen fit to mention it.

"Well, Mister Guthrie, I noticed he was carrying a couple of large packages, one long and thin, one squat. I couldn't for the life of me decide what they must contain," said Hastings.

Something in this description alerted Holmes, who said, "What do you mean, long and thin?"

"Oh, perhaps thirty inches long and ten inches wide. The other case was about eighteen inches on a side," Hastings said with the idle curiosity of a man who spends a great deal of time observing the world.

At that, Holmes pulled the steps to and sat forward on the seat. "Take us round to the back, Hastings, at once. And be careful."

Hastings put Lance in motion, and headed for the alleyway between houses. "Is something amiss, sir?" he asked as he maneuvered the reins.

"I hope not. It is possible," Holmes said grimly. "After our interview this morning, I cannot think we should have another—" He broke off, pointing. "There!" he exclaimed.

I saw a man in tradesmen's garments hunkered down behind Sir Cameron's house. He had made himself a blind between the house and the stable that serviced the entire Mews; he had a long-barreled Hungarian boar-pistol in his hands and was practicing his aim as Mycroft Holmes leaped from the still-moving cab and rushed at him. I followed after him, ready to do my part, whatever that might be.

The miscreant lurched to his feet and started to run only to have Holmes slam into him and grapple with him, pulling him to the paving stones.

"Guthrie," Holmes panted. "Secure his hands."

I had nothing in the way of rope, so I removed my tie and used it to confine the gunman's hands at the small of his back. The man fought as best he could, kicking and twisting with all the strength of desperation, keeping silent the whole time; when he was as bound as he could be, Mycroft Holmes tugged him to his feet.

"Gather up his pistol and its case, if it is here, and find that other case Hastings saw," Mycroft Holmes ordered me. "It will be crowded with three of us, but there's nothing for it." He shoved the man toward Sid Hastings' cab. "Get in, sir. And do not attempt an escape. Unless you can outrun a horse, you have no prayer of getting away." The man shot a vitriolic look at Holmes, his teeth flashing in a snarl, but he got into the cab without incident, and Holmes followed him at once. "Guthrie, ride with Hastings. You'll get wet, I'm afraid, but there is nothing for it."

"If Hastings does not mind, why should I?" I said, and climbed into the box.

Hastings shifted his position—not an easy thing, for the box was small and cramped, being designed for one man—and put Lance into motion again. "Most peculiar," he remarked to me as we once again entered Deanery Mews.

I looked at him. "How do you mean?"

"A man, wanting to take a shot at Sir Cameron—if that was what he was doing—choosing to fire in the service alley rather than in the street." Hastings leaned down and called to Mycroft Holmes, "Will you want to go to Scotland Yard, then?"

"I think that might be best," said Holmes. "I suppose they will want to know what this fellow has been up to."

"Right you are," said Hastings, straightening back up.

"There was no cover in the street," I said, in response to his earlier remark.

"What's that?" Hastings asked, confused.

"You said it was strange he should try to fire in the service alley," I reminded him. "He is noticeable in the street, and not so in the service alley. If Sir Cameron called for his coach, then the fellow we have in custody might have had an easy shot, and a great deal of confusion in which to make good his escape."

"I take your point, Mister Guthrie," said Hastings. "That I do. But what if Sir Cameron did not call for his coach? The fellow might have spent the day waiting to no purpose."

"Sir Cameron might not have left his house at all today," I pointed out. "No matter where that man waited, he had no assurance of taking his shot."

"Just my point," said Hastings as he moved his cab between a brewer's wagon pulled by two enormous Belgian draught horses and a Clarence drawn by a spanking pair of matched bays; there was a crest on the panel, but I could not make it out.

I considered what Hastings had said, then exclaimed, "Turn around, Hastings. At once."

"Why should I do that, Mister Guthrie?" asked Hastings so calmly that I was minded to take the reins myself.

"Because you're right. This man is not the assassin. He is the decoy. He was meant to be discovered so that we would not bother to look further for anyone who might intend to do Sir Cameron harm." As I said this, I added to myself that such a list would be long.

"But you don't think someone is going to make an attempt on Sir Cameron's life?" Hastings protested.

"What better time?" I leaned down and quickly repeated to Holmes what I had just said to Hastings. "Well, sir? What do you think?"

Mycroft Holmes sighed. "He's right, Hastings. Turn back."

Beside him, the man we had caught began to squirm, kicking and flinging himself about as much as the confined space would allow. His eyes were angry, but he kept his teeth clenched together even as he struggled.

"Stop it," Holmes ordered him, and when the man did not, Holmes struck him a sharp blow on the side of the head that stunned him. "Next time I shall knock you unconscious," Holmes warned the fellow.

There were cries and curses from other drivers as Hastings turned his cab around and started back toward Deanery Mews. I clung onto the top of the cab as it swayed and lurched about. As I recovered my balance, I saw traffic slowing ahead. "What now?"

"There's a cart down," said Hastings laconically.

"Can you get around it?" I asked, leaning forward in the hope of seeing our way clear of it.

"Not readily," said Hastings. "Look about you, Mister Guthrie. Everyone is at the same impasse."

I swore, and apologized for my unseemly outburst, and was about to ask Mycroft Holmes if he had any instructions for me when the man we had taken in hand staggered out of the cab, and, his hands still tied behind him, began to stumble through the increasing tangle of traffic.

FROM THE PERSONAL JOURNAL OF PHILIP TYERS

MH has still not returned from Sir Cameron's, although it is well passed the hour I expected him. I am not yet worried, but I am not entirely sanguine, either. Sutton has wakened and has offered to disguise himself in order to go about looking for MH and G. I have said it is not wise, and perhaps he is persuaded . . .

The Admiralty have sent word that there will be services tomorrow for the courier. I would like to attend to pay my respects, but MH may not be able to spare me for the morning.

I must go to the greengrocer within the hour to pick up the cabbage I have ordered, and a string of onions. If there are any suitable potatoes, I will buy them as well. Then to the tea-merchant for Assam, Lady Grey, and Darjeeling. How the demands of every-day life intrude on us all.

Chapter Nineteen

I VAULTED DOWN from the box and began to run after the fleeing man. Around me the press of wagons, carriages, vans, and cabs made progress slow, but I forced my way through the crowd, shoving horses and pushing men aside as I went. The rain did nothing to make my efforts easier; I did my best to keep the fellow in sight, but in the confusion I lost track of him, and wasted almost a minute staring about me in the hope of discovering where he had gone. Finally I saw him blunder onto the side-walk, thrusting himself among the passers-by, many of whom drew back in alarm. I hurried after him, using my elbows and shoulders to clear the way, but lost him once again; I was distracted by a coachman who bellowed insults and imprecations down at me in a Cornish accent so deep he might have been speaking a foreign language. I paused to make a gesture of apology before resuming the chase. This time I cast about for some little time, and was rewarded by finding my tie, dropped in a puddle and smirched, as the only trophy of this most frustrating hunt. I picked it up and began to make my way back through the tangle to Sid Hastings' cab, growing more despondent with each step. When I finally reached that vehicle, it had progressed less than fifty feet from where I had left it. I came to the side, and found it difficult to look at Mycroft Holmes. "I'm sorry, sir. I couldn't catch him."

"Small wonder, in all this," said Holmes with a sigh. "Well, there's nothing for it. He chose his escape-site quite strategically. I only wish I could have seen who was in that spider that took him up; a fine pair of matched red-roans pulled it."

"The driver had a patch over one eye," Sid Hastings added helpfully. "They turned west, but that may be nothing more than an attempt to misdirect us."

"Perhaps the Golden Lodge guards saw some of this. They may be able to provide us with information," I said, trying to make the best of a bad situation.

"If they are watching us, and if they are willing to tell us anything, then perhaps they may be worth asking," said Mycroft Holmes. "But I would prefer not to have to rely on them."

"Don't you trust them?" I asked as I got into the cab dejectedly.

"Not entirely. As no doubt they do not trust me; they have their work to do and I have mine," he said, sinking back on the squabs. "I only hope we may be in time."

"You are not going to blame *this*"—I flung my hand in the direction of the traffic jumble—"on the Brotherhood, are you, sir?"

"No," he conceded. "Not that I would put such a ruse past them, but as they needed to make good their escape, this works against them as much as it does against us. That spider might have been enmeshed as we are, and then there would be no escape, for culprit or henchman. I would not be surprised to see them use a traffic snarl to their advantage, as they seem to have done now. But to rely on one to do their bidding, no, I don't think even they would venture anything so foolhardy." He folded his arms.

"And you are sure it is the Brotherhood we are dealing with?" I did not question his conviction, but I was not so willing to believe them capable of so extensive a machination.

"As sure as I may be without having them in my sights; that Hungarian pistol is as good as a signature," Mycroft Holmes answered, a bit of disgust making him impatient. "And now this. It is just the sort of thing they do, Guthrie: throw their opponents into confusion, and then use the turmoil to their advantage. They know how to turn misfortune to their purpose. In this case, the traffic added to their plans; you may be sure they know how to put public disorder of all sorts to use." He was growing as morose as I was. He tapped on the roof of the cab. "Get round this as best you can, Hastings, and return us to Deanery Mews."

"Do you expect an attack to be made on Sir Cameron?" I asked, trying to put myself in a semblance of order.

"I think something may happen that would be detrimental to our current plans." He sat forward again. "They do not want Lady MacMillian to arrive here without her uncles, that much is certain. So I must be on guard against anything that may make such an event more likely, such as Sir Cameron being badly injured. If he is in hospital, then who would think it strange of his wife to rush to his side, uncles in tow? So they will try again to have him incapacitated."

"Or killed," I added.

"That would be a trifle too extreme, I suspect," said Mycroft Holmes as the cab began to move again. "I think they would prefer Sir Cameron paralyzed than six feet under, for with their estrangement still in effect, her claims would be limited indeed."

"I take your meaning, sir," I said, aware that the reconciliation would have greater significance than I had assumed it would. "If Sir Cameron is alive but an invalid, he is at the mercy of his wife."

"And she is at the mercy of her uncles," said Holmes, watching as Sid Hastings expertly threaded his cab through the knot of vehicles and beyond the worst of it. "Very good, Hastings. I will see you have something for your four children as a sign of my appreciation."

"Most kind, sir," said Hastings, beginning to whistle as we re-traced our route to Deanery Mews.

Beech, the butler, was no more pleased to see us a second time than he had been an hour earlier. "Sir Cameron is in his bath, gentlemen. I am afraid he cannot receive you."

"Never mind. This is not so much for his ears as for yours; in fact it would be as well for him to know nothing of our conversation. I need you to listen and pay attention, Beech," said Mycroft Holmes, and went on confidingly, "As you may know, a shot was taken at your employer on Saturday evening as he was in Mount Street."

"Everyone in this house knows about that incident, sir," said Beech stiffly.

"Yes. Well, you will understand how serious it is when I tell you that the assassin is still at large. As we left this house this morning, we surprised a man with a hunting pistol setting a firing place for himself in your service alley."

"Lawks!" the butler exclaimed.

"Exactly." Mycroft Holmes pulled the butler away from the door in order to speak to him in a more confidential fashion. "We tried to apprehend him, but he escaped into traffic, so now we must warn you that Sir Cameron is still in danger, which is why we have urged him to remove from the metropolis for a week or two. In the meantime, everyone in this house must be on his guard."

Beech bobbed his head to show he understood. "You say the culprit was in the service alley?"

"Just so," said Holmes.

"And he got away?" There was real fear in the man's eyes now, and his voice rose by a major third.

"I am sorry to say that he did," Holmes told him somberly. "You cannot imagine how distressed I am by this turn of events. I fear the man may return here to make another attempt. If he should be so brazen, I hope you and the staff will summon the police at once, and do your utmost to keep him from harming Sire Cameron."

"Oh, yes," said Beech. "How terrible it would be if he were injured."

"I see we understand one another," said Mycroft Holmes, giving the butler a gesture of approval. "Err on the side of caution, Beech. Rather be safe than sorry." He made the two old saws sound original and urgent.

"Truly, sir," said Beech. "It was good of you to come back to warn us. I am sure Sir Cameron will be grateful."

I thought that unlikely in the extreme, but I said nothing as Mycroft Holmes went on. "Sir Cameron will need your sharp eyes and your wits."

"Right you are, sir," said Beech. "I will brief the staff at supper. There are only six of us, but I give you my word they shall all do their duty."

"Very good, Beech," said Holmes. "I will stop round tomorrow, or Mister Guthrie will come in my place, to have your report."

The butler didn't salute, but I could see he wanted to. I spoke up. "I will give Mister Holmes your full account, whatever it may be."

Mycroft Holmes was edging back toward the door. "Keep an eye out for any strangers, of any stripe. Tradesmen are as questionable as men in carriages."

"We will be diligent, Mister Holmes, my word of honor." He stood very straight as we reached the door.

"Thank you, Beech," said Mycroft Holmes as we went out onto the front step once more.

Again Sid Hastings pulled up and took us aboard, then said, "Still want Scotland Yard, sir?"

Holmes frowned with thought. "Not just yet. I'll write a note for you to carry round to Inspector Featherstone, and one to Chief Inspector Pryce. I'll try to arrange a convenient time to speak with them today or tomorrow. We'll peel the layers off this conundrum or I'll know the reason why."

"I am certain of it, sir," I said, taking heart from his determination.

"Yes. I have knocked their kingpin out from under them, and now they are going to have to scramble. That may give them away." He glared at the rain. "This infernal weather. I know it is very English, and I'd far rather have rain than fog, but still—" He stopped. "I suppose I should also keep your Miss Gatspy informed."

"I am sure Miss Gatspy would appreciate it, as would her superiors," I said, making a point by leaving out any pronoun whatsoever, of identifying her independence from me.

"Always so proper, Guthrie," said Holmes, amused. "Indubitably, you have the right of it: no doubt she and the Golden Lodge will be more useful if we work in concert on this occasion."

"But I thought you didn't trust them," I remarked.

"I don't," Mycroft Holmes said curtly, and fell silent for the rest of the ride back to Pall Mall.

Tyers was preparing a bag for the laundress when we arrived. "You are back early. I did not expect you for another hour or so," he said as he abandoned his chores and set about putting on the kettle for tea. "Give me your over-coats and I will set them to dry in the kitchen, near the cooker. They will be damp until evening if I don't."

We both complied at once. "Any news this morning while we were out?" Holmes asked as he handed his over-coat and muffler to Tyers.

"There is a note from Baron von Schattenberg; it arrived a quarter of an hour ago. I put it on the table in your study." Tyers took my over-coat, put it on a hanger, and prepared to go back to the kitchen. "Sutton is out for the morning. He's gone over to the theatre."

"Did he say when he'd be back?" Mycroft Holmes asked, interested but unworried.

"He said he would be back by two, no later. He understands that he is to go to the club in your stead this afternoon." Tyers was almost to the kitchen and had to raise his voice to be heard.

"Yes. I have too much to do." He motioned to me to follow him into the study. "You will need a new tie, I fear," he said to me as he sat down. "I will be glad to see you are supplied one from the stores of those Sutton has in the back."

"It isn't immediately urgent," I said, sitting down opposite my employer. "Unless you are expecting callers this morning."

"My dear Guthrie, given the last five days, I hardly know what to expect." he thought for a long moment. "I think it might be best if you go and select a tie now. Then if we have anyone arrive, you will not raise any questions."

"Right away, sir," I said, getting up again and leaving him alone in the study. As I passed through the kitchen, I saw that Tyers was baking some cheese with walnuts to augment our tea. "It smells wonderful," I told him as I went into the rear and began to look at the labels on the drawers behind the racks of clothing. This was the place the courier had been concealed, and I had an unpleasant twinge as I looked about me, recalling the sad fate of that young man. Finally I opened the drawer marked *neckwear* and selected a tie of deep-green with a hint of blue-black in the weave. It was handsome without being showy, and it was proper without being grand. I slipped it around my neck, refixed my collar-stud and knotted the tie using the oval mirror hung there for that purpose. It was set higher in the wall than was comfortable for me—intended for Mycroft Holmes and Edmund Sutton, both of whom were over six foot—but I managed well enough. By the time I returned to the study Tyers was serving tea and Mycroft Holmes was scribbling an answer to Baron von Schattenberg's note; two other sealed envelopes lay beside his elbow.

"Much better, Guthrie," he approved as I came into the room. "It appears the Baron is distressed at Sir Cameron's sudden intention to return to his Scottish estates for the next fortnight. I am about to reassure him that this is a very good thing."

"And what reason have you given for that?" I asked as I sat down and accepted a cup of Lady Grey tea from Tyers.

"I am explaining to him that with the police investigation in full swing, it would hardly be possible to receive Lady MacMillian in the manner she deserves, and that a delay is preferable to embarrassment. I expect the Baron will agree when he thinks it over. His position is awkward enough without Lady MacMillian being present." He signed the note, folded it and stuffed it into an envelope. "Another missive for Hastings to deliver."

"He will tend to it as soon as you like," said Tyers, as he took the envelope and prepared to leave the room.

"And the police—what about them?" I asked as I tasted the tea; it was still hot enough to scald, and I set the cup down again.

"I will have notes for them, and for Chief Inspector Alexander of Customs; I will also send word to Inspector Strange for his opinion of our most recent developments." He saw me look at him in some confusion, and he explained, "I have a question or two about Lionel

Featherstone's investigation, and Customs should be able to bring me abreast of matters."

"Is this something Inspector Strange recommends?" I asked.

"In part," said Holmes, volunteering nothing more on that head, but adding, "I am aware that there are more issues here than those we have discerned so far. If I can review all the opinions held by the police and others, I might be able to make some sense of it all."

"You are going to put them against one another," I said, as much warning him as describing his tactics. "You will have more of Scotland Yard distressed than Inspector Wallace."

"Had Wallace kept to his work, he would have had nothing to fear from me; he was slipshod and took too much for granted," said Holmes, dismissing my concern without more than a slight frown. "Let his fellow-officers learn from him."

I knew there was nothing more to say that would soften his sense of the police. "Do you think you will have a quick response?"

"I had better." Mycroft Holmes took out another sheet of paper and began to write on it.

I tried my tea again and was just able to swallow it. "What would you like me to do, sir?" I asked when I had drunk half a cup.

"For the moment, I would like you to review the sailings for yesterday and today, from the London docks." He nodded to a stack of papers that were under the seal of the Admiralty. "I want to know what ships have departed, or are scheduled to depart."

"Departures?" I repeated, surprised at the request.

"Yes. I will need to have that information to hand shortly, I think," he said as he continued writing. "This is to Inspector Featherstone, and I hope it will bring us information at once." He put the note in the envelope, sealed and addressed it. "This is to Chief Inspector Pryce; I am informing him of Sir Cameron's imminent journey to Scotland. This, too, should elicit a swift response." When he finished writing this note, he made its envelope ready for delivery, then began another note for Chief Inspector Alexander of Customs. "As soon as these are in the hands for which they are intended, I shall expect a flurry of developments. I will weigh what I am told against the information Inspector Strange provides me." He began another note, writing swiftly, and he addressed another envelope, then he sat back and looked at what he had done; there was a hard amusement in his grey eyes. "You will see how quickly these men will spring into action."

"And if they do not?" I inquired.

"That, in itself, will tell a tale," said Holmes. He completed his notes, rose, and took them to Tyers in the kitchen.

I sat drinking the last of my tea, trying to put behind me the sensation that there had been a change that made us more closely involved in these complicated cases. I put my teacup down and did my best to anticipate all that I might be called upon to do. There were so many avenues I might explore that I was nearly overwhelmed by them all. I was reviewing what we had been told of Jacobbus Braaten's arrival in England over the last several days, when there came a sharp knock on the door. I rose automatically, prepared to answer the summons if Tyers should still be with Mycroft Holmes; it wasn't necessary, for Tyers hastened down the corridor and Holmes strolled back into the study.

"I admit I am curious," he said, acknowledging the knocking from the front door.

"Do you have any notion who it might be?" I asked.

"I have guesses, not notions," said Mycroft Holmes, sitting down and pouring more tea into his cup. "Here, Guthrie. Have another cup."

I did as he required, listening all the while to the urgent sound of the caller. I could not make out the words, but the tone of voice was unmistakably concerned.

A minute or two later Tyers came to the study door and said, "Inspector Lionel Featherstone to see you, sir."

"And he hasn't yet received my note—impressive, to be so beforehand," said Holmes. "His errand must be pressing, indeed. Send him in, Tyers."

"Shall I remain?" I asked.

"Of course, dear boy. I rely upon you to pay close attention to all we hear." He stood up again as if performing a necessary duty, and prepared to greet Inspector Featherstone.

I, too, rose, and a moment later, Inspector Featherstone bustled into the study, his face flushed, his hair damp, and his expression dismayed.

"Inspector Featherstone. What am I to do for you?" Holmes asked, indicating one of the straight-backed chairs that stood about the study.

"The boy's body is missing, and the Turk is gone," the Inspector announced without any introductory remarks or even a greeting.

"Good gracious," said Mycroft Holmes, not nearly so astonished as I was. "And when was this discovered?"

I realized now why Holmes wanted to know about the sailings from London docks yesterday and today; I wondered when he had realized something of this sort might happen.

"The body must have been taken last night, very late, as far as I have been able to determine," said Inspector Featherstone. "I can't put an exact hour on it, but the morgue attendant who came on duty at six in the morning said he discovered it was gone. I made a thorough search of the morgue myself, to be sure the body had not been mis-placed, but that was not the case; the corpse has vanished. The night morgue attendant must not have noticed anything unusual, for he said nothing to the orderly who brought a new body down shortly after midnight, but I believe the late-night attendant slept half his shift, if what I have been told about him is true." Having laid out so much, he sat down. "I have questioned the other attendants, but no one at Saint Elizabeth's saw anything to rouse their suspicions, or so they claim. I have surmised that the theft was planned carefully. So the body was most likely removed between three and six, when activity is at its lowest."

Mycroft Holmes touched the tips of his fingers together. "Did you happen to ask if a patient left in a wheeled-chair, or a body in a coffin?"

"No, not as such, and yes, I did make such inquiries as soon as the loss was reported to me," said Inspector Featherstone. "But there is no record of such, or of a hearse coming to the carriage-entrance during the night, and only two cabs were summoned between mid-night and five. I have the attendant's statement on the incidents and the times. I have also made inquiries among our informants who know about the working of body-snatchers. Nothing from any of them so far." He pulled his notebook from his waistcoat pocket. "One cab departed at two forty-eight, the other at three twenty-one. The first carried a woman whose father had succumbed an hour earlier, the second was summoned by a surgeon. The desk attendant says that no one entered Saint Elizabeth's from one-thirty-two to five-oh-six."

"So it might be possible that the body was removed earlier, and some misleading bundles were put under the sheet and were not re-moved until last night," said Mycroft Holmes. "You may want to ask which of the various attendants actually checked on the bodies. If no close review was made, the body of the young man might have been missing for more than twelve hours before its loss was reported." He regarded Inspector Featherstone with interest. "Don't tell me such a possibility has not occurred to you."

"Well, yes, I have thought it might have happened that way," said Featherstone.

"Indeed," said Holmes. "I should think, given the nature of the murder, that it is highly likely that the body was gone long before it was missed. What intrigues me is the attempt to delay the recognition of its disappearance." He sat forward. "When did you receive word of this?"

"Shortly after six, sir," said Inspector Featherstone. "I came on duty and the report was the first one handed me."

"I see. And did you go to Saint Elizabeth's?" He was clearly trying to establish times for these events.

"Almost at once. I arrived there shortly before seven. I was pleased that the staff that had been on duty—with one exception— had remained after their shift ended." The Inspector shook his head. "I still have not spoken to the late-night morgue attendant."

"Do you know where to find him?" asked Mycroft Holmes sharply.

"He is said to lodge at the *Spotted Dog*, two blocks from Saint Elizabeth's," said Inspector Featherstone. "I called there on my way here, but the landlord claimed his room was empty. I will stop back there later today to see if I can find him."

"Do so, by all means," said Mycroft Holmes, "but I doubt you will find him. I predict he will have disappeared, as well. Did you happen to learn how long he had his post at the morgue?"

"Yes. He was recently hired, on"—he consulted his notebook—"November fifth. They tell me that men do not stay long in that position. Their two day-time attendants have worked in that capacity for more than a year, the man taking the afternoon shift having been there for nearly four years." He closed his notebook again. "Not the kind of work most would like to do, I'd think."

"Very likely," said Holmes. "But your night-man will be gone, I tell you."

"Perhaps," Inspector Featherstone allowed. "I will still go to the *Spotted Dog* this afternoon, if you don't mind."

"I've nothing against your doing that," said Holmes.

"Why do you suppose the man is gone?" the Inspector could not resist asking.

"He had served his purpose. Now it is in the best interests of his true employers to have him out of the city." Holmes sat back in his chair and stared up at the ceiling. "When a check is made on him, he will be found to be a non-entity, a man without a history. He is probably the man who took away whatever had been used to give the appearance of the body being under the sheet, although he is not the only one who had such an opportunity. I am convinced that the body was removed yesterday afternoon, so that Halil Kerem could take it with him on his departing ship."

"You mean his brother stole the body to take it home?" Inspector Featherstone asked.

"Halil Kerem was no more that poor lad's brother than I am," scoffed Holmes. "Kerem was sent to claim the evidence and get rid of it. His story was almost plausible enough to permit him to do this without question. We do not usually suppose that a man would come on a long voyage for no purpose but to dispose of a body."

"He did not expect to find a body," said Inspector Featherstone. "He wanted to find his brother."

"So he said," Mycroft Holmes agreed. "And he set out from Turkey some time before the lad was killed."

"Yes," said Featherstone, his eyes brightening. "Just so."

"But he arrived prepared to take a body with him, according to Inspector Alexander's Customs report; he filed an application to ship a body to Istanbul," Holmes said, unctuous as a cat.

I was engrossed in this account; I knew Mycroft Holmes had such an assumption, but I did not realize he had taken the time to pursue it, or to support his thesis.

"Why do you say that?" Inspector Featherstone wanted to know. He took out his notebook again, and a blunt pencil, and began to make terse memoranda to himself as Mycroft Holmes explained.

"The first mistake he made came when he arranged to transport a coffin one day after his arrival. The second mistake—more egregious than the first—was his claim that the tattoo on the young man was an old one, when it was patently newly done. He soon understood his error and he knew he had to get the body out of the morgue and out of England before the inquiry went any further. He urged me to help him gain its release, as a means of accounting for his intense interest. He wanted to appear at the mercy of English whim, so that we should discount him as a suspect." Holmes spread his hands as if this were obvious.

"Then the story of the . . . the prostitution ring of young foreign men was a fabrication?" said Inspector Featherstone.

"On, no; that is quite real. And I would suppose Halil Kerem is one of its suppliers. I assume it was he who provided the Turkish lad to the panderers here in England. But I gather the boy learned more than he should, either about the ring itself, or its . . . clientele, and had to be disposed of." Holmes took a deep breath. "A lad of that sort is all but invisible at the best of times. In a case such as this one, he vanishes, figuratively and literally."

Inspector Featherstone sat staring at Mycroft Holmes. "You can't be serious."

"As serious as I ever was in my life," Mycroft Holmes responded. "That new tattoo is the mark of a nefarious organization that has done much to corrupt the leadership of all Europe. Its appearance in England is a warning to us all."

"So you believe the lad is in a coffin on his way back to Turkey?" Inspector Featherstone pursued. "Might we wire Turkish Customs to deal with him when he lands?"

"There is someone in the coffin, no doubt. But I expect the boy will be got rid of at sea, so that no more questions can be asked of him." Mycroft Holmes looked over at Inspector Featherstone. "I wouldn't be amazed to learn the morgue attendant lies in a Turkish grave, one day."

The Inspector blanched. "No. Surely you cannot think they would do anything so . . . so . . ."

"I know this organization of old, Inspector, and there is no atrocity of which they are not capable." Holmes' expression was granite-like.

"Then how is this case to be solved?" Inspector Featherstone asked.

"I shouldn't think it could be," Holmes told him, and reached out to pour him a cup of tea.

FROM THE PERSONAL JOURNAL OF PHILIP TYERS

I have returned from carrying the messages for MH, and brought back a note from CI Pryce, which I have handed to MH. Inspector Featherstone left some twenty minutes since, still very much distressed by what he has learned here.

I will prepare supper to have it ready upon Sutton's return, which should be within the half hour . . .

Chapter Twenty

"DO YOU REALLY think Mister Kerem is the villain you described to Inspector Featherstone?" I asked as I finished making a list of Turkey-bound ships; the Inspector had been gone for more than an hour and I had been occupied with the task Mycroft Holmes had set for me earlier in the day.

"Most certainly I do: don't you?" Mycroft Holmes said as he stood up and stretched. "You have been in that part of the world recently. Do you suppose the degeneration of the government is due entirely to the Turks? I know the touch of the Brotherhood when I see it. You said yourself that there were foreign influences in the Ottoman world that contributed to the venality you so deplored."

"Yes, yes, I know," I said. "But it troubles me that the Brotherhood has made such inroads, if that is what has happened," I added the last conscientiously.

"It is," Holmes declared. "Jacobbus Braaten was not in Istanbul for his health." He shook his head. "You cannot ignore the villainy he represents. I must suppose he has used coercion, blackmail, extortion, and every other kind of despicable act in order to advance the goals of the Brotherhood. He has certainly used intimidation and bribery, as you have seen for yourself. I doubt he would stop at any act, no matter how heinous."

"Including running the prostitution ring you depicted? Or did you choose that as an example, not a direct—?" I got no further.

"Of course I meant it specifically. I have had information to hand for almost a month that depicted the activities of that reprehensible trade; I had not found the means to bring it to the attention of the authorities without exposing the men who have done their utmost to inform me on this scheme, or I should have urged action against them before now, a course I am persuaded would serve only to alert the Brotherhood to our awareness, and thereby give them an opportunity to dismantle their criminal ring here and relocate it elsewhere, where we may not as easily surveil them." He stared at the fireplace. "I have no desire to put any of my agents at risk, not if there are means to protect them: the Brotherhood uses traitors ferociously, as an example."

I recalled what he had told me about his time in the Brotherhood as an agent of the government, and that he still had not told me how he managed to escape their vengeance. "This is from experience, is it not?"

"Yes, Guthrie, it is," said Holmes drily. "I am not willing to put anyone at hazard, not with the Brotherhood, which I would do if I divulge the names of those who have helped me." He took the sheets I handed him. "I will need to review the passenger lists for these ships, but I will wager that Mister Kerem is not on any of them."

"But he told us he had reserved space on a ship leaving yesterday," I reminded him.

"And you believed him?" Holmes asked incredulously. "Guthrie, I thought you had a better measure of that man. He had every reason to lie, and no reason to be truthful." He pinched the bridge of his nose. "No. I am afraid we have lost Halil Kerem—if that is his name."

I shook my head. "I shall go round to the shipping companies myself, if you like, and make inquiry."

"No. I have more need of you here. I will send one of the young officers from the Admiralty; the shipping companies will pay more attention to such a messenger than they would to you, in any case," he said bluntly. He was about to go on when there was a loud rap on the rear door and Tyers went to answer the energetic summons. "Sutton returns," Holmes said to me.

"In good time," I said, looking up at the clock next to the French secretary: it read ten minutes before two.

As if to confirm his arrival, I heard Sutton announce to the air, "Beatrice Motherwell is a termagant."

Holmes rose and went to the study door. "And why is that, dear boy?" he called.

"She wants to change the Sleepwalking Scene to allow her to add lines of her own—*lines of her own!*" The enormity of this outrage made Sutton speak as if he were addressing the uppermost seats in the gallery.

"Dear me," said Holmes, trying to keep a serious demeanor.

"Oh, you may laugh, sir," said Sutton as he came striding into the study. "But this is not some paltry fustian by Colly Cibber or Van Brough. This is Shakespeare, and one of his best-known plays. No matter what she may think, Beatrice Motherwell cannot improve upon the lines, or make the audience think her invention is equal to Shakespeare's." He dropped down into his favorite chair. "You should have heard her when our director refused. A fishwife would have been shocked."

"Well, the run is almost over," Mycroft Holmes said by way of sympathizing.

"Yes, and I don't want it said that our last performances were marred by a Lady MacBeth who ad-libbed the best-known scene of her character." He flung up his hands. "We have done so well, and now this! What worse may befall us, I ask you? No wonder they say the play's cursed."

"You must not be over-set by this, Edmund," Mycroft Holmes advised in that tranquil manner of his that is often enough to make one want to pull hair. "You have secured the recognition you deserve, and not even the rambunction of your leading lady can cast any shadow upon you."

"I would like to think so," said Sutton. "But a play is not the talent and effort of one, it is the sum of all." He leaned his head back and closed his eyes. "I would like a brandy, if you don't mind."

"Certainly," said Holmes, going to fetch a snifter and to fill it from the decanter in the sitting room. When he returned, he handed the generous libation to Sutton, saying as he did, "Here you are. It will ease you."

"Thank you," said Sutton, straightening up and taking the snifter in his hand, swirling the brandy to warm it. "You're very good. I know I should not let this discompose me, but all has been going so well, and I was in a fair way to thinking the worst was past." He took a pull on the brandy.

"You are not the only one to fall into such error," said Mycroft Holmes. "We have had a similar comeuppance to deal with in our investigations." He did his best to look self-deprecating but only managed to look as if he had been sucking lemons.

"Oh? Have there been developments?" Sutton was genuinely curious, and he regarded us with undisguised interest.

"A morning's worth," said Holmes, and recounted what had happened since we called at Sir Cameron's leased house in Deanery Mews; halfway through his account, Sutton began to chuckle, and by the time Holmes had reached the account of the corpse's disappearance, Sutton was into whoops. Holmes finished his report stiffly. "And why any of this should amuse you, I cannot think."

"Oh, don't take umbrage, pray," said Sutton, bringing his mirth under control. "It is so like the popular dramas, full of incidents in an ever-increasing avalanche of events." He looked at Holmes and saw that our employer did not share his amusement. "I know it is a serious matter to you, and I do not mean to belittle what you have done, but as an actor, I can only say that your life, since last Friday, would play as a great adventure."

Somewhat mollified, Holmes was able to smile ruefully. "No doubt you are right. If it took place in South America, it would be worthy of Professor Challenger."

"My point exactly," said Sutton, in an uncanny imitation of Holmes' voice and manner. He was about to enlarge on his observation when Tyers announced that dinner was served in the sitting room, and we obligingly made our way to that chamber for the veal stuffed with sage and cheese, and roast onions, followed by a salad of winter vegetables cooked in cream. There was fresh bread and new butter, and a fine Côtes du Rhone to wash it down.

"An excellent repast," Holmes declared as he passed round the port and Stilton at the end of the meal.

"That it is," said Sutton; equanimity had been restored between them and both were about to light up cigars.

I did not join them in smoking; it is one taste I have not acquired, although from time to time I am not adverse to lighting a pipe. I was content to sip at my port and enjoy the drawing in of the afternoon.

"I'll do the club, of course," Sutton said after a companionable silence. "You said you had to speak to Baron von Schattenberg again, am I right?"

"Yes," said Holmes. "I am sorry I shall miss your performance tomorrow night. Ordinarily I would be at theatre but—" He shrugged. "I am afraid tomorrow night I will be otherwise occupied."

"It isn't as if you haven't seen the production. So long as you can spare Hastings to bring me back here, all will be well. And I will use this evening, upon my return from the club, to review my blocking one last time." Sutton smiled at Holmes' evident consternation.

"You memorized that weeks ago," Holmes reminded him. "And you have played it for the whole of your run."

"So I have. All the more reason to go over it again, so I do not become stale." He made a theatrical gesture. "Oh, come. You did not mind having me pace out every scene as I was learning the part; why should one more go at it trouble you?"

"You're right, of course. It isn't you I am disgruntled with— that's terrible grammar but a true emotion, nonetheless. I am aware that I am not as much caught up with the Brotherhood's machinations as I hoped I would be; I had hoped that by now we would have turned the tide. I am aggravated that Mister Kerem has managed to escape when I thought the delays of Customs would be sufficient to keep him in London for a few more days. I am annoyed that Vickers and Braaten have probably found a way to reach England and may, in fact, be here now. I should have anticipated such a ruse, but I failed to perceive it." He spun the stem of his port-glass in his fingers, watching the dark liquid swirl. "I had thought that by tonight at least one of the criminals would be in gaol, and that we would be in a fair way to getting Vickers or Braaten behind bars. But I have botched that as well."

"You do know the nature of the trouble you face," said Sutton. "Many times you have said that is more than half the battle."

"I know, and ordinarily I would feel a certain satisfaction, but . . ." He let his words trail off.

"You have expectations of yourself that the rest of us do not share," said Sutton. "And if you want to spend the next hour or so finding fault with yourself, I will excuse myself and have a short lie-down. I don't like to see my friends abused, particularly by themselves." He got to his feet, saying in a more relaxed voice, "Fortunately my MacBeth make-up is not too different from my make-up to look like you, or I would have a rush to go from the club to the theatre. As it is, all I need do is emphasize what is already begun." His expression lost its jocularity. "You ought not berate yourself. It is a waste of time and it does nothing more than blunt your sensibilities, as you have reminded me when I have been unflatteringly reviewed."

Holmes sighed and leaned back. "You're right; I know you're right. If I could see my way through the whole of this muddle, I would not be so disheartened. I thought this morning we were in a fair way to taking the lead in this damnable game. But this has been such an exhausting several days, I begin to think I am at my limit."

Sutton chuckled. "Never. You are despondent, and who can blame you for that? But you have not yet put your strength to the test." He put down his empty port-glass. "You are discouraged, but that will pass. Won't it, Guthrie?"

I was shocked to hear my name called, and it took me a moment to recover myself enough to make a good response. "We shall all come about, sir, you'll see. This is only a lull before our next attack."

"No doubt you're right, Guthrie," said Mycroft Holmes, putting his port aside and stubbing out his cigar. "I will be the better for activity. I must change for my return to Herr Amsel's house, and my next discussion with Baron von Schattenberg. I don't suppose this time it will go too well, not with Herr Kriede's killer still unapprehended, and Lady MacMillian's arrival postponed yet again. Although I am glad that we have managed to delay her arrival; that is something in our favor." He rose, and glanced at Sutton. "Go have your lie-down in the withdrawing room. And thank you for doing my stint at the Diogenes Club."

"My pleasure," said Sutton. "It is preferable to waiting in my rooms to discover if I have been cast in *Volpone* or not." He bowed as if to hearty applause, and left the sitting room.

"He's right, I know," said Mycroft Holmes. "I should not be down-cast."

"No," I said. "You should not."

Holmes looked down at me; he deliberately did not comment on my remark. "You'll do well enough dressed as you are."

"But you intend to change," I said, knowing he would want to set the right tone for the meeting, which was likely to be difficult.

"Yes. Nothing too grand, for the Baron and his aides will be in mourning, I should think." He strolled to the door. "Half an hour, Guthrie. Have a cup of tea, if you like."

"I think I will," I said, for though I enjoyed the port, on a cold wet evening, tea would do me more good. There was enough left in the pot that I didn't bother Tyers to make another. The tea was very strong and had a bitter taste, but that, too, was not unwelcome. I drank slowly, trying to prepare myself for this next venture.

Mycroft Holmes achieved a nice balance between formal evening wear and dress for diplomatic occasions. His coat, though black, had a velvet collar of deep-grey, just the proper touch. His waistcoat was a deep-grey shadow stripe, setting the right note. He stood in the doorway. "It is time we were off," he said. "Hastings will be waiting."

"I suppose I should bring my portfolio," I said, preparing to take up this object from where I had put it down hours ago.

"No; I think your leather-covered notebook would be most appropriate. We will not be making any finalized agreements, I should think, and we do not want the Baron to think we are keeping track of his every word—even if we are." He called to Tyers for our overcoats and umbrellas, which were still in the kitchen.

"Here you are, sir," said Tyers as he brought the garments and umbrellas to us. "It is going to be very cold tonight. You may want to carry a lap-rug for your return." He had one, all folded and put in an oilskin pocket. "If you give this to Hastings, he'll have it for you."

"Excellent," said Holmes, taking the pocket. "And now, out into the rain."

The day was closing in fast, most of the light had faded from the sky, leaving only leaden clouds beyond the rain. Sid Hastings was waiting at the rear of the building in the service alley, perched on his box in his engulfing oilskins, apparently impervious to the weather; Mycroft Holmes and I scrambled into his cab and sat back.

"To the German's house?" Hastings said, to be certain.

"In Berkeley Mews," Holmes said as we left the service alley and started westward.

"Are we being followed?" I asked Holmes when we had turned north.

"I believe we have one of the Golden Lodge guards behind us in a covered milord. The other must be on duty at the flat still." He pursed his lips. "I suppose the Golden Lodge could provide useful information, if I were willing to impart what I have learned."

"You are still uncertain about them," I said. "In spite of all they have done."

"Guthrie, I do not subscribe to that aphorism that *the enemy of my enemy is my friend.* The trouble with such thinking is that one can end up in very rum company indeed if it is followed too strictly." He looked out into the streaming sepia sunset, his countenance set in ruminative lines. "I will allow that just at present, the Golden Lodge has been most useful, most helpful, but I am aware that could change in an instant. I do not mind providing them such information as must be immediately useful to them and to us, but I will not open the whole of my files to their scrutiny, nor will I volunteer one iota of intelligence beyond what is needed to secure their present support."

"We have benefitted from their presence," I said.

"And that has included Miss Gatspy." He held up his hand. "Don't bother disclaiming any interest in her. You have insisted upon that point any number of times. You will allow that you have been glad of her attendance."

"I should say so," I exclaimed. "She has probably saved my life."

"And has before, and may do so again," said Mycroft Holmes as if this were expected of her.

"Are you implying that she does not deserve my gratitude?" I demanded.

"Nothing of the sort. But I do hope you are aware if she has saved you, it is not just for your beaux yeux." His faint smile almost took the sting out of his cautionary reminder.

"I am aware of that, sir," I said.

"Oh, don't cut up stiff, my boy. I do not mean to impugn her motives, only to say they are not simply sprung from concern for you. She is an agent of the Golden Lodge first and foremost." He made a gesture of dismissal; I knew he would not discuss it any longer, for which I was relieved. "When we get to Berkeley Mews, I would appreciate it if you would take a little time to talk to Eisenfeld and . . . Farb—whatever his name is."

"Farbschlagen," I supplied, surprised that Holmes was too preoccupied to remember; most of the time he had all names readily available.

"Yes. Paul Farbschlagen. I am curious to know how they are dealing with the death of their fellow-aide. I am especially interested because, as I recall, on the afternoon he died, Herr Kriede was nervous. I would like to know why." Holmes had become more business-like, and I took my tone from him.

"Is there anything in particular you would like to know?" I asked.

"No. But I am curious about the fellow. If he had trouble in his life, it might account for his apprehension. It may be wholly unconnected to this case, but I need to know that, so that I will not have to pursue the matter. Unless, of course, it *is* connected to the cause of his death, in which case I will need to know everything you can find out. I rely on your good judgment to gauge the business appropriately." He shook his head, a self-deprecating smile flicking at the corners of his eyes. "This is so much more the sort of case my brother deals with than I am used to."

"Do you think so?" I asked, not wholly in agreement with him.

"Well, murders in London are a speciality of his," Mycroft Holmes observed. "Conduit Street. We are nearly there."

I rubbed the steam from the lozenge-shaped window at my shoulder and looked out. There were blurs of light around us, and steadily moving traffic. Nothing proceeded in a hurry, but no one stopped for very long, either. Those walking were huddled into their coats and ducked under their umbrellas. "A dreadful night to be out," I said.

"Isn't it?" Mycroft Holmes concurred. "Well, at least we will be indoors." He fell silent, and so did I.

"I'll be back in a hour, sir," said Hastings as he pulled up in Berkeley Mews. "I'm going along to get a pastie, and a pint o' bitters, but I'll be here again in an hour, for as long as you need me."

"Thank you, Hastings. That should be satisfactory; I've left a lap-rug in the cab, for our return." said Mycroft Holmes as we got out of the cab; Hastings touched the brim of his cap in acknowledgment before he gave Lance the order to walk on. Holmes and I trod up the steps to the front door and knocked.

The butler opened the door without haste, and brought us inside. "The Baron is in the library, Mister Holmes. I will announce you and Mister Guthrie," he said when we had surrendered our coats and umbrellas.

"Thank you," said Holmes, very much at his ease; he followed the butler down the same corridor we had walked before, to the library door. The butler presented us as he opened the door, and withdrew at once.

Baron von Schattenberg looked much older than the last time we had seen him. In the last two days, the shadows had taken charge of his face, and he stood as if supporting an immense weight. "Mister

Holmes," he said, with no more greeting than that. "My aides will join us shortly."

"As you wish, Baron," said Holmes. "Let me express my sympathies to you once again—"

"I accept your condolences," the Baron interrupted. "Your help was most appreciated. No doubt the whole terrible event would have been more distressing were it not for your quick thinking. That said, I must tell you I am perturbed by recent developments. It is bad enough to have policemen at the house at all hours, but now I understand that you have encouraged Sir Cameron to return to Scotland before his wife arrives in London, when she has been waiting only for the weather to clear so that she may join him. I am most troubled by this." He finally looked directly at Mycroft Holmes. "You will explain yourself, if you please."

It was precisely the question Holmes was expecting. "In my position, Baron, you would have done the same thing," he said in his deferential-but-assertive manner. "Think for a moment, Baron, on the unpleasant events of the last four days. Sir Cameron has received threats before now, but they have not been acted upon. Yet, since he has come to London, evidence suggests he has been in harm's way. There was an attempt made on his life, perhaps two. You cannot be sure that Herr Kriede's death was not another such attempt gone awry. Rather than put Sir Cameron—and possibly Lady MacMillian—in danger's path, it seemed wisest to send him back to his own estates until we may be sure he and his wife may meet without fear for their lives."

Baron von Schattenberg heard this out politely. "Then you believe Herr Kriede might have been killed in Sir Cameron's stead? I thought you did not support that theory."

"I have not been persuaded either way," said Mycroft Holmes, still standing. "But as long as that remains a possibility, I cannot think it would be to your advantage, or ours, to bring the two together. What would such a reunion avail anyone if it ended in tragedy?" He made a sign to me indicating I should go to the alcove beside the fireplace; I complied as inconspicuously as possible. "Consider, Baron, what trouble our two governments would have if it turns out that Sir

Cameron has been the target of more than one attempt on his life and it is learned that we did nothing to keep Lady MacMillian from sharing his risks."

"I think it should be her decision," said Baron von Schattenberg, a little of his former animation returning.

"If she has all the facts, as we know them, to hand, and is still ready to undertake a visit, then I might agree with you. But as the police have not yet determined the reason for the poisoning, I, for one, do not think I can advise her." Holmes walked toward the window where the velvet draperies were drawn over the dismal evening. "If you are prepared to do this—"

"No," said the Baron. "Put that way, no, of course not." He sat down as if exhausted. "I do not want to ask her to wait longer, but perhaps you are right."

"If any hurt should befall her, it would not redound to your credit, or mine," Holmes said, driving the point home with every sign of concern. "I shouldn't think the police would encourage such a visit at this time, either. If you want to consult Chief Inspector Pryce, then do so, by all means. I am persuaded he would not like you to bring Lady MacMillian here until some progress has been made."

Baron von Schattenberg clasped his hands together and I noticed for the first time that his knuckles were swollen with arthritis. "If it weren't for this miserable storm, Lady MacMillian and her uncles would have been here last week. Then we should not have had to bother with these concerns."

"Oh, yes," said Mycroft Holmes. "Then we should have had to account to her uncles why we had permitted her to come into peril without giving them warning of it. And we might have had a double catastrophe to deal with, instead of just the one." He finally took a seat across from the Baron. "You may not think so now, but this storm has served you very well."

The Baron was eager to be convinced. "What should I tell her uncles when I wire them?"

"If I were you, I should be candid about all that has happened. Only fools would insist on pursuing the visit under such circumstances," said Holmes, marshaling his arguments and heading into the fray. I took out my notebook and prepared for a lengthly spate of memoranda, for I had no reason to think that Mycroft Holmes would not make the most of this opportunity to bring Baron von Schatten-berg around to his point of view.

FROM THE PERSONAL JOURNAL OF PHILIP TYERS

It is almost eight and Sutton has not returned from the Diogenes Club; he has maintained MH's habitual visits to the minute before now, which should have brought him back here no later than seven-forty-three or -four. I am somewhat troubled by this unprecedented delay. It is most unlike Sutton, who, if nothing else, is punctual. If I cannot find Sutton on the street, I will ask for him—in the persona of MH—at the club. If I can learn nothing there, I will speak to the Golden Lodge guards, to find out if they noticed anything irregular. I do not like to assume the worst, but I am truly worried that I have not seen him, even if he decided, for some unknown reason, to approach the flat from the rear . . .

Chapter Twenty-one

I WAS STILL busy talking with Egmont Eisenfeld about Herr Kriede—Paul Farbschlagen having been reluctant to discuss his late colleague—when the butler came into the library, saying, "Excuse me, Baron, but there is a young lady here to speak to Mister Holmes. She says it is urgent." From the butler's expression, this was highly suspect.

Mycroft Holmes glanced at the mantle clock, which had just chimed half-eight, and said, "What is the nature of her errand?"

"That she would not impart to me," said the butler in condemning accents. "She claims it has something to do with your club."

Holmes looked mildly surprised. "Did she?" He rose and inclined his head to the Baron. "If you will excuse me a moment, I will attend to this."

"A young woman looking for you?" said the Baron with ponderous humor. "My dear Mister Holmes, take your time."

"—and he was hoping to advance in diplomatic service, as we all do," Eisenfeld was saying. "His family were wholly landed people, so they did not encourage him, though they knew it could be to their advantage—" He broke off as I lifted my hand. "Yes?"

"Mister Holmes is leaving the room," I said, and waited to see if he called for me. When nothing more happened, I gave my attention to Herr Eisenfeld once again. "You said that he had some money of his own?"

"An annual stipend. Nothing extravagant." He shrugged.

"So would you expect him to have money troubles? You said he didn't gamble or bet on horses. Could there have been anything else?" I had heard nothing so far that made me suppose that anyone in London was angry enough with Herr Kreide to want to kill him.

"Nothing he ever mentioned. He did spend time in public gardens, as I told you, but he did so because of his love of flowers." Egmont Eisenfeld did not share Herr Kriede's weakness, I supposed from his faintly contemptuous expression.

I was about to try another avenue of inquiry when Mycroft Holmes came back into the library abruptly. "I must—Guthrie." He was white around the mouth, and although his demeanor was not much changed, I could tell he was in distress. "Baron, a thousand apologies. I fear I must leave at once. Guthrie come."

"Has something happened?" the Baron asked as he half-rose to his feet. "Have you had news?"

"Yes. Yes, I have had news," said Holmes. "I must attend to— Forgive my departure, Baron."

"Does it have to do with this case?" Baron von Schattenberg asked.

"This case?" He blinked once as if trying to comprehend. "Oh, yes, I would think so," he said, motioning to me.

"Then Godspeed, Mister Holmes," said Baron von Schattenberg with genuine encouragement.

I gave a little bow to Herr Eisenfeld and went to Mycroft Holmes' side. "At your service, sir," I told him.

"Come. Miss Gatspy has brought us a message that requires our immediate and personal response." He paused at the door to bow, then left the library with uncustomary haste.

"Miss Gatspy?" I asked as the door closed behind us.

"Yes. Tyers sent her." Holmes had lengthened his stride so that I had to run to keep up with him. At the door the butler handed us our over-coats and umbrellas and let us out onto the porch with a minimum of fuss.

Miss Gatspy was standing at the foot of the steps, wrapped in a cloak of boiled wool, and holding the stay-rein of her horse harnessed to her sylphide. "We had better hurry," she said. "I will tie my carriage to the rear of Hastings' cab so we may talk on the way back to Pall Mall." She suited action to words as quickly as may be, then climbed into Hastings' cab as Mycroft Holmes and I came down the steps.

It took a minute or two for us to settle into our cramped accommodation, and I was keenly aware of Miss Gatspy's driving-habit pressing against my side. "Pardon me," I said as I endeavored to pull out the lap-rug in its sleeve.

"Never mind that, Guthrie," said Holmes as he closed the door and tapped on the roof to signal Hastings to start. "If it weren't raining and dark, I'd tell him to push his horse," he muttered, then collected himself. "Now, Miss Gatspy, tell me everything you know. Be as concise as possible, but leave nothing out."

Miss Gatspy clasped her hands together. "Tyers found me on watch duty, and told me that Sutton, who should have returned from the club at seven-fifty at the latest, had not returned by ten-past-eight. He went down to the club to see if something might have arisen that had kept Sutton there—in your stead, of course—and was told that Mister Holmes had departed at his usual hour. Tyers then went to search for my fellow watchman, and asked him if he had noticed anything out of the ordinary at the time Mister Holmes usually came back to the flat. That man told Tyers that the rain had been too heavy for him to see clearly, but he recalled there had been an accident almost immediately in front of the club at the time Mister Holmes crossed the road. He said that the whole affair had been settled swiftly, the vehicles went on their way without apparent damage, and he supposed that Mister Holmes had—"

"He was distracted," said Mycroft Holmes heavily. "Since last Friday, my life has been filled with distractions, but none of them as unbearable as this one. If anything has happened to Edmund Sutton, I will—" He stopped himself. "When did you come into the picture?"

"My colleague told Tyers that I was on duty at the rear. Tyers made sure of his information, and very sensibly, I thought, came and found me, and asked me to come to get you. I agreed with him, and set out. I told Tyers to remain at the flat in case Sutton should come back, or some word be sent." She took a deep breath. "That is the sum of what I have been told."

"I see," said Holmes quietly. "And do you have any suppositions you'd care to impart to me?"

"I suppose I must have fears similar to your own: I think some-one has kidnapped Sutton under the misapprehension that he has captured you," said Miss Gatspy, putting words to the idea that had filled my thoughts.

"Is there any other possible interpretation?" Holmes asked. "Might he have been injured in the street, and taken up to be carried to hospital?"

"My colleague made no mention of such a possibility," said Miss Gatspy, and went on more diffidently. "For the time being, it might be as well for it to appear that you *have* disappeared. If Sutton is in the hands of your enemies, his safety can only be possible if they believe they have taken the right man."

Mycroft Holmes nodded slowly. "Yes. I concur. Galling though it is, I must leave most of the investigation of this dreadful incident to you and Guthrie." He went silent for the better part of a minute. "I am disinclined to bring in the police, or the Admiralty, at least not yet."

I finally spoke up. "I think that may be the most prudent course. You cannot be certain that the secret would be kept if it was put in the hands of the police. I mean the secret of your abduction, not of Sutton's," I added, to make myself clear.

"Just so," said Holmes. "Time enough to deal with the Admiralty if questions are asked. For now, the fewer who know of this, the better."

"I will make sure my colleagues are aware that your life will be in danger if they reveal anything," said Miss Gatspy. "Members of the Golden Lodge know how to keep silent."

We had turned onto Piccadilly now, and Hastings urged Lance to a trot; we were jostled by the increased sway in the cab, but none of us complained of it.

Something occurred to me. "Sutton has a performance tomorrow night, and for the following two nights," I reminded Holmes.

"It is not time for that yet," said Holmes sharply.

"But if he has not come back, or if he cannot . . . perform?" I didn't want to imply anything more unpleasant than that.

Mycroft Holmes sighed. "Well, he has taken my place often enough; I suppose I shall have to take his."

Both Miss Gatspy and I were struck dumb by this possibility; finally she said, "Well, that would certainly preserve the deception. It is audacious enough that it might work."

"But, sir," I protested as the complexity of the task struck me. "How can you?"

"I trust I will not have to," said Holmes. "But I know the lines and I have seen the production several times, and I have the advantage of having Sutton's sides for his notes. If I must do it, I should not fail too utterly."

"Well," said Miss Gatspy energetically, "that's settled. Now let's consider how we're to handle this investigation."

The cab slowed as we turned down Saint James Street, and the way grew dimmer, as if in collaboration with our secrecy.

"Tyers is crucial to our success," said Holmes. "He must maintain the appearance that we are continuing on our usual tasks."

"I have a notion," I said, unaware of the idea until I spoke. "Why mayn't Tyers put it about that you have suffered a minor injury and are confined to your bed? This will keep anyone from questioning your absence from your usual activities, it will convince the kidnappers that they have succeeded, and it will lessen the chance that the police may take it upon themselves to intrude. I know, sir, that you are never ill and you have rarely been incapacitated in any way, but in this instance, I think it may provide you with the chance you need."

Mycroft Holmes tapped on the roof, and called out, "Take us in by the rear, Hastings."

"I planned to, sir," the jarvy assured Holmes.

Then Holmes turned to me. "It goes against the grain, but it will answer very well," he said in that calm, measured way that indicated he was thinking very rapidly. "Yes. As you say, it is paramount that the kidnappers believe they have succeeded. For the rest, the device is a useful one. We must do all that we can to protect Sutton." He rubbed his face. "You are a resourceful fellow, Guthrie. I don't say it often enough, but it is true."

We entered King Street and Hastings pulled his horse to a walk. "Just looking about, sir," he called down softly. "In case."

"Good man, Hastings," said Holmes.

"It seems empty enough," Hastings said twenty seconds later.

"Go ahead then," said Mycroft Holmes, sitting as far back in the cab as possible so he could not be seen accidentally by anyone who happened to glance at the vehicle. He was silent as we entered the service alley at the rear of the buildings that fronted on Pall Mall on the south and Saint James' Square and King Street on the north.

"Hastings," I said as we drew up, "will you go round to Curzon Street for me and tell Missus Coopersmith that I will be staying at my employer's flat tonight. Ask her to pack a valise for me, so I will not have to run in tomorrow morning for a change of clothes."

"Right you are, Mister Guthrie," said Hastings as he let down the step for us to get out of his cab. "You'd best huddle together. The rain is getting heavier," he advised, and Miss Gatspy and I contrived to conceal Mycroft Holmes between us—no easy task, for he was taller and of greater girth than either of us. But we did manage to present a confusing impression to anyone who might be attempting to watch us on this forbidding night.

Tyers must have heard our approach, for the rear door opened as we reached the second floor landing. "Come in, do," he said, bundling us inside into a darkened room. "Give me your coats, and then go into the library. I have closed all the shutters and no one can see in, no matter what vantage-point they may secure."

We blundered about in our haste to do as he ordered, and then we made our way to the library. I recalled, in that odd way you do when the stresses of life run high, that when I first went to work for Mycroft Holmes, six years ago, this had been a large storage room; he had changed its use when the books in his study and sitting room had reached a point of impossibility, overflowing their cases, the tops of tables, and the seats of unoccupied chairs. Then its two small, high windows had been considered something of a problem; now we were all glad that there was so little access from without.

"Tyers," said Holmes as he took a turn about the room, "have you any news?"

Tyers did not waste time in recapitulating Miss Gatspy's report; he looked directly at our employer and said, "Nothing, sir, not beneficial or otherwise."

"Has there been any communication since Sutton was abducted?" The words came out roughly but he did not flinch from them.

"There was a note sent round by Chief Inspector Alexander, and another from Inspector Featherstone." Tyers retrieved these from his inner waistcoat pocket and handed them to Holmes. "I believe both men expect an answer."

"And they shall have one, but not tonight," said Holmes. "Can you make us some sandwiches and soup? We will need something to keep us going through the night, but I don't want to stop work for a proper meal."

"Of course, sir," said Tyers, and prepared to withdraw.

"Oh, and Tyers?" Holmes stopped him.

"Yes, sir?" Tyers paused in the doorway, ready for instructions.

"If you will send word to the Admiralty that I have contracted a febrile cold and am laid up in my bed, I would appreciate it. Also inform the club that I may be missing for a day or two, for the same reason." Holmes had opened the notes and held them up to the lamplight.

"Very good, sir. I shall attend to the latter this evening, and the former first thing in the morning." He left the three of us alone to-gether.

"Chief Inspector Alexander says he has not found any record of Mister Kerem's departure, but that a Greek man, Hilarios Kosmos, left for Cyprus on Monday." He nodded. "H and K. It is likely that this is Hilel Kerem, or that we are meant to think it is. Alexander says that the man traveled with a number of large crates, two of which were found to contain upright pianos." He put the note down, musing, "I suppose there are less elegant coffins than a piano-case."

"Do you think he had the body with him?" I asked.

"I think it is what we are intended to believe. But if this Greek is our Turk, and if he concealed a body in a piano-case to take it with him, it must mean that it was gone from the morgue far longer than we reckoned. Not that it is impossible, though it is improbable," he added as he looked over the second note. "Inspector Featherstone is worried," he said at last. "I think he has extended himself too far." He did not explain this any further; he put the note in his jacket pocket and pointed to Miss Gatspy. "You are, perforce, part of our efforts. I trust you will not put yourself in jeopardy because of it."

"If you mean my superiors at the Golden Lodge might object, they have said I am to aid you in any way I can, at least until the matter of Vickers and Braaten is resolved." She smiled winningly at him. "So, for the time being, I am yours to command—on their behalf."

"I must remember to thank them, in future," said Holmes drily. "Guthrie, go into the study and fetch the memoranda and other papers you sorted for me. We have a great deal of reading to do."

I hastened to obey, moving as quickly as I could. I noticed a light was on in Mycroft Holmes' bedroom, and I realized that Tyers had begun to shore up the fiction of Holmes' illness. In the study I found the papers in question, gathered them up, along with a number of pencils from the French secretary, then hurried back to the library, trying to prepare myself for a long night.

Holmes had moved two end-tables together in front of the fire, and he motioned to me to put down all that I carried on this surface. "You've done an excellent job so far. I think we must look for anything having to do with the incidents of the last five days. Guthrie has already winnowed out those bits of information that have no bearing on . . . our developments." He cleared his throat as he sat down. "I am almost certain that Vickers and Braaten are in England, and may have been for more than a week. I know we have intelligence to the contrary, but I am beginning to think that this is another example of misdirection. This whole venture is a triumph of sleight-of-hand." He made a pass with his hands as if to perform a magic trick.

"Including the abduction," I said. "To make it appear that nothing actually happened."

"Yes, Guthrie. You're right," said Holmes. "The device of drawing the attention to a minor collision was most effective. One of the vehicles might have been used to carry Sutton off. We won't know that until we find him." His voice tightened again. "All the more reason to act swiftly."

Miss Gatspy nodded her agreement. "I believe you are right about Vickers and Braaten. They were at pains to make it appear they were trying to get to England, and that kept all of us from looking to see if they were already arrived."

"I haven't been caught napping like that for many years," Mycroft Holmes said, embarrassed by this admission. "How very lacking in me."

"Had you not been kept busy with other matters, no doubt you should have discovered it sooner," I reminded him. "These last few days have been much occupied, as you have, yourself, remarked. You have been caught up in so many pressing incidents that you haven't had the opportunity to review the whole." I patted the papers before me. "Now that you are supposedly missing, you have that opportunity. It is the one signal failure the Brotherhood have made."

"So long as they do not find it *is* a failure," said Holmes warily. "And being preoccupied is no excuse."

"Then we must be sure they don't learn of their blunder. We will not allow anyone to speak with you or to see you. This will persuade the Brotherhood that you are missing, and will convince others that you are truly ill," said Miss Gatspy, reaching out to the stacks of notes. "For now, I will take these—having to do with the Baron and Herr Kriede. That leaves the attempts on Sir Cameron's life and his presence in London for Guthrie, and all the rest for you: the courier, the police, the disappearing body, and anything else." She was so wonderfully determined that I felt compelled to follow her example.

I gathered up the stack of papers. "I should think that it would be best to stop at one-hour intervals for the purpose of reviewing what has been found thus far. Unless we discover a crucial point, and then we should discuss it immediately."

"Yes. That will enable us to compare what we may discover before we lose sight of it again," said Miss Gatspy. "You may hold all such details in your mind, Mister Holmes; I doubt Guthrie and I are as accomplished. And this way we will know what all of us have learned. It may trigger off a thought or two when we share our gleanings."

"I agree," said Holmes with much more humility than I would have expected. He rose and went to the door. "Tyers. Make that tea very strong."

"That I will, sir. And I will stand by to do whatever you may require," came his answer.

"The club?" Holmes asked.

"When I have brought you tea and sandwiches, I will cross the road. There is still a fair amount of time to deliver the news that you are ill." Tyers kept his voice low enough to be heard only in this flat, in case anyone might be listening outside.

"Very good. I suppose I should withdraw to my bedchamber some time tonight," he said to us. "It would be prudent."

"But it isn't necessary yet," I said. "The only persons who might want to call would be those associated with the kidnapping, to see what we are doing to account for your absence."

"I take your point, Guthrie. Arriving too soon after the incident would only create suspicion." Holmes sat forward. "What if a ransom is demanded?"

"What if one isn't?" Miss Gatspy countered. "Deal with that when it happens," she recommended, and turned her full attention to the material in her hand. "You have an elegant fist, Guthrie," she added. "It will make my reading easier."

"Most kind," I said, feeling heat in my face.

"And mine is abominable," Holmes said, making my discomfiture complete. I was glad to begin to read, looking for anything that might reveal useful tidbits of information.

Tyers came with a tray of tea and sandwiches, and the promise of soup in an hour, then he left to cross the street to the club, returning some ten minutes later with a note from one of the senior members offering to send his physician to consult on Holmes' case. "I told him if you were not improved in a day or two, you might agree to it."

"Sensible as always," Mycroft Holmes said, looking up from the pages he perused. "Thank you, Tyers."

"I should add, I think, that Sir Marmion Hazeltine was there, and sent his hopes for a quick recovery," Tyers remarked. "He was with Marlborough."

"Um," Holmes said, to indicate he was listening. As soon as Tyers went away to the kitchen to work on his soup, he said, "Something more has occurred to me: I think we should make pages where we enter the events since Thursday evening, the time when they happened, and who participated. That way, we may discover a pattern."

"I'll set up a chart," I said, and went to fetch large sheets of graph paper from the study. When I returned, I spent ten minutes or so preparing the pages. "There," I told them when I was finished.

"Yes. Very good, Guthrie," said Mycroft Holmes. "If you, Miss Gatspy, would be willing to make note of who among your guards was on duty, and at what position, during these times, it would be helpful."

"I doubt the Golden Lodge would object to that," she said, and took the Thursday sheet and began writing down the watch-schedule and the names of those who kept it.

"When it's finished, I'll tack it to the bookshelves, so we may refer to it while we read," I volunteered.

"Do that. And when this is all over, we must burn the pages. They will have too much information on them that could be used by our enemies." Mycroft Holmes took his pencil and began to write on the Friday sheet. I did the same with Saturday. By eleven the chart was complete and we were back at our reading.

Hastings has brought G's valise, and a note from his landlady asking that he inform her when he plans to return to his rooms. Hastings has agreed to be here at half-eight tomorrow and to remain at our service for as long as he is needed.

I have made up MH's bedroom to make it seem it is occupied, but not so occupied that the Brotherhood will not suppose that this is a clever deception on our part. In the morning, I will send for Watson, just to make it appear that the illness is being treated by a medical man.

I shall bring up another load of logs for the fires, and when I do, I will strive to look about me, to see if there is undue attention being paid to this flat. It is of the utmost importance that we maintain their conviction that they have MH for as long as possible, for if they realize their error, Sutton's life will not be worth a groat.

To that end, I will carry a note to CI Alexander about ships sailing from seven-forty on last night, and what might sail today. I fear the Brotherhood will want to spirit MH—that is Sutton—out of the country as quickly as may be. I must also carry a note to I Strange, so that we may be more alert to the reliable men among the police . . .

The rain has lessened, but it has not yet stopped, nor do I expect it to do so before the end of the week.

Chapter Twenty-two

BY FOUR IN the morning, we had reached a point of exhaustion where our thinking was sluggish, and no amount of tea would change it for the sharper. I had caught myself yawning several times, as had Miss Gatspy. Even Mycroft Holmes, for all his energy and tenacity, was feeling the effects of our demanding studies. It was he who rose and said, "If we rest until eight, we should be able to come back to our work with keener eyes."

"I will keep on longer, if you want," I said, and felt my bones protest.

"What I want, Guthrie, is a sharp pair of eyes and a fully alert mind. At the moment, I have neither from you, or from Miss Gatspy. Or myself, for that matter." This final concession was a telling one. "Guthrie, you take the settee in the sitting room, and Miss Gatspy may have the day-bed in the withdrawing room. I will remain here, on the couch."

I looked at him, somewhat startled. "Your room is more than ready, sir."

"All the more reason for me not to go there, as I am missing," he said. "No, I shall remain here, with the shutters closed. That way I will be as invisible as I can be." He paused a moment. "I must make some provision with Tyers to serve for what looks like two, not three. I'll let him sort it out." He stretched. "Well, go on, you two. Morning is coming."

I was more glad of this opportunity than I cared to admit. "Would you like me up at seven?"

"Yes, but I prefer you rested enough to work for the whole day and well into the evening," said Mycroft Holmes. "So I will encourage you to sleep well; perhaps you will find something we have missed thus far while you sleep."

Miss Gatspy managed to look fairly fresh as she rose. "I think this is a wise plan. I know I will not be much good to you without rest." She put her hand to her head. "I can't hold two thoughts together for more than a heartbeat."

"Then off you go, Miss Gatspy. Tyers will call you at eight," said Holmes with as much gallantry as I have ever known him to display. "You, too, Guthrie. Yvgeny Tschersky told me a Russian proverb: *Morning is wiser than evening.* Let us hope it may be so." He wandered over to the leather couch and dropped down upon it.

I noticed he was a foot taller than the couch was long. "Would you prefer the settee in the sitting room, sir?" I suggested. "I can't imagine you'll be comfortable on that."

"I probably won't be, but I'll be safe," said he. "You should be in the sitting room, for any watchers will make it a point to know that you are here. If they see you have slept on the settee, it will further persuade them that you are making every effort to keep the illusion of my presence." He waved me away. "I'll draw one of the chairs up to the couch, and contrive something. I have slept on far worse."

"No doubt," I said, and made for the door. Miss Gatspy was there ahead of me, and I held it for her. "I am sorry you have been put into such an awkward situation."

"How is it awkward? You mean the lack of chaperone?" She shrugged. "Tyers is here. And if my superiors are not bothered by our sleeping under the same roof—but hardly more than that—why should I feel it is inappropriate?"

I did not know how to answer her. "If you prefer, I can make—"

"If you are proposing to absent yourself from this flat for the sake of my reputation, I thank you, but I see no necessity." She shook her head. "I am not here on a lark, Guthrie, nor are you. You may want to keep that uppermost in your mind."

I felt her rebuke most stringently. "You are right, of course. But I cannot help but be concerned on your behalf."

"I know," she said. "And it is most . . . most dear of you. But there are more immediate demands on us both than the dictates of good society." She had reached the withdrawing room door, which she slid open. "Sleep well, Guthrie, and quickly." With that, she slipped inside and closed the door behind her.

I turned and went to the sitting room, just opposite the withdrawing room, where I found Tyers had left a duvet across the settee. I took off my boots, my coat, my collar, cuffs and tie, and stretched out, making the duvet into a cocoon. I doubted I would be able to fall asleep any time soon, so active was my mind; I anticipated tossing and turning from now until dawn. And then Tyers shook me awake, a fresh cup of tea in his hand. The room was filled with milky light of a rainy morning; Tyers built up the fire a little. "Thank you," I said, scratching my hair and increasing its disarray.

"There is a razor set out for you in the bathroom, and I have taken the liberty of supplying you with clean collar and cuffs."

"Very good of you, Tyers." I sat up. "Did *you* sleep?"

"Yes, and sooner than you did. I took a nap from one until three, and slept from just after four until half-six." He paused in the doorway. "You may want to go along to the bathroom now. I am about to wake Miss Gatspy."

"Oh, yes," I said, taking the cup-and-saucer with me. "I shan't be long. Do tell her I will not remain in the bathroom over-long."

Tyers nodded, faint amusement in his eyes. "I am going to send a note round to the Admiralty as soon as Hastings arrives, informing them of Mister Holmes' illness; breakfast will be served before I leave," he said as I went by him and down the hall.

I nodded my endorsement of this plan, then hurried along to shave and tend to other demands of nature as quickly as possible. I was determined to be ready to work in twenty minutes, and not to keep Miss Gatspy waiting. As soon as I was through, I went into the library and found Mycroft Holmes already up and in a change of clothes. I greeted him at once, saying, "I haven't any new insights to offer, that I am aware of, at least."

"Hardly surprising. I would like to think you would subject all such revelations to intellectual scrutiny before presenting them. If they are nothing more than impressions, we will waste valuable time trying to shape them to our needs." Mycroft Holmes was more brusque than usual, but I took no umbrage.

"I agree, and I hope that this morning we'll be able to review all we put forth last night." I had more faith in such reconsideration than I did in inspiration, in any case.

"Exactly my plan," said Holmes. "I have been looking over our time-charts, by the way, and I keep thinking I am missing something, something obvious." He went and stared at the Saturday page. "We have certainly been busy."

"That we have," I said. "And the end is not in sight." I was about to sit down when I heard the sound of the doorbell being wound.

Mycroft Holmes turned to me urgently. "Out. Go out. Use the study. You know what to say: I am ill and cannot be disturbed." He all but thrust me from the room.

I went at once to the study and sat down at the table where I usually work of a morning, and waited for Tyers to bring the new arrival to see me. I hoped that Miss Gatspy would remain out of sight, for her presence would be hard to explain. I was beginning to fret when the door opened and Chief Inspector Pryce came in, very dapper for a policeman, and frowning. "Good morning, Chief Inspector," I said, rising to meet him.

"Good morning, Mister Guthrie," he replied. "I am told Mister Holmes has taken ill."

"Yes. A feverish cold," I said, pleased that I sounded convincing. "Is there anything I can do for you?"

"I hope so," he answered, but said no more.

"What is it you want?" I asked when he remained mute.

"I want to know why you persuaded Sir Cameron to return to Scotland," he said at last, as if uneasy about the answer.

"Well, you know, there had been at least one attempt on his life, possibly two, and it struck Holmes that having him remain in London—with or without his wife—was taking a risk that would make the investigation more complicated than it need be." I saw him nod, and I added, "You cannot tell me that you wanted him during your investigation."

"No. I am delighted to have him out of the way, for many reasons, as you may guess. But when I spoke to him about leaving, all my pleas fell on deaf ears. I was wondering how you managed it?" He came to sit down, his manner becoming more affable.

"I think Mister Holmes convinced him of the many problems he would have to contend with to have his estranged wife caught up in a murder inquiry, particularly if another attempt should be made on his life," I said, wanting to seem helpful and forthcoming. "There was more than a marriage to consider, as both Sir Cameron and Lady MacMillian have estates and fortunes in their respective countries, and there is a great deal at stake. You know what these reconciliations can be. To add such physical danger seems inexcusably reckless. The Germans would be seriously distressed if anything happened to their noblewoman, and that would put Sir Cameron in a most difficult position in regard to the government here, or his inheritance there."

"I see," said Chief Inspector Pryce with a doubtful air.

I decided to expand a bit on my response. "I think Mister Holmes also mentioned some of the problems that might develop regarding—"

"Money?" The Chief Inspector laughed once. "I know what titled families can be like in that regard—none better." He shook his head. "Oh, you need not apologize for that, Mister Guthrie. I grew up watching my father's relatives circling like sharks."

"And you resented it?" I asked. "I fear Lady MacMillian might."

"I resented their treatment of my mother, not their preoccupation with the estate. I knew it was worth little and it took as much money to keep going as it provided. I didn't want to spend my life doing nothing more than struggling to hold onto something I didn't want. I was sorry my mother was treated so shabbily, but I do not feel I have been deprived of a treasure, no matter what my father's family may think. I took the small parcel of land my father left me—no one wanted it because of the nearness of the railroad—and I turned it into a third-partnership in a repair yard for locomotives; I provided the land and reap the benefit of the business. I am considerably better off than any of my relations, little though they may believe it." He rose. "I appreciate your candor, Mister Guthrie. I don't mind your asking about my circumstances, for it clears the air. I would do the same in your place. I'll do what I may to preserve your confidence." He took a step back. "I won't keep you. Your work must be doubled with Mister Holmes ill."

"I have a good amount on my plate," I said, making no excuse but at the same time not being specific.

"Tell Mister Holmes I hope he is better soon. In weather like this, colds are the very devil to deal with." He went out, and a moment later I heard Tyers escort him to the door.

"Well, well," said Miss Gatspy, coming into the study as the front door closed, "he was out early."

"I suppose he didn't want anyone to know he was coming here," I said. "Holmes is in the library, and Tyers will give us breakfast shortly."

"I know. I was sent to fetch you." Her fine blue eyes shone with mischief. "Mister Holmes is as restless as a caged tiger, but I think he will not do anything that will endanger Mister Sutton. He has been complaining that he should be out and about, tracing all Sutton's movements, but he is afraid he might put Sutton into greater danger. I have advised him to sit quietly for a time, but I will own myself astonished if he will do so."

I nodded. "It would be most unlike him," I said as I left the study and crossed the hall to the library. Entering that room, I delivered a quick account of Chief Inspector Pryce's visit, then said, "I didn't get the impression that he had any secondary motives in coming here."

"You like the man," said Holmes. "And so do I. That may color our impression."

"Well, I have no opinion of him either way," said Miss Gatspy, "and he has not the feel of a man seeking to confirm a crime. If there is someone among the police who is aiding the Brotherhood, I do not think it is he."

"No more do I," Mycroft Holmes admitted. "If he is two-faced, he accomplishes it better than anyone I have ever seen. No, I believe we must look elsewhere for someone in the police." He sat down. "I am disheartened to say it. I will admit I hoped we might find questionable motives in Pryce."

"It *would* be reassuring to have Chief Inspector Pryce be the culprit; it fits our expectations so neatly," said Miss Gatspy. "I will see if the Golden Lodge has any information on him that would indicate he is at fault, but, frankly, I would be shocked if it turns out to be so."

"As would I," Holmes conceded. "But we must remain alert for any member of the police whose actions are questionable." He motioned to me. "Tell me, Guthrie, what do you make of Inspector Featherstone?"

"He is industrious and ambitious enough to be diligent, and he has taken on some difficult cases with success," I said. "Beyond that, I know little about him beyond my impression of the man; your files have only a sentence or two about him." I looked toward the door as Tyers came in, butler's table in hand, with breakfast laid on it.

"There is food for all of you, and the plates are all doubled. If anyone saw this, they would assume two are being fed, not three." He put the butler's table down. "I will bring in more cups directly, but just now there are only two."

"I will wait," I said.

Mycroft Holmes glanced at me, his grey eyes sharp. "If this is not a gesture of self-denial, I will permit it."

"I am more hungry than thirsty," I said truthfully. "Go ahead, sir."

"Well, I am ravenous," said Holmes, drawing up his chair and sitting down while I fetched a seat for Miss Gatspy. "This inactivity is worse than all the careering about we have done."

"Thank you, Guthrie," she said as I seated her. "Now then, Mister Holmes, let us review what we know about Sutton's disappearance."

Mycroft Holmes was busy serving himself poached eggs topped with cheddar cheese and scones. He paused in his activity to say, "It is all on the chart."

"Not all of it, if you will forgive me saying so," she told him. "I spoke with our guards, as you recall, and I am not satisfied that one of the vehicles in the collision was the means of removing him. I think he may have been seized and taken off by other agents of the Brotherhood. I say this because it would not have been remarkable had a constable happened by, and he would surely have detained the vehicles in order to make a report of the accident. No, upon consideration, I believe that the accident was a diversion that made it possible for comrades of the men managing the collision to take Sutton away while everyone was distracted by the supposed accident itself. The Golden Lodge guard did mention that a van went by just after the worst of the collision was cleared. He mentioned it only because it had a caduceus on the side, and he wondered if anyone had been hurt." She poured a cup of tea and selected a scone and pot-cheese, then said, "I doubt whether a constable would detain a medical van."

Holmes was listening intently. "You didn't mention this last night."

"I discounted it, as I realize now I was expected to do. But this morning, it struck me that this could have been the real key to the abduction. It wasn't an ambulance-van," she added. "It was one of those used used to transport other patients, and bodies, those who are not emergencies."

"Aha," said Mycroft Holmes. "Yes, indeed. I take your point, Miss Gatspy. I comprehend your reasons for your suspicions, and I think it would be advisable to find out which hospital had such a vehicle abroad in this part of London last night, and where it was bound." He ate eagerly, preparing for a long day.

"I shall put our men on it," said Miss Gatspy. "You have other matters to occupy you." She looked over at me. "What of Featherstone? Do you think we should check him out?"

"Do you mean, should we go to Scotland Yard to speak with him?" I asked.

"Yes, that is what I mean," said Miss Gatspy. "Beard the lion in his den, as it were?"

"No," said Holmes as he helped himself to another scone and dipped it in the smears of egg-and-cheese on his plate. "That gives him too much of an advantage. If you want to learn anything from him, he must come to you."

"Shall I send for him?" I asked, glad to see Tyers come in with a fresh pot of tea and two more cups-and-saucers; he left these and withdrew at once.

"I wouldn't recommend it; again, he would have the advantage of a warning," said Holmes. "If he is going to come of his own volition, that will tell its own tale. In the meantime, you must be ready to do all that you can to summarize the progress that has been made in various cases. I want to be able to use that information to assess our current predicament."

"You mean the closer we have come to solving a problem, the likelier we are to find the source of our problem?" I said, pouring out the new tea and trying to smile my confidence.

"That may be part of it. It may also be that Kerem's escape might have been a signal of some sort, that set these wheels in motion." He caught his lower lip in his teeth. "I wish I had not let Sutton go to the club in my stead. If they were after me, they should have had me."

"You cannot mean that," said Miss Gatspy in a stern voice. "Our only hope of finding him and saving him is you. With all credit to Sutton, were the circumstances reversed, he would not be capable of the necessary inquiries." She had spread pot-cheese on her scone and had broken off the end to eat. "He is a most accomplished fellow, but intrigue on this level is not his metier."

Holmes shook his head. "If anything should happen to him—" He stopped.

"We will do our utmost to be certain that it doesn't," I promised him.

"That is what I am depending upon," said Holmes as he poured a second cup of tea. "It is infuriating to be cooped up as I am. If I could go about without endangering Sutton, I would."

Miss Gatspy offered him a winsome smile. "I thought about that as well."

"And what did you decide upon?" His question was abrupt, but Miss Gatspy didn't seem to mind.

"Well, if Sutton goes about in all manner of disguises, so can you: you have done so any number of times in the past. And anything is better than having you cooped up and surly as a tiger." She actually laughed a bit as Holmes turned a thunder-struck look on her. "Do not tell me you haven't been fretting to put on your motly and go hunting for these men?"

"Of course!" he exclaimed. "I have been wanting to do just that, but I hesitated. I do not want to put Sutton at any greater risk than he is already. Still, I am sure you are right. Miss Gatspy, I am in your debt more than I can say." He swung around and looked at me. "Guthrie, I want you to inform Sid Hastings that he is going to be carrying an elderly invalid out to Saint Elizabeth's Hospital; he is to wait while we settle a few matters inside. Then he is to carry us back here."

"You are still trying to find out about the stolen body," I said. "Why?"

"Vans of the sort Miss Gatspy reported are often used to transport bodies to Potter's Field. It is somewhere I can begin." He helped himself to another two eggs and began to consume them with gusto.

"Isn't Hastings carrying Tyers to the Admiralty? It's not far, but in such rain . . ." I let my thought trail away.

"He is, but that isn't important now. It will be a matter of half an hour before he returns, and I will need all of it to make myself ready. The real problem here is to distract any watchers enough to keep them from noticing from which flat this invalid comes, or not to come from this flat at all." He sat very still, lost in thought. "It will be a bit awkward, but I can get onto the roof of the building next door and from there I can go another number down Pall Mall. That is two buildings away, and I can enter there from the roof. Getting back will be a bit more difficult, but not impossible, especially if Tyers will arrange to have a ladder at the crucial place."

"Shall I come with you?" I asked, anticipating his answer.

"I think not, Guthrie. I have no wish to give the watchers any reason to associate the invalid with me, and you could provide the very link I wish to avoid. They will not think about the invalid unless we give them reason, and your presence could well be enough to jar their thoughts. No, this is one I must attend to on my own." He took another scone and buttered it. "You must see it is as well if you remain here, dancing attendance on your supposedly ill employer; the kidnappers will assume you are waiting for word from them, and everyone else will accept your devotion as typical of you." He beamed at me; he was almost himself again.

"And Miss Gatspy?" I asked, wondering how he would assign her.

"She has information to get, and I hope she will do so quickly." He directed his gaze to her once more. "I hope I am not being presumptuous, Miss Gatspy, but I am convinced that we must act promptly, or lose the little advantage we have."

"I agree," she said. "Your plans do not bother me in the least. I will return by noon and give you all the information I can."

"Excellent," Mycroft Holmes approved. "Thank goodness I shan't have to be idle all day, else I would be climbing the walls. This may finally put us in a strong position at last. I dislike being forced into a defensive posture." He cocked his head. "While I am gone, Guthrie, your task will remain as before, evaluating all we have put together about the last several days. I have a theory that will depend upon you making as comprehensive an assessment as possible."

"As you wish, sir," I said, taking a scone and dipping it into my tea, as I had done as a boy in Scotland; my mother had often chastised me for ill-manners, but did it herself, upon occasion. "When do you plan to return?"

"From this first venture? No later than one o'clock. I assume I will have more to do before the day is over." He finished his breakfast with a flourish.

"And there is the theatre tonight," I reminded him.

"What do you mean?" Mycroft Holmes asked, arresting his cup on its way to his lips.

"You said that if Sutton was not back this evening, you would take his place in *MacBeth*," I reminded him.

"So I did, and so I shall, if I must," said Holmes stalwartly, then added, "I hope we may have Sutton back with us before then."

"As do I," I told him. "But it may not be possible, in which case—"

"I know, I know," said Holmes impatiently. "He has done more than that for me every day," he went on, somewhat displeased with the possibility looming ahead ahead of him. "I am prepared to do what I must to preserve our fictions for both our sakes." He put his plate aside, saying decisively, "I am going to look at what Sutton has available for disguises."

"He seems improved," said Miss Gatspy as soon as Mycroft Holmes left the library.

"Let us hope it continues," I said.

"Do you doubt it will?" Her large, celestial eyes revealed her own apprehension.

All I could say was, "We shall see."

FROM THE PERSONAL JOURNAL OF PHILIP TYERS

I have just returned from informing the Admiralty of MH's illness only to find MH himself rigged out in an outrageous disguise, complete with white hair and beard and a massive walking stick. He has outlined his plan to me, and now is preparing to go rollicking off across the roofs of our neighbors' buildings to escape notice. He has instructed me to leave a ladder at the study window, and to be ready to admit him by that route between half-twelve and one.

G has gone down to talk to Hastings, and Miss Gatspy has left for the morning, leaving G and me to deal with unfolding events here ...

Chapter Twenty-three

SOMEHOW THE MORNING faded away more swiftly than I had thought possible. I had occupied my time as Mycroft Holmes had ordered me, and now I had eight pages of comprehensive summary to present to him upon his return. It was not the same as being out, pursuing various clues, but it was useful and necessary, as I reminded myself every twenty minutes or so. I had managed to find several suspicious points in the events of the last six days, yet none of them, by themselves, would seem anything significant: seen together, they became ominous. My head ached from effort and apprehension, and I had, to my chagrin, begun to feel my lack of sleep again.

Tyers brought me another pot of strong black tea, saying as he did, "You are doing well, Mister Guthrie, and no doubt about it."

"Thanks for the encouragement," I said, far from convinced of it myself. "I shall have material to present, and that is important."

"It is," Tyers agreed. "The Admiralty have said that Mister Holmes is to notify them when he is sufficiently recovered to resume the daily visits of the courier, and when he will be able to return to his duties. I have assured them both would be done in a timely manner." He made ready to leave the library, but I stopped him.

"What if we don't get Sutton back? What then?" I had been wrestling with that possibility most of the morning, but now that I actually voiced my fear, it redoubled.

"It would be most inconvenient not to, so it must be done. Mister Holmes has much need of Sutton; he relies on him for many skills, and if anything became of Sutton, it is unlikely that Mister Holmes could find such another as he," said Tyers calmly. "I do not suppose that he will remain missing much longer."

"Why do you say that?" I asked, hoping Tyers had some special information that had not come my way.

"Because Mister Holmes would rather face the Brotherhood's inner circle than tread the boards at the Duke of York's Theatre." He smiled once, and let himself out.

I wanted to be amused, but could not rise from the gloom that possessed me. I got up and went to pace in front of the day charts again, hoping to see something I had missed before; I continued to think I had not seen something obvious. I was staring at Friday's events when a sharp knock on the door at the rear of the flat announced Miss Gatspy's return. I gathered up my pages and prepared to welcome her back to our efforts.

"Thank you, Tyers; I'll admit myself," her voice declared; I felt a shiver go through me as the door opened. "There you are, Guthrie," she said. She had taken advantage of her absence to don a new ensemble, this one a walking suit in bottle-green with a heavy silken scarf of the same color wrapped around her throat; her cheeks were pink from the cold and drops of water shone in the wisps of hair around her face where her hat—now most certainly in Tyers' hands, along with her coat—hadn't covered them.

"Is it noon already?" I asked as I glanced at the clock.

"Twenty minutes past," she said, a bit ruefully. "I have my sylphide outside in the service alley, under the stairs. I hope no harm will come to it."

"Your colleagues are on duty," I said to reassure her.

"That may not be enough," she told me as she went to sit down. "Were there any callers while I was gone?"

"No," I said, hoping to make this good news.

"Nothing from the kidnappers?" She looked closely at me.

I hated to have to disappoint her. "Nothing," I said sadly, and then, not wanting to dwell on such unproductive ruminations, asked, "Are you planning to go out again soon? Is that why you have your carriage with you?"

"I hardly know what I will be doing, but I thought it might be advisable to have more than one vehicle at our disposal, considering the diverse matters we have before us to investigate. Hastings can't be constantly driving all over London, you know. This way, if more than one excursion is wanted, we need not rely on hire-cabs, or other transport." She noticed the papers in my hands. "It appears you've made progress."

"I have done a synopsis. I am not sure yet that it is progress," I told her with more honesty than I had intended.

"It is better than having confusion," she pointed out. "If nothing else, it will help us to eliminate those events that are unconnected to our inquiries."

"Did you find out anything useful?" I asked her, trying to find something that would be more rewarding to us both.

"I may have. Mister Holmes will have to determine if what I have learned is useful, when he can spare us a moment." She looked about again, as if expecting to find him sitting in the shadows; she turned back to me and held out her hand. "Let me see what you've done."

"If you wish," I said, and handed my pages to her; while she read I went to the door to ask Tyers to bring a fresh pot of tea.

"Already thrilling, sir," Tyers responded from the kitchen.

"Oh, yes, *please*," said Miss Gatspy. "I am longing for something warm."

I could think of nothing to say to that, so I changed the subject. "I suppose your guards are still on duty."

"Yes; one in a carriage and two on horseback. They want to be able to follow us and continue to watch the flat." She made a gesture of helplessness. "I cannot convince my superiors that I can function as a guard as well as an ally in this situation."

"You mustn't mind their concern," I said, marveling again at how easily this delicate woman faced terrible danger.

She was about to say something, but changed her mind. "We'll discuss that later. I want to read through this, to see if what you have coincides with what I have learned."

I inclined my head, deferring to her, and I waited for Tyers to come with the tea. I did my best not to stare at Miss Gatspy, or to disturb her in any other way, but I found myself watching her, trying to read her expression; I was eager for her comments, and hoping she would be pleased with my observations.

"Here is the tea, Mister Guthrie," said Tyers as he came into the library some ten minutes later.

I was glad of his arrival. "Thank you, Tyers. Have you seen anything of Mister Holmes yet?"

"I checked the window not five minutes ago, to put the ladder in place, and I saw no one on the neighbors' roofs," he said. "He should be back shortly."

"Thank you," I said again as Tyers left the room.

"Do you mean that Mister Holmes is not here?" Miss Gatspy spoke sharply; she had put the papers aside at last. "I supposed he was in another room, or resting. When did he leave?"

"Not long after you proposed the disguise to him," I said, be-mused by her alarm. "He went out a little more than two hours ago; I am sure he was not noticed. You needn't fret. He left from a building down the way." I thought these reassurances would ease her mind; I saw by her expression that I was wrong.

"What on earth made him do anything so foolish?" she demanded. "Now none of my colleagues can watch him, nor do we know what has become of him."

"He went with Hastings," I said, as if that was protection enough. "And, if you recall, it was your recommendation that he use a disguise in order to be away."

"Yes, but not for the entire morning; I assumed he would not be gone more than an hour; I should have known he would press his luck," she said sarcastically. "Do you have any idea where he was going?"

"To Saint Elizabeth's, as he said he would," I replied, a bit sheepishly, for now that she had pointed out the risks Mycroft Holmes had taken, I was inclined to share her indignation.

"In disguise, you say?" She got up and took a turn about the room. "Disguised how?"

"He looked ancient, at least seventy. Before he left, he wrapped himself in a hooded duster of oiled canvas, which will keep him from getting wet and will preserve his make-up from damage. He left out the window onto the neighboring roof, then crossed to the building beyond, and went out to the street from there." I gave a single nod. "Tell me, Miss Gatspy, how do you think he has exposed himself?"

She shook her head. "At least he has taken some precautions. Let us hope they are enough to keep him from being discovered, for Sutton's sake. In weather like this, I suppose he might count himself safer than he would have done on a clear day."

"So he thought," I said, wanting to show her that Holmes had not been as reckless as she assumed he was. "He will return the same way. Unless the Brotherhood know of this, and have posted assassins on the roofs of neighboring houses, and can see through mizzle, he must be safe. And why would they do that if they assume they have Holmes as a captive?" I was speaking very fast, as if quickness made my comments more convincing.

"I see," said Miss Gatspy, her voice dropping down to a condemning lowness that made me aware I had not yet persuaded her.

"He had a thought, and he wanted to confirm it, or discover he was in error," I added.

"Do you know what he sought to find out?" she asked with asperity.

"I must admit I do not," I told her.

She glared at the tea-service. "He is the most infuriating man. I don't know how you endure his employ."

I was wholly conscious of the concern she revealed, but her manner was rather too much for me to accept without challenge. "Dear Miss Gatspy," I said with what I hoped was more hauteur than pique, "You may think what you like about Mister Holmes, but you will not berate him to me, if you please. He is the most capable, extraordinary man I have ever known, and I understand that because of his abilities he is not like most men; I am more than willing to make allowances for him if such are necessary."

"Don't get on your high ropes, Guthrie," Miss Gatspy recommended with a smile. "I am aware of his sterling qualities. And I am aware of yours, as well."

I did not know how to respond to this encomium—if encomium it was—so I remained still, saying only, "I am relieved to hear it."

"And now I've embarrassed you," she said. "Well, don't go about in dismay, if you please." She went back and sat down. "We both will be the better for a cup of tea and a moment's quiet reflection." Without waiting for me to agree, she poured out two cups. "Here. Before it gets too strong."

"Thank you," I said as I accepted the cup and added sugar. I sat down opposite her, and did my best to look at anything but her, so as to quieten my thoughts.

"Guthrie," she said a bit later, "you and I are both worried on Sutton's behalf. Let us not take out our apprehension on one another."

It was such a sensible remark that I could only nod. "I will try to heed your advice," I said.

"Good," she approved. "If you wouldn't mind, I'd like to review your—" She stopped as we heard the rattle and scramble of Mycroft Holmes' return.

"Tyers," he cried out. "Come take the ladder. I have brought it in." He sounded a bit out of breath, but there was no lack of enthusiasm in his voice, which implied his journey had been successful.

I went to the door and found Holmes stumping down the hallway, his oilskins flapping around him, his wispy white hair in disarray from the hood he had just thrown back; he half-dragged, half-carried a ladder over his shoulder. "It is good to have you back, sir," I said, prepared to assist him.

"Good to *be* back, Guthrie," he declared in stentorian accents. "Has Miss Gatspy returned?"

"She has. We are taking tea in the library." I reached out for the ladder only to have Tyers arrive, ready to tend to all.

"Excellent," Holmes approved as he gave the ladder to Tyers. "I will be with you directly."

"I take it you have discovered something," I ventured.

"Indeed I have. And it is just as I thought: it has been under my nose the whole time, and I failed to see it for what it was," He pushed past me, and began peeling off his oilskins.

I went back into the library. "Did you hear?"

"I certainly did," Miss Gatspy said. "Well, we must take this as a favorable omen. How long do you think it will take him to change?"

"Ten minutes," I said, returning to my seat.

"Then let us finish our tea," she recommended. "We cannot learn what he has discovered through contagion or osmosis."

In the event, it was more than fifteen minutes until Mycroft Holmes joined us, still toweling his wet hair. He was in his own clothes once more, and he had removed all traces of the make-up he had worn. As he looked toward Miss Gatspy, he said, "I take it you have something to report to me?"

"That I have," she said. "I have our records on Inspector Feather-stone. You may find them interesting."

"If you mean his Irish mother's alliance with certain self-proclaimed revolutionaries back on the 'auld sod,' you needn't bother," Holmes said, and chuckled as we stared at him. "I should have realized that her maiden name—Collins—innocuous enough, but with certain associations—revealed ties that are not the ones we would want our policemen to have." He sat down. "I'm ravenous," he announced. "It has been a busy morning."

"That it has," I agreed. "And no doubt you have done more than visit Saint Elizabeth's."

"Yes. I called on Inspector Strange, and he was kind enough to allow me to review the records that worked so much against him when he was forced to leave Scotland Yard." He was almost thrumming with energy now, and he put his hand to his chest in a show of mock humility that made me chuckle. "I was astonished to discover how much he had amassed in his files. Most interesting reading."

"Which he did not provide you until now?" I was perplexed by this reticence on Inspector Strange's part.

"He considers his information dangerous—and he is right to do so—and would rather offer briefs than the material itself. In a case such as this, however, he was willing to allow me access to the files themselves. I had to give my word to examine only those records that bore on our current cases, and to look at no others." He looked around. "Is Tyers going to provide us with dinner soon?"

"I should think so," I said. "Tell us what you discovered, sir. We have been on tenterhooks."

"Oh, I think you can rest assured that we have the key at last." He rose and went to the day charts. "It is all right here, if only you know how to look."

"I am willing to believe that," I said, mustering my patience. "You say it is obvious, but we have not seen it. The only person we have—" I stopped. "Sir Marmion Hazeltine," I said.

"Bravo, Guthrie," said Mycroft Holmes.

Miss Gatspy, for once, looked surprised. "What?" She put down her tea-cup and went to stand beside Holmes; she scrutinized the time and events associated with his name. "It is far from obvious."

"If you don't know what you are seeing," said Mycroft Holmes. "As it was intended we should not."

I looked at the charts, trying to make out what Holmes meant.

"I have made some interesting discoveries in regard to Sir Marmion," said Holmes in a steely voice. "I am ashamed that it took me so long to realize that he had a role to play in all this." He made this confession with difficulty. "Had I not so many other—" He broke off. "That is no excuse."

"Excuse or not," I said, "it was the same for all of us." I went to my summaries and began to skim the pages, looking for mentions of Sir Marmion's name.

"That may be," said Holmes, "but our blindness has cost us dearly." He went back to his chair. "I dislike being played for a fool."

Miss Gatspy shook her head. "No one does; but you should let them believe you haven't figured this out yet, so they will not be on guard against you. Remember that they do not know you are hunting them. They assume they have stopped you. This is very much to your advantage. Even if they should suspect otherwise, it would be more strategic to let them assume you are unaware of how they have deceived you, so that they may become sloppy, and make it easier for you to find Sutton, and perhaps to bring Braaten and Vickers to justice."

"You have a most persuasive argument, Miss Gatspy," said Mycroft Holmes. "Galling thought it is, I concur. They must still suppose they have captured me, and not Sutton, which is, as you say, also to our advantage. I see the value in not giving up our slightly improved understanding." He coughed diplomatically. "I have a theory regarding Sutton."

"Oh?" said Miss Gatspy; I listened intently.

"I believe that he was taken in that hospital-van to Hawtrees, Sir Marmion's asylum. What better place to hide a captive than to lock him away, beyond help? And how like the Brotherhood. No doubt they have locked him up, and no doubt they have isolated him." Mycroft Holmes gestured impatiently. "I found out at Saint Elizabeth's that such vans are used to transport patients who have become violently overset from hospital to asylum. No policeman would be likely to stop such a van, nor would they want to examine what it carried, be it corpses, the crippled, or the mad." He held up his hand. "You may say I have insufficient evidence to make this assumption, but I can think of nothing else, and I must take action on what I have rather than delay in the hope that I will learn more. I would do this under other circumstances, but with Sutton's life in the balance, I cannot wait any longer."

"And why are you so sure you will find him at Hawtrees?" I asked, not wanting to question him too closely, but wanting to be assured on this crucial point. "If we go charging in there, and it turns out he is not there, we will never have such an opportunity again."

"Then we must be right," said Holmes. "And consider. If Sutton claims he is anyone, whether he identifies himself, or says he is Mycroft Holmes, who will believe him, in an asylum. No doubt there are other residents who say they are Napoleon or Caesar or Moses, and they are not believed. The more I consider the possibilities, the more likely it seems to me that that is where he has been taken. Sir Marmion practices galvanic therapy there. He has used it most successfully on the most extreme cases. If he administers such shocks to a healthy brain, who knows what damage it would do?"

I could hear the anxiety in his voice, and I shared it. "You don't think he would do such a thing, do you?"

"I am certain he would," said Mycroft Holmes. "Out of scientific curiosity, if not out of his desire to show his worth to the Brotherhood."

"Then you are satisfied he is a member?" Miss Gatspy asked. "Have you proof, or it is supposition?"

"I have some minor proof, and every reason to suppose; I know I can lay the death of the courier at his door, beyond cavil," said Holmes. "I want to have the opportunity to reveal his perfidy to the medical community, but only after I have Sutton back and safe." He looked at the clock. "It is approaching two. Where is dinner?"

I started toward the door, hoping Tyers would be there, ready to set out the meal. The corridor was empty. I went down to the kitchen, and discovered Tyers just coming in from the back. "Mister Holmes is eager for his dinner," I told Tyers, who laughed aloud, not unkindly, and made a gesture of compliance.

"In fifteen minutes, in the sitting room," he told me, and put down the loaves of fresh bread he had just fetched from the bakeshop.

"Very good," I said, and went back to the library with this news.

"Excellent," said Holmes. "As I was saying to Miss Gatspy, I have stumbled upon information that links Sir Marmion to the courier's death. It was really quite brazen." He paused to be sure he had my full attention. "He told us he intended to stop by the hospital to see the courier. Later that day the young man died. What I discovered was that Sir Marmion remained with the courier for almost half an hour, at the end of which time, he reported the courier was having trouble breathing. Sir Marmion departed, and the physicians strove to restore the young man's lungs, but could not. The autopsy notes indicate that the courier's fingers were bluish in tinge, and his skin had a grey cast, all consistent with failing lungs. It is also consistent with certain poisons."

"Which you now suspect Sir Marmion may have administered to him," I said, comprehending the nature of his remarks.

"Which I *know* someone gave to him, for I recommended tests be made for poisons; the test came back with indications for cyanide. There is no doubt he was poisoned, and the only person who had such an opportunity, other than the nurses, is Sir Marmion." Mycroft Holmes all but pounced on the name.

"Isn't there a distinctive odor to cyanide?" asked Miss Gatspy.

"There is, and there is also a distinctive odor to hospitals, rather more overpowering. The courier was being treated for infection, and that also had an overpowering smell. I do not fault anyone for failing to diagnose the problem." He lowered his head, as if preparing to butt his way through the wall. "I do think it unfortunate that no one thought to question Sir Marmion before now; I include myself in the ranks of those who failed in that capacity."

I coughed gently. "Will you be able to gather sufficient evidence to charge him with that crime?"

"Not yet," Mycroft Holmes allowed. "But by the time we have Sutton back, there should be no difficulty in bringing him before the bench."

"If we can find him tonight and get him out of the asylum without harm," I said.

"Precisely what you must do," agreed Holmes before heading toward the door and his dinner.

FROM THE PERSONAL JOURNAL OF PHILIP TYERS

It is all arranged: MH will travel with Hastings, and G will travel with Miss Gatspy to the asylum, and once they arrive, they will study the place. They have agreed upon a ruse to gain entrance, which is for G and Miss Gatspy to do, for MH will have to return to the theatre to perform in Sutton's stead. I will remain here, although I would truly relish seeing MH perform.

The rain is heavier again, and the traffic is slowed because of it. The Times *today reported a sinking in the Channel of a Portuguese merchantman. Nine of the crew were saved, but all the cargo was lost . . .*

Chapter Twenty-four

THE CLOCKS WERE striking three when we descended to our various vehicles, all of us carrying such equipment as we thought we might need to effect the rescue we had undertaken. Mycroft Holmes, who went down the front stairs, had donned an impressive set of side-whiskers and a uniform of a General in the Austrian army; he walked with a limp for which he carried a cane with a sword concealed within it. He complained loudly about the English who coddle themselves, and swore to return.

Miss Gatspy and I went down the rear to her sylphide. She took a little time to explain to her Golden Lodge colleagues what we were about, although with no particulars as to Sutton's function in Holmes' life. They all agreed that the two on horseback would follow us, so that one could go with Holmes and one remain with us at Hawtrees if it proved necessary; then she buckled the Albermarle on her horse. That done, we got into the small carriage, she backed her horse expertly, and swung out toward the road. I stowed my valise under the seat and did my best to sit in some manner that would not bring us into constant contact, for I knew it would be presumptuous of me to do anything that might interfere with her driving. I was acutely aware of her nearness, for all I did my best to ignore it.

We headed west, going along Piccadilly to Park Lane, then to the left again into the Bayswater Road. For almost half an hour we kept silent, Miss Gatspy concentrating on the traffic, I trying to anticipate any problems that lay ahead of us. Then, as Bayswater Road became Notting Hill Gate, she spoke up.

"Do you think we'll be able to get him out as readily as Mister Holmes says we will?" There was little nervousness in her voice, only an eagerness to be getting on with it. "I have been thinking about the plan, and I am not as certain as Mister Holmes is of its success. Too many things could go wrong. If we bungle this, we lose more than our element of surprise."

"Do you have anything else in mind?" I asked, at once curious and determined to stand by Mycroft Holmes' scheme.

"Not yet, but I cannot rid myself of the fear that we have made the whole too complicated, and that we are depending too much on all elements being perfectly executed." She gave a slight tug on the rein to check the mare's pulling. "Do you believe we can actually carry out the whole?"

"I hope we may do," I said, and could not keep from adding, "I still don't like the idea of having you inside such a place as that."

"I am not delighted myself. But I do not believe it is our only chance to succeed; if we fail now, they will know they have the wrong man, and I fear Sutton will pay the price," she said as she passed a lumbering coach with two positions and two footmen, all bedraggled in the rain; Miss Gatspy had the advantage with the smaller, lighter carriage, which was far more maneuverable than the cumbersome covered landau.

"Sadly, I have no better recommendation to make," I admitted. "It is most unfortunate. I have tried to think of an alternative, but none comes to mind."

"You are the one who will be most at risk, not I. You must make them believe you are mad, and trust that they will treat you as Sir Marmion claims those in his charge are treated. All I have to do is present the picture of a sorrowing, devoted wife. If I droop and weep, no one will pay any attention to me. They expect wives to languish when their husbands are confined." She achieved a seraphic smile. "You cannot imagine how relieved I was that Mister Holmes had a suitable ring for me to wear. It lends just the right touch: two small diamonds and a minuscule ruby."

"All that is Sutton's doing," I said, feeling more edgy at the mention of our missing friend. "He has two boxes of various rings, bracelets, necklaces, and the like."

"Well, bravo Sutton," she said, and drew in as the traffic became more congested as we neared Shepherd's Bush. "It's the Uxbridge Road we want, isn't it?"

"Yes." I had taken the time to study the map before we set out. "There is a great deal of cross-traffic here."

"Hardly surprising," said Miss Gatspy as she muttered at a house removal van not far ahead of us; one of the leaders was tangled in the traces and the driver had stopped to tend to the horse and harness. Any number of drivers were shouting imprecations or offering advice to the poor man, who, by the look of him, was soaked through and ready to fight anyone foolish enough to speak to him unhelpfully.

"He can't very well pull to the side under the circumstances," I said, hoping to ease her distress.

"You aren't to take his part, Guthrie," she said sternly. "You mustn't."

"That wasn't my intention, Miss Gatspy," I said in hasty apology. "I only meant that he is as helpless as we are in this situation. There. You see? He has put matters to rights. He will soon be underway again. And so will we."

As we commenced moving, she said, looking straight ahead at

the road, "Guthrie, I know you want to keep my spirits up, and to cheer me on, but I must tell you, I don't need that. You are kindness itself to attempt this for me, but I do not stand in need of your assaults on my morale. You should know me well enough by now to realize that I am always within myself before undertaking any new venture. It is not a sign of weakness, it is only the nature of my character."

"I have no wish to cause you distraint," I said, a bit curtly because I was somewhat affronted by her remark.

"Distraint? You have not," she said. "But you will if you continue your efforts to cheer me." She guided her sylphide toward the confluence of Holland Park Avenue—which Notting Hill Gate had become—with Holland Road, Shepherd's Bush Green, Uxbridge Road, and West Latimer Road. The round-about there was in constant confusion, today much like any other.

I did my best to keep silent while she negotiated the difficult course, steering around any number of carriages, and even an occasional motor-car; I saw a number of horses balk at the noisy machines, and I could not blame them for their reaction. One man in a Benz single-seater was trying to drive around an old-fashioned tilbury pulled by a fractious Welsh pony and driven by an elderly gentleman both of whom audibly disapproved of the invention, the pony neighing and the man berating the motoring enthusiast with his opinion of such nonsense. Miss Gatspy's horse had better manners, but not a much better response to the motor-car than the pony, and minced around the two vehicles, making for the Uxbridge Road at a slow trot, but wanting to gallop.

"Have you ever ridden in a motor-car?" Miss Gatspy asked as soon as we were clear of the round-about.

"No! I am grateful I have never had to." I looked back and saw the carriage and the motor-car were still in the same position.

"I have," said Miss Gatspy, actually smiling. "It was quite wonderful. I actually drove it for several miles."

"I daresay," I told her, having to say something; I could not picture her bowling along in one of those ridiculous contraptions, but I held my tongue on that account; I did not want to know where this had taken place, either.

She sensed my disapproval in my silence. "Oh, Guthrie," she said in mock condolence, "not you, too?"

"I fear so," I said, doing my utmost to look contrite. "I can see no earthly use for those inventions. I cannot think they are anything more than a passing fancy."

"You may be right; any number of distinguished men think as you do," she said, a bit wistfully, it seemed to me. "But if they were faster and, oh, more reliable, if they could carry heavier loads, then there might be use for them."

"Those are a great many 'ifs,' Miss Gatspy," I pointed out, and then shrugged deliberately. "We shall see."

"We shall," she agreed, and guided her vehicle through another knot of carriages and wagons.

We were getting nearer to Hawtrees, and I could not deny the excitement that had been building within me. I wanted to look around, to see if Hastings was far behind us—he had not been ahead of us—and, if I could see him, try to reckon how long it would be until we met for our shared mission. I heard an unmelodious church-bell sound four o'clock and remarked, "We have made very good time."

"Seven miles an hour is about the best we can do," agreed Miss Gatspy. "We should be at Hawtrees in about ten minutes." She let her horse slow a bit. "It won't do to exhaust her, will it?"

"No. We may need her very fresh indeed," I said as I contemplated what we had planned to do.

"Then we may allow her a short time to recover. I hope she may have water and a little gruel while we are at our work." She frowned a bit as we passed a neat pub—Georgian by the look of it—with a livery stable beside it. "Perhaps we should leave it here."

"It is still half a mile at least to Hawtrees, and we do not know what condition Sutton may be in when we get him out. It is still raining, and that will slow us down. We will not want any delays, particularly for—"

She stopped me. "You're right, Guthrie. Perhaps I will ask Bury to bring the sylphide and mare back here once we are underway in our efforts."

I had not heard her mention her colleague by name, and it startled me that she should. "Will he do it?"

"I can't think why he wouldn't," she said. "He can leave the horse and carriage for an hour, and bring them round to the place we specify . . ." Her voice trailed off. "I think that is the turn we want," she said, pointing to a long avenue beside a tall, well-trimmed box-wood hedge that appeared to run for some distance.

"Yes," I said, noticing how dim the light had become. "I can't make out the road-sign, but it is in the right place."

"Then let us turn," said Miss Gatspy, and put her words into action. We entered a pleasant avenue with handsome cottages set well back from the road to the right of us, and the hedge to the left. About a quarter mile along from the turn, a high brick fence replaced the hedge, a narrow lane running between them, isolating the brick wall.

"Hawtrees," I said, recalling the description we had been given. "That wall is a good ten feet tall."

"So it is," said Miss Gatspy. "We must look for a break in it." She kept her sylphide moving, and admonished me, "Keep a look-out, Guthrie. We will have to know how to get out."

"I will," I said. "But given the nature of the place, I doubt it has easy access at any point." We were almost to the main gates: they were wrought-iron, elaborate and imposing. "We couldn't get through those."

"Not even unclothed and soaped," Miss Gatspy seconded; I felt myself blush in response to her remark. "Oh, Guthrie. You needn't color up that way."

"I'm not," I said, and felt it grow worse for my white lie.

We reached the end of the road, and turned left along the brick fence, still hoping for a breach we could later use to our advantage. I hoped we would find a means of escape that would not involve in-creasing our risk. As we rounded the next corner, I saw a tree, a massive old oak, its branches spreading over the fence.

Miss Gatspy saw it at the same time. "You're right," she said as I began to speak. "I think Bury could be persuaded to climb into the branches and hoist us out."

"That seems a bit . . . problematic. If he is discovered, then what would we do?" I asked her, not wanting to take so great a chance as she proposed.

"It may be the best we can hope for; I see no other way out but the gate, and Mister Holmes' plan depends upon us getting beyond the wall," she said as we continued on around the property, only to see Hastings drawn up at the beginning of the avenue. "I suppose we should go and consult with Mister Holmes." She turned her sylphide to the right before I could say anything one way or the other.

"What do you think?" Mycroft Holmes was standing outside Hastings' cab, waiting for us at the foot of the lane, waiting for us, he was smoking a cigar as if to account for his stopping in this place.

"There is a tree-limb that may serve as our means of escape," said Miss Gatspy. "So long as we have help to get into the tree."

Mycroft Holmes gave this his consideration. "If you take care that there is no hint of such a possibility as the help you describe, it may work. Your aid cannot be discovered before you make good your escape. Still." For punctuation he dropped his cigar and ground it out with his heel. "We must make the most of what is immediately to hand." He rocked back on his heels. "I wish I did not have to be at the theatre at seven. I will have to leave here at fifteen minutes of six in order to arrive on time or our efforts are for naught."

"You do not have to wait with us," I said, aware that he was not unknown to Sir Marmion. Nor, for that matter, was I.

"I will determine if Sir Marmion is at the asylum. If he is, we will have to find the means to lure him out." Holmes folded his arms. "Well, let us get it done, Hastings. Let's go up to the gate to make inquiry."

"Right you are, sir," said Hastings without a trace of hesitation. He waited while Holmes climbed aboard, and then started Lance down the long avenue, all but vanishing in the misty dusk.

"I hope the ploy works," I said to Miss Gatspy as I fought my own forebodings.

"If Sir Marmion is away, it should," she said. "He ought to have left for the day, and should not be back until tomorrow."

"Or so we suppose, from what information we have," I added.

"It is better than having nothing to go on," she said.

"Only if it is correct," I told her. I did not want to argue the point with her, so I said, "Do you suppose Sir Marmion knows Mycroft Holmes has a brother? I cannot for the life of me remember if anything was said on that point."

"He must do," said Miss Gatspy. "He is interested in accomplished men; he said so. It stands to reason that he will know about Holmes' brother."

I remained silent; I was too much on edge to be sanguine about our current situation. We had improvised many times in the past, but this time there was much more to lose, and we were in greater London, which somehow made our position more precarious. It was not long before Hastings' cab came back from the gates and pulled to a stop in front of us.

Holmes opened the front of the cab. "Hastings did very well. You shall have proof of my thanks," he called up to the box. He had shed his wiskers and replaced his German military tunic with a sensible hacking jacket half-covered by a coachman's cloak.

"Not necessary, sir," said Hastings.

"He went and rang for the attendant, then told him he had Mycroft Holmes' brother in the cab, and that he was anxious to talk to Sir Marmion. Didn't you, Hastings?" Holmes prompted.

"Just as we practiced it," said Hastings, almost smugly.

"The attendant said that Sir Marmion does not remain at Hawtrees at night, that he would return tomorrow morning at ten, and he begins his rounds at eleven and treatments are given after one: did I want to make an appointment?" Holmes reported. "I said it was important that I speak with him as soon as possible; I would appreciate having a quarter hour of Sir Marmion's time in the morning, and that there was some urgency to the matter."

"The fellow on the other side of the gate said it would be arranged." Hastings took up the narrative. "He advise us to arrive at half-ten, in order to see Sir Marmion before he begins his rounds. I said we would be here."

"So it appears that the night is clear, at least as far as Sir Marmion is concerned," Holmes finished, then straightened up as a man on horseback approached; his hand went under his cloak to the pistol I knew he carried.

Miss Gatspy held out her hand. "No, Mister Holmes. That's Bury."

"One of your Golden Lodge men," said Mycroft Holmes, easing back in his seat. "Yes. Welcome, sir. I am glad of your arrival."

Bury inclined his head but did not speak; he was wrapped in a nautical cloak and deep-brimmed hat that kept out the rain and made him as anonymous as any man could hope to be. He brought his horse alongside Miss Gatspy's sylphide. "What shall I do?" His voice had a faint Dorset twang to it, but nothing so obvious that he could be readily identified.

"You must watch this lane for anyone going to the asylum. If anyone attempts to enter after we have gone in, you must stop him by whatever means you must, short of murder." Miss Gatspy glanced at Mycroft Holmes as she said this, as if making a concession to him. "Then, at ten-thirty, when the attendants go off-duty, you are to climb into the oak-tree around on the west side of the wall. Take a stout rope with you and wait until Guthrie and I, and another man, come to you. Then you must help us climb out, and accompany us back to Pall Mall."

If any of this struck Bury as odd, he gave no indication of it. "I will. How long must I wait for you?"

"Until we come, or until sunrise," said Miss Gatspy. "If we are not out by sunrise, you must return to Mister Holmes and inform him of what has happened." She noticed Holmes' grim little nod. "Once we are inside, I want you to take my carriage around to the livery stable near the pub—you passed the place shortly before you turned off the high-road."

"I noticed it," said Bury.

"See my mare is watered and given warm gruel and two hours of rest. Then bring her and the sylphide back to the base of the tree." Miss Gatspy could see the hesitation in Mycroft Holmes' reaction. "We must have the carriage ready to go," she pointed out. "We do not know what condition your friend will be in when we get him out."

"A sensible plan," said Holmes reluctantly. "Go on."

"We will come to Pall Mall if we are not pursued. If we are, we will go to a house the Golden Lodge maintain near the region of

Sudbury and Harrow," said Miss Gatspy, very pointedly being unspecific. "We will send word to you if we are forced to go there."

Mycroft Holmes was not entirely satisfied with these arrangements, but he was aware that he could expect nothing better, given the short amount of time we had to accomplish our goal. "Very well," he said in concession. "I will remain here until fifteen minutes before six, when I must leave." He made an abrupt motion with his arm. "If only we could bring him out now," he sighed.

"Do you want to try?" asked Miss Gatspy, mischief back in her face.

"If I thought we had a chance . . ." Mycroft Holmes said, unwilling to add that it was impossible.

Then Miss Gatspy said four words that filled me with dread: "I have an idea."

"What would it be?" I asked, although I doubted I wanted to know.

Holmes regarded her appreciatively, his grey eyes shining in a way I found ominous. "Tell me," he said.

Miss Gatspy was ready to explicate. "You have already posed as Mister Holmes' brother. We know Sir Marmion is absent from the place, and we know the longer we wait, the greater our chance of discovery."

"Yes?" Holmes said, by way of encouragement.

"What if we were to go in now. Say that Guthrie is Mister Holmes'—Sutton's—solicitor, and must remove him at once. If there is any resistance, we can cause a ruckus. I will say I am Holmes' betrothed, and have an interest in his well-being." She was positively grinning now—the way a fox grins at the sight of chickens.

"Dear me," said Mycroft Holmes speculatively, a faint upward turn of his mouth hinting at his emotions. "Dear me."

I could see both of them were intrigued by this mad course. "We would need pistols," I pointed out, hoping this might lessen their burgeoning ebullience.

"I have brought mine, and Hastings is armed," said Holmes, dismissing my concern. "Miss Gatspy? And Mister Bury?"

"I have my pistol," said Miss Gatspy. "So has Bury. And I know you have a pistol in your valise, Guthrie," she added.

"It is a reckless, impetuous thing to do," Mycroft Holmes said merrily.

"And for that reason, it is not what they expect. The Brotherhood think they have you, and they might expect some effort on Guthrie's part to rescue him, they are most likely not prepared for a blatant attack," Miss Gatspy said. "Our immediate risks are greater, but our chance of success is also better than if we carry through our other plan. Bury will remain here, on guard, in case we are forced to make a hasty retreat and need someone to cover our backs." She looked his way and saw his confirming half-salute. "We won't have a chance for such a surprise again."

"You are most persuasive," said Holmes, nodding. "All right. How do you propose we manage this?"

"Up to the gate and summon the warden," said Miss Gatspy. "Indignation is the order of the day. You must make it very clear that you are not going to leave without your brother. Threaten to send for the police, if you must."

"I am for it," said Mycroft Holmes. "But we must be out before half-six." His despondency had fallen away completely, as had his obvious apprehension. "Let us get on with it," he declared, and climbed back into the cab, remaining standing as Hastings put Lance into motion. "Up to the gate again, Hastings! *Once more unto the breach!*"

Miss Gatspy actually chortled as she drew her sylphide behind the cab and we all drove up the avenue at a crisp trot; neither the rain nor the increasing darkness deterred our advance. "Get out your pistol, Guthrie. Make sure you have it with you."

"That I will," I said, for now that we were embarked on this escapade, I saw no reason not to use every weapon at our disposal. I pulled my valise from under the seat, opened it, and rummaged in it for my pistol; I was careful, for I knew it was loaded. I found it and slipped it into my pocket. "Where is your pistol, Miss Gatspy?" I asked as we neared the gate.

"In my muff, of course," she said, as if it were the obvious place to keep it.

"Oh," I said as I put my valise back under the seat just as we drew to a halt.

Mycroft Holmes was out of the cab and facing the gate, calling out loudly. "If I must summon the police, you will answer for it!"

I could just make out a man approaching with a lantern in his hand. He came to the gate. "It is against our policy to admit anyone after Sir Marmion has gone for the day," he informed Mycroft Holmes as if that would settle it.

"Just a moment, fellow," said Holmes imperiously. "You have my brother in there, and he is there without the authorization of any of his family, for reasons none of us have been told. Now, I am here with his fiancée and his solicitor to determine if his detention here is appropriate. I know my brother, sir, and I cannot believe that this is necessary, nor have I any report from his physician or any officer of the court that he is incompetent to attend to himself. So I insist you admit me, and these good people. If you do not, I shall be forced to ask the police to—"

The warden had taken a step back, preparing to retreat. "I—"

"You will not depart, sir. You will admit us, or you will answer me in court to account for your actions," Mycroft Holmes announced. "Your employers will also have to answer, all for your want of conduct."

This last appeared to have the desired impact on the warden, who came back to the gate. "This is most irregular," he complained as he turned the key in the massive lock.

"Confining someone without just cause is most irregular," said Holmes, pushing the gate open as soon as the key was withdrawn. "Come," he said to us, and swung his arm to direct us through the gate. "Hastings, you'll remain with our vehicles. The rest of you, as soon as we reach the asylum itself, keep with me. We must not got wandering around the grounds. We don't want to cause any disturbance."

The warden, walking beside the cab, laughed harshly. "Such a way you have of showing it."

"Not at all," said Holmes. "Had you brought my brother to me, none of this would have been necessary." He led us directly up to the door of the fine brick house that had once been a royal hide-away but now housed the mad. It was a large building, built on the noble lines of the Regency period, very well-maintained and elegant. The front door was standing half-open, and the warden went to stand in it, as if hoping to keep us away without incident, a tactic that Holmes treated with the contempt it deserved.

As I helped Miss Gatspy down from the sylphide—a gesture she would ordinarily have refused—I said, "Be very alert."

"Of course," she said, slipping her hands into her muff as we started toward the open door.

I could not entirely subdue a shudder as we crossed the threshold into the wood-paneled entry-hall that faced a graceful double-staircase leading up to a gallery and the wings of the house. The air was filled with moans and cries and other scarcely human noises, so mixed as to sound like the storm-driven sea.

The warden put his foot on the first step, preparing to ascend to the first floor when there was a muffled pop and the man collapsed, clutching his chest from which blood was spurting, sending regular geysers spraying over the paneling, the stairs, and, as the warden turned, ourselves. Scampering footsteps from behind the staircase indicated the murderer was in flight.

FROM THE PERSONAL JOURNAL OF PHILIP TYERS

Word has just arrived from CI Pryce that I Featherstone has been found shot in his office, an apparent suicide. I am told he left an account of his activities that led to this development, and very distressing they are. CI Pryce was very much shocked to learn the extent to which Featherstone had been caught up in illegal and subversive activities, and said he will provide a full copy of this document to MH by tomorrow. It appears that, among other things, Featherstone arranged for the removal of the body from the morgue and turned it over to Mister Kerem, whom he helped to leave the country. There are other aspects of Featherstone's work that have bearing on Braaten and Vickers, and how they got to London. "You may tell Mister Holmes that he shall see it as Featherstone wrote it," he assured me, which is most encouraging. "I will not deliver a gutted carcase for him to ponder. He will have all that Featherstone said, as he said it, for I know Mister Holmes is a discreet man, and the government trust him implicitly."

I have given my word that MH will be available to discuss the information by Friday, and suggested that CI Pryce stop around for sherry at six, which invitation he has accepted.

There is no word from MH or G yet, and it is not late enough to trouble me, but I cannot rid myself of certain uneasy thoughts. That plan they made is a precarious one, and if it should not succeed in every point, it is possible that the Brotherhood will have more than Sutton in their hands . . .

Chapter Twenty-five

"GET THE KEYS! Mycroft Holmes shouted down to me as he sprang up the stairs. "We must hurry!"

"But shouldn't we stop . . . ?" I cried, even as I went to the mortally wounded man and wrenched the keys from his belt; he was hardly breathing and his face, even in the glow of the gas-lights, was pasty; his wretched state was accentuated by an incoherent chorus of shouts and other noises of distress coming from the rooms above us as the inmates of this place gave voice to their apprehensions.

"Not for him, and not for the shooter. Bury will tend to him. Come!" He ran to the gallery, and looked down the halls; shouts, curses, laments, and laughter all had erupted at the sound of the shot and rose in crescendo as we hurried to do what we had come to do.

I took the keys—and there were a great many of them—and went up the stairs two at a time to Mister Holmes. "Here," I said.

From the foot of the stairs, Miss Gatspy called out, "I am going to remain here, as guard. It appears we need one. Carry on, gentlemen."

I was torn between endorsing her good sense and wanting to spare her any more distressing incidents; I ended up saying, "Mind the doors inside as well as out."

"I'm not a complete novice, Guthrie," she reminded me, and waved me on about my task.

"Take the northern wing, Guthrie," Holmes said. "And the cross-corridors. Look in each room. If you find Sutton, yell for me, as I shall for you. Keep your pistol ready." He was already turning toward the southern wing of the building, holding his pistol in one hand, the keys in the other.

"That I will," I said, and tightened my grip on the little weapon as I went into the corridor. I wondered where the attendants were, since I saw none of them about. The first chamber I looked into was occupied by an emaciated man, dressed only in an old shirt, who stood in the corner making hooting sounds; he paid no attention to the tray of food on the floor beside his bed. As I peered in at him, he bent down and defecated as if to express his disgust with his circumstances. I concluded this was not one of Sir Marmion's successes and I quickly passed on to the next room where a young man was industriously struggling to arrange matchboxes on the floor in a pattern of his own devising; he occasionally raised his head and uttered a shriek as if of mortal terror, then went back to his arrangement of matchboxes.

I had got to the end of the corridor and had turned into its L when I came to a room in which there was a great deal of very modern equipment, including a galvanic-current monitor and a shallow zinc tub in which, I supposed from the many covered wires leading to and from it, was where treatment was given. At another time, I would have been curious to examine this most ingenious machine, but I could not linger. I could see a shower-room beyond the treatment room, and was about to pass it, when I decided it would be prudent to check on it.

There was cold water dripping from the enameled pipes overhead, and the light was dim, so that I did not at first see the crumpled body in the far corner, or if I did, I mistook it for a pile of sheets. But the figure moaned, and I rushed to it, taking care not to slide on the slippery tiles; I thrust my pistol back in my pocket so there would be no chance of an accidental discharge.

"Hang on, man," I said, as I felt the clammy skin. "I'll get you out of here." I tried to listen to nothing but the sound of his voice, over the babble and clamor in the rooms beyond these.

The man's face was swollen on one side, red as butcher's meat where it was not darkening with bruising. One eye was swollen shut, and the other blinked unbelievingly. "Guth . . . wie?" he asked through distended lips.

"Egad!" I exclaimed. "Sutton. Sutton! What the devil have they done to you?" I tried to lift him, but he was too heavy for me.

"Gafe me . . . mow . . . phia," he said painfully.

"It doesn't matter. We're here now, Sutton. We'll get you out of here in two shakes of a lamb's tail." I was still trying to wedge my upper body under him to get him onto his feet, at least enough to get him out of the shower-room. "I'll call to Holmes as soon as I get you out of those soaked clothes and wrapped in a towel." I could feel that he was beginning to tremble from cold. I was struggling with Sutton, my boots sliding on the slick floor, so I was not paying attention to the door. When I heard the sound of footfall not far behind me, I hardly turned, assuming I was in the company of Mycroft Holmes and this capricious venture was almost at an end. "You've come in good time."

"I wish I could say the same of you," said Jacobbus Braaten, motioning me to rise with the barrel of his pistol. He had lost flesh since I had last seen him and the lines of dissipation in his face were etched more deeply, yet he still had that powerful, malign energy about him that so many found attractive enough to be drawn to him. He wore a dust-colored smock over his regular clothes, marking him as a part of the staff.

I released Sutton in my effort to right myself; I would apologize later, I thought, if I had the chance. "I should have known you would be here," I said, knowing it was expected of me, and aware that as long as I could keep him talking, he would not shoot us. "A madhouse is an excellent place for you."

"I would be insulted were it not for the fact that I have the pistol," said Braaten, as coolly as a banker calculating interest. "Bravado doesn't become you, Guthrie."

"Sorry to disappoint," I said, hoping my nerve wouldn't desert me. "No doubt you will exact a price for my failure."

"That, and your damaging my leg." He glared as if the explosion had just occurred. "Vickers and I had it so well-arranged. We have been taking the night shift here for Sir Marmion. The cooks and the warden leave at half-ten, giving us until seven in the morning to tend to our own projects. It was going so well. Then Holmes had to thrust his oar in."

I realized that he was unaware that it was Sutton lying on the floor, which gave me what I hoped would be an advantage. "Sir Marmion came to Mister Holmes," I reminded him. "Through no office of yours."

"Ha! He came to do my bidding, to make Holmes want to come here, to whet his curiosity, to intrigue him, to sound him out," said Braaten angrily. "To find out what he was doing in regard to Lady MacMillian. We knew Holmes was the cause for the delay in her visit, and it was intolerable. If he had just been forthcoming—" He put his free hand to his mouth. "I should not tell you any of this. I should just shoot you. It is what Vickers would do."

"Where *is* Vickers?" I asked, as if I cared to know. Just speaking his name left a bad taste in my mouth. "I should have thought he would be with you."

"He left as you arrived," said Braaten, spitting to show his contempt. "He is as ambitious as he is foolish. Suffice it to say he is gone to another place." He sighed with false sympathy and came a step farther into the shower-room. "Which you will never find because you—and Mister Holmes—will be dead."

I didn't trust myself to speak, so I curled my lip. I wondered if

I could reach my pistol and fire it before he killed me? It didn't seem likely. It was hard to believe that I had only minutes to live.

At my feet, Sutton groaned and rolled onto his side.

"Tomorrow was to be his full treatment of galvanic shock," said Jacobbus Braaten. "Today it was just a taste, with morphia to lessen the impact. Tomorrow—well, tomorrow, he would have glowed by the end of the day, and no morphia to deaden the treatment." He aimed his pistol at Sutton. "A pity there won't be time to reap the contents of that wonderful mind. Had you not come, he would have lived a while longer—little as he might want to."

I felt Sutton move, his arm flung out, and I feared he would hasten the lethal moment; Sutton shook, then went limp.

Braaten took another step forward. "I want to see the life go out of your—" His dire words ended on a yelp as he stepped on the film of undiluted liquid soap Sutton had managed to put in his path. His pistol discharged into the pipes and water sprayed down on us. I reached into my pocket and pulled out my pistol, aimed, and fired. I had the satisfaction of seeing Braaten fall to his knees, his hand clasped to the side of his chest, his pistol fallen to the tiles, his thinning hair plastered to his skull by the cold water.

More howls and laughter greeted this noise; inwardly I felt a kinship with their distress, for my sense of approbation was rapidly fading as I watched Braaten's suffering. I did not know if I could remain standing over him, waiting for him to die, without some qualm moving me to pity. I did my utmost to maintain my resolve, trying to observe him with indifference although I was unnerved. I might have tried to render Braaten some wholly useless assistance, but in less than three minutes, I heard Mycroft Holmes calling my name through the cacophony.

"At the end of the rear hall!" I shouted back, in competition with the general uproar. "In the shower-room."

"Are you all right?" His voice was nearer and I could heard the sound of his steady running. "Guthrie! Answer me!"

"A bit shaken, but well enough," I answered. "Sutton is here. So is Jacobbus Braaten." As I spoke this last name, I leveled my pistol at him. "Stay where you are."

Braaten had fallen onto his uninjured side and was pulling into a tight ball. Frothy blood welled from where my bullet had struck. He attempted to speak, then began to cough; his sputum was bloody.

Mycroft Holmes came through the door, his pistol in hand, his expression fixed in an aggressive snarl. He hesitated in the doorway, but only to take stock of the room. Seeing Sutton, he started forward to help him.

"Mind the soap," I cautioned him, just as he slid on the tiles. His arms sawed the air, but he contrived somehow to remain on his feet long enough to regain his balance. Then he dropped to his knees beside Sutton. Water continued to pour down on us.

"Are you all right, dear boy?" Mycroft Holmes asked as he laid his hand on Sutton's shoulder. "Tell me. My word, Sutton, what have they done to you?" he asked as he started to move his double; he could not conceal the horror he felt. He swore, and strove to lift Sutton to his feet.

"I'll . . . man . . . ath," said Sutton, trying to help, but losing his balance. "I'm dithy . . ."

"Small wonder," I said, my pistol still aimed at Braaten. "Do you remove him, Holmes," I recommended. "I'll keep guard on Braaten here—"

Mycroft Holmes stared. "Is that Jacobbus Braaten? By Jove; you're right!" He shook his head. "Age hasn't been kind to him; I shouldn't have known him on a superficial glance. He is very seriously hurt, I see now I come to look at him." He paused to scrutinize the man as best he could from his current vantage-point. "It seems you've punctured his lung, Guthrie."

"I believe so," I said, feeling a bit sick for all it was Braaten I had shot. "I don't think he'll last long."

"Very likely not. But take no chances." Holmes was half-carrying, half-dragging Sutton out of the shower-room. "I'll see if I can turn off the water."

"Much appreciated," I responded.

"I'll ready Sutton to leave," he said, as if his actions had to be explained.

"You'll need dry clothes," I pointed out.

"So will you, Guthrie," said Holmes as he finally got out of the room. "So will you."

I had to admit it was true. I was wet to the skin, and I was alone with my enemy. I had a pistol in my hand. For some little time I considered firing a second shot. But that would be murder, and I knew if I condemned Jacobbus Braaten for committing such a crime, I oughtn't to do it, no matter how great the temptation he presented. As I wrestled with my conscience, the water finally trickled, then stopped, and the last of it ran, red, down the drain.

A series of spasms went through Jacobbus Braaten, and then he lay limp at my feet, all the tension gone out of him along with his breath; the blood, which had foamed out of his wound, no longer flowed, and his eyes were half-open and unfocused. I went out of the shower-room to fetch a sheet to put over him. That done, I got a towel and began to blot. There was a roll-top pull-over in my valise—which was in Miss Gatspy's sylphide. I would have to change into it or end up with sore muscles and a cold. I made my way down to the ground floor, where Miss Gatspy was waiting. The body of the warden had been pulled aside, but the spatters of blood were still everywhere.

"You look a sight," she said, taking stock of my appearance. Then she became more serious. "What about Braaten?"

"He's dead. This time I waited until I was sure." I dropped the towel I was holding onto the stairs. "I wanted to be glad of killing him, but I wasn't."

"Poor Guthrie," said Miss Gatspy with genuine sympathy. "It is never an easy thing to do."

"I shouldn't want it to become easy," I said, oddly pleased that my hands weren't shaking. "Is Holmes—"

"Putting Sutton into Hastings' cab. He has a number of blankets to keep him warm. We are to await his signal before going outside." She glanced at me again. "You might do with a blanket or two as well."

"I have something in my valise that will help, if you will allow me to change my coat and shirt." It was an awkward thing to speak of such personal matters to her.

"You can do that while we drive back. I promise you I won't look," she added as I stared at her. "We must leave as soon as possible. I am worried that Vickers may still escape."

"Was it he who shot the warden, do you think?" I asked, nodding in the body's direction. "Did Holmes venture an opinion?"

"It seems a reasonable conclusion to reach," said Miss Gatspy. "He is probably still on the grounds somewhere, hiding."

"Or setting a trap," I suggested uneasily. "He is not one to accept defeat or to be willing to retreat in any circumstances."

"I will have Bury remain, to watch for him," said Miss Gatspy as matter-of-factly as she might send a man to fetch a pound of bacon from the butcher.

"You might expose him to danger," I reminded her, thinking of what I had done not a quarter of an hour ago.

"Which guarding you is not?" she countered, her demeanor incredulous. "He is part of the Golden Lodge, and he—"

"—eats grizzly bears for lunch, as the Americans say," I interjected. I hoped Mycroft Holmes would summon us quickly; I was not minded to sustain another rebuke from Penelope Gatspy.

There was the flash of a lantern in the dark, and I sighed with relief, going toward the door, Miss Gatspy a step or two ahead of me.

"Guthrie!" Holmes shouted as we stepped out of the door. "What are you doing?"

Before I had a chance to answer, the lanterns flashed again, then came a volley of gunfire and the sound of a motor car coming from the rear of the property toward the gate: a Daimler vis-a-vis was coming across the lawn at a good clip. Two trunks occupied the front seats, and Vickers sat in the rear, one hand steering the vehicle, the other firing a long-barreled pistol.

Hastings dropped down from his box, and I feared as I watched that he had been shot, but then I realized he had gone to quieten his horse while Mycroft Holmes stood over Sutton on the far side of the cab, protecting him from any stray bullets. Bury was occupied trying to keep Miss Gatspy's mare from bolting, and so could not go after Vickers.

The shooting stopped abruptly—I supposed he had run out of cartridges and would have to reload before he could fire more-shortly before he reached the gate, where he leaped down from his motor-car, flung the gates wide, then climbed back into the Daimler and swung out into the avenue, the two lanterns marking his progress down the road.

"Quick, Guthrie!" shouted Holmes as the motor-car continued out of our sight. "You and Miss Gatspy go in pursuit of him. Bury, you remain here, in case he should double back. I must get Sutton to safety."

Hastings soothed Lance, then said, "I don't know how fast we can go, Mister Holmes; he's that tired."

"I know, Hastings. But we must do our best." He resumed his task of getting Sutton aboard the cab. "You two. Off you go. Bury, stay alert. If nothing happens by ten, come along to Pall Mall."

Miss Gatspy paused for a moment as if she was ready to question these orders, then thought better of it. "Quickly, Guthrie. Vickers is getting away." She got into the sylphide and motioned to me to get in beside her. I hurried to do as she wished, hanging onto the side of the carriage as she set the mare in motion again, following after the Daimler, which was nearing the end of the avenue. As I swung myself into the narrow seat, I looked over at her. "It is most inappropriate, but I must get out of some of these wet things. If I keep my valise between us, I should not offend you too much."

"Oh, Guthrie," Miss Gatspy said in an exasperated tone. "Do get on with it. I have to concentrate on driving; you will not astonish me if you remove your coat, your waistcoat, your shirt, *and* your singlet."

I could say nothing in response to her that would not give modesty its nimiety. "I will be as quick as I can."

"Good. I need your eyes to help me." She kept her mare going at a jog-trot—as fast as was safe in the dark on such wet roads.

"There are no other motor-cars that I can see on this road," I said as I struggled to get out of my suit-coat. It was like peeling the wet rind off a tropical fruit, but eventually I managed it, and flung the garment onto the floor at my feet just as the sylphide rocked as it swung into the Uxbridge Road. I clutched my valise as if it would afford me balance, and waited to remove my collar, tie, and cuffs until we were on steadier ground.

"He's turning to the right," said Miss Gatspy, leaning forward as if to urge her mare on. "He may be heading toward Brentford or Kew."

"Or the Great West Road," I said, thinking this the more likely choice. "He could very well want to get out of the London area." I was down to my shirt, and about to extricate myself from its moist embrace.

"My thoughts as well, Guthrie," said Miss Gatspy. "But I fear we will not be able to keep up with him." There were already three carriages and a bicycle between us and the Daimler; we had little chance of closing the gap, for the mare was tired and beginning to flag. As I watched, the motor-car turned west again and was quickly lost to sight. At the next left turn, Miss Gatspy swung to the east and let the mare set her own pace back into the soggy bustle of greater London.

I took my roll-top pull-over and a clean singlet from my valise; I donned the singlet quickly, then pulled on the pull-over. "We hadn't a chance," I said after we had gone about two miles.

"No, we hadn't," Miss Gatspy conceded. "Although there was always a chance the motor-car would overturn, or it would suffer an accident of the motor in this rain."

"A shame it didn't happen," I said as I put my valise behind my legs under the seat. "I would have been delighted to pull him out of a wreck of his vehicle."

"Well, at least Braaten is no more," said Miss Gatspy. "Now all we must hope is that Sutton is all right."

"He did not appear all right," I said warily. "His face was quite . . . quite bruised." It was not the whole of it, but it summed up the most obvious aspect of his appearance. "He was given morphia, and he is not . . . himself."

"He will be better," said Miss Gatspy. "They didn't have him long enough to habituate him to the drug." She looked at the traffic ahead as we once again approached the Uxbridge Road. "I suppose we should go back to Pall Mall."

"Yes," I said. "But would you mind stopping on the way in Curzon Street long enough for me to change my clothes and drop of these things?"

"Of course, if you want. But what on earth for?" Miss Gatspy tried to mask a yawn with the back of her hand. "If you'd rather remain there, I will see you tomorrow morning."

"Oh, no," I said, a bit of my energy returning. "After I call in Pall Mall to see how Sutton is doing, I am planning to go to the theater."

She stared at me. "Why on earth?"

I laughed. "You've forgotten? Mycroft Holmes is going to play MacBeth tonight at the Duke of York's Theatre and I wouldn't miss it for all the tea in China," I cried aloud, and was pleased when Miss Gatspy looked at me with renewed vitality. "Would you care to join me, Miss Gatspy?"

She cocked her head flirtatiously. "Mister Guthrie, I would love to."

FROM THE PERSONAL JOURNAL OF PHILIP TYRES

MH returned here at six-forty, with Sutton, who is now installed in MH's room where he will remain until he is more himself. I have been given the task of caring for Sutton until MH is once again in the flat. Sutton is in poor shape, his face showing signs of ill-usage, and patches of his hair shaved for a purpose he has not been able to describe. I am preparing a hearty broth for him, and I will feed him regularly until he is once again restored to good condition. Sutton is still under the influence of the morphia he was given some hours ago, and it will be some hours more before his body is rid of it; it has left him a bit delirious and drowsy, so that he is unable to hold thoughts together for more than a minute or so. He has also been kept in cold, wet clothing, which has left him much depleted of energy, and inclined to shiver at the least touch of a draught. I have built up the fire in MH's room and taken another comforter down to help him restore himself.

G came by not ten minutes ago, dressed for an evening out, and eager to learn as much as he can about Sutton's current condition; he was relieved to learn that MH sent for Watson before he left for Saint Martin's Lane; the good doctor is expected here at nine. Thank goodness he is the soul of discretion. G also asked if there had been any new information brought to this flat since MH and he went out to find Sutton. I told him—as I had told MH somewhat earlier—that there was a dispatch bag brought round about half-five, and that I believed it had to do with some developments bearing on her Herr Kriede's death. It appears there was more to that event than seemed the case at first. MH resolved to examine all his evidence in the morning, when he has recovered from the demands of this night.

I am sorry I cannot leave to attend the performance; MH left here wrapped in mufflers and his caped cloak, with a driving hat pulled down low over his brow, so that none of the company will have a good look at him until he has donned costume and make-up for the play. I will have to rely upon G's report of the event, to which I look forward with great enthusiasm . . .

Chapter Twenty-six

BEATRICE MOTHERWELL, IN her medieval finery as Lady MacBeth confronted her husband, her eyes blazing. "*We fail.*" She reached out and took hold of his tunic, pulling him near to her. "*But screw your courage to the sticking-place/And we'll not fail.*" She moved around behind him, her head pressed against his shoulder as she went on to describe how she would ply Duncan's servants with wine while MacBeth murdered the King.

"She's making changes," I whispered to Miss Gatspy.

"Not in the text," was her equally soft answer.

"No, in her movements. She hasn't done it this way before." I frowned as I said it.

"She didn't do this with . . . our friend?" Miss Gatspy asked, and was shushed by the man behind and one seat away from her.

"Not when I have seen it," I said, barely louder than breath. "I wonder why she changed it?"

"Watch the play," Miss Gatspy recommended.

In the third act, in the first scene with the murderers, Mycroft Holmes—in the persona of MacBeth—stumbled in the speech, *Your spirits shine through you.* I wondered if anyone noticed, or if they did, they assumed he had done so for dramatic reasons; none of the actors appeared to be aware of it, but it would not be likely that they would.

During the interval, while Miss Gatspy and I drank tea together, she said, "I think he is doing very well. It is a pity his injured friend cannot see him. I think he would approve; it is a very creditable interpretation."

I could not help but smile at her clever conceit. "It is," I agreed. "It is likely that he would be pleased with the performance."

She gave me a quizzical look. "The play isn't over yet."

"And . . . er . . . *the play's the thing?*" I quoted Hamlet.

"Tonight it certainly is," she said, her words containing many levels of meaning.

In his fourth act scene with the Witches, Mycroft Holmes struggled with the visions of Banquo's descendants who were destined to reign after him. "*A third is like the former. Filthy hags! Why do you show me this?*" Fortuitously his voice cracked as it rose; I thought it was a very skillful device—either that, or he was growing tired; much as I wanted to believe the former, I was more sure of the latter.

By the third scene of the fifth act, I could see that Holmes was flagging; apparently some of the actors were aware that he was not at full strength, as well, for they kept moving him downstage, and turning him more toward the audience—Sutton called that dressing—and helping him to make the most of his tired voice.

"*Bring me no more reports; let them fly all: Till Birnam Wood remove to Dunsinane I cannot taint with fear.*" Arrogance covered the beginning of panic in MacBeth's assertion. "*The spirits that know/All mortal consequences have pronounced me thus: 'Fear not, MacBeth; no man that's born of woman/Shall e'en have power upon thee.'* "

He made the same grand, sweeping gesture that Sutton did, but a trifle slower and with a more ironic bow. As I continued to watch, I was glad the play was almost finished, for I recognized the exhaustion that was giving its impetus to Holmes' performance now.

"*Tomorrow and tomorrow and tomorrow,*" Mycroft Holmes intoned as if sounding a funeral bell, "*Creeps in this petty pace from day to day . . .*"

"He's really doing very well," Miss Gatspy whispered to me. "In spite of the way his Lady MacBeth was behaving."

She was vehemently hissed by a man behind her, who was much annoyed at her expressions of approval from the first rising of the curtain.

"*. . . have lighted fools/The way to dusty death . . .*"

Because I knew Mycroft Holmes fairly well, I distinguished his personal discomfort in his position for what it was, and did not see it as the abandoning of hope that most of the audience perceived. I also felt an uncomfortable twinge of memory of Jacobbus Braaten earlier today, watching him die. Until this moment, I had been able to put that behind me and lose myself in the play.

"*. . . That struts and frets his hour upon the stage/And then is heard no more . . .*" The poignant words struck me as the farewell I understood them to be: Mycroft Holmes would not walk this stage again, nor any other, if he could arrange it. "*Full of sound and fury/Signifying nothing.*"

I remembered the battle was coming, and I hoped that Sutton had gone over the moves of it enough times for Holmes to copy them perfectly, for I suspected this would be the most difficult part of the play for my employer to perform. In spite of all the excitement on the stage, and the double tension I experienced—that of the drama itself, and that of knowing Mycroft Holmes was playing the lead role, not Edmund Sutton—fatigue was catching up with me. I was in no danger of nodding off, but I had slumped a bit in my chair, and I was aware of aches I could ordinarily ignore. I could not help but wonder if Miss Gatspy was enjoying herself, or if the exigencies of the day had robbed her of delectation.

The last fight came, and, as the Bard decreed, MacDuff triumphed. The play ended, the curtain came down, and there were curtain calls—all the usual ritual of the theatre. I applauded along with the rest, and felt assuagement of Holmes' behalf that this ordeal was almost over.

"We should go backstage," said Miss Gatspy, plucking at my sleeve. "We should congratulate him for getting through it in such good form."

"Perhaps," I said, not knowing if Holmes would welcome our visit.

"At least we should try," she said, and began to edge her way toward the aisle. "He can always refuse to let us come in. The doorman will know."

I could not say no to her, nor did I want to, truth to tell. I meekly followed after her, out of the building and around the side of the theatre to the stage door, where I stood while Miss Gatspy approached the doorman, saying, "We are here to visit Mister Sutton. He may have left our names: Mister Guthrie and Miss Gatspy?"

The doorman did not bother to consult the list. "You're not on it," he announced, and looked away from her.

"Oh, but I think you are mistaken," said Miss Gatspy, going up to the stand where the doorman sat, and pointing to a grubby sheet of names. "There. You see? Gatspy and Guthrie. Along with Tyers."

The doorman sniffed as he stared down at the sheet as if it had only just materialized in front of him. "Oh," he said with such tremendous boredom that I wanted to call him to task. "You may go in. It's the second door at the top of the spiral staircase, prompt side."

"Thank you," I said formally as we went into the dark, starkly functional world of backstage. The spiral staircase the doorman mentioned was beyond the banks of ropes and counterweights that raised and lowered scenery, curtains, and certain special lights. There was a faint smell of gas from the lights, but not enough to be alarming. We passed the stagehands—rough men in work-clothes—and a few supernumeraries in archaic armor and false beards before we came to the wrought-iron staircase that corkscrewed up to the dressing-rooms above; the whole structure gave off an unmelodious clang as I put my foot on it to begin our ascent.

"Be careful, Guthrie," said Miss Gatspy, following me upward. "Someone may want to come down."

"I will," I said, and went on without incident to the narrow metal balcony that marked the start to the corridor. The second dressing-room had a label tacked to it: EDMUND SUTTON it read. I knocked and said, "It's Guthrie, sir, and Miss Gatspy, come to congratulate you."

"Come in," said an exhausted voice I hardly recognized; we went in and found Mycroft Holmes in a dressing gown, his make-up partially removed. The dressing-room was small, and painted a shade somewhere between green and cream; it smelled of sweat and greasepaint and cologne. Gaslights flanked the mirror, giving a bright, even luminescence to everything before it. A small clothing rack mounted on wheels held the costumes Mycroft Holmes had just worn, and next to it, a butler's chair held his engulfing street-clothes. I watched as Holmes went on smearing white cream on his face and wiping off the resultant smear of color with a bit of butcher-paper. He indicated a stool, and I offered it to Miss Gatspy, who sat down and watched this process. "And the devil of it is, I must put on more before I leave, so I may maintain some semblance of Sutton's appearance."

"I think Sutton would have been pleased, sir, had he seen you tonight." I wanted to say more, but Holmes help up his hand.

"Had Sutton been able to see me, I shouldn't have had to do this." He took a last swipe under his chin. "I had no notion how tiring it is to project the voice for a full play. And the lights are distracting, as well as hot."

"No one suspected," I said.

"Why should they. Although La Motherwell noticed Sutton was not quite himself; you saw how she carried on in the earlier scenes. I said I had a touch of a cold. I am not entirely sure she believed me." Holmes folded his hands and met my eyes in the mirror. "I rely on you to leave with me. I don't want to be detained by any of this troupe. Actors are canny folk; I might fool them on-stage for a performance, but I cannot continue to do so now that the performance is over." He looked down at the pots of color and the tub of powder. "Is it still raining?"

"Yes; it's getting heavier again," said Miss Gatspy before I could answer.

"I see," said Holmes. "Well, that is in our favor. I will have excellent reason to be engulfed in my cloak. I shall have to give it to Sutton, or questions may be asked if he doesn't wear it again." He selected a tannish-pink shade of color and patted it onto his face, taking care to smooth it with a wedge of sponge. "I can't change the color of my eyes, but I can put a little dark-blue on my lashes, to make my eyes seem bluer. My hair will be covered. Fortunately the cloak is voluminous, so it will conceal my bulk. I must say, I am pleased that the costumer wanted to make Sutton look bulkier. I took the padding out of the costumes; Sutton will have to put it back again." He continued working on his face, using shading to diminish the lines in his face, creating an eerily younger appearance. "Hastings should be waiting for me shortly. I want you to accompany me out of the theatre."

"So you said," I reminded him.

"And I want you both to come back to Pall Mall with me. There are a few matters we need to discuss." He continued to refine the make-up until it no longer looked applied. "This has been a most demanding week, Guthrie."

"So it has, sir," I said.

Holmes pushed back from the mirror. "It isn't quite over yet, but very nearly. If we can but put one or two matters to rest, we will be able to conclude the whole by Friday." He ran his fingers through his hair, muttering something about the wig he had worn. "Miss Gatspy, you have been most helpful. I hope this does not in any way compromise your position within the Golden Lodge."

"You needn't worry on that account," said Miss Gatspy. "In this instance, our goals and yours have been in accord." She favored him with a seraphic smile.

"Miss Gatspy, you unnerve me." Holmes rose. "If you will both be kind enough to wait outside, I'll complete my changing."

"Of course," I said, and held my hand out to Miss Gatspy, in case she needed assistance in rising in these cramped quarters.

"Thank you, Guthrie," she said, so demurely that I wasn't at all sure she wasn't mocking me. She allowed me to escort her from the room, and then she pulled me to the head of the corridor where there was a small bench. "It has been a very exciting day, hasn't it?"

"A very exciting—if that's the word I want—week, I should rather say," I responded.

"But today—had we been in Italy, it could have come from Missus Radcliffe's pen. Disguises. Unscrupulous villains. Mysterious doubles. Insane asylums. Cross-country chases. Not that she would have had a motor-car in her tale," she added hastily, her blue eyes bright with amusement. "But you will admit it had a touch of romance."

"I should think more along the line of Wilkie Collins," I said. "And he is more contemporary than Missus Radcliffe."

"Yes," she agreed, and fell silent as Beatrice Motherwell approached.

Out of her medieval raiment, she was a handsome woman with a generous figure that she was at pains to show off in a nip-waist princess gown of sapphire-blue. Her hair was done up fashionably and she wore a diamond dog-collar and a rope of pearls around her neck. She was accompanied by a man, at least a decade her senior, in evening clothes with the unmistakable air of wealth and privilege about him. As they passed us, she nodded to us, saying, "You're Sutton's friend, aren't you? Shame he was having an off-night. Still, he is a trouper, to play in spite of it. His voice was off. It must be his cold." With a smile that was almost a smirk, she was gone, making her way down the circular stairs with the ease of long practice.

"Well!" said Miss Gatspy. "*Frailty, thy name is Motherwell,*" she said in an undervoice. "I can see why Sutton speaks about her as he does."

"That was a touch too much," I agreed.

"Guthrie, you are a nod-cock," said Miss Gatspy in kindly rebuke.

I was about to ask her why she thought so when the door to Sutton's dressing-room came open and Mycroft Holmes surged out, once again wrapped in his cloak and a long muffler with his hat pulled down low. He coughed for effect. "Guthrie. Come," he exclaimed, and clapped me on the shoulder before propelling me toward the stairs. "You, too, Miss Gatspy."

"As you wish," she said, her voice still tinged with inner merriment.

We trooped down the stairs, our steps sounding like hail in a smithy. As we reached the main floor, one or two other actors hailed Holmes—as Sutton—but didn't detain him, seeing he was with company. The doorman hardly deigned to notice our departure.

"Where is your carriage?" asked Holmes as Sid Hastings brought his cab up in front of the theatre; now that most of the audience had left, the place seemed deserted and a bit sinister, for all its decorative facade and shining lights.

"Around the corner," said Miss Gatspy.

"Then we shall meet again in Pall Mall," he said, as if there could be no argument on that head.

"Yes. That we shall," said Miss Gatspy, and slipped her hand through my arm. "Come, Guthrie."

I went along with her, thinking as I did that the theatre is truly a haunted place. We rounded the building away from the stage door and started to where her sylphide had been stalled for the evening's performance. All but one or two of the various carriages and buggies were gone, giving the place a forlorn look, like a ballroom after everyone had left. We had just got inside the sylphide when the mare whinnied loudly and tossed her head as if in protest of having to continue to work. I was about to say something about this when Miss Gatspy motioned me to silence. "What is it?" I mouthed, for I was keenly aware that she was abristle with distress.

"The mare's been crippled," she said barely above a whisper. "Someone is trying to trap us."

"Are you certain?" I asked in the same hushed voice.

"She is not moving because her tendons are cut," said Miss Gatspy in such a tone of fury and sadness as I never hope to hear from her again.

"How can you be certain?" I asked.

"Because there is blood on her legs and she is in pain," said Miss Gatspy. "And we are trapped."

I remained still, listening to the rain and any other sounds from the night. I thought I heard the snick of a pistol being cocked, and I dropped into a ball on the floor, Miss Gatspy immediately beside me.

The shot went off and the mare neighed again, struggling to run, and instead falling, tangling herself in her harness.

"I have had *enough*," whispered Miss Gatspy, and reached into her muff for her pistol. "Guthrie, get ready to run."

"I have my pistol with me, as well," I told her softly. "If we both move simultaneously, we might be able to stop them—whoever they may be."

She nodded agreement, and drew her pistol. "Ready? Set. Go."

We both rolled out of the small carriage, she on the left, I on the right. We both landed crouched and aiming our pistols into the dark; a figure in a flapping cloak stopped not six feet from the carriage and turned to run.

"Stop!" I cried, and started after him. I chased him into Saint Martin's Lane, and up toward Long Acre, but he had a lead on me, and I could not stop him from slipping between two buildings on the edge of Covent Garden. Fearing to leave Miss Gatspy alone, I turned and ran back toward the Duke of York's Theatre only to hear a single shot just as I approached. "Miss Gatspy!" I shouted, dreading what that might portend, and arrived to find her standing over her mare, tears shining in her eyes.

"She was suffering," she said, and handed her pistol to me.

"My dear Miss Gatspy," I said, putting my arm round her shoulder to comfort her. "What a dreadful thing."

"It's one thing to shoot at us," she said in a small, tight voice, "for we can defend ourselves. But to cripple a blameless horse for no reason but to make it easier to fight us—that is the utmost cowardice."

"Yes, it is," I said, truly agreeing with her. What on earth were we going to do now? I asked myself. How were we to disengage the carriage and harness from the dead horse, and how were we to dispose of the animal? It was all perplexing and inconvenient.

"Don't worry," said Miss Gatspy, as if reading my thoughts. "My colleagues will take care of this."

"Ah, yes, your colleagues," I said. "Just where were they when your horse was cut?" Little as I liked the notion of being followed, I dislike the lack of diligence even less.

"They were seeing Mister Holmes home," she said. "They thought we would not need their attention."

"Not much help," I said, trying to keep my temper in check.

"No; they will have to account for their lapse to our superiors." She put her hand on my arm, keeping her muff on the other; she made no mention of her pistol, so I put it into my trouser-pocket, away from my own pistol. "Pall Mall isn't so very far. We could walk back, if you don't think it would be too great a risk?"

"We can certainly try," I said, the fatigue I had been feeling vanishing as if by a fairy's spell. "If we take too long, Hastings may well come in search of us."

"Or my colleagues," said Miss Gatspy. "Down Saint Martin's Lane to East Pall Mall and thence to Mister Holmes'." She did her best to smile. "It isn't much more than half a mile, would you say?"

"More or less," I replied, not caring about the distance. It was a sweet ending to what had been a most trying day, and one that wasn't yet over. I thought that a few more minutes in Miss Gatspy's company would lessen the sourness of what was to come, and solace her loss of her mare. So I did not walk as fast as I might, and I only worried that the rain might damage Miss Gatspy's gown, or chill her. We saw few vehicles on the street, and not many men on horseback until we were almost opposite Cockspur Street, when a rider approached us, hailing Miss Gatspy by name and asking why she was not in her carriage.

"You will see why when you go back to the theatre. I leave you and Langford to tend to it." Her tone was sharp, but I could hear the distress she strove to hide.

"Right you are, Miss Gatspy," said the man, lifting his hand in salute before he rode on toward Saint Martin's Lane.

While they had spoken I became acutely aware that her hand was still in mine in the crook of my arm and that she had made no attempt to remove it. It was a heady sensation, and one I feared I was making too much of: she had endured a most trying day, one that ended in her having to dispatch her own mare with her pistol. It was only to be expected that she would require succor; I was determined not to refine upon it too much, or to attach any significance to it beyond her inclination to be comforted.

"Tell me, Guthrie," she said as we resumed our walk, "are you glad that you rid the world of Jacobbus Braaten?"

The question was so blunt that it took me aback. "I am glad he isn't alive to plague innocent people any longer. But I am not glad to have killed him. If I were, it would make me such another creature as he was."

"Imitation being the sincerest form of flattery?" she paraphrased inquiringly. "Well, *I* am glad of it."

Much as I disliked admitting it, this bit of praise lifted my spirits. "You are very good to say so, Miss Gatspy. It isn't the sort of thing that a man should take pride in."

"Of course it is," she said, chiding me gently. "We give soldiers medals for killing every day."

"That is different," I told her. We were nearing Mycroft Holmes' building, and I wished we did not have to go up at once, though I knew we must.

"Only in your mind, Guthrie." She preceded me up the stairs to the second-floor flat.

As we climbed, I asked her, "How are you going to get back to your . . . accommodations tonight?" It struck me then that I had no idea where she stayed in London, or with whom.

"My colleagues will attend to that," she answered obtusely, and continued upward.

Tyers admitted us promptly. "He's in the study. So is Sutton." He wore the look of a man much put-upon. "It is bad enough having one of them quoting Shakespeare, but *two*—"

"We'll take care of that for you, Tyers," said Miss Gatspy, and led the way into the study, where we found Sutton sitting in Mycroft Holmes' usual chair, a blanket wrapped around him over his dressing gown, and a pillow behind his head, Mycroft Holmes standing in front of the hearth, the make-up cleaned from his face, a snifter of brandy in one hand and the poker in the other which he was just now wielding in a mock display of theatrical swordsmanship.

Seeing Miss Gatspy, he lowered the poker, saying, "We were about to send out the hounds."

"There was some trouble," said Miss Gatspy, as if it were nothing more than a broken wheel-spoke. "We walked."

Sutton sat forward, although it was clearly a painful effort. Parts of his face looked like raw meat and when he tried to speak, his voice rasped and he gave up uttering the sympathies he wished to express.

"What sort of trouble, Guthrie?" Holmes asked, his grey eyes narrowing.

"We were attacked," I said, hoping to make light of it, for Miss Gatspy's sake.

"Attacked?" Holmes repeated. "By whom?"

"Someone all in black. I chased him, but lost him near Covent Garden. You know what a warren that place is. Not that that's an excuse," I added hastily.

"It is certainly an explanation," said Holmes. "Sit down, the two of you. Tyers will bring us food directly, and I must say, I am famished." He looked over at Sutton. "I must say I cannot imagine doing performances night after night. I'm quite enervated."

"One becomes accustomed, if one loves it," said Sutton, the sound raspy, but a great deal more like himself than he had been earlier this evening. There was no lingering vagueness, and no lethargy beyond that brought about pain and fatigue.

"Yes, I suppose so," said Mycroft Holmes thoughtfully. He turned and regarded us for a long moment. "There have been developments," he said at last. "Inspector Lionel Featherstone is dead."

"How?" I asked.

"Who did it?" Miss Gatspy demanded in the same instant.

"He seems to have done the deed himself," said Holmes. "It appears he was being coerced by the Brotherhood to be their agent within the police. Chief Inspector Pryce has sent me a preliminary report and will provide me with a copy of Featherstone's account of his activities."

"But coerced? How?" I could not grasp this at all.

"His mother has associations in Ireland who are against the English, men who would embrace any cause, no matter how reprehensible, if it was dedicated to the destruction of England. Somehow they made common cause with the Brotherhood, and through extortion gained Featherstone's cooperation. When he could not endure their demands any longer, he stopped them the only way he knew how—by putting an end to his life, and his compromises." He paused to drink a little more brandy. "They must have someone else in the police, and higher up, for Featherstone was often assigned those cases in which the Brotherhood had an interest. I hope Inspector Strange's files may shed some light on this."

"Then the Kerem debacle was given to him so that he could influence its outcome," I said, keenly aware that this would account for a great deal.

"Yes. It was he who arranged for the removal of the body, and it was he who concealed the removal for more than twelve hours. He, himself, removed all traces of the deception, with Sir Marmion's help." Holmes' face darkened. "I still blame myself for not seeing his part in this earlier." He cleared his throat. "Only Sutton sensed there was something off-plumb about him; I should have listened to you, Edmund. Indeed I should."

"It was as much my distrust of science as anything about the man," Sutton conceded, his statement ending in a burst of tight little choking sounds. He waved his hand to indicate he had more to say. "Science always purports to high ideals, but often results in oppression and cruelty."

"That is not the fault of science, but of the men who use it," said Holmes austerely.

"Perhaps," Sutton allowed, unwilling or disinclined to argue.

"Sutton has a point," said Miss Gatspy. "Science may be as you say, but all scientists are men, subject to the needs and vagaries of men. It is probably astonishing that we have made as much progress as we have, given the nature of men."

Mycroft Holmes bristled at this. "You cannot mean that you, too, decry science because of the use to which men put it?"

"No," she said, "I won't go that far. Yet you must allow that even the most enlightened scientist may have a dark side to his nature, one that will turn his most laudable intentions to despicable acts: Sir Marmion most certainly has such a blight on his character."

Holmes stared at her, unable to answer for at least five seconds—something of a record for him—and then he bowed. "I cannot dispute that in Sir Marmion's case, his application of his science is far from pristine."

Miss Gatspy decided to press her advantage. "Isn't that the underlying theme of *MacBeth*? Isn't that the very point of your performance this evening?"

"Ah," said Mycroft Holmes at his most beatific, "the play, dear Miss Gatspy, is fiction. Shakespeare makes no mention of the fact that the historical MacBeth reigned for almost seventeen years. Not to take away from Shakespeare's genius: his compression of events, and his dramatic interpretation of history may have that as a theme, but history, like life itself, is rather more complex than that."

Sutton made a cry of protest. "Who would remember MacBeth but for Shakespeare?"

Holmes considered this. "You have a point," he said at last. "Truly, Sutton; you have a point."

FROM THE PERSONAL JOURNAL OF PHILIP TYERS

MH, Sutton, G, and Miss Gatspy are having their midnight supper, and I must shortly finish putting the kitchen to rights before retiring. In the morning, CI Pryce will come, and they will begin to unravel this complex knot of interlocking cases. It is likely to be a very busy day, one which will be as exacting in its way as the ordeal of the last week has been . . .

Sutton is still rocky, but no doubt he will improve and recover. It may be just as well that he has only two more performances of MacBeth *to go. He will need to rest for at least a week when it is done. I would hope that MH would be willing to rest for a day or two as well, but I suspect he would not be willing to give in to such indulgences . . .*

Epilogue

CHIEF INSPECTOR VAUGHN Pryce apologized for his visit. "I know I told you on Friday that I would not call again until Wednesday, but there have been developments." He stood in the entryway brushing the snowflakes off his shoulders.

Mycroft Holmes was in the study door; I was a few steps behind him. It was very nearly noon on Monday, our first day attempting to return to our usual schedule of activities. "They must be significant, or you would only send a message round."

"Yes, they are." He handed Tyers his coat and came toward us.

"I reviewed Inspector Featherstone's account with great interest; thank you for providing me a copy of it," Holmes said by way of welcome.

Chief Inspector Pryce merely nodded his acknowledgement. "Do you mind if we talk this over confidentially?"

"My dear Pryce," said Holmes. "You may say anything you like in the presence of Guthrie or Tyers. They will not carry a syllable of it beyond these walls." He did not add that Sutton was asleep behind the closed doors of the withdrawing room; he stood aside and allowed Chief Inspector Pryce to enter the study. "Tell us what has transpired."

Now that he was in the room, Pryce seemed unable to decide what to tell us. He paced the confines, and finally stopped in front of the shuttered windows. "I was called to a house in Hayes End, in Drayton Road. The local constabulary had discovered something that needed my attention, they said." His distress grew more emphatic. "We found Sir Marmion Hazeltine—or most of him."

"Gracious," said Mycroft Holmes.

"He had been done to death most terribly," said Chief Inspector Pryce. "I was very much shocked, and I am not easily put off trim." He sat down in the nearest chair. "He appeared to have been the sacrifice in a blasphemous ritual. His hands and male parts were missing. So were his eyes."

Holmes looked very somber. "There was a triangle carved in his chest? Enclosing a wound to the heart?"

Chief Inspector Pryce looked startled, and then sighed, nodding. "I thought you would know."

"Why?" Holmes asked, troubled by this remark; I could see him reach for his watch-fob and begin to twiddle it.

"Because there was a note, and Sir Marmion's journal. The note was addressed to you." Chief Inspector Pryce bit his lower lip.

"Which said?" Mycroft Holmes prompted. "I am sure you have read it."

"It said: *this round goes to you. The next is ours.*" The Chief Inspector's voice sounded hollow, as if just speaking the words added to their weight on his mind.

"No signature, of course," said Holmes.

"No," said Chief Inspector Pryce. "But there was a long-barreled pistol of some kind holding down the note and the journal."

"Oh, dear," said Holmes, aghast, his voice dropping to a near-whisper. "So he thinks this was a game?"

"Apparently so," said Chief Inspector Pryce. "Their aim appears to have been two-fold: one, to bring Sir Cameron MacMillian under the absolute control of his estranged wife; I cannot discern why." He shot a suspicious glance at Holmes, whose visage gave away nothing. "The second was to distract you with as many demands on your attention as they could muster, to see if you would become lost in the tangle. The criminals involved apparently wanted to drive you to the limit so as to operate undetected, or so it would seem, given as much as I have to go on." He looked down at his hands as he flexed his long, knob-jointed fingers. "Sir Marmion seemed to think you were kidnapped and held in his asylum."

"Did he?" said Mycroft Holmes in a tone that revealed nothing whatsoever.

"Yes," said Chief Inspector Pryce. "He planned to examine you under galvanic-shock, to force you to reveal all you know. Apparently this didn't happen. This all was intended as preparation—I do not know for what." He waited, hoping for some comment; he got none. "In any case, Sir Marmion's failure to wring information from you caused his associates to . . . to kill him."

"He may have deserved the full judgment of the law, but he did not deserve slaughter," said Holmes with utmost sincerity. "I should have preferred to see him hang."

"Should it have come to that?" asked Chief Inspector Pryce.

"Oh, yes, I think so," said Holmes as if discussing the change in the weather. "He was involved up to his neck, beyond doubt."

"Involved in what?" Pryce demanded.

"Activities against Britain, and against her citizens." It was all the answer Holmes was prepared to give. "If I were you, Chief Inspector, I would handle the evidence in this case most circumspectly. You have stumbled upon a significant record of villainy. It may prove embarrassing to many if it should become generally known."

"Is that a warning or a threat?" Pryce was growing restive; he fiddled with his notebook.

"From me? A warning. I have nothing to fear from that book. Let them try to do their worst." He stopped worrying his watch-fob. "But there are others who may not feel as I do, and some of them are influential."

Chief Inspector Pryce sighed. "It may be time for me to retire," he said. "I have money enough to last all my life long. I thought I could rectify some of the injustices I have seen through becoming a police officer, but I am not so sure anymore."

I saw he was in dismay, and so I said, "If you have done some good, you have accomplished more than most." It wasn't much in the way of comfort, but it was the best I could offer; it was often all I had myself.

"Thank you, Guthrie," said Chief Inspector Pryce with a sarcastic smile.

"Ta," I replied.

Pryce looked back at Mycroft Holmes. "I don't suppose we'll ever find out who killed Helmut Kriede. The Germans won't like that."

Mycroft Holmes blinked in astonishment. "Why, my dear Chief Inspector, it's patently obvious that Herr Kriede was the victim of his own poison."

Chief Inspector Pryce favored Holmes with a bemused stare. "And how is it patently obvious?"

"Look at the accounts of Farbschlagen and Eisenfeld. Both men say that Kriede was agitated before Sir Cameron arrived. We already knew there was an agent of the criminal organization called the Brotherhood among the Germans—"

"And how did we know that?" asked Chief Inspector Pryce.

"Certain agents working clandestinely in Europe warned us of that possibility," said Holmes, and did not elaborate. "Since it was not the Baron von Schattenberg himself, it had to be one of his aides. Kriede must have had instructions to poison Sir Cameron, and had applied the poison to the top cup, knowing it would be given to Sir Cameron. His nervousness was the result of having already put the poison in place. Having done that, he could not refuse to drink the tea without exposing himself to the very kind of discovery he dreaded. So he drank his own poison rather than betray the Brotherhood."

"If Sir Marmion is any indication of how they treat their traitors, I might have done the same and drunk the poison," said Pryce.

"Precisely what Kriede must have thought," said Mycroft Holmes. "We may never be able to prove it in a court of law, but I am satisfied on that point, just as I am satisfied that Vickers has escaped again." This last admission did not please him, and he frowned ominously. "If he intends to continue this so-called game of his, he will be back. And I will have him."

Chief Inspector Pryce shook his head. "I don't want to know any more about it." He rose. "If you have any suggestions as to what I might tell the Baron regarding Kriede?"

"Certainly: tell him that Helmut Kriede was the victim of an attempt on Sir Cameron's life. It is, as far as it goes, the truth." Mycroft Holmes held out his hand. "You have been very diligent, Chief Inspector. It would be a shame if Scotland Yard were to lose you. Give me your word you will think over your retirement for at least a week before coming to a final decision." He held out his hand.

Pryce took it. "All right; I will give it a week." He started toward the door. "I may have to call upon you again."

"I look forward to it," said Holmes as Tyers appeared to usher Chief Inspector Pryce out the door. When he was gone, Holmes looked back at me. "This is a bad business, Guthrie. Vickers will be out for vengeance now."

"Hasn't he always been?" I asked.

"Yes, of course. But he has failed on two crucial points, and the Brotherhood will not reward him for that. So it follows he will want to exact a price for his chagrin." Mycroft Holmes stood staring into the middle distance. "He surely holds me responsible for his defeat. The Brotherhood will not tolerate another such debacle on his part, so he will have to annihilate me in order to remain one of their number."

I felt a cold chill go through me at his choice of words, and my recollection was nudged. "You never did tell me how you escaped from the Brotherhood once they found you out," I reminded him.

"I didn't, did I?" said Holmes. "Well, that is more Tyers' story than mine. You must ask him about it one day." He returned to his seat and began to read over the latest dispatch from the Admiralty when Sutton strolled into the room.

"Good morning," he said genially. The bruises were fading from his face, leaving his complexion a greenish-yellow shade that not even Sutton could make appear suitable. "You've been entertaining the police again, I hear."

"Yes," said Holmes. "He was helping us tidy up some loose ends from last week."

Sutton gave a single nod of his head. "Loose ends. You might well call them that," he said seriously. "Shakespeare has something to say on that head."

Mycroft Holmes shot him a warning look. "If you mean to quote *MacBeth* to me, I may throttle you."

"No, no; I've done with the Scottish Play," said Sutton. "I had another in mind."

Knowing one of us would have to ask, I said, "Which one?"

Sutton beamed. "Why, *All's Well that Ends Well,* of course."